THE
MAGISTRATE

ALSO BY BRIAN KLINGBORG

Thief of Souls

Wild Prey

THE MAGISTRATE

AN INSPECTOR LU FEI MYSTERY

BRIAN KLINGBORG

MINOTAUR
BOOKS
NEW YORK

First published in the United States by Minotaur Books,
an imprint of St. Martin's Publishing Group

THE MAGISTRATE. Copyright © 2023 by Brian Klingborg. All rights reserved.
Printed in the United States of America. For information, address
St. Martin's Publishing Group, 120 Broadway, New York, NY 10271.

www.minotaurbooks.com

Designed by Omar Chapa

The Library of Congress Cataloging-in-Publication Data is available upon request.

ISBN 978-1-250-85501-5 (hardcover)
ISBN 978-1-250-85502-2 (ebook)

Our books may be purchased in bulk for promotional, educational, or
business use. Please contact your local bookseller or the Macmillan Corporate and
Premium Sales Department at 1-800-221-7945, extension 5442, or by email at
MacmillanSpecialMarkets@macmillan.com.

First Edition: 2023

10 9 8 7 6 5 4 3 2 1

If you've come this far, this one's for You

CAST OF CHARACTERS

(In accordance with Chinese naming conventions, surnames are placed first)

Raven Valley PSB:
Chief Liang
Sergeant Bing
Constable Fatty Wang
Constable Li, "the Mute"
Constable Huang
Constable "Yuehan" Chu
Constable Big Wang

Criminal Investigation Bureau Team:
Ma Xiulan, Forensic Pathologist
Jin Miao, Supervising Technician
Lu Fei, Deputy Chief, Raven Valley PSB
Sun Huizhen, Constable, Raven Valley PSB

Nangang Benevolent Society:
Mr. Chen, Director of Nangang Investment Inviting Corporation
Mr. Liu, Director of Nangang Public Rental Housing Corporation
Mr. Zhao, Director of Nangang State-owned Building Investment Corporation
Mr. Cai, Head of the Nangang Procuratorate Arrest Section
Mr. Pang, Mayor of Nangang District
Judge Ren, President of Nangang People's Court

Mr. Xu, Chief of Harbin Homicide
Mr. Hong, Chief of Nangang Public Security Bureau
Mr. Wan, Nangang Deputy Mayor and Party Secretary
Mr. Yu, Chairman of Nangang Standing Committee
Mr. Tang, Businessman

Chief Xu's Team:
Detective Han
Detective Pangu

Magistrate's Team:
Mr. Zhang
Mr. Li

Others:
Gao Yang, disgraced ex-politician
Ling Wei, Gao's ex-wife
Hak, North Korean operative
Sister Kim, leader of underground church

PROLOGUE

Chen steps out of the crowded, stifling bar for a breath of air. It's ten thirty on an overcast October evening. A fine silver mist blurs the headlights of passing cars. Chen tilts his face up to the heavens and sighs as a crisp autumn breeze soothes his overheated flesh.

They say the human body is sixty percent water. In Chen's case, after several hours of concentrated boozing, it is verging on equal parts water, beer, and whiskey highball.

The occasion of his inebriation—as if he really needs an excuse—is Golden Week, an annual holiday commemorating the founding of the People's Republic of China. For most citizens, Golden Week is observed with fireworks, parades, and a week's vacation. For Chen, it's a pretext to go out drinking every night and sleep until noon the next day.

Chen feels his head spinning like a propeller. Perhaps he's overdone it. He opens his eyes and shuffles over to lean against a wall. He belches, feels hot liquid rush into his throat, thumps his chest with a fist. He lights a cigarette and hungrily smokes it. A pair of pretty women totter by in short skirts and high heels.

"Have fewer children, raise more pigs!" Chen shouts.

This is an old slogan from the late seventies, when the one-child policy was strictly, and sometimes brutally, enforced. Now that the country is experiencing a population decline—today's youth is overworked and undersexed—the needle has swung one hundred and eighty degrees back the other direction.

Chen knows this, of course. He just thinks he's being funny. He laughs uproariously, but the women are not amused. They clutch each other for safety as they hurry past.

Chen finishes his cigarette—the nicotine has vastly improved his condition—and tosses the butt onto the sidewalk. He smooths his hair and looks at his watch. One more for the road. Maybe two. He stumbles toward the bar entrance. He doesn't see a car roll up to the curb and a tall man dressed in a drab suit and a cotton face mask hop out. The man makes a beeline for Chen.

"Director Chen?"

Chen stares blearily at the man. The mask doesn't trouble him—nowadays mouth coverings are de rigueur for citizens with the sniffles or who fear the latest rumored outbreak of coronavirus. "Yes?"

The man flashes an ID. "Harbin Metro Public Security Bureau, Financial Crimes Division. Would you come with me, please?"

Chen cups an ear. "What?"

"Harbin PSB, Financial Crimes. Please come with me, sir."

"There must be some mistake."

"You are Chen Jianguo, director of the Nangang District Investment Inviting Corporation?"

"Yes—"

"Then no mistake. Let's go." The man takes Chen's elbow and tugs him toward the car.

"No, wait! I don't—"

"Don't make a scene, Director. It will only serve to embarrass you. And your fellow conspirators."

"Conspirators?" The warm liquor sloshing around Chen's belly abruptly turns to ice water. "What is your name?"

"You can call me Zhang."

"I will make a call." Chen reaches for his cell phone.

Zhang snatches it from his hand. "No calls."

"How dare you!"

"Get in the car, please." Zhang herds Chen into the backseat, climbs in beside him, pulls the door shut. The driver, likewise wearing a face mask, eases into traffic.

"I think you'd better tell me what this is all about," Chen says after a few minutes. Zhang doesn't answer. "I have powerful friends, you know!"

Zhang gives Chen a short, vicious uppercut to the chin. Chen's head snaps back. He sees stars. Then crashes painfully back to earth. He touches his mouth—his fingers come away bloody. His fear turns to fury. He wings an elbow at Zhang. Zhang deflects it and jams a black device into Chen's neck.

Chen experiences a violent, shuddering jolt, followed by intense shooting pain. His body stiffens, then goes limp.

"Be still," Zhang says. "Be quiet. Understand me?"

When Chen can speak again, he gasps: "You're not the police!"

"I said, be quiet."

They drive for twenty minutes. Chen racks his brain: Who are these men? Why do they want to harm him? Sure, he has stepped on a few toes to get to where he is now. He's used and discarded women. Played fast and loose with other people's money. Leveraged what political influence he possesses to benefit himself. But no more so than anyone else would do in his position!

The driver parks in an industrial no-man's-land. At this hour, the windows of the surrounding factories are dark, their parking lots empty. Zhang hauls Chen out of the car and tosses him onto the ground. The driver opens the trunk, removes two thick bamboo sticks. He tosses one to Zhang.

"Thank you, Mr. Li," Zhang says.

"You're welcome, Mr. Zhang," Li says. He keeps a stick for himself.

Chen makes a run for it. Zhang catches up and cuts him across the back of his thighs with the stick. Chen stumbles and falls. Zhang and Li stand over Chen and take turns thrashing him, like railroad workers pounding a spike. Chen shrieks and flails, seeking shelter from the blows, but there is none to be found in the cold pavement.

Afterward, Chen lies bruised, broken, weeping.

Zhang squats down, slightly out of breath. "The Magistrate sends his regards."

Zhang and Li return to the car and drive away.

Exactly one week and a day later, Director Liu of the Nangang District Public Rental Housing Corporation boards an elevator at the Four Seasons luxury apartment building and presses the button for the lobby. As the car descends, he checks his appearance in a mirrored panel on the wall. Hair combed. Clothes free of stray hairs. No trace of lipstick on his face.

Liu does not live at the Four Seasons, but his mistress, Ms. Hu, does. She's twenty-four, slim, with an adorable melon-seed-shaped face and perfect alabaster skin. They met at a restaurant when Hu was twenty-two and Liu was forty-one. On their first date, Liu took her shopping at Prada and bought her a dress, scarf, and wallet, paying thirty thousand yuan. Later that night, she demonstrated her gratitude by emerging from the bathroom of their suite at the Shangri-la Hotel wearing the scarf—and nothing else.

Aside from paying for Hu's apartment and monthly living expenses, Liu takes her on an annual holiday somewhere sunny and lavishes her with small gifts. In return, she launders and folds the clothes he keeps at her apartment, rubs his head when he wakes up with a hangover, and listens patiently while he complains about work. And there is sex, of course, depending on the ebb and flow of Liu's libido.

Liu checks the time. *Cao!* It's later than he realized. His wife doesn't much care where he spends Friday night, but on Saturdays she prepares an elaborate meal and expects him to eat with her and the children. If the soup gets cold because of his tardiness, she'll give him a tongue-lashing.

It's Ms. Hu's fault. After breakfast she insisted—the naughty minx!—that they attempt a pair of rather acrobatic Daoist sexual positions: Spring Phoenix Ascends the Jade Pillar; Hungry Tiger Cub Enters the Flesh Grotto.

How could he possibly refuse?

The elevator reaches the lobby; Liu rushes outside to flag a taxi. He is pleasantly surprised to find one already idling out front. He waves at the driver, who gives him a terse nod.

Liu opens the back door. "Waiting for someone?"

The driver is wearing a hat, glasses, a cotton face mask. "Just dropped a customer off. Where you headed?"

Liu gives him the address. The driver agrees to take him. Liu slides onto the backseat and pulls the door shut.

They travel a few kilometers down the road before detouring down a side street.

"Where are you going?" Liu asks.

"Traffic ahead," the driver says. "Shortcut."

"What traffic? On a Saturday?"

The driver turns down another street. Liu leans forward to look at the ID placard on the dashboard. "Driver Li, do you suppose I'm a tourist and you can gouge me by taking backstreets?"

"No."

"Then where the hell do you think you're going?"

"Here." Li turns once more and pulls to a sudden stop.

Liu's anger grows. "What are you doing, you idiot?"

"Just one moment, sir."

Wang ba dan!" Liu reaches for the door. But before his fingers can grasp the handle, the door opens, and a man pushes his way inside.

"Hey!" Liu protests.

"Hey, yourself," Zhang says. He jams a Taser into Liu's neck and gives him a jolt. He pulls the door shut. Up front, Li shifts into gear and speeds down the street.

"Sit quietly," Zhang tells Liu. Like Li, he is wearing a hat and mask. "Don't make a move. Don't make a sound."

"Is it money you want?" Liu gasps, probing the seared flesh of his neck. "I'm not rich, but—"

"Give me your cell phone."

Liu hesitates. Zhang brandishes the Taser. Liu hands over his phone with a trembling hand. Zhang tosses it out the window.

Now Liu is no longer angry. He is afraid.

Li drives to a quiet side street and parks behind a white van. He gets out and opens the van's rear door.

"Let's go," Zhang says. He manhandles Liu into the van and pulls the door shut. It's dim inside, but Liu can just make out an apparatus bolted to the floor, one that looks very much like a "tiger chair"—an ugly metal contraption used in Chinese police stations and black jails to keep suspects immobilized during interrogations. "Sit," Zhang says.

"Who are you people?" Liu asks, voice quavering.

Zhang shoves Liu into the chair. Liu struggles. Zhang tases him again, then straps Liu in—ankles, wrists, lap, chest. Up front, the engine starts and the van rolls forward.

Zhang makes himself comfortable on the floor. Liu wheedles and begs until Zhang threatens to tase him again. They drive for a while and then stop. Li opens the back door, climbs in, and pulls it shut behind him.

"Please—" Liu begins.

"Don't bother," Li says. He lifts the bottom of his mask, places a cigarette between his lips, lights it. He holds his hand in front of his mouth, the cigarette protruding between stubby fingers.

Zhang flicks on an overhead light. He hums an old pop tune as he picks up a plastic box and opens the lid. He removes an object that resembles a big fat stylus.

"What is that?" Liu moans.

Zhang clicks a button. The tip of the stylus whirrs and vibrates. "I'd advise you to be very still. Otherwise, I might poke an eye out."

"No!" Liu wails. "I'm begging you!"

"Quiet!" Zhang lowers the stylus and presses his other hand on Liu's forehead to keep him immobilized. Liu whimpers as the tip inscribes a searing pattern onto his cheek. After several excruciating minutes, Zhang switches off the stylus and steps back. "What do you think?"

"You're no Wang Xizhi," Li says. He is referring to a famous fourth century scholar who, as legend has it, practiced his calligraphy beside a pond, dipping the tip of his brush into the water to wash off the ink; such was his diligence that the pond eventually turned completely black.

Zhang smirks beneath his mask. "For a man who can barely read, you've got high standards."

Li drives them back to a residential neighborhood. Zhang unstraps Liu from the chair and pushes him out onto the street. "The Magistrate sends his regards," he calls out. He pulls the door shut and the van speeds off.

Liu scrambles to his feet and runs like a madman. He passes several pedestrians, who hasten out of his way. Eventually he grows exhausted and slumps onto a bench at a bus stop. As he catches his breath, he considers what to do.

Go to the nearest PSB station? No—he doesn't know why these men targeted him, and until he does, it's better to be circumspect. Find the nearest medical clinic? Yes, but first he wants to see what they've done to him.

Liu walks to the nearest parked car and looks at his face in the side mirror.

He is shocked and appalled.

His cheek is red and inflamed and it bears a sloppily rendered tattoo of a Chinese character in black ink: 贼.

THIEF.

霜降
EARLY FROST

ONE

The phone rings just before midnight. Lu Fei, deputy chief of the Raven Valley Township Public Security Bureau, groans. At this hour, a phone call can only mean one thing.

Trouble.

Lu Fei doesn't want any trouble. What he *wants* is for the phone to stop ringing and to remain right where he is—in a warm bed, pressed up beside a warm body.

Especially because the bed and body belong to Luo Yanyan. His girlfriend.

Lu smiles to himself in the dark. *Girlfriend*. He likes the sound of that.

When contemplating his relationship with Yanyan, he pictures a wisteria plant: a slow-growing creeper, requiring a great deal of patience; only recently showing signs of blooming after years of diligent cultivation.

While they have not articulated the parameters of their relationship in so many words, they are, more or less, a couple. Lu sleeps over at Yanyan's house a few nights a week. If he stops by the Red Lotus after work, she is less reticent to openly display her affections for him—gently resting a hand on his arm when she serves him a drink, bringing him a cup of tea at the end of the evening when she's decided he's had enough, that sort of thing.

And when alone, they simply cannot keep their hands, lips, and other body parts off one another. It's as if they are two randy teenagers who've been given the keys to the Pent-up Lust Suite at a tawdry love hotel and told to indulge in their wildest fantasies.

Even at this hour, despite the incessant ringing of the phone, Lu's proximity to Yanyan leads to feelings of arousal. He snuggles up behind her and reaches around to cup one of her breasts. "Marry me," he says. He makes this request at least once a day.

"Are you planning on letting that ring all night?" Yanyan growls.

"*Ta ma de!*" It's times like these Lu regrets he was reinstated as deputy chief after his recent suspension. He rolls over and fumbles for his cell phone. "What?"

It's Constable Sun, whom Lu has come to regard as one of the most reliable and competent members of his team. "Sorry to bother you at this hour, Deputy Chief. But we have a body. A homicide."

"Where?"

"Off the expressway. Near the bridge where it crosses the river on the west side of town."

"How do you know it's a homicide?"

"The body was set on fire," Sun says. "And it has no fingers. Or teeth."

"I'm on the way."

Lu dresses with the lights off and kisses Yanyan goodbye. She waves him off grumpily. He goes downstairs and walks a block or so to where he's parked a patrol car. He feels justified in retaining the vehicle for his personal use because Chief Liang, Lu's boss, is usually steeped in whiskey and beer at some local karaoke joint by 9:00 P.M. Consequently, whenever something happens after hours, it is Lu who gets the call.

Lu yawns as he cruises through a dark and somnolent Raven Valley. He sees only a handful of cars on the road. Folks in these parts are early to rise and early to bed. Especially now that autumn has arrived and temperatures are already dipping below freezing at night.

He drives to the outskirts of town, passing a few lonely and isolated farmhouses before reaching the bridge. The *paichusuo*'s other patrol vehicle is parked there, red and blue lights flashing. Lu pulls over, takes a flashlight from the console, and climbs out. His breath steams in the night air as he fetches a pair of paper booties and latex gloves from the trunk. He switches on the flashlight and picks his way down the steep grade to the riverside, where Constables Sun, Li the Mute, and Fatty Wang are huddled beside a dark splotch lying in the weeds.

As Lu draws near, he catches a whiff of charred meat. A sulfurous stench of burnt hair. A taste of copper on his tongue.

Constable Sun briefs him: "A car passing by on the expressway saw flames and called it in. Fire and Rescue got here first. The body was smoldering, so they sprayed it down and tossed a fire blanket over it."

"I hope they didn't wash away all our evidence. What time was the call?"

"Log says eleven twenty-two P.M."

"What time did you get here?"

"Just after Fire and Rescue."

"Let's have a look." Lu dons the paper booties and gloves. Fatty Wang and Li the Mute remove the silver blanket covering the corpse, then step away. Lu shines his light on it, head to toe, then back again.

He sees a body, male, nude, skin blackened, arms and legs warped and twisted. He leans closer. The mouth is a gaping silent scream. As Sun said, no teeth. The victim's hands are curled into unnaturally truncated fists. No fingers, either.

"The murderer doesn't want us to ID the body," Fatty Wang offers.

"Looks like," Lu says.

"No speed cameras along this stretch of the expressway," Li the Mute offers. "No video of the body being dumped."

Lu is shocked. Not by Li's policework, which is just common sense, but by the fact that Li has spoken of his own volition. Li so rarely opens his mouth; Lu half expects a puff of dust to emerge when he does. "Thank you, Constable Li." He takes a moment to organize his thoughts. "Constables Li and Wang, please get some tape from your vehicle and rope this area off. I'll want to return at first light and search the area thoroughly. Will you two be all right safeguarding the scene until then?" Lu raises a hand. "Don't bother answering, that was a purely rhetorical question."

Lu takes Sun with him back to town. He has her call the county coroner while he drives. Afterward, they ride in silence, Sun uncharacteristically quiet. Lu assumes she's just tired—it is the middle of the night, after all. But eventually she clears her throat and says: "Can I discuss something with you?"

"Sure."

"I'm . . . I'm getting married."

"What? Congratulations!" Lu didn't even know Sun was dating someone. "Who's the lucky guy?"

"His name is Yao Jun. His father owns the Fengman organic food processing plant."

"No kidding? That's a big plant! I guess he's kind of rich, then."

"Well, his dad is kind of rich."

"Where'd you meet?"

"Tantan."

Lu could have guessed as much. Tantan is a popular online dating app. Such modern conveniences have gradually replaced more traditional ways of meeting a mate in the People's Republic.

"The thing is . . . ," Sun continues.

Lu thinks, *Other shoe dropping in three, two . . .*

"He's thirty-five. And I'll be thirty in a few months. And he's eager to start a family."

"Right," Lu says. "Well, I haven't looked into the specifics, but I think you're allotted ninety days of maternity leave, and I'm sure you've accrued additional vacation time."

"Yes, but . . . he doesn't want me to work anymore. He's traditional that way."

"By *traditional,* you mean he wants you to stay home and change diapers and have supper on the table when he comes home from a hard day at the plant?"

"No need to make it sound so awful," Sun says.

"Sorry," Lu says. "It's just that—you strike me as someone who enjoys her independence. And you're a very good police officer. With tons of potential. Who knows—maybe you'll even be chief of your own station someday?"

"He doesn't want to be married to a police officer."

"Why? Because it's dangerous?"

"I don't really want to talk about it," Sun says. "I'm just giving you notice that I'll be resigning soon."

"And your mind is made up?"

"Yes."

"This is what *you* want?"

"I want to get married."

Lu sighs. The role of women in society has changed a lot over the years, but the pressure to marry, have children, continue the family line, remains strong. "Can I meet him?"

"Why?"

"If I'm losing my most trusted constable, I want to at least make sure she's in good hands."

Sun hesitates before answering. "Are you going to be nice?"

"Aren't I always?"

"Not really."

"Well . . . I'll be on my best behavior."

"Will you bring Ms. Luo?"

"Sure."

"All right. I'll ask him."

Lu drops Sun off at her home and drives back to Yanyan's house. He undresses and climbs into bed but can't sleep. He finally gets up an hour before dawn and goes downstairs to make tea.

TWO

For Choi Hyunjoo, age sixteen, and Lee Eunji, nineteen, the universe consists of a tiny room, windowless, a peeling vinyl floor, scuffed white walls, two narrow beds with threadbare flower-print sheets—and, for upward of sixteen hours a day, twin laptop computers featuring the latest in webcam technology.

The two young women are let out periodically to use the restroom or take meals in the apartment's cramped kitchen. On rare occasion, they may be granted a few minutes on the roof under the watchful eye of the man they call the Director, or his wife, whom they have been instructed to address as Umma, meaning "Mom" in Korean. The Director is Korean, but his wife is Chinese, and her Korean language skills are those of a six-year-old child.

Choi has been in China for thirteen months and her Chinese is, if anything, worse than Umma's Korean. It's not really Choi's fault—she spends most of her time in this room, and, aside from Lee, the Director, and Umma, interacts exclusively with men from South Korea who pay for her time—and other things—online.

Choi is from North Korea. As a child, she endured gnawing hunger, bitter cold, and regular beatings from her disciplinarian father. The cold and hunger, at least, are a familiar part of most childhoods in North Korea. But Choi's generation had the benefit (or curse, depending on your perspective) of something previous ones did not—access to the wider world through a burgeoning black market that offered knockoff luxury goods, counterfeit fashion, pirated movies, and foreign music.

Consequently, Choi and her friends knew just enough about life outside the Hermit Kingdom to know what they were missing.

At the age of fourteen, Choi decided to defect. She spent the next year searching for a broker who would smuggle her across the Tumen River into China, where she dreamed of working in a high-end department store and marrying a rich, kind, and handsome Chinese husband, like the ones she saw on pirated Chinese soap operas.

But when she finally found a broker, instead of helping her secure a job or husband, he sold her to a sex trafficker. The trafficker forcibly took Choi's virginity and then resold her on down the line, and so on, until she ended up here, in this squalid room in a run-down apartment building in Harbin.

Even so, Choi considers herself one of the lucky ones. Yes, she is forced to smile and flirt with men who pay to chat with her online. And sometimes, if they pay more, take off her clothes and even perform pornographic acts that would make her poor mother's hair turn white. But at least she is not working in a roach-infested brothel, servicing a dozen rough and drunk men in a single night.

Most days, Choi and Lee clock in before noon and are up until three or four in the morning entertaining clients. As long as someone is willing to pay, they are expected to perform. Disobedience earns them threats, slaps, withholding of food, and—what Choi and Lee hate worst of all—excruciating pokes with Umma's knitting needle directly into the soles of their feet.

But Sundays are a typically a slow night, and at this hour—nearly 2:00 A.M.—both Choi and Kim are supposed to be sleeping.

They are not. Because tonight—tonight they will escape this hellhole.

It started three weeks ago, when Choi met a new customer online. He introduced himself as Mr. Hak. Choi found that her clients generally fell into one of two categories: desperately lonely men who were seeking some sort of human connection, even if they had to pay for it—and lustful swine who regarded her as a tool designed solely for their sexual gratification.

Hak was neither of these. To begin with, he was younger than her average customer by at least a decade and, judging from what she could see on the computer screen—broad shoulders, arms corded with muscle—ruggedly handsome. He didn't complain about his sad life or make salacious, voyeuristic demands. They simply chatted, like two normal people. And she could immediately tell from Hak's accent that he was from the north.

"Yes. I'm from near Pyongyang," Hak confirmed. "You?"

"Onsong."

"Oh, that's really in the sticks."

"You aren't in Korea now?"

"I'm in China. Crossed the border two years ago. You?"

Choi had been warned by the Director to remain circumspect about her personal details. She was meant to be a blank canvas upon which her clients could project their prurient fantasies. But the thrill of speaking to another North Korean trumped her caution. "Just over a year."

"You came looking for a better future, is that it?" Hak asked. "Have you found it?"

Choi didn't answer at first, then smiled brightly. "Of course! I'm very happy here, talking to new friends like you."

Hak smiled back, a bit knowingly. "Where are you now? What city?"

Choi fiddled with her headset. "I can't really say."

"Why not?"

"Some guys get too attached. They come looking for you."

"I'm in Harbin. And I think you are, too."

Choi gasped. She glanced up from the computer to make sure the Director or his wife were not looming in the doorway. She turned to Lee, who was sitting on her bed, naked, legs spread toward the laptop camera, a vacant expression on her face. Choi recognized that expression—she had worn it many times herself.

"I can help you," Hak said. "I've helped many girls in your situation."

"I don't understand what you mean."

"I think you do."

"I'm sorry . . . I . . ."

"I can get you out of there and across the border to Vietnam, where a charity organization will sponsor you—provide food, shelter. Eventually a real job. A real life." Hak paused to let his offer sink in. "I promise you, I'm not a broker or a trafficker. I'm a *liberator*."

Choi burst into tears. Lee didn't stop what she was doing, but she shot Choi a quick glance. It was not so unusual for one or the other of them to suddenly break down. The terrible things men said to them, the awful things men wanted them to do on camera—sometimes it was just too much to bear. Choi shook her head to let Lee know she was okay.

"Sorry, I don't mean to upset you," Hak said. "And in any case, it's not safe to talk like this. But I can send you a link to a messaging app. We can communicate in secret."

Choi swiped her cheeks. "I have to go."

"As long as you're young and pretty, they'll keep you online," Hak said. "But the second you no longer make the daily minimum, they'll sell you to a brothel. And as you get older and less pretty, you'll be sent down the ladder, each situation worse than the one before, until you die or kill yourself. That will be your fate. Unless you let me help you."

Hak's offer was terrifying—and thrilling. What if the Director found out? What if she tried to escape and got caught? But . . . what if Hak *could* help her get free?

For the first time since crossing the Tumen River just over a year ago, Choi felt an inkling of hope.

A few nights later, after lights-out, Choi crawled into Lee's bed and told her about Hak. Lee was wary. "What if he's just another guy like the Director trying to poach us? What if he sells us to someone who forces us to do dirty movies? Or worse?"

"It's a risk. But I trust him. And I want to get out of here."

After a moment, Lee found Choi's hand and squeezed it. "Then I'm going to trust *you.*"

Over the next couple of weeks, Hak and Choi frequently communicated through the messaging app. Hak asked many logistical questions. What was the layout of the apartment? What kind of security measures were in place? What was the Director's daily routine?

He soon chose a date for the escape.

Hak: *I'll make sure the Director is out of the picture.*

Choi: *How will you do that?*

Hak: *Don't worry, it's my concern. Minus the Director, that will just leave his wife. We'll do this in the middle of the night, so hopefully she'll be asleep. But if she wakes and tries to stop you, you may have to deal with her.*

Choi: *What's that mean? Deal with her? I'm only sixteen. She's twice my size.*

Hak: *There are two of you against one. And you want to get out of there, right? Do whatever it takes.*

And now, finally, the moment has arrived. As Hak promised, the Director went out earlier in the evening and has not returned. Umma is asleep in her bedroom after drinking her customary nightcap—two cans of Harbin Hapi Gold beer.

Choi and Lee pack their few belongings—hairbrushes, some extra under-wear, one jar of face moisturizer—in a plastic bag. They sneak out of their bedroom.

They can feel the rumble of Umma's snoring through the cheap parquet floor of the hallway.

They go out to the living room, ignoring the front door—it is outfitted with some sort of industrial lock they have no hope of opening without a key. Instead, they lever open the window. It screeches indignantly in its rusted frame. Umma's snores abruptly cease, and the two young women freeze, their hearts pounding. Ten seconds go by. The snoring resumes. Choi and Lee breathe a sigh of relief.

Umma keeps a basket of yarn in the living room—the needles she wisely keeps locked in her bedroom. Lee takes the largest ball of yarn, wraps a length around her hand, tosses the remainder out the window.

After a moment, she feels a tug. She pulls the yarn up and finds a rope tied to the end. She hitches the rope around the sturdiest piece of furniture in the room, a sofa leg. She and Choi exchange a quick hug. It has been decided ahead of time that Choi will go first. They don't voice the logic behind this decision, but it's understood that Choi is lighter. If the rope is going to break, it will be when Lee is climbing down. This way, at least one of them is likely to make it.

"Good luck," Lee whispers.

Choi nods. She loops the plastic bag around her thin wrist. Her tiny hands white-knuckle the rope as she lets herself out into empty space.

The apartment is four floors up. There is no safety apparatus here—it's just

Choi and the rope and a cement sidewalk twelve meters below. The coarse fabric of the rope burns Choi's palms. She has not had any regular exercise since she came to China and her arms quickly begin to burn. She descends slowly, haltingly, one anxious handhold at time. As she nears the sidewalk, she hears Hak speak words of encouragement in a low voice.

"Another few meters," he says. "Nice and slow. Almost there."

She feels his hands steadying her feet, then clutching her legs, taking some of the weight off her arms.

"Let go," Hak says. "I've got you."

Choi drops into Hak's arms. He gently lowers her to the sidewalk. She lies there utterly spent. Hak tugs three times on the rope. Overhead, Lee's legs swing out over the edge of the windowsill.

Then comes a shrill voice. Hak sees Lee look back into the apartment. "Come on," Hak mutters to himself. "Come on, girl."

Lee starts down. As Hak watches, the head and shoulders of a woman pop out from the window above. A clawed hand reaches for Lee, grasps her hair. Lee, to her credit, grits her teeth and keeps going. Umma ends up with a fistful of thin black hair. She tosses it after Lee and disappears back inside.

Lee descends a few meters and then stops. Like Choi, she's weak from inactivity, not enough food. She clings to the rope, too tired to climb down, too high up to let go.

"Hurry!" Hak urges, raising his voice.

Lee feels a rhythmic vibration travel along the rope. She knows what this means: that cruel bitch is up there sawing away with a kitchen knife. Lee forces herself to open her right hand, clutch the rope farther down, the same with the left, her palms on fire. Right hand, left hand, feet seeking whatever purchase they can find. The vibration of the rope intensifies.

Hak watches. He doesn't think she's going to make it.

He's right.

The rope abruptly gives way. Lee plummets like a stone.

Into Hak's arms.

His body shields Lee from the worst of the impact. They hit the sidewalk with a crunch. Hak grunts in pain, but immediately shifts Lee's weight off, gets to his feet, pulls her toward the van parked at the curb. He worries that passing drivers have seen the rope and the girls dangling from it and wondered what the hell is going on. Someone might have already called the police.

Hak returns for Choi, herds her into the van, slams the back door, goes around front, starts the engine. He makes it half a block before he is forced to stop at a light. Despite the tense circumstances, he does not panic. Years of training under the most extreme conditions have taught him to control his emotions.

The light takes an eternity to change. When it finally does, he accelerates, but not too fast. He's less concerned about pursuit—the Director is dead, and his wife isn't likely to report the kidnapping of two sex-trafficked girls she's kept trapped in her apartment—than getting pulled over for a driving infraction.

"There are water bottles in a bag," he says over his shoulder. "Help yourself."

Initially, Choi and Lee huddle on the floor, arms trembling with exhaustion, hearts pounding with fear. But after a few minutes, a sense of elation creeps in. Choi bursts into giddy laughter and hugs Lee. Lee hugs her back, but remains wary of Hak.

"Why are you helping us?" she asks.

Hak pictures a young woman, about Choi's age. A white shirt and blue skirt. Bobbed hair. Despite crooked teeth, a bright smile.

And then he sees an image of the same young woman, filthy and bruised, a dark and squalid room, a bowl of food on the floor, as if she were a dog. A man on top her, grunting like a pig. He grips the wheel, his thick knuckles whitening. "What they did to you was wrong. No one deserves that kind of life."

Choi crawls forward, leans over the seat, and wraps her arms around Hak. "Thank you, Brother Hak. Thank you, thank you, thank you!"

Hak brushes her off gruffly. "I'm driving!"

"Sorry."

Hak softens. "Get some rest. You have a long journey ahead of you."

Choi crawls back to Lee. They hold hands and sit huddled together, soothed by the rhythmic motion of the van.

Lee sniffs the air. She lifts Choi's hand to her nose. "You smell like gasoline."

Now that Lee has mentioned it, Choi can smell it, too. She figures Brother Hak likely spilled on his hand as he was fueling up before rescuing them. She shrugs—no big deal.

The smell of gasoline never killed anyone.

THREE

Monday morning finds Lu Fei, Sergeant Bing, Sun, and the other constables on duty conducting a grid search of the area off the expressway. If there was any evidence worth noting, Lu fears Fire and Rescue have washed it away.

"We should at least be able to narrow down the vehicle the suspect used," he tells Sergeant Bing. "The incident was called in at eleven twenty-two P.M. Let's check the nearest speed cameras east and west of here for, say, between ten thirty and midnight. Can't imagine there will be many."

Bing purses his lips. "Maybe a few dozen."

"A few dozen isn't a hundred. Get a list of license plates and run them down."

"Unless the suspect had the victim lashed to his hood, how will we know which of those dozens of vehicles he was using?"

"Check time stamps. If there's a vehicle that took an especially long time to transit between the two cameras, you have your man."

"What if he drove down from Harbin, dumped the body, and then drove back? He'd only pass one of the cameras."

"Then same thing, Sergeant. Estimate how long it would take to drive to this spot, dump the body, and drive back."

"What if the driver is just coming out to the country to gaze at the moon or catch frogs?"

"Are you always so contrary this early in the morning? Perhaps you need a nice strong cup of *wulong* tea?"

"Sounds lovely. Do you have one?"

"No. I might have an old pack of cucumber chewing gum in the glove compartment of my patrol vehicle."

"Hard pass."

Lu leaves Bing to manage the scene and canvass nearby residents about any suspicious activity in the night while he and Sun drive to the county hospital to observe the autopsy of the victim.

The ME is a cheerful sort for someone who earns his living elbow-deep in dead people. He practically rubs his gloved hands over the corpse. "This looks like an intriguing case!"

"I prefer my mutilated murder victims to be dull and lacking in intrigue," Lu says.

"Don't be a spoilsport."

The ME confirms the victim was male, between thirty-five and fifty years of age, 167 centimeters in height, and approximately eighty kilograms in weight. "Hard to gauge weight accurately with burn victims," he explains. "Loss of fluids and so on."

"I'm curious to know if the teeth and fingers were removed pre- or post-mortem."

The ME examines the victim's hands with a magnifying glass. "Edges of some of the cuts are a bit ragged. I'd say he was moving around a bit." He pries opens the victim's mouth and probes inside. "Hard to say with the teeth. There's going to be a lot of damage if you yank them out with a pair of pliers no matter how you slice it."

Despite the degraded condition of the skin, the ME discovers traces of tattoos on the victim's chest, upper arms, and back. "Tattoos this extensive usually indicate membership in a criminal gang."

"If you can find something recognizable, maybe we can use it to help with an identification," Lu suggests.

The ME searches the body and finds a small undamaged section of skin. "Here."

It takes Lu a moment to reconstruct the jumble of inked images—a glaring eye, twin curving whisker-like appendages, a dagger hilt, and hint of fish scales. "It's . . . a fish with a knife in its mouth?"

"A koi, I think," Sun says. "Those are barbels." She points at the whiskers. "Koi use them to taste things."

"Right," Lu says. "A knife-wielding koi. Exceedingly rare in nature."

"A gang tattoo, obviously," the ME says. "But *which* gang?"

Sun leans in. "There's some Korean writing." She reads slowly: "*Gur . . . Yong . . . Ma . . . Eul*. Guryong Village. That's a famous slum area in Seoul."

"You read Korean?" Lu asks, surprised.

"I studied it in school," Sun says.

"Is there no limit to your talents, Constable Sun? In any case, I guess we can safely assume this guy was a *Korean* gangster. That gives us a starting point. We can check our criminal gang database, narrow down some names based on age and location."

"But if he's listed in our criminal database as a Korean gangster, wouldn't we have deported him already?" Sun asks. "Which means he's probably in the country illegally. And therefore, there's no record of him."

"Unless he was arrested, deported, and then snuck back across the border," Lu says. "Which is a pretty gangster thing to do."

As the autopsy progresses, the ME locates a knife wound between the fourth and fifth ribs on the victim's left side. "The apex of the heart lies just to the left of the sternum there," he explains. "If I were going to cleanly dispatch someone with a knife, this is the exact spot I'd choose." He looks up. "In other words, the suspect knew exactly what he was doing."

"A gang enforcer?" Sun asks.

The ME looks doubtful. "I've seen a fair number of gang-related stabbings. Terribly sloppy work. Multiple entry wounds, slash marks, and so on. I'd have to say *this* looks more like the work of someone with a great deal of training. Such as a military guy. Special forces or the like."

"Great," Lu says. "Just what I need first thing Monday morning. A homicidal commando."

Back at the *paichusuo*, Sun combs through criminal databases and Lu reads up on the latest Interpol organized crime reports. They meet in the late afternoon to compare notes.

"Did you know there are more than a million ethnic Koreans living in China?" Lu says. "I had no idea it was that many."

"Sure," Sun says. "Koreans have been here for hundreds of years. There's even an autonomous Korean prefecture in Jilin Province. It used to be sixty percent ethnic Korean, but the government encouraged a lot of Han Chinese to move there, so now it's only half that. Many of the locals still speak Korean and keep traditional Korean culture, but the younger generation has mostly assimilated and views itself more Chinese than Korean."

"Nobody likes a know-it-all, Constable."

"Sorry."

"Anyway . . . compared to the yakuza and triads, Korean criminal gangs are small fry. There are maybe ten thousand in all South Korea. This Guryong Village group appears to be one of the newer ones. They make their living in the usual way—drugs, extortion, prostitution, sex trafficking. They mostly stick to South Korea, but there is some cross-border cooperation with Japanese yakuza and Chinese triads. Perhaps our victim was representing the Guryong gang's interests in the local drug or sex trade. Did you have any luck in identifying him?"

"I only found records for three criminals known to be associated with that gang," Sun says. "One is deceased. Murdered, in Jilin in 2020."

"Unless this is the start of a zombie apocalypse, we can check him off the list. Next."

"The second was deported to South Korea last year."

"Could he have snuck back over the border?"

"He's twenty-two and weighs about fifty-eight kilos. Too young and small to be our victim."

"Hopefully you hit pay dirt with number three?"

"Unfortunately, no," Sun says. "He's still alive."

"That *is* unfortunate," Lu says. "But maybe he knows who the victim is. Where can we find him?"

"Locked up in a pretrial detention center."

Chinese law allows for a criminal suspect to be placed in a detention center for up to two months while an investigation is carried out. In certain circumstances, this detention may be extended another five months. In practice, such detentions often last much longer. A year, even two.

The conditions at these facilities are legendarily awful. Suspects are packed into dirty cells without heat in the winter or air-conditioning in the summer. They are denied basic rights, such as the ability to meet with their lawyers or seek treatment for illnesses. They are harassed and interrogated and often beaten.

It's not a stretch to say detention centers are less a means to safeguard a suspect until a trial can be carried out and more a means to crush their spirit and pry a confession from them.

"Location?" Lu asks.

"Yanji City, Jilin Province."

"Shit. That's far."

"Perhaps we can set up a phone call."

"No. When questioning a suspect, you must be close enough to read the expression on his face, smell his sweat, and hear his bowels churn. We'll go out there and make a day of it. Don't forget to pack your baton in case we need to beat some information out of him."

Sun laughs, but she can't really be sure if Lu is joking or not.

FOUR

Of Harbin's nine city districts, the second smallest of them—but arguably the most significant—is Nangang.

The district is split neatly into two distinct halves. The northern portion is a densely populated modern metropolis that pierces the heart of Harbin like a jagged sliver of glass. It is home to prestigious schools, luxury apartment buildings, thriving retail businesses, shopping centers, a railway station, and several beautiful parks. It is also where the administrative offices for Heilongjiang's provincial government are located.

To the southwest, concrete and steel give way to expansive agricultural fields and livestock farms. Scattered within this bucolic patchwork are tract housing developments, food-processing factories, and small manufacturing plants.

One such housing development is a neighborhood called Jin Shan Cun (Gold Mountain Village). No one knows how this name was derived—certainly, if there was ever any gold to be discovered there, it is long since gone. Likewise, if there once existed a mountain, it was leveled long ago, its soil washed away by rain and floods or carried off to replenish cabbage patches and vegetable gardens.

Yet the name persists.

In the center of Jin Shan Cun is a spacious compound with a main residence and two smaller buildings set among meticulously tended gardens of flowers, trees, and manicured bushes. The buildings are constructed in a turn-of-the-century European style with red brick and white cornerstones. A two-meter wall runs the circumference of the property.

Those who know of this place, and the depraved things that occur there, call it the Little Red Palace.

Its lord and master is a man named Tang Fuqiang. Tang is tall, slim, and still handsome at the age of fifty-one. He originally hails from a small village in the Heilongjiang hinterland—a coal-mining town. After watching his father spend his daylight hours crawling into a dark, dirty, and dangerous hole in the ground, only to emerge with a case of black lung that rendered him unable to walk without gasping for breath while not yet forty, Tang resolved to not let such a fate be his own.

After graduating from high school, Tang found work as an apprentice tailor. His good looks, brash charm, and eye for fashion proved a popular combination, and soon he had outgrown his small town and moved on to the nearest big city—Harbin. He arrived on a bus with only a few yuan in his pocket, a desire to get rich, and a willingness to do whatever was necessary to achieve that goal. He found work in a Harbin sweatshop, but the pay and conditions were not to his liking, so he impulsively decided to become a barber. He didn't know a thing about cutting hair, but in those days standards were not high, and any idiot with a decent pair of scissors and a comb could set up shop on a street corner and lure in the occasional victim.

In between customers, Tang entertained himself by sitting on his stool and making conversation with passersby, especially women, many of whom were beguiled by his quick tongue, tight trousers, and colorful silk shirts. One afternoon, a woman twenty years his senior—Ms. Meng—paused to exchange a few words. Ms. Meng found Tang witty and engaging—and much better looking than her elderly husband, who always reeked of the Zheng Gu Shui liniment he insisted she rub into the sagging flesh of his back and shoulders each night.

One thing led to another—a date for tea, a morning walk along the Songhua River—and soon they were meeting at his tiny roach-infested apartment for sex once or twice a week.

Ms. Meng had no illusions that they might run off to forge a new life together. Truth be told, she really had no desire to ditch her husband, repulsive as he may be, for some penniless street barber. But Tang made her feel alive and desirable in a way she hadn't for years.

Given Tang's precarious financial circumstances, Meng didn't mind paying when they went out for a meal. Tang would sometimes offer, pulling a wad of crinkled yuan out of his pocket with a sheepish grin, but no, she insisted. And she bought him gifts: A new shirt when she noticed his cuffs were fraying. A sweater when cold weather set in. Nothing outlandish or too expensive, nothing that might arouse her husband's suspicions.

But one thing Meng hated about her affair with Tang was his squalid apartment. She often suggested they get a room at a hotel, but Tang wouldn't hear of it.

"Why waste money when we have a perfectly good bed right here?"

"What about renting another apartment, then? A nicer one?"

"I'm cutting hair, not spinning gold. And anyway, if I had extra money, I would put it toward opening my own salon. A proper one with adjustable chairs, lighted mirrors, a sink with hot water. Thick, fluffy towels. Botanical shampoos and Western styling creams."

"A wonderful dream, Fuqiang."

"Yeah, but I'll never make it a reality. Not at this rate."

Inevitably, after some consideration, Meng offered Tang a modest loan. He refused the requisite three times, then gratefully accepted. Over the next few weeks, while they lay on sweat-soaked sheets after their exertions, he rattled on about his business plans. First he would rent a small space, outfit it on the cheap, and hire two other barbers to work for him. As business improved, he would upgrade, and then open a second salon, and a third.

Meng barely paid attention—she couldn't care less about what kind of electric razor Tang coveted, what color scheme he planned to use for his uniforms—but she took pleasure in his happiness.

One day, Tang phoned Meng to tell her he had the perfect spot picked out—available at a good rent, but if he was to secure it, he needed to come up with some fast cash. He quoted a sizable sum, more than Meng had anticipated. She asked to see the place. He took her to a vacant storefront. Cement floor, bare walls, exposed pipes, air ducts in the ceiling. Tang hummed with excitement as he showed her where he would put a trio of barber chairs, a table for complimentary tea, a sink for washing hair. That very afternoon, she withdrew the money from her bank account. She put the cash in an envelope and sealed it with the imprint of her lips.

Tang's eyes glistened with tears when he took it from her hand.

And then—nothing. He stopped answering Meng's phone calls and texts. She went to his apartment—the landlord told her Tang had moved out. She rushed to the vacant storefront. It remained empty. The owner told her Tang never signed a contract for the space.

In desperation, Meng left a hurt and angry message on Tang's voice mail threatening to go to the police. Not five minutes later, he called back.

"Listen, you bitch. You and I both know you won't go to the police because that would require you to tell them you gave me that money of your own free will—because I was giving you something your husband couldn't. How do you think he'd react if he heard that?"

"Fuqiang! How can you be so cruel?"

"How can you be so stupid?"

Meng choked back a sob. "Do you feel nothing for me?"

Tang snorted into the receiver. "A cow like you? I was strictly after the milk, darling. Now, don't call me again, or I'll drop a note to your hubby with all sorts of salacious details."

That was the last Meng heard from Tang. And in retrospect, she would not have been surprised to learn that she was only one of several women Tang romanced and dumped after being similarly misused.

FIVE

Despite the deceptive way Tang obtained the funds, he did use them for their stated purpose—to open a small salon, in one of the seedier parts of Nangang District.

But any customer unfortunate enough to wander into Tang's salon off the street would no doubt find it just a bit . . . odd. The front room was cramped, with barely enough space for a cheap couch and three secondhand barber chairs. Beauty supplies were minimal: a few combs floating in jars of green antiseptic like medical specimens, a shelf holding an anemic collection of shampoos and conditioners.

And, at any given time, up to three young women lounging in the chairs, dressed in matching uniforms of tank tops and short skirts, idly scrolling through their phones with an air of apathy.

If our prospective customer was foolish enough to persist in his quest for a haircut, one of the girls might grudgingly be convinced to give it a go. But the customer would surely be disappointed with the results, because none of the girls could cut hair worth a damn.

The real action in Tang's salon took place in a few small rooms in the back, where thirty minutes with one of the girls cost three hundred yuan—less than fifty dollars U.S. When he first opened for business, Tang had the girls make the rounds of various bars and clubs, handing out business cards to prosperous-looking middle-aged men. After only a few months, the salon was turning a modest profit, which Tang frugally squirreled away in anticipation of expanding his operation.

It was around this time that Tang received a visit by a uniformed PSB sergeant. The sergeant was short and squat and had lips that reminded Tang of a flounder.

"My name is Xu," the sergeant said. "Vice Division."

Tang had been expecting such a visit and was as cool as a sea cucumber. "Would you like some tea, Sergeant?"

"What I'd like is to have a look around." Without waiting for an invitation, Xu opened the door leading to the back and disappeared inside.

The girls were nervous—they knew the stakes. Any evidence pointing to the true nature of the salon's business—even a single unused condom—would be sufficient to charge them with prostitution and earn them a stint in a reeducation center. They whispered and fretted until Tang told them to shut up.

While Xu was poking around in the back, Tang poured a cup of tea and slipped five thousand yuan into an envelope. When Xu returned, Tang offered him a seat. He set the envelope down, with the teacup on top of it.

Xu lowered himself into the chair, crossed his legs, and lit a cigarette. "Rooms with cots. Reeking of bleach."

"Those are so my girls can rest between customers," Tang said.

Xu laughed. "Sure, sure." He eyed the girls appraisingly and took a sip of tea.

"Would you like a . . . haircut?" Tang asked. He called one of the girls over and had her twirl for Xu.

Xu smiled but shook his head. He took a final drag on his cigarette and dropped it into the teacup. He took the envelope, counted the contents, and slipped it into his pocket. "All seems to be in order. Have a nice day."

Thereafter, Xu returned around the first of the month to collect an envelope. The third time Tang offered him one of the girls, Xu said: "No. I like them a bit . . . younger."

When it came time to open another salon, Tang discussed his plans with Xu. "There's someone you should meet," Xu suggested.

A sit-down in a private room at a restaurant was arranged. In attendance was a man in his fifties, dressed in a Western suit and smoking a Western cigarette.

The man wore thick black glasses and was draped in an invisible, yet tangible, cloak of authority. Xu made introductions.

"This is Mr. Gao—Nangang deputy mayor and party secretary."

"I'm honored," Tang said.

"You should be," Xu answered.

Gao waved dismissively. "Please, sit. Let's talk. I understand you have big plans. Perhaps I can, in some small way, be of assistance."

Thus began a long and mutually rewarding relationship.

Tang's one salon turned into two, and two into three. Gao assisted with permits and bureaucratic red tape. Tang was clever with his money and parlayed his earnings into side ventures. Gambling dens. Legitimate real estate. As his fortunes rose, Gao introduced him to other influential members of the Nangang elite. Tang's *guanxi* network broadened and deepened. It was easy to make friends when he was generous with his bribes, women, and booze.

Time passed as water flows down a river. Tang grew rich and powerful in his own right. And, as every king needs a castle, Tang built himself one in Gold Mountain Village—the Little Red Palace.

Meanwhile, Xu was promoted to head of the Nangang PSB and then, later, chief of Homicide for Harbin; as for Gao, he was arrested and sent to jail on charges of corruption and lost absolutely everything.

Since its humble beginnings as a cheap salon-cum-brothel, the LRP has evolved into an opulent den of vast and varied iniquity. Millions in yuan are won and lost there on the toss of a single die. Meals of contraband bushmeat, Kobe steak, raw fish, French cheeses, and decadent desserts are washed down with oceans of imported champagne, beer, and cognac. Girls from China, Korea, the Philippines, Vietnam, and Thailand are on hand to fulfill the feverish fantasies of rich and powerful men.

And, following Gao's arrest and imprisonment, the local elite who fluttered around him like moths to a flame shifted their orbit to Tang and his Little Red Palace. He is less their titular leader than a fat and cunning spider at the center of a web that ensnares them through vice or money or, in most cases, a generous allotment of both.

These men call themselves—informally, confidentially, and with a hint of sarcasm—the Nangang Benevolent Association.

And at this moment, all eleven members of the NBA are seated around a long mahogany table in a wood-paneled room at the Little Red Palace, smoking cigarettes, drinking their beverage of choice—and clucking like chickens in a slaughterhouse.

SIX

The members of the NBA are scattered throughout the highest strata of Nangang District's executive, legislative, and judicial branches. Taken individually, each of their official positions has the potential to bring in a great deal of money. Not legitimately, of course—civil servants in the People's Republic are paid a pittance—but the opportunities for influence peddling, insider trading, patronage, bid rigging, collaboration with criminal networks, and so on, are as bountiful as individual grains in a mountain of rice.

Meanwhile, their collective stranglehold on Nangang politics and business provides them with a power equal to that of pint-sized Sicilian Mafia.

To take just one example, there is the matter of affordable housing.

Prior to 1988, most citizens in the People's Republic were allocated housing based on their *danwei,* or work unit. After this system was abolished, housing development skyrocketed, but so did real estate prices. While many entrepreneurial urban residents were able to take advantage of new and improved housing opportunities, others were left in the lurch.

The central government soon realized it had a problem—a lot of angry people accustomed to state-provided housing, no matter how squalid, who were now basically homeless. It quickly issued new policies aimed at ensuring most middle-class and low-income families could find an affordable place to live. But, for the sake of efficiency, it left the actual construction, financing, and management of such projects to local authorities.

Sitting around the table in the conference room of the Little Red Palace at this very moment are the select few in charge of all public housing in Nangang: Mayor Pang; Deputy Mayor Wan; Director Liu of the Public Rental Housing

Corporation; and Mr. Zhao, head of the state-owned Building Investment Corporation. Together, these worthies appropriate land for public projects, review construction bids, appoint developers, monitor costs and profits, and decide which lucky citizens receive access to new apartments.

The situation is much the same when it comes to the administration of justice. The NBA counts among its brotherhood Chief Hong, head of the local Public Security Bureau; Judge Ren, president of the district court; and Mr. Cai, head of the Nangang Procuratorate Arrest Section. And, of course, there's Xu, chief of Harbin Homicide.

The NBA's membership is rounded out by Director Chen of the Investment Inviting Corporation and Chairman Yu of the District Standing Committee.

These ten officials, plus Tang Fuqiang, equal eleven men. Eleven crooked pillars supporting a rotten shrine dedicated to sex, greed, and power.

The NBA generally meets once a month to discuss various business matters, but on this particular evening, the talk centers on a series of questions uppermost in everyone's minds:

Who—or *what*—is the Magistrate? What *exactly* does he know about the Nangang Benevolent Association?

And most importantly—what the *hell* does he *want*?

Wan is in his late fifties, short and round-faced. He smokes Panda cigarettes, like his role model, Deng Xiaoping. Although he is the deputy mayor and therefore officially number two in the hierarchy of the civil government, he also serves as secretary of the district Chinese Communist Party. That makes him the most powerful politician in the room. "This Magistrate—as he or *they* call themselves—clearly has it out for us." He waves his cigarette around the table. "We are all in danger."

Wan's titular senior, Mr. Pang, purses his thin, bloodless lips. "We can't be certain of that, Brother Wan. Maybe it's just *some* of us." He smiles patronizingly at Chen and Liu. Chen's right eye is a startling shade of purple. Liu has a white bandage taped over his cheek. "Have you two been cooking up some clandestine deal we don't know about, and upset the wrong person?"

Liu angrily rips the bandage from his cheek. "Are you suggesting I've been stealing petty cash from under everybody's nose? Is that why I have this obscene thing on my face?"

Pang shrugs. It's not inconceivable that Liu had some side deal going he didn't tell the others about and it went sour.

"Brother Wan is right," Chen says. "The Magistrate obviously knows who we are, and you'd better watch your asses, because he's coming for one of you next!"

"But *why*?" says Chief Hong.

"That's a—excuse me for saying—stupid question," Chairman Yu sniffs. "Who among us has not stepped on dozens of toes? Cultivated a host of bitter enemies on our rise to the top? Tall trees cast long shadows."

"But how would this person—or entity—know our identities?" asks Procurator Cai. "It's not like we carry membership cards."

Judge Ren swirls cognac in a crystal goblet. "Inside man?"

The table erupts into a chorus of competing voices. Tang allows the men to speak over one another for a moment, then raps his knuckles sharply on the wood. "Gentlemen, please. This is getting us nowhere." The hubbub subsides. "I don't think we need to start searching for knives hidden behind our backs just yet. While we don't publicize our fraternity, there are plenty of outside business partners and rivals who know at least something of our unspoken affiliation."

Zhao's voice quivers: "Keep in mind, these . . . assailants . . . have substantial resources. Vehicles. Knowledge of our movements. *Tasers*."

Yu shifts his frown over to Chief Hong. "Has your investigation turned up not even a shred of evidence?"

"The suspects wore masks," Hong says. "The car they used was a Bentian." *Bentian* is the Chinese pronunciation for the characters that make up the Honda brand name. As there are millions of Hondas on Chinese roads, this information is next to useless. "And they were careful to avoid areas with CCTV cameras."

Wan toys with his glass of scotch. "Does that mean they have access to classified information regarding the city surveillance network?"

"It's easy enough to find that information online," Hong says. "If you do a bit of digging."

Yu turns to Xu. "And you, exalted chief of Homicide? Anything useful to share?"

Xu takes a leisurely drag of his cigarette before answering. "Has a homicide occurred that I am not aware of? Because until it does, these crimes are not in my jurisdiction, and were I to get involved, it might the arouse the suspicions of my superiors, no?"

Wan grunts. "What about media coverage?"

"I haven't filed any incident reports," Hong says. "There's nothing for the media to cover."

"What happens in Nangang stays in Nangang," Pang says smugly.

Judge Ren generally bangs a gavel when he wants attention, but here he settles for ostentatiously clearing his throat. "I suggest for the time being we all proceed with extreme caution. Never travel alone. Vary your routine. Take an alternate route to your office and home."

"Sure, fine," Zhao says. "But until we discover who's behind this, we'll all constantly be looking over our shoulders."

"We have assembled here the finest minds in local law enforcement," Procurator Cai says. "It seems to me we should be able to approach this like any other crime. Starting with a likely suspect. Or suspects."

Tang lights a fresh cigarette. "I think we can safely rule each other out. It's not as if Brother Zhao can eliminate Brother Ren and take his place on the district court, right? Or I could depose Brother Pang and become mayor. We each have our roles and our revenue streams. Targeting one another gains nothing, and in fact weakens us considerably."

"Who, then?" Zhao says. "A rival who wants to take over your prostitution operation? Have you reached out to your *hei shehui* contacts to ask if they know anything?" This term, *hei shehui,* literally means "secret society," but refers specifically to the criminal underworld.

"I've put word out," Tang says. "If I hear something of interest, I'll let everyone know."

"The answer seems rather obvious to me," Yu says. He pauses for dramatic effect. "Gao is behind it."

There is a moment of uncomfortable silence. Then Xu says: "Unlikely."

"How do you know?" Yu asks. "He has every reason to be bitter. To want revenge. We sold him down the river. We picked over the remains of his carcass."

"We had an understanding," Tang says. "There was simply no logic to all of us going down."

Yu smiles thinly. "Maybe someone whispered in his ear about you stealing his woman."

Xu intervenes to preempt a brawl. "Gao is, by all accounts, much diminished. A shell of his former self. Penniless, apart from the small sums we see fit to send him. I don't believe he could mount an operation of this complexity."

"What about his mental state?" Ren asks. "Have you visited him since he got out? Has any of us?"

No one answers. No one has.

"Perhaps," Wan suggests, "that would be a logical first order of business. Go around there and have a look. And may I suggest, Brother Hong, that you peruse his phone and bank records? See if anything raises a red flag?"

"Of course," Hong says.

Xu's sigh is punctuated by cigarette smoke. "I suppose it falls to me to pay a visit to him."

Before the meeting concludes, Tang brings up one final matter—his missing director and escaped cybersex girls. "This is the third time one of my cybersex dens has been compromised this year. I've lost five girls and, as you all know, one of my directors was found floating facedown in the Songhua River recently. I can only assume this latest one has been murdered as well."

"It's not just you," Pang says. "I've heard rumors of similar problems in other districts."

"It's these damn Christian missionary organizations," Hong says. "Masquerading as vocational schools. Nonprofits. Meanwhile, they're running a highly sophisticated underground railroad spiriting girls out of the country. Even with orders from Beijing to stamp them out, they're like knotweed. Rip one out and two more spring up in its place."

"Well, each of these girls costs me five or six thousand yuan," Tang says. "It adds up. Can't you do something about it?"

"No witnesses?" Hong asks.

"Just the director's wife. All she saw was a van and a man."

"All right. We'll check local traffic cams to see if we can get a license plate. Which will probably be stolen."

"If what you say is true and someone's murdering your directors," Ren says, "it would appear these religious organizations are oddly lacking in the compunction not to kill."

"Fanatics," Tang says. "On a mission from God."

The meeting adjourns. A handful of the men stay behind to enjoy various diversions—Judge Ren plays cards; Xu takes one of Tang's newer and younger girls up to a room. Chen and Liu get drunk in the lounge and commiserate at their rough treatment by the Magistrate.

Zhao would like nothing more than to join in the fun, but it's only Monday and he has an important and stressful presentation to make to the Asset Supervision and Administration Commission tomorrow—so he decides to head home and get a good night's rest.

A prudent decision—and one he will soon regret.

SEVEN

When Zhao emerges from the front entrance to the Little Red Palace, his driver is waiting behind the wheel of gleaming black Trumpchi sedan parked in the courtyard. Zhao climbs in back.

"Home," he says.

A guard opens the gates, and the driver exits, zigzags through residential streets, emerging onto a two-lane road heading north. Zhao leans back against the white doily covering the headrest and closes his eyes. He is on the verge of dozing off when the driver curses, decreases speed, and pulls over.

Zhao sits up. "What's going on?"

"Police," the driver says.

Zhao glances through the back window. He sees red and blue flashing lights. "Were you speeding?"

"Only a little," the driver admits.

Zhao lowers his window. "I'll sort these fools out."

A man dressed in a police uniform and cotton face mask approaches from the rear.

"Look here," Zhao says, sticking his ID out of his open window. "My name is Zhao and I'm the director of the Nangang Investment Inviting—"

"I'll deal with you in minute, sir," the officer says. He taps his flashlight on the driver's window. "Lower your window." The driver does. "Unlock your doors and put the key on the dashboard."

"What is this about?" Zhao says.

The officer shines his flashlight in Zhao's face. "I *said,* I'll deal with you in a moment." He turns back to the driver. "Door! Key!" The driver unlocks the door and drops the key on the dashboard. "Put your hands on the steering wheel," the officer says.

"Why?" the driver asks.

"Please comply with my instructions immediately."

The driver grudgingly puts his hands on the wheel. The officer reaches in and slaps a handcuff on the driver's left wrist, then locks the other end to the wheel.

"Hey, what the hell are you doing?" the driver growls, tugging at the cuff.

"This is outrageous!" Zhao shouts.

The officer reaches in and frisks the driver. He finds no weapons, just a cell phone, which he tosses on the floor in front of the passenger's seat. He takes the car key and puts it into his pocket, then opens Zhao's door.

"I'll have your job for this, you maniac!" Zhao shouts.

"Move." The officer shoves Zhao over and climbs onto the seat beside him. Zhao scrambles for the opposite door—but it opens and a second uniformed officer forces his way in.

Zhao, too late, understands what is about to happen.

The first officer—Zhang—tases Zhao. The second officer—Li—cuffs Zhao's right wrist to the headrest of the passenger's seat and his left wrist to the driver's seat.

Zhao's driver starts slamming his palm onto the car horn and shouting out the window at passing cars. Zhang reaches over and tases him in the neck. "Quit making a fuss," he says. "Just sit quietly. We're not here for you."

Zhang and Li pull folded rain ponchos from their pockets, shake them out, shrug into them. They slip their hands into latex gloves.

"Ready?" Li says.

Zhang takes a deep breath. "Ready." He removes a knife from his pocket. The blade is serrated, like a shark's tooth.

Zhao flails in panic. Li wraps his arm around Zhao's neck, pulls him close, holds on tight.

Zhang grips Zhao's left wrist and places the edge of the knife on Zhao's forearm.

Then he begins to saw.

Zhao's driver leans into the steering wheel and claps his hands over his ears to shut out Zhao's shrieks and the revolting sound of the knife cutting flesh and bone.

Blood spurts across the car's faux-leather and vinyl wood-grain interior. Zhao mercifully faints. After thirty more seconds of forceful knife work, Zhao's severed hand pops free with a wet squelch. Li releases Zhao's limp body. He ties a length of rubber tubing around the stump of Zhao's forearm and wraps it in a roll of gauze.

Zhang and Li, drenched with blood, get out of the car. They strip off their ponchos, turn them inside out, and wad them into balls. Zhang leans down to speak to the driver. "When he wakes up, tell Zhao the Magistrate sends his regards." He and Li return to their car. The flashing lights switch off.

As they speed past, Zhao's driver can see they are driving an ordinary sedan—a Bentian.

He reaches down and fishes on the floor for his cell phone. He dials emergency one-handed. The operator comes on the line and the driver begins to explain the situation, but then Zhao revives, sees his severed hand dangling in front of his nose, and starts screaming.

EIGHT

Tuesday morning, Lu and Sun depart Raven Valley at first light to catch a train for the four-hour ride to Yanji City. Lu brings a laptop and catches up on some administrative work. Sun buries herself in a book, making occasional notes with a pencil.

"What are you reading?" Lu eventually asks. Sun shows him the cover. It's a Korean language textbook. Intermediate-level. "This inmate is Chaoxianzu," Lu says, using the term for an ethnic Korean who resides in the PRC. "I'm sure he speaks Mandarin."

"Maybe he'll appreciate hearing some Korean—as a sign of our sincerity."

Lu smiles at her naivete. "These career criminals are way past such niceties. He'll just want to know what we can do for him in exchange for any information he provides."

"Well . . . it can't hurt," Sun says, sounding a bit wounded.

Lu wants to tell her to toughen up, especially if she plans to make a career in the PSB, but then he remembers she doesn't—so what's the point? "Have you and Mr. Yao set a wedding date yet?"

"No, we just got engaged. Sometime next year, I expect."

"And when do you plan to resign?"

Sun sighs and closes her textbook. "Perhaps this summer."

"Why so soon?"

"It will be a big wedding. Lots of planning involved."

Lu mutters something under his breath.

"Sorry?" Sun asks.

Lu doesn't answer at first. Then he says: "It's just that . . . I'll hate to lose you."

This admission catches Sun by surprise. She reopens her textbook and buries her nose in it.

Lu turns to stare moodily out the window at the flat, gray autumn landscape.

They arrive in Yanji, the capital of the Yanbian Autonomous Prefecture, a few hours later. It is a modest city of about four hundred thousand residents. Lu notices that all the street signs are written in both Chinese and Korean.

At the train station, he buys a carton of cigarettes, a cheap lighter, and a prepaid cell phone. He and Sun hop into a taxi and ask to be taken to the detention center. As they pass through the city, Lu finds himself impressed by Yanji's modern architecture, wide streets, and general cleanliness.

The detention center, like most such facilities, is a foreboding and cheerless place constructed of steel and cement, surrounded by walls and watch towers, prioritizing security over fitness for human habitation. They enter, relinquish their valuables, sign paperwork, and wait for thirty minutes until a guard comes to fetch them. The guard leads them down unheated corridors that echo with the sound of clanging steel and disembodied human voices. Their path terminates at a metal door—the guard unlocks it and shows them into an interview room.

"Wait here," the guard says. He leaves, slamming the door behind him.

Sun shivers. "Colder in here than outside."

That's only a slight exaggeration. Lu takes a seat at a wooden table. Sun paces back and forth. The room smells like damp rot. There are splotchy stains on the wall—could be mildew; could be blood. Lu sees that Sun is anxious and asks her to refresh his memory regarding the details of the inmate to help settle her mind.

"Park Jinhua," Sun recites from memory. "Age twenty-five. Born in Yanji to parents who immigrated from South Korea in the eighties. Busted for running a cybersex operation using trafficked female defectors from North Korea. He was identified as a Guryong gang member upon arrest—by means of his tattoo.

Previously, he was busted on some misdemeanors, for which he was placed under *guanzhi*."

Guanzhi—literally "control"—is a lesser form of punishment levied on criminals convicted of relatively minor offenses. It requires them to keep local authorities apprised of their movements and activities and limits their freedom of speech, assembly, and protest.

"I expect he's looking at some serious time now," Lu says.

"If he's guilty of what he's accused of, he should be executed," Sun says.

Lu is somewhat shocked by Sun's vehemence, but he can't disagree.

The sexual abuse and trafficking of North Korean women and girls is a serious and growing issue in China. Hundreds of North Korean women defect every year, seeking relief from famine and repression, and hopeful for a better life. Go-betweens often promise them a job in a restaurant or factory—then sell them to brokers who force them into marriage, prostitution, or cybersex work. To make matters worse, the Chinese government regards these victims as illegal immigrants rather than refugees. If they go to the authorities, they are simply repatriated back to North Korea, where they will likely serve time in prison camps under horrific conditions.

While he waits for Park to arrive, Lu opens the carton of cigarettes and removes a single pack. He puts it in his pocket and places the remainder of the carton under his chair.

There is a sharp rap on the door. The door opens and the guard leads Park in.

Park is handcuffed and dressed in loose-fitting blue pants with white stripes down the seams and a blue jacket with stripes on the shoulders and breast pockets. The guard sits Park in a chair across the table from Lu.

"You can leave his hands free," Lu says.

"You sure?" the guard asks.

"Is this inmate known to be violent?"

"Not particularly."

"No need for cuffs, then."

The guard shrugs. "Suit yourself." He removes Park's cuffs and goes to the door. "Knock when you're ready." He leaves. Lu hears the clunk of a key twisting in the lock.

Park keeps his eyes on the table. His face bears the signs of a recent beating—a purplish bruise under one eye, a scrape on his nose and chin. Lu wonders if that was the work of another inmate, or the guards.

"I am Deputy Chief Lu Fei of the Raven Valley PSB," Lu says. "This is Constable Sun."

Park doesn't react.

"According to your police record, you are a member of the Guryong gang," Lu says. "Members of your gang use a tattoo of a carp holding a knife in its mouth as an identifier. Correct?"

No response.

Lu nods at Sun. She produces a folder. Lu opens it and removes a photograph of the dead man's torso. He points to the tattoo detail. "One like this. Look!"

Park lifts his eyes, glances at the photo. His brows knit briefly, then he looks away.

"This tattoo was discovered on a body that was dumped on the side of the Tongjiang Expressway Sunday night," Lu continues. "The victim was doused with gasoline and set on fire."

Park shrugs infinitesimally.

Lu removes the lighter and pack of cigarettes from his pocket. He picks open the foil of the pack and shakes out a cigarette. He rests it in the center of the table. He keeps the remainder of the pack by his elbow.

After a few seconds, Park makes a grab for the cigarette. Lu slaps his hand over it. "We want to know who this dead person is."

Park leans back and folds his arms. He meets Lu's gaze with a defiant stare.

Lu turns to Sun. "Did you bring that baton like I told you?" He smiles, picks up the cigarette, and offers it to Park. "You're already listed as a gang member in our criminal database. Identifying the body isn't going to cause you any additional trouble. Why not help us out?"

Park snatches the cigarette. Lu lights it for him. Park inhales deeply. "Why do you care, Chinese policeman? Just another Korean gangster, right?"

"This victim was dumped in my jurisdiction. I consider that a personal insult. The killer must think I'm too stupid to catch him."

Park smokes furiously, as if any moment his cigarette will be confiscated.

"Can you help me or not?" Lu asks.

"I don't know," Park says. "Can you help *me*?"

"With your case? Absolutely not. You deserve everything that's coming to you."

"But I'm innocent."

"Said every criminal ever." Lu pushes the photo across the table. "Who is this dead man? You must know him. There aren't so many of you Guryong boys in Northwest China."

Park blows smoke from the corner of his mouth.

Lu understands Park's reticence. If he provides Lu with the victim's identity, he knows Lu will investigate the victim's background, associates, possible motives for his murder. In the process, he may turn up additional incriminating evidence on Park himself. Lu pushes the open pack of cigarettes across the table. "Here."

"That's it?" Park says. "You're offering me a lousy pack of cigarettes?"

Lu retrieves the carton from under his seat and sets that on the table. "Feel free to smoke yourself to death. All I'm asking for is the victim's name."

"Think you can buy me as cheaply as some desperate little bitch from North Korea?" Park sneers.

Sun takes Lu by surprise—she steps forward and snatches up the folder, finds a photograph of the victim's clawed hand, slaps it down. "Your friend was tortured hideously before he was murdered. First, they beat him. Then they cut off his fingers, one by one."

Park makes a show of studying the cracked and peeling paint on the ceiling.

Sun slaps another photograph down, this one of the victim's mouth pried open by the medical examiner. "After that, they pulled out his teeth! Look!"

Park flicks ash on the floor, takes another drag on his cigarette. Lu reaches over and slaps it out of his mouth. "The constable told you to look at the photo, so look, damn your mother!"

Park curses under his breath and stares at the photo with exaggerated interest. "There! I looked! Satisfied?"

Sun's face has gone white, apart from two circles of bright red on her cheeks. "Can you guess what they did after they chopped off your friend's fingers and yanked out his teeth? No? They cut off his . . . his private parts. They made a little pile of them on his chest, doused him with gasoline, and lit him on fire!"

Sun is obviously embellishing, but Lu doesn't contradict her.

"We don't care about you," Sun continues. "We don't even care about your dead friend, to be honest. But we aren't about to let the kind of monsters who would do something like this to go free. They must be brought to justice. Will you help us or not?"

Lu inches the carton of cigarettes across the table. "A name is all we ask."

"How the hell should I know who this dead person is?" Park snarls. "I haven't spoken to anyone on the outside since I got here. They won't even let me call a lawyer! I'm completely cut off!"

Lu was expecting this. He takes the prepaid cell phone out of his pocket, sets it on the table. "Make some calls to your friends. Ask around."

"In return for smokes? You'll have to do better."

"Right. Let me think. How about this carton of cigarettes—and I won't beat the living shit out you."

Park snorts.

"Have you no loyalty to your gang?" Sun asks. "No honor?"

"What would you know about it, little girl?" Park shouts.

"I know if someone did this to my brother, I'd want to avenge him, without regard for my own skin."

Park snorts again. "Then you're a fool. This is real life, not a kung fu comic book."

"I'll see that you get a lawyer," Lu says.

"How?"

"I'm a deputy chief in the PSB. I can make it happen."

Park grunts skeptically.

"Give me a name and I'll get a lawyer in here by the end of the week if I have to pay his initial retainer myself."

Park chews on that for a moment, then reaches for the phone. "Can I at least have some fucking privacy?"

Lu knocks for the guard and then he and Sun go out into the corridor. They wait ten minutes. When they return to the room, they find Park with his feet propped on the table, smoking a cigarette, cackling on the phone like the neighborhood gossip. Lu holds his hand out for the phone. Park clutches it protectively to his chest.

"Tea break is over," Lu says. "You got a name?"

"Maybe."

"Give me the phone."

"Hell, no. You'll see who I called and go hassle them."

"Erase the numbers, then."

"What am I, stupid? As if you can't hack a phone."

Lu's patience is wearing thin. "Destroy it, I don't care!"

"Let me keep it."

"Not on your life."

"Then I'm not telling you shit."

Lu lunges for the phone. He and Park engage in a mildly embarrassing tussle until Lu snatches it away. He hurls it to the floor and stomps on it. "There! Problem solved! Now—a name!"

Park curses in Korean, words Lu does not understand, but he gets the gist. "Sung Jongmin. Missing since Sunday night."

"What was Sung's role in your gang?" Lu asks.

"What gang?"

"The one tattooed on your ass, Park. Come on, don't make this any more difficult than necessary."

"He operated an internet chat den."

"You mean a cybersex operation?" Sun says.

"No. Just a site where lonely men can chat with pretty girls."

"Where was this?" Sun asks. "Are the girls still being held there?"

"No. They're gone."

"What do you mean, gone?" Lu asks.

"They climbed out the window the same night Sung went missing."

"I see," Lu says. "Is this the work of a rival gang encroaching on your business? Killing your people and stealing your girls?"

Park shrugs. "Maybe it's just the local cops going into business for themselves."

"What was Sung's address?"

"Harbin. That's all I know. Me and Sung weren't buddies or anything. He did his thing in Harbin, and I did mine here."

"Harbin," Lu says. "Right." He starts gathering up the photos to place back in the folder. "Enjoy your cigarettes, Mr. Park."

Outside in the parking lot, Lu says, "Good work in there."

"I lost my temper. Sorry about that."

"Not at all. One must find a way to cut through the bluster with these thugs, and I think your shaming him is what ultimately did it."

"I think it was you promising him a lawyer. Are you going to follow through?"

"Hell, no. Let him rot."

Sun is a tad surprised by Lu's duplicity, but also not inclined to defend Park. "Where do we go from here?"

"You heard him—Sung is from Harbin. We'll turn the case over to Harbin Metro."

"We came all this way and went to all this trouble just to let *them* have it?"

"It's their jurisdiction."

"But the body was found in Raven Valley."

"My guess is the killer dumped Sung there because it was sufficiently remote. The nexus of the case remains in Harbin."

"But—"

"Constable—that's how these things go. Let's just move on."

Lu understands Sun's disappointment. Nothing makes a police officer feel quite so alive as hunting a killer. And he knows the case will be remanded to the Harbin Homicide Division which is run by a man he loathes—Xu.

But never mind. Lu is not welcome in Harbin, and Sung Jongmin is no longer his responsibility.

NINE

Xu sits in the back of his unmarked SUV as it jockeys through Harbin morning traffic. His hulking driver, a detective nicknamed Pangu, makes liberal use of the lights and siren to bypass particularly crowded patches.

Xu pops the lid off a bottle of Baoji pills, tosses the contents down his throat, and rubs his roiling stomach.

In ordinary times, work is stressful enough—meetings, paperwork, speeches, official appearances, unrelenting pressure from higher-ups, the constant threat of a knife in the back from departmental rivals. The tension never lets up, even for a second.

But now, adding fuel to the fire, there are Tang's missing cybersex girls and dead director—the director's identity confirmed by a police report sent over to Harbin Homicide just this morning—and a madman (*madmen?*) calling himself the Magistrate.

Xu is not overly worried about the two missing girls. Sex trafficking is a porous business, susceptible to breaches of security. You can't keep humans penned up like livestock forever. And the girls will be too frightened of being deported to go crying to the authorities, so Tang need not fear blowback on that score.

The murder of the director, however, is more troubling. When Tang's first director turned up dead, Xu was willing to chalk it up to an unpaid gambling debt, a rivalry for a woman's affections, a beef with some other tough guy—the motives for a killing among such bottom feeders are as abundant as fleas on a wild dog.

Now the body count has risen to two. Is the assassin, as Tang suggests, a fanatical Christian missionary steeping himself in the blood of sinners? Maybe, maybe not. Whoever he is, one thing's for sure—he has high-level skills.

Despite the seriousness of the matter, Xu allows himself a smile when he thinks of the director's body turning up in Raven Valley. That stuck-up bastard Lu Fei thought he'd finally caught a decent case after years of handing out speeding tickets and investigating stolen tractor batteries, only to have to hand it over to Harbin Homicide. What a bitter pill to swallow!

Xu's smile quickly fades when he considers the enigma that is the Magistrate. Seemingly well funded, organized, adept at surveillance, abduction, and violent assault. And escalating rapidly. Chen beaten. Liu tattooed. And now Zhao—his hand lopped off.

Xu believes the alias—the "Magistrate"—to be an important clue. In the dynastic era, magistrates were local officials who carried out the will of the emperor. They supervised the populace, collected taxes, enforced the law. When it came to the administration of justice, the magistrate decided which civil and criminal cases to consider, gathered evidence, and questioned witnesses, often by means of torture. And he alone determined guilt and innocence and meted out appropriate punishment.

In choosing this title, the Magistrate is signaling that he considers himself judge, jury, and executioner.

And that brings Xu to his current assignment. A visit to his old friend and erstwhile mentor, Gao Yang.

When he and Xu first met, Gao was a rising star in local politics. And it was partially through Gao's patronage that Xu and the others—Mayor Pang, Deputy Mayor Wan, Chairman Yu—ascended to their current positions.

In those early days, the central government was still under the influence of Deng Xiaoping and his "principle of collective leadership"—a system in which the most powerful men in the central government ruled by consensus. Deng's goal was for the country to never again suffer chaos and instability under an unassailable cult of personality such as the one surrounding Mao Zedong. But he failed to account for the cultural features—distance, environment, dialect, economics, clan loyalties—that give rise to regional rivalries. So, while Deng was aiming for one big happy family, what he got instead was a new political arrangement that eventually became known as "one party, two factions."

The party was, of course, the CCP, and the factions were the Shanghai Gang, a coalition of urban coastal elites, and the Chinese Communist Youth League (CCYL), an alliance of populists rooted in the countryside. Both groups engaged in blatant patronage. When Jiang Zemin of the Shanghai Gang succeeded Deng, he installed his trusted compatriots in important government positions. When Hu Jintao of the CCYL succeeded Jiang, he did the same. Over time, there was a natural ebb and flow as one leader gained influence, promoted his protégés, and they in turn promoted their subordinates. Surprisingly, this system, although creaky and ethically challenged, worked—because, despite naked favoritism, the presence of both Shanghai Gang and CCYL members at senior levels of government provided a check and balance on each other's worst impulses.

Gao was a Shanghai Gang protégé, and he came up quickly through the ranks during Jiang's tenure, eventually securing an appointment as Nangang deputy mayor and party secretary in the early 2000s. And he appeared destined for even more lofty achievements—mayor of Harbin, or even governor of Heilongjiang Province.

Gao was riding high in his private life as well. He had a luxurious home. Wealth and connections. A luxury automobile, a driver, and bodyguard.

And a beautiful wife.

Even now, thinking of her—Ling Wei—Xu feels a stirring in his groin.

Ling was an aspiring singer more than twenty years Gao's junior, plying her trade in smoky lounges and cheap cabarets. In Xu's estimation, Ling's voice was only middling at best. But she had the face of an angel. And the body of a goddess.

Together, they were the ultimate power couple. Gao, the charismatic politico. Ling, the perfect complement to his ambition.

And then Gao ran into a brick wall. Namely, an anti-corruption campaign carried out by the newly appointed President of the People's Republic, Xi Jinping.

Like Gao, Xi came from solid revolutionary stock and enjoyed a privileged upbringing—until Mao Zedong purged his father for a perceived lack of dedication to socialist principles. During the Cultural Revolution, Xi was "sent down to the countryside" to live among the peasants of rural Shaanxi Province. This later turned out to be an advantage, as he was able to portray himself simultaneously as an elite, *and* as a man of the common people. Xi's dual pedigree helped him rapidly ascend the ranks of provincial and national politics until he was eventually appointed Hu Jintao's successor.

Once at the tiller, Xi moved quickly to consolidate his position. His efforts were assisted by a perception among CCP leaders at the time that the government had lost its ideological direction. One of Xi's first moves was to launch an anti-corruption campaign to root out, as he called them, "tigers and flies"— crooked high-ranking officials and ordinary party functionaries. For this effort, he relied heavily on a government agency called the Central Commission for Discipline Inspection (CCDI). The CCDI had the authority to investigate reports of corruption, imprison suspects without a warrant, and, like the magistrates of old, conduct interrogations and elicit confessions through beatings, sleep deprivation, and seizures of property.

Thousands of high- and mid-level bureaucrats of both the Shanghai and CCYL factions were caught up in the CCDI's net. Many, if not most, were in fact guilty of corruption. Others were simply the victims of factional power conflicts. A large number were targeted because they were rivals to the authority of the newly emerging "Xi Gang."

As for Gao, no one knows who originally reported him to the authorities, or why the CCDI elected to take up his case. No matter—he was quickly accused of "wavering in his ideals and beliefs, turning his back on party missions and values, violating regulations, bathing in the pomp and circumstance of his special privileges, practicing favoritism . . . ," et cetera, et cetera. All these accusations were indisputably true, but Gao was no better or worse than any other politician of his ilk.

Long story short, Gao's goose was cooked. An emergency conclave was convened at the Little Red Palace. Gao could not attend—he was already locked up.

The eleven members of the Nangang Benevolent Association came up with a proposal. It fell on Xu to deliver it.

He visited Gao at the detention center. Although Gao had only been there a week, he had seemingly aged a decade. Xu made his pitch. Gao was going down—that much was certain. And to be brutally honest, if questioned by the CCDI, Xu and the others would have no choice but to denounce and disavow him.

Gao understood. He was nothing if not a pragmatist.

In return for Gao's silence regarding the complicity of the others, the NBA was offering support upon his release. To ensure he was provided for until the end of his days.

But Gao had something else on his mind. "Ling Wei is divorcing me."

Xu was not surprised. A dish like Ling could have any man she wanted. Now that Gao was disgraced and penniless, it only made sense that she would move on to the next *gan die*—sugar daddy.

"I don't care what happens to me," Gao continued. "But I want you and the others to swear that you'll watch out for Weiwei. Keep her safe. Make sure she is comfortable."

"Of course, Brother Gao," Xu said. "On behalf of all the brothers, I swear."

That was the last time Xu laid eyes on Gao. Soon after, he was convicted and sentenced to five years in prison.

As promised, Gao kept his end of the bargain. None of the eleven were implicated in his crimes. In return, they set up a modest fund on his behalf and provided him with an apartment in a middle-class neighborhood upon his release ten months ago.

By all accounts, prison was not kind to Gao. He suffered deprivation and illness. A minor stroke rendered him partially incapacitated. All his riches and influence were gone. He was a broken man.

As for Ling Wei—to the surprise and consternation of the other brothers, each of whom coveted her himself to some degree, she soon fell in with Tang Fuqiang. Although they are rarely seen together in public—perhaps she has the decency to feel ashamed of her betrayal of Gao—it is common knowledge that she is Tang's mistress.

Xu does not to relish visiting Gao under these circumstances. But of all the possible suspects, it is Gao who possesses the most conspicuous combination of insider knowledge and motive.

All this runs through Xu's mind as Pangu pulls to a stop outside of a nondescript apartment building. He hops out and opens Xu's door. "Want me to come in with you, boss?"

Xu belches sour bile and massages his aching stomach. "No, stay with the car. This shouldn't take long."

TEN

Xu rides the elevator to the third floor. The hallway smells of fried food, cigarette smoke, medicinal herbs, and incense. Xu hears, through closed doors, loud conversations, TV programs, the shrill crescendo of Peking Opera.

Chief Hong has already perused Gao's phone and bank records and discovered nothing suspicious. Of course, Xu knows any intelligent person who is up to no good would avoid using his official phone to carry out illegal activities or pay for such services through an easily tracked bank expenditure. And Gao is no dummy. So, despite the lack of evidence, it remains possible that he is behind the attacks on Chen, Liu, and Zhao.

Xu knocks on Gao's door. When it opens, he finds himself facing a young man dressed in white pants and a gray tunic.

"Yes, may I help you?" the man says.

"Who are you?" Xu asks sharply.

"My name is Kong. Can I help you?"

"Where's Mr. Gao?"

"He's inside. What is this about?"

Kong looks exceedingly fit. Broad chest and shoulders, forearms corded with muscle, big blue veins popping out of his rounded biceps. Xu flashes his police ID. "Who are you, exactly?"

"I'm Mr. Gao's home care aide."

"Well, I want to see him."

"Is there a problem?"

"We're old acquaintances."

"Right. I'll just see if Mr. Gao is up to receiving visitors. One moment, please."

Kong moves to close the door, but Xu puts a hand on it. Kong doesn't persist. He turns and goes over to a bedroom door, knocks, and enters. Xu steps inside, closes the front door, and snoops around the living room.

He sees a rattan couch, a coffee table and a couple of chairs, a round dining table, a few odds and ends. Not much in the way of furnishings, to be honest, and what there is appears to be of poor quality. To the right is a door leading to a kitchen alcove. Windows across the back wall face out onto a courtyard, empty at this hour apart from a few old folks dancing to folk songs played on a portable CD player.

Xu hears low voices coming from the bedroom. After a moment, the door opens and Kong reappears, holding Gao's elbow.

Xu is shocked. What a dramatic difference five years has made. Gao's hair has gone all white. He trembles and shakes as he walks. His skin is sallow and mottled with age spots.

Kong helps Gao sit on the couch. "I'll make tea." He disappears into the alcove.

Gao looks at Xu with eyes that are bloodshot yet still piercing. "So," he says.

"Hello, old friend," Xu says.

Gao laughs bitterly. "Old friend," he repeats, in a mocking tone.

Xu sits. He offers Gao a cigarette.

"Ah!" Gao's face lights up as if he's been offered an ingot of pure gold. He takes the cigarette with a trembling hand. Xu lights it and then his own. Gao inhales deeply and blows smoke through his nostrils.

"How have you been?" Xu asks, although the answer is abundantly obvious.

"Wonderful, just wonderful," Gao says. "My house, gone. Fortune, confiscated. Reputation, ruined. Friends, nonexistent. Wife, divorced." He waves the cigarette around the room. "Some days I wonder why I bother to keep breathing."

Kong rushes out of the kitchen and snatches the cigarette from Gao's fingers. He glares at Xu. "Mr. Gao is not permitted to smoke. And I'll have to ask you to put your cigarette out immediately."

Xu almost lays into Kong, but then shrugs, takes one last drag, and hands the butt over. Kong takes both cigarettes and returns to the kitchen.

"Where did you find that one?" Xu says in a low voice.

"He was assigned by a home health care company. One of the few social services I still qualify for."

"I didn't realize you were in such bad straits, Brother Gao. I'm sorry to see it. And I'm sorry I did not come to see you sooner. But . . ." Xu pauses.

"It's not good for you," Gao offers. "To be seen with me. The stench of corruption might rub off on you."

Xu doesn't answer.

Gao shakes his head. "Ridiculous. I'm a broken old man who had paid his debt to society a thousand times over. Nobody gives a damn about me anymore, Xu. Do you suppose the CCDI has agents posted in my lobby, making a note of who comes and goes?"

"No, of course not."

They make awkward small talk until Kong appears with a pot of tea and two cups. He pours for Gao and hands him a cup. He does not pour for Xu. Xu gives him a cold stare. "Why don't you take a little walk?"

"I don't think that's a good idea," Kong says.

"It's all right," Gao tells Kong. "Give us a few minutes."

"Just a few minutes." Kong turns to Xu. "Mr. Gao tires easily and needs his rest."

"Go on, boy. I won't make him do calisthenics."

Kong leaves with a dark look on his face. Xu laughs. "A regular mother hen, isn't he?"

Gao shrugs. He uses both hands to sip from his cup, sloshing tea over the rim. He shakily sets the cup down. "So, why are you here, *old friend*?"

Xu clears his throat. "Perhaps you've heard that some of our mutual acquaintances were recently assaulted?"

"Assaulted? No. Who?"

"Liu, Chen, and Zhao. They cut Zhao's hand off."

"*Cao!* Who's *they*?"

"We don't know. At least two perpetrators who say they are working for 'the Magistrate.'"

"The Magistrate. Are we suddenly back in imperial times?"

"Excellent question, Brother Gao."

Gao stares off into the space, and then suddenly understands. "Wait. You think that . . ."

"I don't think anything," Xu says. "But in any crime, there is a means and a motive. You are the only one who knows the identities of all the members of our little club . . . and who might have reason to wish us harm."

Gao's voice rises querulously. "How dare you, Xu!"

"Now, Brother Gao, don't excite yourself."

Gao points a crooked finger at Xu's face. "Ungrateful prick. I spent five years in prison so that you all could live in your big houses and drive your gleaming luxury vehicles, eat your expensive meals, and bed your beautiful mistresses! And you have the gall to come here and accuse me of plotting against you?"

"Well—to be fair, you just summed up the long and short of it, didn't you?"

Gao pauses openmouthed, then clacks his teeth together. He slumps into the cushions of the couch. "Ungrateful and disloyal—the lot of you."

"You understand why it makes sense to pay you a visit, though. Right?"

"I don't know who this Magistrate is. I don't know anything about the assaults. I sit in this apartment all day, watching TV or playing cards with Kong. I have nothing, I do nothing. I'm just waiting to die."

"I'm truly sorry about the way things turned out, Brother Gao." Xu eyes the room. "We really should have arranged for better living conditions. I'll speak to the others about that. And we'll increase your monthly stipend. We owe you that."

Gao waves a hand morosely, then fixes his watery eyes on Xu. "What about Weiwei? Have you seen her? How is she?"

Xu shifts uncomfortably. He was afraid of this. "I haven't seen her, but I believe she is safe and healthy and wants for nothing. As promised."

"You can do me the favor of getting a message to her. Tell her . . . it's been too long. I would like to see her. Just to make sure she's all right."

"I'll do that, Brother Gao." Xu watches Gao's thin, bent body nearly swallowed up by the threadbare couch cushions. Could this withered old man be the

Magistrate? Where would he get the money to hire thugs? To obtain vehicles and equipment? "Sadly, I must get back to work."

"You'll get a message to Weiwei?"

"Yes, of course. No need to get up. I'll see myself out. Take care, Brother Gao."

Xu leaves Gao to his wretchedness and goes downstairs. He finds Kong cooling his heels in the lobby. Kong smiles thinly. "Leaving so soon?"

"What of it?"

"I hope you didn't give him any more cigarettes. Or rile him up. Mr. Gao has a weak heart."

"How's about you just stick to making tea and wiping Gao's ass?"

As Xu walks back to his SUV, he makes a mental note to have this Kong checked out. He seems a bit too full of himself to be just a simple home health care aide.

ELEVEN

Sister Kim hosts religious services in the living room of her Harbin apartment three days a week. She staggers congregants so that only half a dozen or so are gathered at any one time. Given the current atmosphere of repression, she's reduced to operating her church like a spy cell, tending to her vulnerable flock in waves to minimize the risk of having them all rounded up by the police in one fell swoop.

The congregation is exclusively Korean, and exclusively female. Korean churches lean toward the patriarchal; and providing support and refuge for women who suffer oppression, violence, and exploitation at the hands of the men in their lives is Sister Kim's mission.

Hers is one of hundreds, perhaps thousands, of underground churches spread across the People's Republic. It is a risky endeavor. The Chinese government takes a dim view of religion, not only because of the Marxist axiom that it "is the sigh of the oppressed creature, the heart of a heartless world, and the soul of soulless conditions; it is the *opium* of the people"—but also because the Communist Party rightly recognizes that belief in a higher power is an existential threat to its ideological control.

And lately the authorities have been cranking up the heat. Churches and Christian charities shuttered, missionaries arrested, interrogated, sometimes under torture, then expelled. It's open season, and Sister Kim lives in constant fear of a knock at the door, a visit by the Ministry of State Security; or the Bureau of Ethnic and Religious Affairs.

Yet, she persists. Serving her small congregation—and carrying out her other, even more secretive work—is why God put her on this earth.

During services, which consist of a simple prayer, Bible reading, and perhaps a few hymns sung quietly, worshippers sit in fold-out chairs in front of a wall that Sister Kim keeps bare apart from a single item—a large crucifix. The crucifix is plain and unadorned, just two pieces of wood fitted together, sanded, and varnished. Sister Kim doesn't go in for those garish depictions of Jesus on the cross, his lean, muscular body naked apart from a tattered loincloth, a look of ecstatic anguish on his chiseled features. In Sister Kim's estimation, such visual representations border on the obscene.

After services are concluded, congregants enjoy tea and biscuits, talk about their worries and fears, and provide mutual comfort. Then they depart in twos and threes to avoid arousing suspicion.

On this day, Sister Kim cleans up after everyone has left, then eats a simple lunch and walks twenty minutes to the nearby Children's Park where she finds an empty bench. A handful of people walk past—grandmothers pushing baby strollers, old men getting a bit of exercise. It's chilly, but not freezing, and the air smells refreshingly of pine.

A man in drab clothing, a hat, a cotton face mask, ambles by. A minute later, he returns. He sits on the bench and pulls out a cell phone.

Sister Kim raises a newspaper to her face. She speaks in Korean: "Trouble?"

Hak pretends to read something on his phone. "No. The girls should reach the border in a week or so."

"How about the people who ran the operation?"

"Like I said, no trouble."

Sister Kim does not inquire further. The girls are her focus, not the monsters who so callously use them. "There is a young woman in Tumen who needs our help. She's holed up at the apartment of a friend of mine, Pastor Lee. He'll be expecting you. A simple job. Pick her up, hand her off to the next link in the chain."

"Sure. What about that brothel in Dalian we discussed?"

"Too dangerous," Kim says.

"I can handle it."

"I'm sure you can, but we can't afford to draw attention to ourselves with a mission of that scope. It will be messy. The police will be all over it."

"Those girls are suffering, Sister Kim."

Sister Kim takes a pained breath. "I know they are. But we must pick our battles." She sets the newspaper down on the bench and stands. "Thank you, Brother Hak. You are truly doing God's work."

She leaves. After a moment, Hak picks up the newspaper and opens it. Inside is a piece of paper with an address, a phone number, and an envelope of cash. He memorizes the address and number, then lights the piece of paper on fire with his cigarette lighter. When it has burned itself out, he grinds the ashes into dust beneath the sole of his shoe.

TWELVE

Tang Fuqiang typically wakes midmorning and takes his breakfast, weather permitting, on the third-floor balcony outside his private quarters, overlooking a neatly tended garden. The garden is planted with bamboo, pine, and plum trees surrounding a small pool of clear blue water. Rising from the shallow depths of the pool is a two-meter "scholar's rock" inscribed with Chinese characters reading FEN FA ZI QIANG. Given the ambiguity of classical Chinese, this saying can be translated in a variety of ways, but Tang's preference falls along the lines of "Get rich or die trying."

Unless it is a matter of the utmost urgency, Tang's staff knows not to disturb him while he's breakfasting. It is his time to quietly reflect, regroup, and steel himself for the pressures of the day.

Today, he is nursing a bit of a hangover, so he eats rice congee with chicken, onion, garlic, and ginger, and drinks several cups of good-quality Dragon Well tea. Then he smokes a post-meal cigarette before going into his bedroom and dressing in crisp black slacks, a silk Gucci shirt, and a pair of Italian loafers.

He takes the private staircase at the back of the building—accessible only by key cards possessed by Tang, his head of security, and his housekeeping manager—down to the first floor. The guard on duty in the rear foyer bows obsequiously. The guard is dressed, as are all of Tang's security staff, in a dark suit and clean white shirt.

Tang walks through the rear passage, poking his head into the kitchen and dining room along the way. He emerges into a spacious lobby—marble floors, a double-height ceiling, a staircase with a wrought-iron railings curving up to the second-floor mezzanine, a life-sized sculpture of a peach tree in its center.

He turns left and enters the lounge; plush carpeting, comfortable seating, a bar in the back, karaoke stage up front. He checks ashtrays for smudges, the seating for lint, the surface of the bar counter for sticky residue. Tang runs a tight ship and any dereliction of duty by his staff will result in a heavy fine.

Next, he heads up to the second-floor west wing and inspects the bedrooms where his hostesses service clients to make sure the sheets have been changed, trash emptied, supply of condoms and lubricant and sex toys replenished. He traverses the mezzanine to the east wing, unlocks the door with his key card, and walks down a hallway lined with offices on either side. A facility as grand as the Little Red Palace requires a great deal of administrative work, and already his staff is hard at work, crunching numbers, paying bills, ordering supplies.

At the far end of the hallway, opposite Tang's personal office, is a reinforced door leading to a control room. Only two people have a key card that will unlock this door—Tang and his head of security, a big ex-fighter nicknamed Chaiyou—"Diesel." Tang unlocks it now and enters to find Diesel sitting at a monitor reviewing CCTV footage from the night before.

"Morning, boss," Diesel says.

"Anything good?" Tang says.

"Pull up a chair."

Tang lights a fresh cigarette while Diesel cues up video of the director of Heilongjiang's largest steel manufacturer attempting to have drunken sex with one of Tang's hostesses.

"I'd say he's less of a steel magnate," Tang jokes, "and more of a *dofu* peddler!"

In addition to the standard security measures one expects—cameras at the front and back gates, the entrances to the main residence, scattered around the grounds—there are hidden feeds in LRP's lounge, gambling room, and bedrooms. Naturally, Tang's guests don't know they are being filmed—if they did, there would be hell to pay—but the cabinet lining the back of the control room is stuffed with fastidiously labeled hard drives commemorating the sexual hijinks of some of Harbin's most important citizens.

Even some of Tang's own brothers in the NBA, including Chiefs Xu and Hong, Deputy Mayor Wan, and Judge Ren, make guest appearances.

Tang keeps these hard drives both for his own amusement and for a rainy day. He sleeps better at night knowing he has the equivalent of a nuclear arsenal in his back pocket.

Tang and Diesel conduct a quick review of the night's footage and decide what to preserve for posterity; the rest, they erase. Afterward, Tang walks across to hall to his office and spends the remainder of the morning making phone calls relating to his various business concerns.

After lunch, he meets with his food and beverage manager to sign off on new orders of foreign booze, cigars and cigarettes, fresh seafood, and imported steaks. In the early afternoon, he meets a certain Mr. Chow, who hails from Guangdong Province and speaks Mandarin with an excruciating Cantonese accent. Chow is, among other things, a procurer of young women for sex work. His girls tend to be young and attractive—aspiring singers or actresses who fell just short of the looks, talent, or contacts to make it in the business. Today Chow has brought a Eurasian woman he's discovered working as an escort in Macao. She gives her name as Cynthia. Tang is immediately taken with her biracial exoticism—it will be a selling point among his clientele. Unfortunately, she does not speak Mandarin well, so Tang is forced to use his limited English skills, which he feels puts him at a disadvantage.

"How old?" he asks.

"I'm twenty."

Tang smiles and shakes his head. "How old?"

Cynthia frowns. "Okay, so I'm twenty-four. But I can pass for twenty."

"If you full Chinese, maybe. Instead, you pass for twenty-four. Daddy American?"

"British."

"Where now?"

Cynthia shrugs. "Who cares?"

"Mama?"

"She's in Hong Kong. We don't get along."

"You see my place?" Tang waves his hand. "Very high-end. Exclusive clientele. They pay lots of money. And my girls give them what they want. Whatever they want."

"I'm willing to do that . . . within reason."

Tang looks at Chow, confused. He doesn't understand *within reason*. Chow translates into Mandarin.

"Oh." Tang nods and looks at Cynthia. "Like what? What not okay?"

Cynthia sighs and asks herself for the thousandth time how it has come to this. "No rough stuff. No hitting. No filming. No bareback." She can see that Tang doesn't understand this last stipulation, so she says: "They have to wear a *tao*." A *cover*—a condom.

"Ah," Tang says. "No problem. But you don't speak much Chinese?"

"Not much," Cynthia admits. "Why? Do your clients come here mainly for conversation?"

Tang laughs. He likes this girl. And she will add something new to his stable. "You wait outside, I talk business with Chow."

Cynthia leaves the office. Tang offers Chow a cigarette and lights his own. They haggle a bit and then agree on Chow's commission. Tang calls Cynthia back into the office and presents her with an offer.

Cynthia was hoping for more. She wants to make enough money to quit this life in five years, buy a house far, far away from the sweltering stink of Asia, open a flower shop, and forget about the first thirty years of her existence. But the terms seem fair, and more than she was making in Macao. She agrees.

Tang summons an older woman wearing distinctive cat-eye glasses he introduces as Ms. Su. He instructs Su to draw up a one-year contract.

"You go with Ms. Su," Tang tells Cynthia. "Sign contract. You have place to live in Harbin?"

"I'm at a hotel."

"I have dorm on grounds, nice, very cheap. I take rent out of your pay. Okay? Go now. You have any problem, question, ask Ms. Su."

When they are gone, Chow smirks. "Pretty, right? Going to try her yourself?"

Tang ignores Chow's question. He opens his safe and counts out Chow's broker's fee. "Stick around and have a drink at the bar. First one's on the house."

"Your generosity is boundless," Chow says dryly.

Midafternoon, Tang selects two of his hostesses and they all pile into the back of his luxury sedan. His driver takes them to an upscale hotel in downtown

Harbin, where Tang has reserved a suite. He and the hostesses check in and go upstairs. They wait for thirty minutes before there is a knock on the door. A handful of men enter. Two of them are high-ranking members of a local criminal organization. The others are their thugs.

Tang and the two gangsters sit. The hostesses fix drinks and then go into the bedroom and shut the door. The thugs just stand around looking tough.

Tang asks the two men if they've heard any rumors of rival gangsters looking to muscle in on Nangang District.

"Why?" one of them asks. He is his early seventies and, given his age and experience, Tang politely addresses him as Uncle Number Three. "You've had some trouble?"

"No real trouble," Tang says. He downplays matters because he doesn't want to appear weak or ill-informed in front of the triad bosses. Although they are all swimming in the same water, so to speak, these men are sharks—they will go into a feeding frenzy at the first scent of blood, never mind if you are friend or foe. "Just an uptick in street crime."

The other gangster is in his forties. His nickname, "Ice Pick Brother," was earned when he made his first kill at the age of sixteen with the aforementioned tool. "It wasn't my boys."

"Mine, either," Uncle Number Three says. "Maybe just some punk kids."

"Can you ask around?" Tang says. "Street crime is bad for everyone's business."

"Sure," Uncle Number Three agrees. "Now let's talk about those construction contracts."

Thirty minutes later, business concluded, Tang opens the bedroom door and crooks a finger at the hostesses. "Show our guests a good time," he says.

The hostesses put away their phones and stub out their cigarettes. They aren't looking forward to getting pawed at by Uncle Number Three and Ice Pick Brother, but they know the men will tip them well. "Time to earn that Cartier bracelet," one says to the other.

Tang leaves them to it. He goes downstairs and summons his driver. He's got just enough time to make his next appointment—a dinner date, with Ling Wei.

THIRTEEN

A foursome is seated at a table in Raven Valley's best hot-pot restaurant, the Nine Dragons. Although it's a bit early in the season for hot pot—it is a meal best enjoyed when the body needs warmth and nourishment to bolster against icy winds and subzero temperatures—there is something about the communal ritual of eating hot pot that promotes a feeling of community, friendship, family.

But tonight—not so much.

The party consists of Lu Fei, Luo Yanyan—looking chic in black jeans—Constable Sun, and her fiancé, Yao Jun.

Yao is tall and a bit plump, as befits his status as the scion of one of Raven Valley's richest families. Lookswise, he's only average, for which Lu cannot fault him. You don't get to choose the shape of your nose, the set of your eyes, the prominence of your cheekbones.

Short of cosmetic surgery, Lu amends.

What you can choose is the way you treat other people: as human beings, or as props in a role-playing game of which you are the star.

It doesn't take Lu long to understand Yao tends toward the latter.

He is not surprised. China is teaming with "little emperors"—boys born during the one-child policy, raised with an excess of attention and material comforts, and as a result suffering from extreme narcissism.

Yao starts the evening off by showing up twenty minutes late, and when he does arrive, he doesn't apologize. He's only been in his chair for thirty seconds before he starts snapping his fingers for a waiter. "You like foreign wines?"

"Yanyan does," Lu says. "I prefer Shaoxing."

Yao wrinkles his nose at the mention of Shaoxing. He peruses the wine list and suggests an Australian pinot noir.

"Shall we also order a bottle of Shaoxing?" Sun offers.

"I'm fine with beer," Lu says. He turns to Yanyan. "What about you?"

"The pinot sounds good."

The waiter soon returns with Lu's beer, the wine, and a pot of soup broth, which he sets on a lit burner at the table. While waiting for the broth to simmer, Yao expounds at length on the travails of owning a food-processing plant— draconian government regulations, difficulty in finding reliable workers, the overhead costs. Later, when the waiter sets down bowls of vegetables, meat, and seafood, Yao launches into a diatribe about the advantages of organic over non-organic foods. He shows them a wilted leaf of cabbage. "This is definitely from one of those corporate mass-production fields where they irrigate with polluted water from the Songhua."

"I admire your passion for your work," Yanyan says. "Speaking of passion, tell us more about what attracted you to Constable Sun."

Sun smiles shyly and tells Yanyan: "No need to be so formal. Please call me Huizhen."

"Only if you call me Yanyan."

"I don't dare!"

Yanyan waves Sun's protest away. She turns back to Yao. "You were just about to tell us what made you fall in love with Huizhen."

Whereas Yao was previously quite chatty, now he seems at a loss for words. "Well . . ." He tosses the wilted cabbage into the soup broth and gives it a stir. "She's very kindhearted."

"And intelligent," Lu says. "She's probably the smartest constable I have."

Sun is unaccustomed to such compliments. She covers her face with a hand.

"I take it you like a woman with an independent streak?" Yanyan asks.

"I don't know about *that*," Yao says. "As I said, she's very kindhearted. She'll make a wonderful mother for our children."

Yanyan adds a few slices of meat to the pot. "How many do you plan to have?"

"Oh, perhaps just two," Yao says. "I mean, Huizhen is no spring chicken."

Lu sees a tiny line form between Yanyan's eyebrows—an impending sign of danger. He clears his throat. "One of the wonderful things about the progress we've made in society is that many women still work, even after having children. Wouldn't you say?"

"I would not," Yao says. "No wife of mine will work. Especially as a police officer."

"Is that because you're worried about her safety?" Yanyan asks.

"Sure, and also I don't think women should be hanging around lowlifes all day."

"And by lowlifes," Lu jokes, "you are referring to her colleagues?"

Yao laughs. "I meant thieves, drunkards, criminals."

Lu adds bean sprouts to the pot. "Well, I must say I'd love nothing more than to have more female constables. Female sergeants, even. Hell, even female chiefs! A police station staffed only by men is like a high school boy's locker room. Belching, farting, drinking, smoking, off-color jokes. Endless juvenile pranks. The presence of a woman is a moderating influence."

"You just proved my point," Yao says. "I don't want Huizhen around that kind of environment. It's unseemly."

Yanyan sets down her chopsticks. "Perhaps it threatens you on some level?"

"Threatens me?" Yao says, clearly irritated. "I don't understand what you mean."

"Quick, everyone, eat before the meat is overcooked!" Sun urges. She fills Yao's bowl. The table is silent for a moment, apart from the sound of slurping and chewing.

After a few bites, Lu says, "There are many advantages to marrying a woman with a career, you know."

"Right." Yao smirks. "She can take care of all my speeding tickets, right, Little Pumpkin?"

"I already told you no on that," Sun says.

Yao shrugs. "Then what's the point?"

The rest of the evening passes in similar fashion. When the bill arrives, Lu and Yao fight over it, as politeness dictates, but Lu insists. He's sorry when he sees the price of the pinot noir. He complains about it on the drive back to Yanyan's apartment.

"Forget the bill," Yanyan says. "That guy was a jerk. Pumpkinface?"

"No, no," Lu says. "He called her Little Pumpkin. It's sweet."

"It's not sweet. He said she's an old crone with a dried-up womb."

"Well, she's almost thirty."

"Lu Fei! Plenty of women don't get married until they are thirty. Or older. Or at all! Do you know how old I am?"

"Yes, but you were married before, so your age is not relevant."

"A woman is no longer defined by her husband and her male offspring! Times have changed, for heaven's sake."

"You're right. Sun is in the prime of her life. And Yao was a jerk." Lu slows down and takes a turn and then mutters: "And the price of that bottle of wine!"

"Will you forget about the damn wine? Aren't you worried Sun is making a bad decision out of desperation provoked by men like you who consider a thirty-year-old girl past the age of marriageability?"

"I'm not one of those guys. I like older women." Lu puts a hand on Yanyan's knee. "If you know what I'm saying."

Yanyan slaps his hand off. "I'm serious. I don't want her to make a decision she'll regret for the rest of her life."

"What do you suggest, then? We find a way to break them up?" Lu means this as a joke, but then he thinks: *Hmm* . . . "Perhaps we should put our heads together and come up with a plan."

"For now, the best thing would be for you to make sure she understands how much you value her at work," Yanyan says. "Can you do that?"

Lu nods. "Yes. That I can do."

FOURTEEN

Tang and Ling Wei meet at a French bistro located just a few blocks from her apartment. The apartment is neither spacious nor luxurious, but it is comfortable and convenient. And Ling pays no rent because Tang owns it. He has offered many times to move her closer to the Little Red Palace, into her own house with a garden if she wishes, or alternatively into one of the newer high-rises in downtown Nangang, but Ling always demurs. She tells Tang he has done more than enough for her already.

Tang can't help but agree—he *has* done a great deal for her. After Gao's fall from grace and her subsequent divorce, Ling was left penniless and without prospects. Tang swept in, provided her a place to live, a monthly stipend, access to a car and driver. Five years later, he still lavishes her with expensive gifts. Treats her to expensive meals.

He does not do these things out of the kindness of his heart.

In his youth, Tang was charismatic and stylish in his tailored slacks and silk shirts. Now that he is older, he is still reasonably attractive, but more importantly, he possesses two of the strongest aphrodisiacs in the known universe— money and power.

The point being, Tang has never found it difficult to cajole a woman into his bed.

Except for Ling Wei.

He has attempted to woo her like a lovesick teenager. He's tried guilting her into sleeping with him. He has considered just taking her by force. He is not sure what's prevented him from doing so. It's not that she's a creature of such high virtue—her marriage to Gao, twenty-plus years her senior, proved that she is fundamentally no different than any other member of her sex who makes her way in the world flat on her back.

But if Tang is just after sex, he can have any of the girls at the Little Red Palace or one of his brothels. And even in a relative backwater like Harbin, the streets are teeming with beautiful and ambitious young women, as ripe for the picking as a July peach.

With Ling, it's different. Tang doesn't just want to *have* her physically; he's seeking something a bit more ethereal. He wants her to tremble with nervousness when she sees him. To let out a little gasp when he touches her hand. For her heart to race when she sees his name on her caller ID.

If it were anyone else, it might be tempting to say that Tang is in love with Ling. Tang himself does not think in such terms, however. For him, relationships are either transactional or hierarchical. People are to be used or dominated.

When Ling arrives at the restaurant, she is dressed casually in jeans and a sweater, a simple ponytail, no jewelry apart from a pair of plain silver studs. Tang wishes she would dress more like she did when she was on Gao's arm—in clothes that clung to her body, accentuating her curves. A glitter of jewelry drawing attention to her delicate wrists, her slim white neck.

Tang attempts to plant a kiss on Ling's lips. She turns her head at the last moment. Tang inhales her scent—a heady blend of jasmine, mint, and kumquat. The perfume is Hermès—Tang knows this because he's let himself into her apartment and searched through her things on more than one occasion when she's out.

"You smell delectable," Tang says.

"You're very kind."

Tang orders them a bottle of wine. They make light conversation. Tang knows that Ling has recently returned to singing old standards at a piano bar—in fact, he has arranged it on her behalf. He asks if she is enjoying the experience, and she confirms that she is. Ling, in turn, makes polite inquiries about Tang's business—the legitimate side of it. She is aware of his various illegalities, of course, just as she was with Gao—but, as with her ex-husband, she and Tang prefer to maintain an illusion of propriety.

They have dinner—pappardelle with duck ragù for Ling and a beef fillet for Tang. Ling drinks sparingly. Tang finishes most of the bottle and gets a bit drunk. He offers to share a slice of cheesecake, but Ling begs off.

"Too much."

"You ate like a bird," Tang says.

"At my age, I gain weight easily."

"In all the right places."

Ling's smile is unreadable. Is she flattered? Repulsed? Tang wants to crack her head open and look inside to discern what she is thinking.

"Winter's coming," Tang says. "Why don't we fly to somewhere warm for a long weekend?"

"Thank you, Fuqiang, but no. I couldn't."

"You very well could."

"I have my performances. And my volunteer work with the elderly support organization."

Tang scoffs. "You don't need to actually waste your time making soup for those old biddies, Weiwei. I'd gladly make a generous donation in your name."

"Thank you, but that's not the point. Volunteering makes me feel like I'm doing something useful."

In lieu of dessert, Ling drinks a cup of tea, and Tang, a nightcap. Then he pays the check and offers her a ride home.

"It's only a few blocks."

"It's late. I'll drive you." Tang texts his driver. When they leave the restaurant, the car is waiting out front. He and Ling climb into the back. The motion of the car pulling away from the curb tips Ling into Tang, and he takes the opportunity to put a hand on her thigh. She tenses but doesn't push his hand away. The feel of her firm, warm flesh arouses Tang. He slides his hand higher.

Ling gently plucks his hand off.

Perhaps it is the wine, or the stress of a particularly difficult week, but Tang is suddenly angry. He turns on Ling. "You take advantage of me. And give nothing in return." He thrusts his hand into her crotch.

Ling struggles. "Please, Fuqiang!"

"Without me, where would you be? Spreading your legs for a fistful of cash to pay the rent?"

"I have never asked you for anything!"

"Because I freely give it."

"Take back your apartment if that's how you feel. I'll find somewhere else to live."

"Where? How will you eat? What will become of you?"

"Please stop. I'm begging you."

"You *should* be begging me." Then, as suddenly as the anger appeared, it passes. Tang removes his hand and turns away. "I'm sorry, Weiwei. I don't know what came over me. Too much to drink. Pressures at work." He wipes his forehead. It comes away slick with sweat. "Please forgive me."

Ling says nothing for a moment, then she reaches over and gently takes his hand. "I'm sorry if I seem ungrateful. I'm not. I appreciate all you've done for me. But I meant what I said. The moment you begin to begrudge it, I no longer desire it."

Cao, Tang thinks. *How can you control someone if you don't possess something they want or need?*

The car stops in front of Ling's apartment building. She reaches for the door. "Good night, Fuqiang." She tugs the latch. It's locked. She waits quietly, patiently, until Tang jerks his head at the driver. The driver unlocks the door and Ling gets out.

FIFTEEN

Tang broods on the drive back to the Little Red Palace.

He is positive that Ling doesn't have a lover, because he has taken the precaution of planting spyware on her phone and computer. The staff in the building lobby keep him apprised of her visitors. On the nights she performs at the piano bar, he dispatches one of his men to watch from the audience. He occasionally has her followed as she goes about her daily business—just to make sure.

In some ways, the fact that Ling isn't seeing someone else makes things worse. It means she is not rejecting Tang's affections because she loves another. Instead, it's because she would rather be alone—than with Tang.

Tang's car arrives at the Little Red Palace. Steel gates swing open on oiled hinges. His driver lets Tang off in front and parks the sedan in the garage. A security guard in a dark suit and white shirt greets Tang at the front entrance. Tang gives him a surly grunt. He walks through the lobby, down the back passage, and into the rear foyer. The guard there bows. Tang ignores him. He uses his key card to unlock the door to the stairwell, walks up to his private quarters.

He enters his bedroom, strips off his clothes, and puts on a silk robe. He goes out to the living room, fixes himself a stiff drink, and lights a cigarette. He calls Ms. Su on the house phone. "That Eurasian girl," he says. "Cynthia. Has she moved out of her hotel?"

"Yes, Mr. Tang. She's here in the dormitory."

"Have Diesel send her up."

There is a pause on the line. "Now?"

"Did I stutter?"

"But she just arrived this afternoon. She isn't settled yet. And it's late."

"*Ta ma de niao,* what are you, her wet nurse? Send her up!" Tang slams the phone down.

By the time Cynthia arrives, Tang has had another drink and another cigarette, and his black mood has only grown more tenebrous. He nearly explodes when he sees Cynthia dressed casually in sweats.

"*Wo kao,* you look like you work in supermarket!" he barks, in English.

"I'm sorry, Mr. Tang. It's late and Ms. Su said I wouldn't start work for a couple of days, so I was just—"

"Never mind!" Tang grabs her wrist and pulls her toward the open door of his bedroom.

"Wait!" Cynthia protests. "What are you doing?"

"What look like?"

"But I thought—"

Tang turns and grips her jaw with a clawed hand. "You don't think *nothing*! I say, you do! Understand?"

Cynthia pushes him off. "I'm not your slave."

"Dumb bitch."

"I'm leaving." Cynthia heads for the door.

Tang sneers. "You have money? Place to go? How about passport?"

Cynthia turns. "Ms. Su has my passport. Tell her to give it back."

"Sure. When you make back money I pay Chow. Plus one night lodging in dorm. Transport from hotel. You eat dinner here? Price of dinner, too."

"Bullshit."

"No bullshit. We have contract. Read fine print." He admonishes her with a finger. "Always read fine print."

"Maybe I should just go to the cops?"

Tang goes over to the desk and picks up his cell phone. "Police my close friend. You want to call? Here, I dial for you."

Cynthia curses under her breath. She's lost this battle, and she knows it.

Tang places the phone back onto the desk. "Come." He heads into the bedroom without a backward glance. After a moment, Cynthia lowers her head and follows.

Tang orders her to undress. He takes a bottle of Hermès perfume from his nightstand and sprays her liberally with it.

Then he does to her what he would like to do to Ling Wei.

SIXTEEN

Thursday morning, Xu attends a biweekly "Police Cloud" meeting. The goal of this much-ballyhooed big data system is to take information the government routinely collects on its citizens—birthplace, address, occupation, family relations, religious affiliation—and integrate it with hotel and travel records, CCTV footage, biometrics, consumer information, medical history, and even one's shopping habits, to predict and stop crime before it happens.

Xu thinks it's a great idea—in theory. In practice, these meetings are long droning affairs filled with flow charts, graphs, and statistical analysis that leave Xu struggling mightily to keep awake.

He is on the verge of dozing off for a third time when his phone vibrates. He sneaks a quick look at the caller ID: it's Chief Hong. Xu can't answer right now, so he just slips the phone back into his pocket. A moment later, it vibrates again. This time, with a text: *Call me. Urgent.*

Ta ma de, what now? Xu texts back: *In meeting.*

Hong texts back: *Cai is dead.*

Xu's blood turns cold. What does that mean, *Cai is dead*? A car accident? Did he jump off a roof?

Or did the Magistrate kill him?

As soon as it's expedient, Xu excuses himself and goes out to the corridor to call Hong. "I'm listening."

"Cai's body was discovered in the lobby of an empty apartment building this morning."

"And? Details!"

"I don't want to get into it on the phone. Come see." Hong gives Xu directions.

Forty minutes later, Xu looks down at Cai's body with a sick feeling in his stomach.

It's not that he's disturbed by the sight of a corpse. He's viewed many—homicides, suicides, traffic accidents, old folks who died in their sleep. Even a few who were his own handiwork.

And it's not that Cai was a close friend. With his advanced schooling and fancy lawyer's degree, Cai was a bit too uppity for Xu's taste—though, by virtue of their careers in law enforcement, they were part of a fraternity that even the other members of the Nangang Benevolent Association, apart from Judge Ren, could never share.

No—Xu feels sick because Cai's murder is proof that the Magistrate is specifically targeting the NBA; and his attacks are escalating exponentially. First a simple beating. Then a tattoo. A hand cut off.

And now *this*.

Cai lies crumpled in one of his well-tailored suits, face swollen and purpled, eyes bulging from their sockets, tongue bloated and protruding from his cracked lips. A ring of dried blood crusts his nostrils. A fly sits the glazed sclera of his left eye.

There is a cord wrapped tightly around Cai's neck, just above his starched white collar.

"Strangled," Hong says.

"Brilliant detective work," Xu mutters. "Who found the body?"

"An old lady walking her dog. She didn't get a good look. She thought he was just a drunk sleeping it off."

"First respondents?"

"The two constables over there."

"We'll deal with them in a minute. Any street or security cams?"

"No." Hong waves at their surroundings. "No residents."

They are standing in the lobby of a half-completed apartment building in one of Harbin's so-called "ghost cities." The name is a bit of a misnomer—a ghost city or town usually indicates a place that was previously occupied and is now abandoned. But in Harbin, as in many other major Chinese cities, there are extensive new housing developments that have never once seen a single resident, built by developers as an investment—and then, when the anticipated housing rush or economic development didn't materialize, simply left vacant.

"When's CSI arriving?" Xu asks.

"Haven't notified them yet."

"Then we have some time. Let's talk to the constables."

They approach the pair—one male and one female—who are standing on the front steps outside the lobby.

"You know who I am?" Xu asks.

"Yes, sir," the male says. He looks to be around thirty.

"What's your name?"

"Zheng, sir."

"You?" Xu asks the female constable.

"Fan, sir."

"Listen up, both of you. This is a highly sensitive case. The person in there was a high-ranking functionary of the court system. Sadly, it seems he took his own life."

The female constable, Fan, opens her mouth to say something, thinks better of it, closes her mouth again.

"I don't want you talking to the press about this," Xu continues. "Or your friends, boyfriend, girlfriend, whatever. Understand? Or I'll have your badges. Do I make myself clear?"

"Yes, sir," the constables say in unison.

"You are dismissed," Xu says. "We'll handle it from here."

The constables exchange a look of surprise, then shuffle off to their patrol car. Xu calls Pangu, who is sitting in his SUV parked at the curb, on his cell phone. "I need you. Come here and bring three sets of latex gloves and shoe coverings." He hangs up and lights a cigarette.

"What do you propose?" Hong says.

"We'll stage it like a suicide. After which, you call CSI. As long as those constables don't talk, we should be able to keep this contained."

"Cai was the head of the arrest section of the district procuratorate. We can't just sweep this under the rug."

"I get that. But we need to make sure no one draws a connection between what we have here and the other assaults. Or a pattern may emerge. One that exposes us."

"What about the *next* attack?" Hong says. "We've got to find this maniac."

"I'm open to any and all suggestions, Brother Hong."

"You're sure Gao isn't behind it?"

"I'm not sure about anything." Xu takes a drag on his cigarette and flicks it onto the pavement. "He seemed physically unwell but still mentally sharp. An operation of this scope, though—it requires money, planning, personnel, equipment. Could he be doing it right under our noses? You got that camera installed outside his apartment?"

"It goes in this afternoon."

"And the background check on his beefy nurse?"

"Kong. He served in the People's Liberation Army—he was a medic. Otherwise, he's clean."

"Maybe we should find out where he was between ten last night and six this morning."

Pangu arrives carrying gloves and booties. "Yes, boss?"

"Come inside," Xu says. "I've got some heavy lifting for you to do."

SEVENTEEN

Xu and Hong manipulate the scene to make Cai's death look like a suicide and file a corresponding report. Xu routes the autopsy to a certain medical examiner whom he finds to be generally compliant.

The ME sees evidence to counter the suicide narrative, but experience has shown him that in Harbin a death is often like an onion—layers within layers of political nuance he is not party to. Perhaps Cai was murdered by a prostitute, or a gay lover, and Xu is just trying to avoid embarrassing the procuratorate. Who knows? Who cares? If Xu insists it's a suicide, so be it.

In the weeks that follow:

The remaining members of the Nangang Benevolent Association circle their wagons. Aside from carrying out their official duties, they avoid being out in public. No dinners with friends, nights at the Little Red Palace, evening assignations with their mistresses. They are suddenly painfully aware of how vulnerable a person is just by virtue of going about his or her daily life. Walking to a parked car at night. Jogging down to the corner market for a pack of cigarettes. Taking a drunken cab ride home after a karaoke party.

Within the NBA, Judge Ren worked most closely with Cai and therefore feels his absence most acutely. Luckily, an old crony of Ren's is chosen as Cai's replacement—and so, in the end, it's business as usual in the Nangang justice system.

Chen heals physically from his thrashing but suffers lingering psychological effects and becomes something of an agoraphobic.

Liu pays a great deal of money for laser removal of the tattoo on his cheek. It will take several weeks to complete, and in the meantime, he keeps a bandage over his cheek and tells colleagues he's had a brush with skin cancer.

Zhao nurses his wrist stump resentfully. When he learns of Cai's strangulation, some part of him is perversely pleased—it means that those members of the NBA who have not yet suffered at the hands of the Magistrate are now under the threat of death. This puts the loss of a hand in perspective.

But he can't help but feel a touch bitter that Chen and Liu got off so lightly.

Deputy Mayor Wan, Chairman Yu, and Mayor Pang are obliged to endure an endless merry-go-round of administrative responsibilities, speeches, committee meetings, factory tours, ribbon-cutting ceremonies, CCP obligations, social events. To do otherwise would arouse suspicion. Given their positions, Wan and Pang already have security details assigned to them; and Yu imposes on Xu to find a pair of detectives who are willing to moonlight as his bodyguards for the time being.

Meanwhile, Tang feels quite secure inside the walls of the Little Red Palace, protected by guards, gates, and security cameras. If required to travel for a face-to-face meeting, he takes Diesel along and keeps a handgun tucked in a hidden compartment in his car.

Despite the onset of cold weather, business at the LRP remain steady. Sadly, however, Cynthia has proven to be a major disappointment. She is sullen with Tang, unaccommodating with the guests, and shirks her responsibilities. She is fined repeatedly for her recalcitrance, but this has no effect. The last straw is when the elderly head of one of Harbin's large agricultural conglomerates lodges a complaint. "She was terrible," he grouses to Tang. "Like a wet rag. I had to do all the work!"

Tang looks at the old man, skinny as rail, stooped shoulders, leaning heavily on a cane. *If this bag of bones had to do all the work . . .*

He tells Ms. Su to sort out Cynthia. Su threatens to transfer Cynthia to one of Tang's less refined brothels in town. "How'd you like to be bedding migrant construction workers and PLA grunts?"

"I want to leave here," Cynthia says. "Give back my passport. I don't want to be paid anything; I just want to go."

"You will get your passport when you earn back what we have spent on you."

"That will never happen because you keep adding fees and fines."

"Don't be silly. A pretty girl like you—one who is willing to please—can make loads of money in just a few months."

Two days later, Tang's security cams catch Cynthia trying to escape over the wall. Tang has her brought to his office. "Where you think you going? Back to Macao? With no money? No passport?"

"Please, Mr. Tang. Let me go and I'll find my own work and send you money each month."

"Ha! You think I'm stupid? Pay first."

Of course, Tang knows Cynthia only receives a nominal salary and commission based on the number of customers she's serviced, minus room and board, incidentals, fines, and so on. The system is designed to keep his hostesses in a constant state of debt. And it's an up-or-out policy. As soon as a hostess's revenues dip below a certain minimum, he will transfer her to one of his other, less exclusive brothels, or sell her contract to some other sex trafficker. Very few of his girls will ever get their passports—or their lives—back.

Later that night, one of the hostesses finds Cynthia lying on the floor of a shower stall, the last few drops of blood from her cut wrists swirling down the drain.

Tang has her body transported to a crematorium and pays an undertaker to burn it and dispose of the ashes. It's not the first time he's made such an arrangement, and he doesn't expect it to be the last.

EIGHTEEN

Mayor Pang's vice isn't strong drink, women, or narcotics. It's a card game called baccarat.

A favorite of the British fictional spy James Bond, the rules of baccarat are refreshingly straightforward. The object is to assemble a hand of two or more cards that have a value of nine. A "player" competes against a "banker," with the option to bet one of three ways: the player's hand will win, the banker's hand will win, or there will be a tie. As in the dice game craps, one doesn't have to be a "player" to place a wager—spectators likewise have the option to bet on any of the three possible outcomes.

As a result of its simplicity, and odds that favor the house less than most casino games, baccarat is especially popular with Asian gamblers. It satisfies on a metaphysical level as well. The most desired outcomes in baccarat, a tally of eight or nine points, are homophones for "riches" and "longevity," respectively—and who doesn't want more of those? And even within the gambling community, a notoriously superstitious lot, Chinese bettors are legendarily obsessed with signs and portents. When they discover a baccarat player on a hot streak, they believe that by latching onto him, his luck can become their own.

As for Pang, like a chain smoker on a fourteen-hour flight, he can only hold out for so long before he caves to the temptation of sneaking off for a quick drag in the bathroom. Meanwhile, over the past couple of weeks he's managed to convince himself that Cai's death is unrelated to the Magistrate business. A side deal gone south; a rival for a woman's affection; an unpaid debt; an ex-con Cai had a hand in sending to prison.

Besides, he can no longer stomach being cooped up at home. He needs a change of scenery, to blow off some steam. To get the old juices flowing again.

Pang tells his wife he has a work obligation. Drinks with the chairman of the local People's Congress Standing Committee. After so many years of marriage, Pang's wife tunes out the details. She just tells him not to be home too late.

Pang catches a taxi and has the driver take him to a lively street on the western edge of Nangang District known for its many pubs and cheap restaurants. Pang's ultimate destination is Ruyi Palace, a seafood joint where the cuisine is only middling, but there is a secret casino after hours in a banquet room upstairs.

Pang enters the restaurant and has a word with the manager. The manager snaps his fingers. A waiter materializes to guide Pang upstairs, where he is met by a bouncer who accepts Pang's modest tip, then opens a door and ushers Pang through it.

Inside is a cavernous room, the walls decorated with dragons and phoenixes and Double Happiness characters. Round dining tables have been folded up and stacked to one side, and in their place are a craps tables, a roulette wheel, and half a dozen card tables. Pang gets a drink from the bar and wanders a bit to get the lay of the land.

Of the two tables where baccarat is being played, only one has drawn a sizable crowd. And Pang is helpless to resist its gravitational pull.

A kid sits at the table—he's only about twenty, but already he's riddled with an inveterate gambler's tics—he squeezes his cards tightly, blows on them before peeling up the edges with a glacial slowness to peek at their value, mumbles to himself, checks his cards again, taps his fingers according to some arcane and ritualized code. His method is working, because, as Pang stands there watching, the kid wins three hands in a row.

Pang puts a wad of cash on the kid before the next round. The kid wins again. Pang grins and orders another drink from a passing waitress and throws down more money.

Next hand, the kid draws a nine. An immediate win. Pang chortles. Winning at gambling is better than sex. The only thing that comes close is wielding power.

The next few hands are less kind. The kid and the banker tie, so no money is paid out. Then the kids loses. Pang shrugs. You can't win 'em all. He's sure the odds will swing back in the young man's favor. He places another bet. And the kid draws a nine!

Pang considers the wad of cash he has sitting on the table. Should he let it ride? Take half back just in case? No. He's going to let it ride. This kid is going to make him a bundle. Bets are finalized, cards are dealt.

A short, thin man standing next to Pang calls out to a passing waitress with his drink order: "*Kafei!*" A coffee.

"*Ta ma da!*" Pang growls. "What the hell are you saying?"

"What?"

"That's bad luck, idiot! *Fei,* like 'fly,' as in, *my luck has flown away!* Have you never gambled before?"

"I, uh . . . I just wanted a coffee!"

The kid jitters in his chair, on the verge of having a nervous breakdown. The dealer asks for quiet.

"Brainless dolt," Pang mutters under his breath.

The kid loses the hand and Pang's money. The short, thin man has the presence of mind to make himself scarce. The other gamblers who bet on the kid commiserate on their misfortune. Pang tracks down the casino manager, points out the object of his ire, and insists he be blacklisted from the casino. The manager knows who Pang is, of course. He immediately has the short, thin man escorted from the premises.

Pang gambles for another hour or so, but his luck remains firmly in the toilet. He leaves the restaurant in a foul mood.

Outside, the street is nearly empty, the bars and restaurants closed for the night. Pang summons a car service and waits on the corner for it to arrive, shivering in the cold.

Down the block, a car starts its engine and rolls up in front of Pang without switching on its headlights. A tall man climbs out. He's wearing a coat, hat, and cotton face mask. "Good evening, Mayor Pang. My name is Zhang. I'm with the Central Commission for Discipline Inspection. Surely you are aware that gambling is illegal in the People's Republic of China?"

Pang is at a loss for words. Has he just been caught in a sting operation?

"Please come with me," Zhang says.

"I don't understand," Pang says

"It is not necessary for you to understand. Come along." Zhang reaches for Pang's elbow.

Pang backs away. "Don't touch me." This doesn't make sense. The CCDI arresting him? At this hour? For gambling? Something's not right. He looks at the car. It's a black sedan. A Bentian.

Pang runs. He doesn't get far. Zhang takes him down, tases him, cuffs his wrists, and drags him into the car.

A kitchen worker comes out to toss garbage into a bin just in time to see Zhang spirit Pang away. He doesn't recognize Pang, but he knows a forcible abduction when he sees it. As the car drives off, he rushes back inside to tell the head cook what he's just witnessed.

The cook shrugs and lights a cigarette. "How many of these degenerates do you suppose owe money to loan sharks? How many of them win enough to pay off their debts, or know when to quit? Whatever bad shit happens to them is their own damn fault."

Zhang and Li take Pang to an industrial section of the city where the streets are deserted at this hour, apart from scuttling rats and prowling stray cats. They manhandle Pang into the back of a van. In place of a tiger chair, the van is outfitted with a huge metal vat. Given the limited space, Zhang and Li have some difficulty maneuvering Pang into the vat, but once he's inside, they lift a heavy metal grate over the top and lock it in place.

The vat is three-quarters full of a sticky, viscous liquid. Pang, his hands still cuffed behind his back, fights to keep his head above the surface. The liquid gets into his mouth, and he spits it out, disgusted by the taste. It takes him a moment to identify what it is.

Cooking oil.

Pang feels the van vibrate as the men move around, then hears an ominous hissing sound. The hissing is quickly drowned out by loud music played over the van's radio.

Pang shouts for help. He slips and his head goes under. He manages, with difficulty, to sit upright again. He blinks oil from his eyes and coughs. He yells, but his voice is drowned out by the radio.

In due course, Pang feels the oil begin to heat up. He begs for mercy. He bangs his head against the grate until it bleeds. The temperature of the oil quickly becomes uncomfortable. Then unbearable. Pang pitches, rolls, and flails, choking on hot liquid, his skin burning and blistering.

Zhang and Li sit in the car parked behind the van, sharing tea from a thermos and smoking cigarettes. They give it thirty minutes, then play two rounds of rock paper scissors to determine who will shut off the heat and drive the van. Zhang loses. He curses bitterly. Li laughs.

Zhang gets out and slips his hands into a pair of gloves before opening the van's back door. He is greeted with a blast of hot air and the stench of deep-fried meat. Holding his breath, he leans into the van to switch off the burner under the vat. He goes around front and turns off the radio.

He leaves the van doors open and gives it about ten minutes for the worst of the heat and smell to dissipate. Li finally waves impatiently out the window. Zhang gives him a rude gesture, then slams the back door of the van and climbs in up front. Despite the cold, he drives with the windows down, the lingering stench of Pang's scalded flesh in his nostrils.

He knows it will be a long time, if ever, before he craves a bowl of *baodu*—boiled cow stomach—again.

NINETEEN

An emergency meeting is convened Monday morning. Six men gather around a polished table in a conference room. Six anxious men.

Occupying the seat of honor is the mayor of Harbin, a rotund and normally jovial character, given to sly witticisms and, in private, dirty jokes. Today he has no quips to share. To his right is the secretary of the Harbin Chinese Communist Party—the mayor's ideological counterpart, but in terms of actual political power, his superior. Chief Wu, head of the Harbin PSB, sits across from the party secretary, and beside him is his subordinate, Chief Xu. Rounding out the assembly, and representing Nangang District, are Chief Hong and Deputy Mayor Wan.

Xu has just finished briefing the others on the progress of the investigation, of which, admittedly, there isn't much.

The mayor is confused. "No witnesses. No camera footage. How could that be, in this age of mass surveillance and facial recognition technology?"

"We are combing through public and private footage," Xu says. "Interviewing the decedent's family and associates. I'm sure we will have a suspect or suspects in custody soon."

"How soon?" the party secretary asks. His concern is less for the murder of Mayor Pang and more about potential panic among the citizens of Harbin if word of it got out.

"Chief Hong and I will work tirelessly until we break the case."

"Platitudes are not a plan," the secretary says.

Chief Wu interjects: "Given the nature of this homicide, the perpetrators almost certainly left traces behind. I mean, just the equipment necessary to deep-fry a man—that's not something you buy on Taobao, is it?"

"No, sir," Xu says. "That's why I'm confident we'll have this case closed forthwith."

"You'd better," the party secretary warns.

"I'm thinking we should call in the Criminal Investigation Bureau," the mayor says.

"I don't believe that's necessary," Xu says.

The mayor taps his blunt fingertips on the mahogany wood veneer of the table. "Aren't they experts in this sort of thing?"

"So are we," Xu says.

"What about the guy from the procuratorate?" the mayor asks. "Cai. Is there any connection?"

Xu figured this was coming. He looks at Hong.

Hong clears his throat. "No, Mr. Mayor. Cai's death was a suicide. Pang's was a homicide."

"You're sure about that? The suicide, I mean. It's weird, the two deaths, coming in such proximity."

"Are you suggesting a serial killer is targeting Nangang officials?" Xu smiles broadly to demonstrate the inherent ridiculousness of such an idea. "If so, why make one look like a suicide and use such an outlandish and macabre method to murder the other?"

"I don't know," the mayor snaps. "It's odd, that's all."

"It definitely represents an unfortunate chain of events," Xu says. "But the two deaths are in no way linked. Cai's friends and colleagues indicate that he was experiencing some personal problems recently. Perhaps a bout of depression. And he was known to be a bit of a heavy drinker. As for Mayor Pang . . . well, as Chief Wu says, given the arcane and elaborate murder method, it shouldn't take long to track down the perpetrators."

The mayor turns his attention to Chief Wu. "I don't want to step on any toes, but I really think we should call in the CIB."

Wu purses his lips. He is reluctant for two reasons. One, asking for CIB's assistance is a loss of face for the Harbin PSB. And two: unlike Western countries, where government figures are often targeted by radical elements, officials in the People's Republic are rarely the victims of politically motivated violence.

Which means it's likely Pang was involved in something untoward. And the grotesque nature of the homicide leads Wu to think the motive was revenge.

Although Wu has no knowledge of what Pang may or may not have been mixed up in, he and his subordinate Xu have been colleagues for many years. And they have, when expedient or financially rewarding, cut corners, skirted regulations, broken the law. So Wu cannot say for sure if Xu will be implicated if the reasons for Pang's murder come to light, but he can't rule it out, either. And a chain is only as strong as its weakest link. If Xu goes down, others might end up as collateral damage. Namely, himself. "I think that's premature. Let's let Chiefs Xu and Hong do their jobs for now."

"Agreed," Deputy Mayor Wan says, miffed that no one has asked his opinion.

The mayor leans back in his chair and turns to the CCP secretary. "Your opinion?"

The secretary is something of a unicorn—an honest and forthright idealist who believes fervently in the core values of Marxism-Leninism. "If details of this brutal crime were to leak, it could inspire widespread panic. Remember the chaos surrounding the Gao Chengyong murders in the nineties?"

"The press knows better than to publish lurid stories," Hong says.

The secretary raises an eyebrow. "Someone always talks, Chief Hong. Gossip spreads like a disease. Before you know it, our citizens will be afraid to leave their homes at night. They'll launch protests in Sophia Square, asking why the government and party aren't safeguarding their safety. Our best hope is to catch the killer before that happens." He nods at the mayor. "Let's call in the CIB."

TWENTY

Tuesday morning, Dr. Ma Xiulan and Supervising Technician Jin arrive on the first flight out of Beijing. They are met at the luggage carousel by Chief Xu's right-hand man, Detective Han. Han is the type of policeman who gives the impression of extreme volatility—as if he might erupt into bloody violence at the slightest pretext. Ma takes an immediate dislike to him. Her opinion is not improved when he eyes her up and down in a frankly lascivious manner.

"Just you two?" Han asks.

"Do you require more?" Ma asks.

Han shrugs. "I've got a car waiting outside."

When dealing with the locals, Ma finds it expedient to establish a pecking order right off the bat, so she hands Han a case of equipment. "Carry this, would you?"

Han's mouth twists unpleasantly, but he takes the case. Once their luggage is loaded into the car and Ma and Jin are settled in the backseat, Han climbs up front and nods at the driver. "This is my partner. Everyone calls him Pangu."

In Chinese mythology, Pangu is a primordial hairy horned giant. As the story goes, when he died his breath became the wind; his left eye the sun; his right eye the moon; his body the mountains, rivers, and forests. Even the fleas on his fur transformed, becoming the myriad animals of the world.

From what Ma can see of the back of Pangu's head, the nickname is fitting—he is a big man with thick, straight hair like the bristles on a toilet brush.

Well, when in Harbin, Ma thinks. "Detective Pangu. A pleasure."

Mayor Pang's body awaits them in an autopsy room at the Harbin morgue.

So do a pair of Harbin medical examiners, along with Chiefs Xu and Hong. Introductions are made all around.

"I've read your book," one of the MEs tells Ma. He's referring to *Death Is My Trade,* an autobiography Ma published to no small success—and a substantial bit of controversy—a few years ago. "I found it a bit . . . sensationalistic."

"There was not one fact or incident in that book that was inaccurate," Ma says. "And it served an important purpose—bringing to light the corruption and sloppiness that is rampant in our field."

"You'll find neither of those here," the ME sniffs.

"Glad to hear it," Ma says.

"Deputy Director Song couldn't make it?" Xu says.

"He's in Zhejiang on another case," Ma says. "I'll be acting as the lead investigator here. Will that be a problem?"

"Not at all. I'm just sorry you had to come all this way for such a trivial matter."

"Trivial? If I'm not mistaken, you have a bizarre and brutal homicide on your hands?"

"Yes. But I doubt you will be able to tell us anything we don't already know."

"I appreciate the vote of confidence. Shall I just have your detectives drive us back to the airport now, or might I be allowed to conduct my examination?"

Xu's pendulous lips curve into the semblance of a smile. "No offense intended. Please." He waves a hand at the autopsy room.

Ma is no stranger to a hostile crowd—local cops and coroners who feel like her presence is an insult to their authority and a negative reflection on their abilities. And it often is.

But she doesn't allow herself to get dragged into petty politics or fret about fragile masculinity. She's here to do a job.

She opens the door and grimaces at the smell of cooked meat, boiled organs, rendered fat, and isopropyl alcohol. Someone gags—Ma thinks it's Pangu. She and Jin enter. They slip coveralls over their clothes, place dabs of menthol gel under their noses, and don face shields. Xu, Hong, Han, and Pangu position themselves in the farthest corner of the room. The two medical examiners crowd around the autopsy table.

"Which one of you performed the PMCT scan?" Ma asks. A PMCT will reveal many details a traditional examination of a degraded body will not, including hidden signs of trauma, heat fractures, fluid in airways, trapped gases, and hemorrhages.

"Me." One of the MEs opens a laptop computer to show Ma and Jin a series of digital scans. He concludes, "The victim was alive when he was boiled in hot oil. His wrists were handcuffed. Head trauma indicates he was in a vessel with a metal lid and banged his skull against it repeatedly in an attempt to escape. Cause of death was a heart attack induced by a rapid and massive increase in blood pressure."

"Thank you, Doctor," Ma says. She will review the scans in more detail later, but now comes the actual autopsy. To be more precise, a second one—the Harbin MEs have already conducted their initial postmortem. Given the indignities it has endured, it's no surprise Pang's corpse has the consistency of a bag of soggy mush. The procedure is a messy one. Halfway through, all four police officers—Xu, Hong, Han, and Pangu—retreat to the corridor.

In the end, as Xu snidely predicted, Ma doesn't uncover any startling revelations. Naturally, the local MEs are pleased, their professional pride left intact.

Afterward, Ma and Jin wash up, and then Detectives Han and Pangu drive them to Harbin PSB headquarters and escort them up to their makeshift office—a conference room down the hall from the Homicide Division.

Ma asks Han if he can review the homicide report with her: "Since you're the lead homicide investigator on this case."

"Sure thing," Han says.

"Great. Now, according to a statement from the victim's wife, he left his home at around nine P.M. on Saturday, November fourth. GPS tracking of his phone indicates he went to National Road, an area known for its nightlife."

"Correct."

"And his body was found the next morning at a construction site by a private security guard doing his morning rounds."

"Correct."

"This construction site doesn't have locked gates and security cams?" Ma asks.

"It's four city blocks of razed buildings and empty holes in the ground. Impossible to guard the entire site."

"What about a night watchman?"

"The nearest one was in a trailer a couple hundred meters away from where the body was dumped," Han says. "Probably sound asleep with his teeth soaking in a jar. He's seventy-four years old."

"How about traffic cams on the streets leading to and from the construction site?"

"We're working on it."

"How long might that take?" Ma asks.

"I don't know. To be honest, the surveillance cam coverage in Harbin is a lot spottier than we officially let on. Maybe a quarter of the cameras are just for show and aren't even transmitting. We have some detectives out canvassing the area to supplement what we have available with footage from private cams. But it's a process." Han is chewing gum, and as he speaks, Ma can see it circulating in his mouth like a wet rag in a washing machine.

"I see," Ma says. "Moving on, according to your report, no witnesses recall seeing Pang at National Road. None of the local establishments captured footage of him on *their* security cams."

"Correct."

"Pang was the district mayor. And *nobody* can attest to his presence in a busy nightlife area?"

"Apparently," Han says unhelpfully.

"Was he wearing a fake mustache?"

Han smiles. "It's not like he was a movie star. Nobody really gives a shit about a district mayor."

"Well, the killer certainly did."

That evening, Ma and Jin have dinner at a restaurant near their hotel. After placing their orders, Ma looks around to make sure no suspiciously cop-like patrons are within earshot and leans closer to Jin. "I can't figure out if these people are indifferent, incompetent, or have something to hide. I mean, the fact that we can trace Pang's last known whereabouts to a street filled with restaurants and pubs, yet there are no eyewitnesses or security footage, strains credibility."

Jin slurps his tea. "Well, it's not inconceivable a district mayor and the local PSB would be involved in something shady. And less than eager for us to find out what it is."

"Perhaps it would be prudent to bring in another investigator," Ma suggests. "One who knows Harbin well . . . and the various personalities we're dealing with . . . and who might be able to discern some hidden truths."

Jin sets his cup down. "Are you thinking what I think you're thinking?"

"Probably."

"That's just asking for trouble."

Ma smiles. "Trouble is our business, Brother Jin."

立冬
WINTER

TWENTY-ONE

The next day, Lu Fei arrives at the Harbin PSB headquarters, along with Constable Sun. He presents his credentials to the attendant in the lobby. The attendant calls upstairs for Dr. Ma. As they wait, Lu finds himself feeling nervous. He knows he's not welcome in Harbin, even more so in this particular building. It wouldn't surprise him if a scrum of cops came rushing in to attack him with batons and pepper spray. Instead, Ma appears with a smile of welcome.

"A pleasure to see you again, Inspector Lu!"

"The pleasure is mine, Dr. Ma." It's been nearly a year since Lu has laid eyes on Ma, and in the interim she has grown even more elegant and stylish, if such a thing is possible. He introduces Sun.

"Welcome to the team," Ma says, then stage-whispers, "Watch for snakes in the grass."

"That bad?" Lu asks.

Ma shrugs. "Can't say for sure, yet. That's why you're here."

Building passes are sorted out for Lu and Sun, and then Ma takes them up to the conference room.

Jin pumps Lu's hand enthusiastically. "Hello, Inspector! Welcome to the jungle!"

Ma brings Lu and Sun up to speed. When she's finished, Lu nods knowingly. "Keep in mind, Xu started his career in Nangang District. And Hong is one of his longtime ass-licking cronies. I don't know Pang personally, but as he came up through the district government, I'm sure he and Xu had many opportunities to cross paths. In other words, Nangang is a murky and incestuous little pond."

"Well, one thing at a time," Ma says. "The murder might have nothing to do with Xu and Hong."

"Agreed," Lu says. "But if there is a cover-up, you can bet those two bastards will sabotage us any way they can. Falsify reports. Withhold information. Hell, if it's a choice between smothering us in our sleep or going to prison, they wouldn't think twice."

"Inspector," Ma says, "I brought you here because of your local expertise . . . and we may well find something shadowy going on beneath the surface here . . . but let's not get carried away just yet."

"No, no, you're right," Lu says. He glances at the ceiling of the conference room. "What do you think the chances are they've planted a bug in here?"

A task force meeting is scheduled for 11:00 A.M. Chiefs Hong and Xu will attend. Neither of them is yet aware that Lu is on the case.

Last night, when Ma phoned Lu about joining her team, he was at first hesitant. He departed Harbin under a dark cloud a decade ago—exiled after catching Xu with an underage prostitute. In the years since, he's made peace with his new life and sunk roots into Raven Valley. But somehow he keeps getting sucked back here. If he were a superstitious man, he might be tempted to say the city refuses to release its hold on him until he resolves some unfinished business.

And then there is the issue of Constable Sun's imminent resignation.

A murder investigation is the pinnacle of police work. What higher calling is there for a police officer than the pursuit of a killer? Lu is hoping that the excitement of a high-stakes investigation may be just what Sun needs to realize her life's ambition is loftier than the domestic role her fiancé has chosen for her.

For these reasons, he agreed to come aboard. "But don't tell Xu until it's a done deal," he advised Ma. "Otherwise, he'll do everything in his power to stop you before I even cross the city line."

When Xu and Hong walk into the conference room five minutes later and find Lu sitting at the table, Xu nearly has a stroke. "What is *he* doing here?"

"I've asked Inspector Lu to join my investigation team," Ma says.

Lu spots Detectives Han and Pangu filing in behind Hong. Han's face twists unpleasantly when he sees Lu. Lu groans inwardly. This is going to be worse than he anticipated.

"No," Xu says. "Absolutely not."

"Excuse me," Ma says. "I decide who's on my team, not you."

"You know I fired him when I was district chief, right?"

"So I've heard," Ma says. "I've also heard there are two sides to that story."

Xu nearly erupts like Mount Vesuvius. Then he calculates the odds of winning a battle against a senior CIB investigator and adjusts his tactics. "This man has a deep-seated animosity toward me. He will say and do anything to impugn my reputation."

"He also cracked the Undertaker Zeng serial killer case," Ma says. "I don't think I need to justify his qualifications."

"From your decision to bring him aboard I can only surmise you have some personal ax to grind with me."

"This case is not about you," Ma says. "It's about the murder of Mayor Pang. Unless there's something you'd care to share with the rest of us?"

Xu's flounderish lips work silently for a moment, then he sits down and motions for Hong and the two detectives to do the same. "I'll be speaking to your deputy director about this."

"That is your prerogative. Now let's begin." Ma quickly reviews her autopsy findings. She confirms the details of the police report and the status of the investigation. "Regarding the victim's presence at National Road, I still find it odd that no one recalls seeing him. Might he have been doing something clandestine? Meeting a mistress or outside business associate, for example?"

"There isn't the slightest whiff of impropriety surrounding Mayor Pang," Hong says. "Everyone speaks highly of his character."

"Have you already obtained his financial and phone records?"

"They should be arriving by the end of today," Hong confirms.

"We'll want to look at his work records," Ma says. "Administrative matters or projects he was involved in that might provide a motive."

"Naturally," Xu says. "We've got some detectives over at the district mayor's office as we speak. But I think you'll find the details pretty bland. Rubber-stamping economic development initiatives. Vetoing the expansion of poultry breeding zones."

"Nevertheless," Ma says. She gives Jin a nod. "Supervisor Jin?"

"Any thoughts on the equipment used to boil the victim?" Jin asks.

"Had to have been an industrial cooking pot," Hong says. "The kind used in large-scale food processing, sauce-making, and so on."

"Are there any such pots big enough for a human being?"

"Some," Hong says. "If you modify them. Take out the mixing apparatus."

"And they can get hot enough to thoroughly cook a man Pang's size?"

"From what we understand, they heat up to two hundred degrees Celsius. Might take a while, but that's plenty hot enough."

"I assume you're chasing down recent local orders for such items?"

"Yes."

"There can't be that many."

"Harbin is a city of ten million," Xu says. "And thousands of restaurants and factories. And the perpetrators may have bought the pot secondhand, from a private owner, paid cash. It will take some time."

"Understood, thank you," Jin says.

"I'll be putting together a short list of the victim's friends, family, and colleagues and conducting interviews," Ma says.

"Why?" Hong asks. "We've done that. Seems like a waste of time to duplicate efforts."

"This wasn't a crime of passion," Ma says. "Or a random, spur-of-the-moment murder. It was meticulously planned and executed. And if someone just wanted Pang dead, there are a dozen easier ways. A gun, a bomb, a knife, a brick. Obviously, the purpose in boiling the victim was about more than just committing a homicide. The suspect intended to send a message, or a warning. And I'll wager one of his friends, colleagues, business partners—maybe his wife, or girlfriend if he has one—knows something that will shed some light on the killer's motivation."

Xu leans forward in his chair. "That is a logical theory, Dr. Ma, but let's make sure we're on the same page here. Our goal is to catch a murderer. Not to prosecute Mayor Pang posthumously, or to harass the good citizens of Nangang District. You're just visiting, but we live here."

"I understand."

"Fine. Proceed with your interviews, but please use discretion." Xu looks at his watch. "What else?"

"We'll need access to your criminal records and databases."

Xu nods. "What else?"

"That's all for the moment," Ma says.

Xu stands. "Very well. If you need anything, Detective Han will act as your liaison."

"Thank you for your time," Ma says.

Xu gives Lu a dark look on this way out the door. Lu lets out a silent breath when he's gone.

After discussing a few more administrative details, Hong likewise makes his excuses and leaves. Han shuts the door behind him, then turns and makes a pretense of sniffing the air. "I thought I smelled pig shit when I walked in."

While working as a detective in Nangang, Lu was Han's senior in terms of age and rank. But even then, Han was under Xu's wing, which meant that consistently he flouted rules and regulations without much fear of reprisal.

"Last time I saw you, Han, you were bleeding and unconscious," Lu says. "Which was a considerable improvement in your personality."

Han smirks. "This is going to be fun."

"Can't wait." Lu notices Pangu giving him the evil eye. Lu doesn't know Pangu personally, but he can see Pangu's nose is still crooked from when Lu gave it a nasty crack with a leather sap. "I don't recall your name, Detective, but I never forget a nose I've busted."

"Perhaps while you're in town I can return the favor," Pangu says.

"All right, gentlemen, that's enough," Ma says. "Whatever bad blood you share is a distraction to this case. I won't tolerate dick-waving on my watch. Are we clear?"

Han laughs, a bit shocked by Ma's comment. "Sure thing, Doc."

"Inspector Lu?" Ma says.

Lu nods. "I'm just here to do a job."

"Good," Ma says. "Then let's get to work."

TWENTY-TWO

Following the meeting, Ma, Lu, and Han depart for the construction site where Pang's body was found. Jin and Sun remain in the conference room to comb through the provincial crime database searching for homicides with an MO similar to that of Pang's murder.

They don't find any. Nor did they really expect to.

The homicide rate in Harbin is quite low for a city of ten million—just 0.5 cases per 100,000 citizens. That happens to be on par with the national average, but both Jin and Sun are fully aware that criminal activity is grossly underreported in the People's Republic. The government enjoys touting China's relative safety as a sign of its moral superiority over decadent Western countries, with their drug problems, serial killers, and school shooting deaths. As a result, local police commanders are strongly incentivized to ignore, hide, or find creative ways to adjust their statistics before sending them up the ladder for inclusion in provincial and national reports.

"Well what if a previous murder was miscategorized as an accident or suspicious death?" Jin suggests.

"Suspicious death" is police jargon for a death in which the manner or cause are not immediately obvious. This might include a sudden and unexpected demise with no witnesses, one that cannot be attributed to a preexisting medical condition, or any fatality in which the circumstances are unusual enough to warrant an investigation.

Pangu is loudly snacking on a bag of shrimp chips. "Involving the deep-frying of a human spring roll? We checked. We're not total idiots."

"I'm sure you're not," Jin says. "But in the interests of due diligence, we'll run a search anyway."

Pangu licks chip dust off a thick fingertip. "Due diligence until you're blue in the face, for all I care."

What Pangu says is true. There are no boiling or scalding deaths listed as suspicious, and only a handful of accidents that fit the bill: a laundry worker killed when a steam pipe ruptured; a maintenance person parboiled while cleaning out a defective boiler; a child who tumbled into a hot bath.

"The circumstances of these accidents are all well established," Jin concludes. "And the victims are not similar to Pang in any way."

"Told you that," Pangu says.

"So you did." Jin pushes back from his laptop. "Tea, anyone?"

"Sure," Sun says.

"Canteen's on the first floor," Pangu says. "Can't miss it. Grab me a tangerine C100 while you're down there."

Jin shuts his laptop. "Why don't you come with me, Constable? It's important to take a break now and then, keeps the mind sharp."

They take the stairs down to the first floor, then follow the sounds of metal utensils clinking against crockery. In the canteen they split up: Jin roots around in a refrigerator for Pangu's C100; Sun heads to the tea station.

A group of male constables sits at a nearby table. As Sun pours two cups of tea, one of the constables looks over at her and says something to the others in a low voice. They all laugh. Sun pretends not to notice.

Although there are three hundred thousand female police officers in the People's Republic, give or take, the PSB is still heavily male. Most police colleges even cap their acceptance rates for female cadets at fifteen percent, citing the heavy workload and risky nature of a law enforcement career as justification.

While serving as the only female constable in the Raven Valley PSB, Sun has encountered her fair share of boorish behavior. Initially Chief Liang didn't know what to make of her. He vacillated between treating her like a porcelain doll—something to be placed on a shelf and admired from afar—and an office secretary. When important guests came to visit, he often asked her to serve tea, a request she resented but lacked the confidence to decline. Until one day she brewed the bitterest, most vile-tasting tea she could manage—and that was the last time he made such a request.

The other constables in the *paichusuo* were a mixed bag. Huang, Fatty Wang, and Li the Mute were kind and helpful. Sergeant Bing was gruff but respectful. Yuehan Chu and Big Wang went out of their way to create an inhospitable atmosphere, telling off-color jokes, stopping by her desk to fart loudly, texting sexist memes to her cell phone—all sorts of petty annoyances.

But Sun persevered, and eventually even Chu and Big Wang realized she wasn't going anywhere and grew tired of hazing her.

Now she'll soon be leaving it all behind—the long hours and dull administrative work; the squad room's baked-in stink of body odor and stale cigarette smoke; Fatty Wang's cheerful nature and Li the Mute's sweet shyness; the hilariously inane things that are apt to come from Constable Huang's mouth; the way she feels just a smidgen taller and a touch more confident in her clean and starched uniform.

And, of course, the locals who rely on her for assistance, to address an injustice—or sometimes just to provide a shoulder to cry on.

Back upstairs, Jin gives Pangu his C100 and receives a perfunctory thanks. He opens his laptop and notices the keyboard displays the telltale remnants of shrimp-chip-grease-covered fingertips on some of the keys. He frowns at Pangu.

Pangu contrives to look as innocent as possible. He fails.

TWENTY-THREE

The site where Pang's earthly remains were discovered is a remote section in the midst of four city blocks of leveled concrete, machinery, building supplies, and raw earth. Specifically, in a rubble-strewn lot hidden behind a shed filled with wooden planks and a giant garbage bin that smells of rotting food.

A security guard—ancient, so thin a stiff wind might blow him into the Songhua River—shows them to the spot, now delineated by wooden stakes pounded into the ground and roped off with yellow police tape. Lu asks the guard if he was on duty Saturday night. The guard grins uncomfortably—he has only a few remaining teeth in his mouth—and nods.

There is not much information to be gleaned from those few square meters of churned earth. Aside from the police tape, Lu can see other signs of investigatory work: the prints of police boots, cigarette butts, a wayward paper shoe cover.

Lu asks about security cameras and is told by the guard that this sector of the construction site has none. "Not much to steal here," the guard says. "Unless you're after empty cigarette packs and greasy take-out containers."

Next stop is the district mayor's office, where Lu and Ma interview members of Pang's staff under Han's dour supervision.

Government offices are generally lousy with petty squabbles, sex scandals, and cutthroat rivalries, and this one is no exception—the staff are eager to throw each other under the bus at every opportunity—but everyone is circumspect when it comes to their statements regarding Pang. Either he was a man of few peccadilloes—or his minions are too intimidated to dish any dirt.

They manage to catch Deputy Mayor Wan on the way to a meeting. "Mayor Pang was my friend and colleague," Wan says woodenly, as if facing a wall of bright lights and media microphones. "He was a dedicated party member and tireless public servant."

"And you don't know any reason why someone would want to murder him?" Ma asks. "Especially in such a horrible manner?"

"Perhaps it was a radical political element?"

"What kind of element did you have in mind, Deputy Mayor?"

Wan shrugs. "I don't know. A Uighur?"

"What possible motive would a Uighur have for killing Mayor Pang?" Lu asks.

"That's your department," Wan sniffs. "I must be going. Good day."

As the deputy mayor rushes off, Han glances at his watch and says: "How much longer here?"

"I think we're done," Ma says. "I'd like to head over to the mayor's home and speak to his widow."

"She doesn't know anything. Trust me."

Hearing the word *trust* come out of Han's mouth makes Lu laugh. Han shoots him a nasty look.

"If you don't want to take us, we'll just hop in a cab," Ma says.

Han's mouth twists. "I'll bring the car around."

After Han leaves, Ma turns to Lu. "Don't antagonize him. It's already going to be hard enough to get anything done with his dead weight around our necks."

"Sorry. It just slipped out."

Back at headquarters, Jin and Sun run a background search on Pang. It's all very standard stuff. Pang attended Harbin Number 3 High School and Harbin Normal University. He joined the Communist Party while still a student and then worked his way up through various local administrative posts. He was, by all indications, a quintessential career politician. Married thirty years, no children. No criminal record or official demerits.

A glance at Pang's social media footprint likewise turns up little of interest. No controversial posts on Weibo, just dull and uninspired platitudes. A few mentions on Baidu: Pang presiding over an effort to impose new prohibitions relating to the "renewal of party discipline criteria and ethics"; his latest obligatory statement regarding coronavirus; an article quoting him as bullish on Nangang District investment opportunities. And, of course, there is local media coverage of his murder, heavy on hagiography, light on specifics.

Sun discovers a handful of photos of Pang online—inspecting ice and snow removal efforts during a blizzard; shaking hands with the head of an investment group from Norway; Pang and a younger man smiling for the camera, both dressed in slacks and polos and holding golf clubs, the caption reading: *Nangang District Mayor Pang and Deputy Chief Procurator Cai participate in a charity golf tournament benefiting the Harbin Number One Specialized Hospital.*

"For a senior member of a district administration, Pang hasn't left much of a trace," Sun remarks.

"As it should be," Jin says with a wry smile. "Our government officials are dedicated to the collective good, not their own selfish ambitions."

Later, Jin asks Pangu about progress in analyzing video footage taken from city surveillance cameras.

"Crime Control and Prevention is handling that," Pangu says. "If they find something, they'll tell us."

"Maybe I can sit in?"

Pangu waves a meaty hand. "Sift through hours of raw tape? Waste of your time. Let the grunts handle it."

"Right." Jin gives it fifteen minutes, then says he's going to the restroom. Pangu doesn't even look up when Jin closes his laptop and takes it with him.

While Jin doesn't require permission to go where the investigation takes him, he knows he'll be incurring the potential wrath of the Harbin PSB if he skips over the chain of command.

He doesn't care.

He wanders the halls of the building until he finds what he's looking for—a cavernous amphitheater outfitted with a massive screen on one wall. The screen displays various camera feeds superimposed over a map of Harbin. A dozen or so police officers sit at workstations, searching for scofflaws or just watching ordinary citizens go about their business.

Jin asks the shift supervisor where the footage for Pang's case is being reviewed. The supervisor looks nervous. "Did you speak to Detective Han or Chief Xu about this?"

"Why? Do I require their clearance? Is the footage top secret?"

"No, but . . ."

"Then what's the problem?"

"No problem. But wouldn't you prefer we handle the initial review and notify you when we find something?"

"What I would prefer is that you show me where the footage is being reviewed. Now. Please."

The supervisor leads Jin over to a workstation occupied by a skinny young man in a constable's second-class uniform. There is a can of Hong Niu—Red Bull—at the youth's elbow. When he sees the supervisor and Jin coming, he quickly stashes the Hong Niu under his desk.

"This is Constable Xue," the supervisor says.

Xue stands, nods deferentially. "You're from the CIB, right? How cool is that?"

"Pretty cool," Jin says. "Have you found anything of interest, Constable?"

Xue looks at the supervisor, hesitates. "I'm still reviewing, sir. It will take some time."

"No doubt. In any case, I'll need to include details regarding your search methodology and the city surveillance system in my official report. Mind if I sit?"

"Please."

Jin pulls up a chair, opens his computer, types in a password. "First, I'll need you to provide me with a complete listing of camera locations near where the victim went missing, and within a five-block radius of the site where his body was discovered. I want you to make a special note of blind spots, outages, that sort of thing."

Xue looks like he's swallowed a piece of hot lead. "All right."

Jin turns to the supervisor. "No sense in you standing around while we go through all this. I'll let you know if I have any questions." He turns back to Xue. "Let's begin with an overview of your surveillance system. Brand and model number for the cameras, their capabilities, including facial recognition, network software specs, and so on."

Xue launches in. Jin taps away on his keyboard. After a few minutes, the supervisor retreats to his workstation. Jin lets Xue drone on for a bit, then interrupts him. "You can stop there." He leans in. "Have you really not found anything, Constable? No footage of the victim or possible suspects?"

"Well . . ." Xue fidgets.

"Listen, I don't know why my team is getting so much interference, but if I find out there's some sort of conspiracy afoot to hide evidence, I'm going to open the gates and let the dogs loose. And they aren't too particular who they bite in the ass. Get my meaning?"

Xue smiles nervously. "You're putting me in a tough position here, sir."

"Just do the right thing, Constable. That's all I'm asking."

Xue reaches under the desk and picks up his can of Hong Niu. "Want one?"

"No, thanks. I already have astronomically high blood pressure."

Xue drinks, belches softly, tosses the can in a wastebasket. "We've been told to refer any developments through Detective Han."

"Why do you suppose that is?"

"So we don't waste your time with potentially insignificant details?"

"What do you *really* think is the reason?"

Xue smiles again. "The Harbin PSB doesn't want to be upstaged by a bunch of uppity Beijingers?"

"Perhaps. Does this mean you've found something?"

"Not a lot. But . . ." Xue glances over to check the supervisor's position. "Let me show you." Xue fiddles with his mouse. "I can definitively place the victim on National Road at nine thirty-three P.M."

The monitor displays a snippet of video footage—Pang exiting a car, then walking out of frame.

"Can you see where he went?" Jin asks.

"No, unfortunately," Xue says. "No coverage from that spot down to the edge of the block."

"How can that be?" Jin waves at the dozens of workstations, the huge screen on the wall. "You have the latest technology."

"Yes, sir. But keep in mind, we have two hundred and fifty thousand cameras in a city of six-point-five million. That's thirty-nine cameras per one thousand citizens. A lot, yes, but far fewer than a city like Beijing. Or even London."

"All right. So, you have Pang arriving, but not his destination or his departure?"

"That's the long and short of it, sir."

"Have you checked private security cams from the local businesses on that street? Maybe they have coverage of the blind spot."

"Ah, that's where things get interesting."

"Do tell."

"Unlike city surveillance cameras, which are hardwired, most private security cams are wireless. And a wireless camera can be jammed if you broadcast at the same frequency. Which is what our suspects must have done. As a result, those private cams picked up nothing but static."

"*Ta ma de.* The bad guys are getting smarter every day."

"Yes, sir."

"What about the vicinity of the construction site?" Jin asks. "Same deal?"

"More or less. Spotty coverage there, but I've been reviewing footage and making a note of any vehicles that may have been used to transport the victim's body entering or exiting the general area."

"Are there a lot?"

"Discounting motorcycles, Hongguang minis, garbage trucks, and the like, sixty-four."

"That many? *Wo kao.*"

"Yes, sir." Xue's expression turns cagey. "So, how do you like working at CIB?"

"I like it fine."

"Any job openings? I'm sick of Harbin. The winters are killing me."

Jin laughs. "It's cold in Beijing, too, Constable."

"Not like here."

"You can always check the website or ask your supervisor to recommend you. But it's very competitive."

"Well, I graduated from the Harbin Institute of Technology with a degree in engineering."

"Great school. You must have had a lot of job prospects. Why join the PSB?"

"I watched too many crime dramas growing up. Maybe you can put in a word for me?"

"Perhaps. Back to those sixty-four vehicles you were telling me about."

Xue nods. "Sure . . . it's not much but . . ." He fiddles again with his mouse and pulls up a screen grab of a van. The resolution and lighting are poor—the van could be white, could be gray. "This is a block away from the construction site, one-oh-nine A.M. Out of the sixty-four vehicles, eleven were vans. But this was the only one I couldn't get a full license plate for. I believe the plate was obscured, maybe by one of those lenticular plastic covers that alters the numbers based on your vantage point."

Jin is familiar with such items—popular with drivers who are trying to avoid paying tolls and purchased easily enough if you know where to go. "Do you have any shots of the driver?"

"Tinted windows." Tinted windows are illegal in China, but, like lenticular license plate covers, not uncommon or difficult to obtain. "I followed the van as far I as I could." Xue pulls up a map on his monitor and traces a line from the construction site, through a series of smaller side streets, and then into the southern reaches of the district. "I lost the trail here, around Red Star Village."

"You think that was the van's destination?"

"Not necessarily. That's just where surveillance cam footage peters out. The van could have turned in any direction, or just kept going south."

"Maybe with what you have here—make and model, a partial license plate—the Vehicle Registration Bureau can get us an ID."

"Maybe, but if this is the van used to transport Pang's body, I'm sure the suspects stole the plate."

"It's worth a shot. Anyway, that's good work, Constable. If I leave you my card, you'll inform me personally of any further developments?"

"That might get me in hot water."

"Then don't get caught. But if you do, I've got your back."

"Well, if the CIB has my back, how can I refuse?"

Jin smiles. "You really can't." He takes a business card out of his pocket and slides it across the desk. "This has my cell phone and email information. You can reach me twenty-four/seven."

Xue looks up and his eyes widen. "Trouble at six o'clock."

Jin turns. Pangu is barreling in his direction with a sour look. He turns back to Xue. "You didn't tell me anything you weren't supposed to. Got it?"

"Got it." Xue palms Jin's card and smiles conspiratorially. "I'll have that résumé to you by dinnertime."

TWENTY-FOUR

In keeping with her dead husband's status, the widow Pang lives in a moderately luxurious two-bedroom apartment in a centrally located high-rise. She opens the door only wide enough to show one eye, bruised and puffy from tears or lack of sleep. "I already spoke to the police." Her eye flickers toward Han. "Didn't *he* tell you?"

"We're with the Criminal Investigation Bureau, not the Harbin PSB," Ma says. "You have heard of the CIB?"

"Yes, of course."

"You may consider our presence as a sign of the seriousness with which the Ministry of Public Security regards your husband's case," Ma says. Then, in a gentler tone: "We are here to help, Mrs. Pang."

"I just want to be left alone in my time of mourning."

"We'll only take a moment," Ma says. "May we come in, please?"

The widow grudgingly steps away from the door.

Lu takes in the floor-to-ceiling windows overlooking the boulevard below, the classic Chinese furnishings—lacquered wooden frames set with stiff, square cushions of embroidered red silk, cloisonné vases stuffed with last year's New Year's pussy willows, framed calligraphy on the walls.

Widow Pang slumps into an armchair, Lu and Ma sit on the couch. Han positions himself behind them, looming over the proceedings. The widow lights a cigarette with an unsteady hand.

Lu turns and cranes his head up at Han. "Why don't you have a seat?"

"Don't worry about me."

"Oh, but I do."

Ma asks the widow a series of questions. About the night of the murder. Concerning Mayor Pang's friends and associates, his business dealings. Any reason why someone might want to harm him.

The widow answers in a monotone. "He often went out at night for work or social events. Unless he needed me to come along, he rarely told me where he was going and what he was doing."

Lu is distracted by the ash on the tip of the widow's cigarette, slowly lengthening as she smokes. He wants to warn her to tap it into an ashtray but is leery of interfering with the flow the Ma's interview.

"He didn't say he was going to National Road, or for what purpose?" Ma asks.

"No."

"But there was nothing unusual about that night?" Ma asks.

"No."

"How was his mood? Did he seem anxious? Frightened?"

The widow looks up at Han, then back at Ma. "No." A fingertip's worth of ash finally falls into her lap. She doesn't even notice.

"Have you ever been to National Road with your husband?" Lu asks. "Was there a particular bar or restaurant he frequented?"

"I've never been to National Road. I don't like pubs, and I've heard the restaurants there are nothing special."

"Did he—pardon me for asking—have a girlfriend or mistress?" Lu asks.

The widow shows a flash of anger. "Don't be insulting."

"I mean no offense. These are just standard questions in an investigation."

The widow sighs deeply, leans forward, and stubs her cigarette out. "He wasn't like that. He wasn't perfect, by any means. A workaholic. Perhaps a bit selfish. Arrogant. But not a skirt-chaser."

"What kind of business dealings did he have outside of his regular work?" Lu asks.

"I don't know. Investments." She waves a hand. "The usual things."

"Did you have access to his financial records?" Ma says.

"We have a joint bank account. I'm sure you already have all our records."

Ma and Lu ask a few more questions, attempting to glean something of interest, but without much success. On the way out, Ma hands the widow a business card. "Should you think of anything important . . . or just want to talk . . . call me anytime."

The widow nods, takes the card, and shuts the door in Ma's face.

TWENTY-FIVE

Pangu grumbles about being a glorified babysitter on the way back up to the conference room, but there's not much else he can do or say regarding Jin going rogue. And Jin doesn't make an issue of it—no sense in pissing off the locals more than necessary.

In the late afternoon, Jin tells Pangu he wants to go to National Road.

"We already canvassed the area," Pangu says. "Like the police report says, no one remembers seeing Pang."

"Due diligence, Detective."

"Oh, yeah. *That*."

"You're not obligated to come."

"As if," Pangu says. He fetches the car and drives Jin and Sun across town, making liberal use of his lights and sirens.

Jin has narrowed Pang's final destination to a strip of about ten tightly packed establishments on the east side of the road. He and Sun enter the first one and show Pang's picture around. Pangu sticks to them like glue.

And so it goes until they reach the end of the strip, without success. Jin is frustrated and confused. "It doesn't make sense that no one saw Pang," he tells Sun. "Someone's not telling the truth."

"Maybe he was here with a woman who wasn't his wife," Sun says.

"Or maybe one of these places has a massage parlor on the top floor," Jin suggests. "Let's go back and poke around behind closed doors."

"You can't do that without a search warrant," Pangu says.

"Technically, you are correct," Jin says. "But I don't care about the parlor—I just want to know what Pang was doing here."

"You've already questioned everyone. Let's not be pests."

"You're right. What was I thinking? When conducting a homicide investigation, the primary directive is to not be a nuisance."

Sun and Jin—Pangu their dark and doleful shadow—return to the first pub on the street and ask to have a look in the basement and upstairs. The manager doesn't like it but doesn't dare refuse—no one wants to cross the CIB.

The search proves fruitless until they reach a seafood restaurant midway down the block—the Ruyi Palace. "You were just here," the manager grumbles.

"We want to see your upstairs," Jin says.

"It's just a banquet room. Not in use now."

"We'd still like to take a look."

"Why?"

"Is this going to be problem?" Jin asks.

The manager grimaces. "This way."

The banquet room is as advertised—a large space, carpeted, round tables, a bar alcove, a small stage for speeches and performances.

Sun tries a door in the back. "What's in here?"

"Storage."

"Open it," Jin says.

"But it's nothing!" the manager says, his voice rising. "Extra dishware and kitchen supplies."

"Open it."

"To be honest, I lost the key a couple of weeks ago. I'll have to call a locksmith."

"Quit wasting my time and open the damn door or I'll get a crowbar and do it myself."

"You'd have to pay me for the damage."

"Unless I find something I shouldn't," Jin says. "In which case, *you'll* be the one paying—with hard labor." He softens his approach. "Listen, Uncle. We're just here about the homicide of Mayor Pang. I don't care if you have a stockpile of foreign booze or smuggled rhino horns in there."

The manager sucks air through his teeth, produces a key, and opens the door. Jin pokes his head in and switches on the light. He sees folded-up green-felt poker tables, a roulette wheel, shelves holding cards and chips.

The manager wipes his sweaty palms on his pants. "The mayor came here sometimes to play cards. Just for fun. No actual money exchanged hands."

"Sure," Jin says. "Just for fun. He was here last Saturday?"

"Yes."

"What time?"

"I don't know exactly. He got here before ten. Left an hour and half or so later."

"Did he win or lose money?"

"I told you. It's just for fun."

"Right, I forgot. Did anything unusual happen while he was here? Any strangers around? Did he have an altercation with anyone? Did he leave with anyone?"

"No."

"No to which one?"

The manager licks his lips. "No to all."

"Do you have security cameras on the premises?"

"In the side alley. I already checked the footage as soon as I heard the news about the mayor's death."

"Let me guess," Jin offers. "All you got was static."

"Yes, that's right."

"Show me."

The manager takes them into a cramped room he uses as his office and pulls up footage from Saturday night. It shows an alleyway between the restaurant and the neighboring building, along with trash bins and a narrow view of National Road. The manager shows Jin that the camera was recording as normal until around 10:00 P.M. After that, nothing but snow until approximately 11:30 P.M.

Jin nods. "You'll need to come down to PSB headquarters and make a statement."

"Can we leave the part about the card games out of it?"

"That's up to Harbin Metro."

They depart the Ruyi Palace and find that night has fallen. A bitter wind snatches at their coats.

"Are we good?" Pangu asks. "Or do you want to kick down a few more doors while we're here?"

"What's your hurry?" Jin says. "This is good business for you."

"What do you mean?"

"Nothing." Jin suspects Pangu will circle back to the restaurant later to extort the manager in exchange for turning a blind eye to his gambling operation. But that's none of his concern. He's in Harbin to catch a killer, not investigate police corruption. "Let's call it a day. I'm ready for dinner, a beer, and an early bed."

TWENTY-SIX

Han drops Lu and Ma off at the hotel and tells them a car will pick them up tomorrow at 10:00 A.M. "I wouldn't go wandering around here at night," he says. "This isn't the best part of town."

Lu nods. "And I hear the police are totally incompetent."

Han grins nastily. "On second thought, you should take a long stroll after dinner. See the sights." He cracks his swollen knuckles. "Get some local color."

"Good night, Detective Han," Ma says. She and Lu get out of the SUV and Ma tugs him toward the lobby. "Time for a drink."

The hotel bar lacks ambience, but at least it's quiet and has a decent selection of alcohol. Ma orders a glass of white wine, Lu a beer. They settle into a corner table.

"You saw that Han was doing his level best to intimidate the widow," Lu says. "It wasn't just me, right?"

"I saw. I think she was telling the truth, though. She doesn't know who killed her husband." Ma sips from her glass. "So, what's the story with you three? You and Detectives Numbskull and Numbnuts?"

Lu laughs, then sobers. "We had a dustup last year. Xu wanted them to teach me a hard lesson." Lu tells Ma about the fight in the basement records department of PSB headquarters, which ended with Han and Pangu unconscious, and Lu giving Xu's unmentionables a vicious squeeze.

Ma shakes her head in disbelief. "I can't believe they got away with assaulting a fellow police officer. All three of them should have been fired . . . even jailed . . . for such an infraction."

"This is a big city, but in some ways it's a small town. By the time I was coming up through the ranks, Xu was already connected. And he had an influential and powerful mentor—a local party boss, named Gao. That's how I knew for sure he wasn't going down when I caught him with a prostitute."

"Where's this Gao now?"

"Last I heard he got ensnared in the anti-corruption campaign and sent to prison. Maybe he's still there. Maybe he's dead. The point is, Xu has *guanxi,* so if you throw dirt at him, you'd best be prepared for it to bounce off and smack you dead in the face."

"Who else do you think is dirty in Harbin?"

"Not sure. I've been gone ten years, remember? Certainly Xu is a scumbag. As is Chief Hong."

"Xu's boss? Chief Wu?"

"Don't know him personally. Never worked with him. To be honest, I can't really speak for anyone outside of the Nangang PSB."

"Ready for another drink?"

"Let me get it."

"No. Business expense." Ma goes to the bar and orders a second round. She returns and sets a beer down in front of Lu. "I know Xu got off scot-free when you caught him in the arms of an underage prostitute. But what about the girl? And the owner of the brothel?"

"I took the girl and handed her over to social services. Not sure what happened to her after that. As for the owner—his name was Tang Fuqiang. Rumor had it he started out cutting hair for a few yuan on the street and somehow parlayed that into becoming one of the biggest pimps in Nangang."

"A real entrepreneur. Living the Chinese dream."

"With serious *guanxi.*"

"That was the end of it, then?"

"Well . . ." Lu takes a long swallow of beer and wipes his mouth. "Want to hear a story?"

"Sure."

"Promise never to tell."

"Promise."

"All right." Lu leans forward. "I laid low for about a week after I caught Xu at the brothel—and then I went to Tang's flagship establishment. A big garish monstrosity decorated in neon and chrome . . ."

Lu remembers every detail like it was yesterday. A balmy spring night—the kind that inspires you to have dinner al fresco with a loved one, then take a long walk along the Songhua River.

Instead, Lu arrives at the entrance of the brothel wearing a bulletproof vest under a windbreaker, a balaclava over his head, and carrying a riot baton.

A valet in a white shirt and bow tie was stationed out front. Lu walked right past him and through a set of double glass doors into a foyer, where he encountered a hostess in a red silk dress and a gorilla-sized bouncer. The hostess took one look at Lu and let out a scream. The bouncer moved to block Lu's path.

Lu swung the baton. The dense wood made a resounding crack as it snapped into the side of the bouncer's knee. The bouncer howled and sprawled into the foyer's decorative centerpiece—a shallow pool of water fed by an artificial waterfall and stocked with a dozen sleek goldfish.

The hostess screamed again. The bouncer flailed. One of the fish plopped onto the foyer carpet. The bouncer lurched to his feet, dripping wet. Lu hit him behind the ear. The bouncer crumpled back into the pool. Lu reached down, picked up the errant fish, tossed it in beside the bouncer. He told the hostess to run. She did.

Lu kicked open the door leading to the lounge. Inside was a cavernous and dimly lit room with a bar and karaoke stage. A half dozen men sat by the stage in a scrum of hostesses.

Lu pointed with his baton. "Out! All of you!"

This demand first elicited confusion, and then belligerence. One of the men leaped up, his face red from drink and anger. "Who the hell are you?"

"Last warning," Lu said.

"*Qu ni ma!*" the man cursed, coming at Lu.

"Have it your way." Lu hit the man with the baton. The man dropped like a stone into a low glass table, shattering it into hundreds of pieces.

Screams from the hostesses. The men got the hint—they gathered up their belongings and fled, carrying the semiconscious man along with them.

Lu headed for the bar. He discovered a bartender cowering behind it. "Piss off," Lu said. The bartender edged past Lu and sprinted for the door. Lu slid the tip of his baton along a shelf of liquor, tipping bottles of whiskey, scotch, bourbon, vodka, cognac, gin, and rum to the floor.

He was getting started on the second shelf when two toughs burst through a door in the back. One carried a club. The other, a watermelon chopper. A third man came in behind them. "What the fuck do you think you're doing?" the man shouted. "Do you have any earthly idea who I am?"

"Yes," Lu said. "Tang Fuqiang, a turd-eating, lowlife turtle's egg."

Tang seemed shocked that Lu would know his name and still have the balls to wreck his brothel. "Kill this bastard," he ordered the toughs.

The toughs fanned out. Lu stepped out from behind the counter, his shoes squelching in spilled booze and crackling fragments of glass.

Strategically speaking, Lu preferred to target the Watermelon Chopper first. But the other guy rushed in, swinging for the fences. Lu parried with his baton and the two weapons collided with a shuddering crack. Lu flipped his wrist and flicked the tip of the baton across the tough's face, splitting his lip.

The tough recoiled, angrily wiped blood off his chin, and attacked in a rage. Lu sidestepped, backhanded the baton against the side of the tough's knee. It wasn't a debilitating blow, but it hurt enough to buckle his leg. A quick strike to the back of the tough's skull laid him out on the carpet.

Watermelon Chopper quickly shot forward, blade flashing. Lu pivoted and leaped; a touch too slow. The blade sliced across his back, only the bullet-proof vest saving him from a serious wound.

Lu turned, feinted high, went low, and hit Chopper in the shin, then feinted low before winging a sharp blow across the man's wrist. Chopper's blade dropped to the floor. Lu finished him off with three heavy strikes to the head, each one ringing out like the thud of a baseball bat against a ripe melon.

Tang stuck around long enough to see things weren't turning out as expected, then rushed back through the door. Lu ran and caught the door's edge before it could swing shut. Ahead was a narrow stairwell. Lu raced up it, catching Tang on the second-floor landing.

Tang curled into a ball and begged: "Don't kill me!"

"I'm not a murderer. Lucky for you."

"What then? You want money? I'll give it to you." Tang's face twisted with fury. "But you'll never spend a cent of it. Your guts will be hanging from a lamp-post by dawn tomorrow."

"I'm not after money."

"What the hell do you want?"

"I want to make you suffer." Lu heard a faint wail in the distance—approaching sirens. "Unfortunately, time is not on my side. But I'll be back. Tomorrow. A week from now. A year from now." Lu thrust the tip of the baton into Tang's sternum. "Take my advice, you bottom-feeder. You ball of matted shit on a dog's anus. Shut down your whorehouses and get out of Harbin while you can still walk. Hold that thought—" Lu swung the baton hard against Tang's ankle. Tang screamed in pain and clutched his leg. "I meant, crawl."

Lu exited through the back of the building, stripped off his balaclava, walked briskly down the street, tossed the baton into a Dumpster a few blocks away.

He assumed Xu would know he was the attacker, but given the illegal nature of Tang's business, chances of an investigation were nil.

Nevertheless, two days later, Xu called Lu into his office and informed him he had arranged a transfer to a smaller and less stressful posting. "Where they might appreciate an officer of your limited abilities."

So, in the end, it wasn't Tang who was chased out of town—it was Lu.

"My goodness," Ma says, when Lu is done. "That's quite a tale."

"Every word is true." Lu shrugs. "Anyway, I'm not bitter about leaving Harbin. I'm happy where I am. But I would be lying if I said I didn't yearn to see Xu and Tang pay for their sins." He tips his glass to his lips.

"And I'd be lying if I said I wasn't slightly turned on right now," Ma says.

Lu nearly spits beer all over the table.

"Relax," Ma says. "I know you have a girlfriend. I'm no poacher. How's that going, by the way? Tell me all the sordid details. The more sordid, the better."

"I guess you could say we are officially a couple."

"You guess? You're not sure? Are you sleeping together?"

Lu feels his face grow hot. "I don't kiss and tell."

"Oh, please." The corners of Ma's eyes crinkle. "I hope she's not one of those shrinking violets who only does it with the guy on top and the lights off."

"Dr. Ma, please!" Lu protests. "That's extremely personal."

"Isn't it about time you called me Xiulan? And don't be such a prude. Sex is one of life's greatest rewards. I'm happy for you. *Gan bei!*" Ma's phone vibrates. She glances at it. "Our intrepid colleagues have returned from the wild."

The foursome decamps to a nearby restaurant to have dinner and review the day's developments. They agree that Jin and Sun have pinpointed the likely motive for Pang's visit to National Road, but that this knowledge is unlikely to shed light on the murder itself.

"As for the van," Jin says, "chances are it and/or the license plate were stolen. Besides, we're all familiar with the stink of chicken gizzards boiling in a pot. Can you imagine the stench cooking an entire human body would produce? You'd be able to smell it a kilometer away. Any vehicle they used to transport the body would be rendered unusable. I'm sure the van's already been scrapped or parked in a field and burned to a crisp."

"A dead end," Lu agrees. "But this kid you spoke to. He basically admitted Harbin PSB is engaged in a cover-up."

"Not exactly," Jin says. "He said developments are to be routed through Han. Which, in a sense, is logical, since Han is the lead investigator for Harbin Homicide. But—"

"He's not to be trusted," Lu finishes. "And he's sticking to me and Dr. Ma like a bad reputation."

"Same with his partner," Jin says.

"Do you think this is all leading back to a gambling ring?" Sun asks. "The local PSB gets paid off by underground casinos like the one Pang went to? And Xu doesn't want that to come to light?"

"That is one possible explanation for why Xu and Hong are keeping us in the dark," Ma says. "But it doesn't solve Pang's murder."

"Maybe the murder is incidental to the cover-up," Lu suggests. "Pang had gambling debts he couldn't pay. A very pissed-off loan shark killed him. And, as Constable Sun says, Xu is concerned our investigation will implicate him in a bribery scheme."

Jin isn't buying it. "Loan sharks have a saying: Dead men don't pay interest."

On the walk back to the hotel after dinner, Lu stops at a kiosk to buy a bottle of water. He notices a young man walking thirty paces behind them suddenly stop, turn away, and light a cigarette. Lu makes his purchase, and the group continues on. When they reach the entrance to the hotel, Lu takes a quick backward glance and sees that the young man has maintained a steady distance thirty paces behind.

Inside the lobby, he sees a second young man sitting with a good view of the front entrance and the elevators, studiously reading something on his phone. His buzz cut and tactical boots are a dead giveaway.

He tells the others in the elevator on the way up to their rooms.

"Xu's men?" Ma asks.

"Xu or Hong."

"I can't recall a homicide investigation where *I* was the one under surveillance," Jin says.

Sun finds this revelation deeply disturbing. Back in her room, she spends twenty minutes searching for hidden cameras and listening devices. She doesn't find any, but even so, she dresses for bed in the bathroom with the door closed and the lights off.

TWENTY-SEVEN

Dalian sits at the southernmost end of the Liaodong Peninsula like a shiny bauble balanced on the tip of an outstretched finger. Given its temperate climate, fresh ocean breezes, white-sand beaches, and numerous public parks, it is one of China's most pleasant cities. An eclectic mix of Russian, Japanese, and Chinese architecture lends it an international flavor. So, too, does its bustling international port, a direct shipping link to 160 nations, the numerous American, Japanese, Korean, and European manufacturing plants, and the hordes of tourists who flock to its beaches each summer to roast in the blazing sun like strips of *cha shao* pork.

Given all those tourists, foreign workers, and traveling businessmen, it's no surprise that, aside from the wholesome activities Dalian has to offer, there are some unsavory ones on the menu.

One such is the Fragrant Spring Russian Spa, located in a commercial building near to the central train station. The building's first three floors are leased by the Sunshine Handicraft Company, an exporter of cheap wooden toys. The spa occupies the top floor, and at any given time there are between five and ten so-called "massage therapists" working there, all of them female, all of them defectors from North Korea.

These women came to the People's Republic hoping to escape hunger and poverty; to find a decent job; a fresh start. Now they are compelled to have sex with strange men who care nothing for their bodies, or their souls. And they are watched over by minders who treat them like expendable commodities.

The spa opens for business at 7:00 P.M.—by which time the employees of the Sunshine Handicraft Company have cleared out for the night—and remains open as long as there are paying customers, generally until one or two in the morning.

If you wish to enter, the procedure is as follows: first, buzz downstairs and show your face to a camera. If you pass the initial inspection, the door will be unlocked electronically and you will enter a small vestibule. A cramped and rickety elevator will take you up to the fourth floor and deposit you into a reception area. A hostess will greet you with a smile and a flirtatious touch. A couple of minders will be on hand to wave a metal detector over your clothes and make sure you pay in advance. Then the hostess will press a hidden button and escort you through a door into one of the "therapy" rooms. Each of these rooms is furnished with a padded table, towels, lubricants, and, tucked into a drawer, an assortment of condoms. The rooms smell strongly of bleach.

If any of the other rooms are occupied during your visit, you might hear the low rumble of conversation through the paper-thin walls—as well as noises of a more personal nature.

The hostess will invite you to undress and put on a thin cotton robe and will then depart. After a few moments, there will be a knock on the door and one of the therapists will enter. If you speak fluent Korean, you might have a pleasant chat. If only Chinese, the therapist will communicate with you through signs and simple words, such as: "You like?" "Yes." "No." "Stop!"

Afterward, the therapist will wipe you down with a towel and help you dress. It is expected that you will tip her, after which she will escort you out to the foyer, bow politely, and thank you for coming.

Hak knows all this because he's been surveilling the Fragrant Spring Russian Spa for the past forty-eight hours. And last night he posed as a customer and paid for thirty minutes with a young woman in one of the rooms. They spoke in Korean; she was cagey. Among the only personal details she would divulge was that she was originally from Pyongyang, had been in China for nine months, and was very happy to be working at the spa.

Hak estimated her age at twenty or so. The same age his sister would be now . . . if she is still alive.

When the therapist suggested Hak might want to strip off his clothes and put on the robe, he made some excuse. He had a wife and children at home.

He'd been drinking and decided, rather rashly, that this was what he wanted—but now was having second thoughts.

This frightened the therapist—if Hak left before his allotted time was up, the manager would think she'd failed to provide a pleasurable experience. There would be consequences.

Hak understood. He waited out the thirty minutes, continuing to ply the young woman with questions she was reluctant to answer. Eventually he tried a different tack. "What do you miss most about home?"

The therapist smiled wistfully. "Would you believe *raengmyon*?"

Hak laughed. This was a simple dish of buckwheat noodles in broth, served with a spicy paste and various toppings. "I could go for a bowl of that myself."

When his time was up, Hak left without incident, noting the position of exits and security cameras on the way out.

Now it's three in the morning and Hak is parked in a van down the street. The spa is closed, lights off. The neighborhood is dark and quiet.

Hak doesn't know now many minders are up there, or if they're armed with something more than cleavers and kitchen knives, but he's sure that Sister Kim's assessment was right—this is going to get messy.

Honestly, he doesn't care. He's looking forward to leaving a trail of bloody bodies in his wake.

He has purchased from his black-market contacts a North Korean copy of a Browning Hi-Power nine-millimeter pistol. This is not the best pistol available, but it is one he trained extensively with during his time in the North Korean special forces and he knows its quirks. He's also managed to obtain a sound suppressor.

Hak starts up the van and drives to the front of the building. He shuts off the engine and climbs out. He is wearing a face mask and leather gloves. A thin down coat and sturdy shoes.

The facade of the building is cluttered with exhaust pipes, air-conditioning units, electrical wires, and a metal frame for a projecting sign. Hak has previously chosen his route. He starts up, using what convenient points of purchase the building provides.

He quickly ascends to a window outside the fourth floor and peeks inside.

He spies ambient light coming from a TV—and a man sitting in a chair in front of it. There's an empty bottle of beer on a table beside the chair. Hak assumes the man is asleep, but he can't be sure.

Hak shimmies down an exhaust pipe to the third floor, moves over a couple of meters, and then hooks his fingers onto an air-conditioning unit frame. He pulls himself up, swings a leg over the lip of the unit, and flattens himself on top. He peeks through a dirty window on the fourth floor—and sees only darkness. He waits for his eyes to adjust.

Eventually the gloom reveals a lunchroom—tables and chairs, a refrigerator, a counter. Hak removes a folding knife from his pocket, slips it under the window, and wiggles it back and forth until there is space enough for his fingers. He levers the window up a few centimeters.

With a terrifying jolt, the metal frame holding the air-conditioning unit suddenly shifts. A bolt pops out of the wall and plinks onto the street below. Hak nearly slides off the frame's edge—catching himself just in time by hooking a hand inside the window.

He hangs there, legs dangling precariously, heart in his throat. The window isn't yet open wide enough for him to squeeze through. But he fears that if he applies pressure to lift it higher, the AC frame will completely give way.

As he considers his options, the frame shudders and dips another few degrees.

Hak has no choice—he'll have to risk it.

He gingerly pulls himself closer to the window. Despite the cold, he is sweating under his coat. He tugs at the bottom of the window frame. It doesn't budge. He tugs harder. It raises a couple of centimeters. Then a couple more.

A second bolt pops out of the wall with a metallic *crack*. The AC frame spasms like a dying beast. Hak grips the bottom of the sill and yanks himself forward, his spine scraping along the bottom edge of the window. He plops headfirst onto the floor of the lunchroom and rolls to his feet.

He listens for the sound of the air-conditioning unit crashing to the sidewalk below. At this hour, it will wake the everyone on the block. He hears only the rapid thump of his own heartbeat. *Lucky.*

He takes a breath, holds it, lets it out slowly. And again. He draws his pistol, opens the door to the next room. He confirms that the man in the chair is asleep, a half-smoked cigarette held in his fingers. Hak puts away his gun. He won't need it for this kill.

He unfolds his knife. Steps softly around the rear of the chair. Reaches over, cups the man's chin, pull sharply upward, slits his throat.

He waits until the man stops twitching and gurgling, then releases his hold, wipes the blade of his knife on the man's shirt, folds it, and puts it in his pocket. Draws the gun. Pads down the hall.

The first door on the left leads to a room with two bunk beds. Three men sleeping there. Hak closes the door.

He'll be back.

Farther down, another two rooms face each other across the hall, deadbolted from the outside. This is where the women will be sequestered.

There is one last bedroom at the end of the hall. Locked, but Hak opens it easily with his knife and a bit of wire from his pocket. He puts the knife away, grips the gun, pokes his head inside.

He sees a man and woman in bed. The man—young, early twenties maybe—snores loudly. Hak assumes he is the spa's manager—and the woman is whichever "therapist" he has chosen as tonight's fringe benefit.

Hak gently shuts the door. He returns to the first bedroom. He stands outside and takes a moment to prepare himself. Then he opens the door and enters.

He shoots the two men in the bottom bunks in rapid succession. Head shots, very clean. The gun barks like a small dog. The man in the top bunk sits up, looks for the source of the sound, confusion on his face.

Hak shoots him. Blood hits the ceiling.

Hak exits the bedroom and runs down the hall. As he nears the last bedroom, the panel of the door explodes, spraying splinters. Hak registers a gunshot. He hits the floor.

Shiba! Anyone in a three-kilometer radius will have heard the sound.

"Don't shoot!" Hak calls out, in Korean. "I only want the girl." He repeats this in Chinese.

"*Yeosmeog-eo!*" the manager yells.

Korean, then. "I don't care about you," Hak yells. "Send the girl out and I'll take her and go."

"Liar!"

"You're right to be wary. Tell you what. I'm going to open the door and slide my gun through. Then I'll show you that my hands are empty. And you can just walk out of here."

Silence. Which Hak takes to mean that the manager is considering this proposition.

"Don't shoot," Hak calls out again. He takes a knife out of his pocket, unfolds the blade, slides it up his sleeve. "I'm opening the door." Staying low, Hak opens the door a crack, places his gun on the floor, pushes it across the floor. "See the gun?"

"How do I know you don't have another one?"

"You don't. But I'm going to show you."

Hak reaches his outstretched hands into the room, wiggles his fingers. He nudges the door open, steps cautiously inside.

The manager and the woman are standing on the far side of the bed. The manager has a forearm around her neck. Both are naked. The manager's gun is pointed over the woman's shoulder directly at Hak. Hak lowers his mask to reveal his face.

"Easy," Hak says. "The cops will be here soon. Your gunshot made sure of that. If you want to stay out of a Chinese prison, I suggest you put on some pants and split. Leave the girl, save yourself."

"Maybe I'll kill you first."

"Anyone can kill if they have to. But only some will if they don't. Whatever your sins, I don't think murdering an unarmed man is among them."

"You don't know shit about me!"

"You're right, I don't." Hak sees that the therapist is the same young woman he spent time with last night—the one with a fondness for buckwheat noodles. "Listen, kid," he tells the manager. "I don't want to get caught by the cops, either. Let the girl go. Make a run for it. I won't move a muscle until you're gone."

The manager is scared, Hak can see that. Hak is torn between wanting to get this done before the cops arrive and not spooking the kid into indiscriminately spraying bullets. He waits, precious seconds ticking by.

"Move back," the manager finally says. Hak retreats, hands up. The manager withdraws his arm from around the woman's neck but tells her to stay where she is. She folds her arms over her breasts and shakes with cold and fear.

The manager keeps an eye on Hak while he searches for his underpants. He finds them, sticks a foot through the leg hole, stumbles and nearly falls, looks down to catch himself.

Hak mouths a word in Korean to the woman: *Duck.*

The manager quickly looks up. "Don't fucking move."

"I'm didn't. I'm not."

The manager tugs his underwear up, reaches for his pants. He keeps the gun steady, but his eyes flicker away for a moment.

Hak mouths the word again: *Duck.*

Does she understand? It's hard to say. Her face is a mask of terror.

The manager picks up his pants and slides a leg into them. Then he realizes he'll have to transfer the gun to his left hand to finish the job. He hesitates.

He's going to do it, Hak thinks. *He's going to shoot me.*

The therapist ducks.

Hak flicks his arm down—catches the knife in his hand—cranks his arm up, steps, and throws in one motion. The knife flies across the room and hits the manager. The manager shouts, claps a hand to his shoulder. The gun clatters onto the floor.

Hak is not happy—he was aiming for the throat. He bounds over the bed, punches the manager in the face. The kid's head bounces off the wall. Hak grips the knife handle, yanks it out, slashes the manager's neck, hops back to avoid a spray of blood.

The therapist runs screaming out of the room. Hak collects his pistol from the floor and runs after her, bringing her down midway down the hall. "Don't fight me!" he shouts. "I'm here to save you."

Rounding up the other therapists is no easy task. They are confused, frightened, and reluctant. Hak doesn't blame them, but there's no time to be gentle. He pushes and prods them downstairs and into the van, still dressed in their nightclothes. He cranks up the heater and drives.

He doesn't hear any sirens or see flashing lights as he makes his way through empty streets. Perhaps the neighbors chalked that one gunshot up to the backfire of a car's engine.

"Listen up!" he calls out over his shoulder. "You must trust me and do exactly what I say. I'm going to get you someplace safe. Out of the country. Where you can start a new life."

The women have heard such promises before. They don't know what to believe. They cling to one another like survivors from a sinking ship huddled wet and exhausted in a life raft.

When they reach the outskirts of Dalian, Hak breathes more easily. He tells the women he's taking them to a safe house. From there they will travel three thousand kilometers by means of a secret route, a modern-day underground railroad, to the Vietnamese border. "A team of volunteers will be waiting to take you to a South Korean Embassy," he explains. "You'll eventually be resettled in South Korea or America."

"America!" one of the therapists gasps.

"Yes," Hak says. "America." He reaches into a pocket and takes out a laminated photograph of a teenage girl. He hands it over the back of his seat. "Have any of you run across this girl? The picture is four years old. She'd be twenty now. Her name is Mirae."

The women pass the photo around. None of them have seen Mirae. Hak expected as much, but each time he shows the picture with the same result, he feels the same raw, devastating disappointment.

In his heart, Hak knows Mirae is dead. But he won't ever stop searching for her. Not until he has proof, one way or the other. And he won't stop killing the men who prey on women like her until he is dead himself.

TWENTY-EIGHT

The CIB teams spends the remainder of the week pursuing time-consuming but ultimately fruitless avenues of investigation.

Lu and Ma proceed with their interviews of Pang's friends and associates, with Han constantly breathing down their necks. Han and Lu do not speak or interact directly unless absolutely necessary, but given their proximity, every cramped elevator ride, every passage through a narrow doorway, presents an opportunity for a primitive display of male dominance. Ma's presence tempers their worst impulses, but as she watches them metaphorically beat their chests like mountain gorillas, she is reminded why she has resolved to never, ever marry a police officer.

Jin and Sun have the unenviable task of digging into Pang's personal finances. After an examination of Pang's bank accounts, UnionPay, and WeChat pay records, Jin tells Sun he doesn't see any overt signs of impropriety, apart from the obvious: "Pang's monthly salary was seven thousand yuan. His monthly rent was six thousand five hundred."

"I guess he ate a lot of instant noodles," Sun jokes.

Jin smiles. "Do you know how much our president is paid? He got a nice raise not long ago. Eleven thousand three hundred and eighty-five yuan a month." He snorts. "Nobody in their right mind would assume he and other officials subsist on such an amount. Never in the four-thousand-year history of China has a government functionary ever been paid enough to live on. Hence, institutionalized corruption in various forms."

"So, Pang is . . . dirty."

"Depends on what you mean by *dirty*. We're looking for something more substantial than a local businessman giving him carton of Marlboros and a fat red packet on New Year's."

"Such as?"

"Big money or big politics. A major property development that Pang ushered through, or didn't usher through, which may have bent some noses out of joint. Criminal activity—drugs, sex trafficking, construction contracts. Money he embezzled to buy his girlfriend a boob job. Stuff like that."

"We won't find any traces of something like that in his financial records."

"You are correct. On to his phone records."

This proves equally unproductive. "Any corrupt politician with half a brain will have a burner phone for his covert communications or just conduct his personal business face-to-face," Jin remarks.

"So what now?"

"We dig into his work records." Jin looks at Pangu, who remains the silent partner in this process, apart from the sound of rattling snack bags. "Detective, can you drive us over to the mayor's office?"

"We have a couple of detectives looking through his files already," Pangu says. "Why not spare yourself the agony?"

"This is my job," Jin says.

"People's hero." Pangu levers himself out of his seat. "I'll bring the car around. Meet me in front."

While Jin and Sun wait in the lobby for the car to arrive, Jin provides some background: "As you know despite the supreme authority of the Chinese Communist Party, politicians like the late Mayor Pang enjoy a large measure of influence and authority in their jurisdictions. And because of that, they have plenty of opportunities for bad behavior—patronage, influence peddling, graft. But keep in mind, Pang was not the most powerful official in Nangang District—that distinction belongs to the party secretary. Wan, I think his name is. So, anything Pang has signed off on has likely passed through Wan's fingers as well."

"Then we're investigating Wan, too."

"By default, yes. And Wan or his factotums will probably be watching us carefully. So, if you find something of interest, keep it between the two of us until we know whether or not it's significant."

"Got it."

Pangu swings around with the car and they drive to the mayor's office. A secretary shows them into a conference room, where a pair of Harbin detectives are already knee-deep in file boxes, old food containers, and paper cups half filled with cold tea.

"Fresh meat," one of detectives says with a cheeky smile. Introductions are made. His name is Tian, and his partner is surnamed He.

"Anything of interest?" Jin asks.

"Depends on your definition of *interesting*," Tian says. "I now know more about waste management than I ever dreamed possible."

"Sounds about right for having spent the past few days shoveling shit," Jin says.

Friday afternoon, Lu arranges to speak to a supervisor from the Organized Crime Division. Han tags along, naturally. When he arrives at the supervisor's office, Lu realizes they have met before.

"Xiao Niu!" Lu says. "*Hao jiu bu jian!*" Long time, no see!

Xiao Niu is the supervisor's nickname, meaning "Little Ox." Lu had few occasions to work with Little Ox in the past, but he remembers him more fondly than some of his other colleagues in Harbin.

Little Ox smiles. "It's Da Niu now." *Big Ox*. He taps the rank indicated on his shoulder board. "I've come up in the world."

"So you have. Congrats! Shall I adjust my form of address?"

"Old friends like yourself are free to call me 'Little.' Just not the young punks!"

Lu asks for a rundown of the local organized crime scene. He is already aware that there are thousands of Mafia-like entities in the People's Republic, ranging from neighborhood toughs peddling drugs and extorting shopkeepers to transnational gangs who cooperate across borders with criminal counterparts in the U.S., South America, Europe, and Asia.

"Nangang District certainly has its share," Xiao Niu explains. "But they're mostly independent operators. Small potatoes. Neighborhood protection rackets and the like. We also have the odd businessman with a loose gang association— hiring thugs as muscle to intimidate rivals, extort customers, and so on."

"And the bigger organizations? Xin Yi An, 14K?"

"They sniff around when they sense an opportunity."

"How about gang connections to government officials?" Lu asks.

"Ah . . ." Xiao Niu sticks a finger under his collar to loosen it. "We are not aware of any such connections in Nangang at the present time."

"And do you suspect the involvement of a criminal organization in Mayor Pang's murder?"

"We are unaware of a connection between Mayor Pang and any criminal elements operating in Nangang," Xiao Niu says woodenly.

"Right." Lu gets the picture. More runaround. "I appreciate your time."

Xiao Niu smiles, relieved to be off the hook. "Glad to help."

Lu stands. "Oh, one other thing."

Xiao Niu's smile fades. "Yes?"

"A body turned up in my jurisdiction not long ago. A guy named Sung, part of the Guryong Korean gang. He'd been tortured and set on fire."

"Really? Brutal."

"I sent the report along to Harbin Homicide. Seeing as how it's probably gang-related, I'm wondering if it ever crossed your desk—and if a subsequent investigation has turned up any leads."

Xiao Niu glances at Han. "Did you ask Detective Han?"

"We haven't confirmed that the victim belonged to the Guryong gang," Han says. "So that case hasn't yet been referred to the Organized Crime Division."

"I guess the statement of a fellow gang member isn't enough for you?" Lu says.

"When's the last time a gang member told the cops the truth about anything?"

"How about the big-ass tattoo of a carp holding a knife on Sung's back?"

"We reviewed the coroner's photographs. We could barely make out any details."

Lu shakes his head. "I'd like to say I am surprised. But I'm not."

When Lu returns to their assigned conference room, he finds Ma typing away on her computer. "Well?" she asks.

"Nobody knows nothing around here."

Lu opens his laptop and positions the screen so that Han can't see it. He logs into the Harbin Homicide database and accesses Sung's case file. It's sparse, apart from the usual biographical data and the report that he submitted weeks ago.

Appended to the file is the report from the Traffic Control Bureau listing license plates recorded by traffic cameras he had Sergeant Bing request following the discovery of Sung's body.

No one has bothered to run the plates. A simple and routine administrative matter.

Lu emails a copy to Sergeant Bing along with a note asking him to follow up.

That night, the team dines at local restaurant on crispy chicken, roast lamb, eggplant, and spinach, washed down with lots of beer, apart from Sun, who drinks vodka flavored with plum.

The next morning, Saturday, Ma and Jin fly back to Beijing. There's no sense in Lu and Sun cooling their heels in Harbin, so they return to Raven Valley by train.

The investigation will resume Monday morning.

TWENTY-NINE

Lu arrives in Raven Valley in time to have a pleasant lunch with Yanyan. Then he regretfully kisses her goodbye and heads to the *paichusuo* to catch up on paperwork. He is surprised to find Sergeant Bing at his desk in the squad room.

"Brother Bing! Here on a Saturday!"

"And why do you suppose that is, when I could be home in my sweatpants watching hockey on TV?"

"You enjoy the smell of unwashed socks and Fatty Wang's leftovers?"

"Wrong."

"Because Chief Liang pushed all my work off to you while I'm in Harbin?"

"Correct. Also, I'm running down your vehicle license plates."

"Thanks for that. Any results?"

"I have a short list."

"How many?"

"Four. I got full plates for three and ran them. None of the registered owners have records or warrants, but I'll give you their contact info and you can reach out. I only got a partial plate for the fourth vehicle. Near as I can tell, the driver had one of those films over it that obscures the numbers."

Lu thinks of the white van in Harbin. Could there be a connection between a Korean pimp and the murder of a district mayor? It's not inconceivable—a sex ring involving the Guryong gang, Tang, the Nangang PSB. Pang might be paid to ignore it or might even be greasing the wheels in some fashion, issuing business licenses and the like.

"Maybe the driver was just trying to avoid a toll," Bing continues. "But I've identified the model as a Dongfeng Ministar. I'm going to take the partial plate and start plugging in combos until I find a registration for that make and model. Should take about, oh . . . twelve hours or so."

Lu squeezes Bing's shoulder. "I owe you a bottle of whiskey."

"More like an entire distillery."

Lu spends the afternoon in his office working his way through a mound of administrative paperwork. Around six, Chief Liang makes an appearance. "Ah, the prodigal son returns."

"Hello, Chief. Forget your lighter or something?"

Liang plops himself into a chair in front of Lu's desk. He's wearing civilian clothes and is red-faced from the cold. "Any leads in your case?"

"Not really. But I think Xu and the local PSB head are engaged in a cover-up."

"Of course you do."

"What's that supposed to mean?"

"Just what I said. Anyway, I hope you crack it soon, because I want my deputy chief back here where he belongs."

"I'm sure the killer is sympathetic to your plight and will soon give himself up."

Liang smiles wryly. He drums his fingertips on the arm of the chair, crosses and uncrosses his legs.

"Something on your mind, Chief?" Lu asks.

"You know . . . I'll be nearing the age of retirement soon."

"But you're in the prime of your life!"

Liang gives Lu a sour look. "Have you given any thought to your future?"

"Yes. I can see it as clear as day." Lu spreads his hands and looks off into the distance. "Three more hours of paperwork, then two loads of laundry."

"Seriously, kid."

Lu drops his hands. "Perhaps you have some thoughts?"

"Well . . . I figured you might take over here when I retire. That is, unless you want to ditch the country bumpkins of Raven Valley and run off to the bright lights and first-class toilets of Beijing to toil as a faceless cog in the CIB."

"You paint a romantic picture."

"Seems to me they're trying to poach you. And I don't like it."

"Are you feeling protective . . . or possessive?"

Liang shrugs. "I think your place is here. With a certain pretty bar owner."

"Hey, now. That's dirty pool."

Liang smiles. " 'Exploit your enemy's weaknesses, avoid his strengths.' "

"Sun Zi. And I'm not an enemy."

"All's fair in love and war, kid." Liang slaps his thighs and stands up. "Anyway, I'm off. People to see, things to do."

"Alcohol to be drunk, karaoke to be sung."

"Give what I said some thought. You're not getting any younger, you know. Time to settle down. Start a family."

Later that evening, Sun meets her fiancé, Yao Jun, for dinner. Yao is in a dark mood—sales are down—and he has little patience for Sun's breathless summary of her week in Harbin.

"Boiled alive?" Yao says. "*Tian!* Who would do such a thing?"

"That's what I'm trying to find out. Isn't it exciting?"

"Disgusting, more like. And how long do you think you'll be on this case? I don't love the idea of you being in Harbin by yourself."

"I'm not by myself. I'm with the deputy chief and two investigators from CIB. CIB! Me! Can you imagine?"

"Sounds dangerous."

Sun reaches over and puts a hand on Yao's arm. "It's sweet that you're worried."

"Of course I'm worried. This is why I want you to quit. Can you picture us going to a wedding or New Year's dinner with friends and someone asking you about your work? And you telling them you're working on a homicide in which a man was cooked in a vat of hot oil? Everyone would immediately lose their appetites. Not to mention the fact that you're off in another city in the company of strange men. I know what cops are like. Dogs, every one of them."

Sun withdraws her hand. Yao spends the rest of the evening talking about something more to his liking—himself. As he prattles on, Sun fantasizes it is Detective Tian sitting across from her, discussing the nuances of the Pang case, rather than Yao pontificating on fluctuations in the price of organic fertilizer.

THIRTY

Lu and Sun take the first train to Harbin on Monday morning. When they reach PSB headquarters, the eight-to-midnight shift is just beginning to file in. Detectives Han and Pangu haven't yet arrived, and Ma and Jin's plane from Beijing won't be landing until midmorning, so they have the conference room to themselves for a brief, magical moment.

Lu parks his suitcase in a corner. "I'm going to the canteen for tea. Want some?"

"Yes, please."

When Lu returns fifteen minutes later with two Styrofoam cups and a couple of greasy *shaobing* pastries he finds Sun in a giddy mood.

"Look," Sun says. "Someone slipped this into a folder I left here over the weekend." She hands Lu a white sheet of computer paper on top of which have been taped three Chinese characters cut from a newspaper. They read: *Cai Jingdong*.

"What's that?" Lu asks. "A name?"

"Yes. I looked it up. Cai Jingdong was the head of the arrest section of the Nangang Procuratorate."

"*Was?* You mean . . ."

"He's dead."

Lu sets the tea and *shaobing* down. "Cai Jingdong." With an effort, he conjures up a fuzzy image of a tall, stern man. "I vaguely remember him from before. He was just a junior procurator back then. Dead, how?"

"Suicide. Hung himself, according to the police report. October eighteenth."

"Two weeks before Pang."

"Yes. And he did it in the lobby of an abandoned housing development. Which seems like a strange place to commit suicide."

"It does. Autopsy report?"

"Yes. Cut-and-dried, so to speak. But there's more. I remembered that when I ran a social media search for Pang, I found a photo of him and Cai together." Sun shows Lu the picture on her monitor. Lu reads the caption: *Nangang District Mayor Pang and Deputy Chief Procurator Cai participate in a charity golf tournament benefiting the Harbin Number One Specialized Hospital.*

"So, we have two high-ranking officials from Nangang dead within the space of two weeks," Lu says. "And they at least had a passing acquaintance with one another, if not a close relationship. What's the status of Cai's body? Can we get Dr. Ma to perform another autopsy?"

"Cremated."

"How convenient. Anyway, good work! This is potentially a huge break!"

"I didn't do anything." Sun lifts the note. "Someone wants us to know the truth."

Five minutes later, Pangu slouches in, smelling of cigarettes, and Han, soon after.

Ma and Jin's flight is delayed—they finally turn up around noon. No sooner have they opened their laptops than Lu suggests lunch.

"We just got here," Ma says.

"Lunch," Lu says firmly.

Han and Pangu tag along. Lu leads the group on a bit of a walkabout until he finds a busy restaurant that has two tables across the room from one another. He informs Han the parties will sit separately.

"Why?" Han asks.

"Because looking at your face will make me lose my appetite."

When they are seated, with Han and Pangu out of earshot, Lu fills Ma and Jin in.

"Are you thinking serial killer?" Ma asks.

"I wasn't thinking in terms of a classic serial killer," Lu says. "But two high-ranking district officials dead in the space of two weeks? One of which *might* be misleadingly classified as a suicide?"

The discussion pauses while a waiter brings tea and takes their order. Afterward, Ma says: "We don't know it wasn't a suicide."

"Why else would someone leave us a note?" Lu asks.

"Also, Pang and Cai knew each other," Sun says.

"As you would expect in a district of Nangang's size," Ma points out.

"Was Cai married?" Jin asks.

Sun shakes her head. "Single."

"Girlfriend?"

"None mentioned in the report. The investigation was perfunctory. Very little detail."

Ma turns to Lu. "Did you know him?"

"Only in a professional capacity," Lu says. "I don't recall having any strong feelings about him one way or the other. We didn't travel in the same circles socially. I can't recall any scandal surrounding him."

"Well, minus the body or any other evidence," Ma says, "our only way to learn more is to find whoever it was that left the note. Might be hard to narrow down—there are likely a lot of folks at least tangentially involved in Cai's case. The dispatcher who took the call, the responding officers, their supervisor, whichever detectives were assigned to the case, CSI, the medical examiner . . ."

"Are the first respondents listed on the report?" Lu asks Sun.

"Yes, two constables."

"Then let's start there."

"We can't just walk up to them and ask if they left us a secret message," Sun says.

Lu agrees. "And we can't speak to them at the station without people knowing."

"We'll approach them when they're off duty, then," Ma suggests.

"And by *we,* you mean Constable Sun," Lu says.

Sun is shocked. "Why me?"

"They left the note in your folder, didn't they?" Lu asks. He raises his teacup. "This may be the break we're looking for. *Gan bei!*"

When the food arrives, everyone digs in, except for Sun—she's lost her appetite.

THIRTY-ONE

The two men who call themselves Zhang and Li live together in a tract house in a middle-class residential development not far from Gold Mountain Village. Most of the surrounding homes are occupied by families—two parents, one child, occasionally a set of grandparents. A decade ago, local folks might have found it strange that two unmarried men live together, but times have changed, and no one gives it much thought now. Besides, Zhang and Li are pleasant neighbors—they come and go at odd hours, but otherwise are quiet, courteous, and mind their own business.

If asked, Zhang and Li will tell you they work as graphic designers for a website development firm called Xin Guo Xing, which means "New National Prosperity," or XGX for short.

Their dirty little secret—they have other secrets, but those are magnitudes dirtier—is that Zhang and Li know next to nothing about graphic design and website development. If you put a gun to Zhang's head, he might be able to grind out an amateurish web page using one of the many templates available online. Li can barely figure out how to use his own phone.

The truth is that XGX exists solely for the purpose of routing funds to Zhang and Li without the bothersome complication of creating an actual product or service that can be verified by the Chinese government. Nearly all XGX's ostensible clients are overseas—in the U.S., South America, Eastern Europe. If you examine these clients more closely, you might discover they are shell companies—and there's no way of determining who really owns them.

This is a well-established means of moving money back and forth through anonymous offshore accounts outside the reach of the Chinese government. CCP officials have been doing it for years.

Small wonder, then, that neither Zhang nor Li fit the typical mold of a Chinese entrepreneur. Both come from poor backgrounds and never attended college. Zhang spent many years in People's Liberation Army, rising to the rank of *shang shi*, senior sergeant, before mustering out. He then found job as a bodyguard. Li's background is similar, although instead of the PLA, he worked as a constable in the Nangang PSB, and when he found the hours, pay, and heavy oversight not to his liking, he quit and became a driver and general gofer for a wealthy client.

Money was steady and life was good, for a time. Then both Zhang and Li lost their jobs and, unable to find other suitable work, slowly became poorer, hungrier, and more desperate. When the person whom they call the Magistrate contacted them a year ago, Li was living in his mother's house in the Heilongjiang countryside, tending her vegetables and chickens. Zhang was working security in a Daoli nightclub, hauling drunken patrons out by their collars.

At the present moment, Zhang and Li are sitting at their dining table, smoking, drinking beer—and plotting. Over the past twelve months, they have carefully surveilled the members of the Nangang Benevolent Association, noting their routines, habits, friends, mistresses, favorite restaurants. But now that the NBA knows it is being targeted, it is becoming more difficult to catch one of them exposed and alone.

Zhang wants to take Deputy Mayor Wan or Chairman Yu next. "We can abduct Yu using the police vehicle ruse."

"He's got a security detail now," Li says. "One of Xu's moonlighting cops. Who I'm sure is armed."

"We knew it would get more dangerous as we moved down the list," Zhang says. "Dangerous and messy. We may have to change our tactics. Use brute force."

Li lights a cigarette and exhales a long stream of smoke toward the ceiling. "Do you really think we're going to get them all?"

"That's the plan."

"Seems impossible, don't you think?"

Zhang shrugs. "We'll take it as far as we can."

"Maybe we should focus on the top dogs now," Li says. "Like Tang."

Zhang shakes his head. "We're saving Tang for last. He gets the Death by a Thousand Cuts."

"Honestly, old friend, I don't know if I can stomach that. Cai was bad; Pang was worse. And slicing off an ounce of flesh at a time?"

Zhang understands Li's sentiment. He's still not able to contemplate a bowl of fried tripe without wanting to throw up. "We'll cross that bridge when we get to it. In the meantime, whoever's next is getting his head lopped off, right? So, let's account for that. How long might it take to cut through a man's neck?"

"Got me."

"Aren't you a pig farmer?"

"Chickens, idiot."

Zhang laughs. "I vote for Chairman Yu. He's kind of scrawny."

THIRTY-TWO

Back in the conference room after lunch, Sun looks up Cai's case report and makes a note of the responding constables: Zheng and Fan. She locates them on the interdepartmental directory and is relieved to see that Fan, at least, is female. That will make the approach easier. She jots down Fan's cell phone number and home address and checks the duty roster—Fan is working an eight-to-four shift today.

Around three in the afternoon, Lu's phone rings: it's Sergeant Bing. He goes out into the hall and answers. "What's up? Chief Liang misplace the toilet plunger again?"

Han comes out of the conference room and leans against the wall, making no pretense of giving Lu privacy. "Just a moment," Lu says into the receiver. He lowers the phone. "Piss off."

"I'm just getting some air."

"I didn't realize turds required oxygen."

"I'm laughing, but I'll be laughing harder when I break your face like a porcelain teacup."

"Sure, but later. Right now, piss off."

Han's lip curls. "You don't give me orders."

Lu hisses in annoyance, raises the phone to his ear, and walks down the hall. "Go ahead."

"I found a match for that Dongfeng Ministar," Bing says.

"I'm listening." Lu hears Han's heavy footsteps behind him.

"It's registered to a business in Harbin. A gift shop specializing in Korean imports. Korea Town Market. The owner is a woman named Kim. She's

Chaoxianzu. Born in Yanbian Autonomous Prefecture but living in Harbin for the past fifteen years. She has one citation for violating regulations concerning religious affairs. I'll email you the particulars."

The team works the rest of the afternoon, and then Lu suggests they knock off at five and head back to the hotel.

"So soon?" Han asks.

"I need a nap," Lu says.

"Tough getting old," Han smirks.

"If there's any justice in the world, you'll never find out."

After getting a lift back to the hotel, they convene in Jin's room. Lu is amused but not surprised by Jin's fastidious housekeeping—his clothes are neatly hung in the closet, and he insists everyone take off their shoes and don cheap paper slippers when they enter.

They huddle around Jin's laptop and search various criminal and government personnel databases in order to find additional information about Procurator Cai. They glean a bare-bones sketch of his life—birthplace, schooling, career—but nothing enlightening about who he was as a person.

"It's odd that he was over forty and not married," Lu remarks. "Perhaps he was clandestinely homosexual."

"Do you assume everyone over a certain age who is not married is gay?" Sun asks, with a touch of uncharacteristic tartness.

"No, my point was only that if he was, that would be a good angle to explore. A secret life. Threat of blackmail and so on."

"Check out the female constable who responded to the scene," Ma suggests.

They discover that Fan was born and raised in Harbin, is twenty-nine, single. Her Weibo account displays casual photos of her with friends—posing in front of city landmarks, eating countless meals, ice-skating.

In many ways, Fan reminds Lu of Sun—both are constables, about the same age, and unmarried. He wonders if a woman's chances of finding a suitable match automatically decrease by fifty percent once she joins the PSB.

"What's the plan?" Jin asks.

"Constable Sun will question Fan," Ma says. "And I'd like to swing around and talk to the widow Pang without Han on my back."

"They've got cops in the lobby," Jin says. "Maybe unmarked cars outside."

"Let me do some reconnaissance," Lu offers.

He takes the elevator down to the lobby, notes the presence of a young man, military-style haircut, sitting alone.

Lu wanders into the tiny sundries shop and buys himself a pack of cigarettes and a lighter. He opens the pack and slips a cigarette into his mouth, then saunters out the back entrance and lights it. He coughs and the smoke burns his eyes as he pretends to enjoy his cigarette. It takes him a moment to spot the unmarked car down the block—two shadowy figures inside. He takes out his cell phone and makes a quick phone call, then tosses his cigarette on the ground.

He goes back upstairs and confirms Jin's suspicions. "A guy in the lobby and a car out back. I'm guessing one in front, too."

"How do we get out without being seen?" Jin asks.

"Leave it to me. Let's all head back to our rooms and rest for a bit. I'll call you in about thirty minutes."

It's more like an hour. When the team files into Lu's room, they find a man with a mustache and goatee, shaved head, dressed fashionably in black, sitting on Lu's bed, sipping from a paper cup of tea.

"Everyone," Lu says. "This is my friend Monk."

"Ah," Jin says. "We've never met, but I remember you from Inspector Lu's file on the Zeng case."

"Didn't realize I was immortalized on paper," Monk says, rising and giving everyone a nod.

"Monk has generously offered his assistance in getting us out of the hotel," Lu says.

"I didn't offer. You called, and you're lucky the Black Cat is closed on Mondays, or you'd be out of luck."

"Details, details . . ." Lu points to the bed and an open duffel bag stuffed with clothes.

"What's this?" Ma asks, pulling out a long white coat with faux-fur trim.

"Everything I was able to gather on short notice," Monk says.

Lu explains: "I'm guessing our watchers downstairs have been provided with photographs of us and made a note of our hats and coats—so even if we come out of the elevator all bundled up, they'll still recognize us. Therefore—disguises. Choose an outfit, coat, hat, something completely unlike what you brought with you. We'll put on face masks—no one's going to bat an eye at that—and slip past them."

"I only see women's clothes here?" Jin says, as he roots in the pile.

"Exactly," Lu says.

"You're joking," Jin says.

"Last time I went undercover I got a fake tattoo, dyed my hair, and pierced my ear," Lu says. "And I'm not going to even get into what I had to do to smuggle a camera." He pats Jin on the shoulder. "I think you can handle wearing a dress for fifteen minutes."

Ma and Sun go down first, as a pair. It's dinnertime, and they ride in the elevator with several other hotel guests. The young man on watch in the lobby looks up, sees the crowd moving as a knot, watches them exit.

Two bored cops in a car out front have been entertaining themselves by commenting rudely on passersby.

"She's got a nice bounce to her step," the first cop says, as Ma walks past.

"Can't see her face. And she might be a pig in a coat, for all you know."

"A pig in a coat . . . a tiger beneath the sheets!"

"I'll take her friend." The second cop nods at Sun. "She's tall. I like a tall woman. Makes it easier to have sex in the shower."

The first cop snorts. "You haven't had sex, or taken a shower, since July."

Five minutes later a trio emerges—a bald man with a mustache and goatee and a woman on either arm.

"Look at that lucky bastard," the first cop says. "Two women! He must be rich."

The second cop squints. "Those girls don't look right. They're walking like a couple of marines."

"Good peasant stock. Strong backs and childbearing hips. Able to work all day and keep their husband warm at night."

The second cop yawns. "How many more hours of this?"

"Take a nap. I'll wake you in an hour, and then it's my turn."

"Sure."

The first cop lights a cigarette and watches the trio walk past. After further consideration, he agrees with his partner's assessment. There's something off about those girls.

THIRTY-THREE

Monk's van is parked a few blocks away. Everyone piles in; Monk starts the engine and cranks up the heater. "Where to first?"

"Inspector Lu and I can take the widow Pang," Ma says. "Constable Sun can question Fan, with Brother Jin providing backup."

"I actually have something else I need to do," Lu says.

"I'm sorry, what?" Ma snaps.

"It's related to the case. Sort of. I just need an hour or so. If it pans out, I'll tell you all about it."

"Lu Fei . . . ," Ma warns.

"Please. Trust me."

Ma sighs. "I'll take the widow myself, then."

On the way to Fan's building, Jin and Lu shrug out of their female apparel and into a change of clothes they've brought along. Sun adverts her eyes. Ma watches, amused. "Nice legs, boys. You should consider wearing skirts more often."

"Get stuffed," Lu says.

Monk drops Sun and Jin off. Lu hops out and hails a taxi. Ma and Monk drive on.

Sun and Jin stand on the sidewalk, shivering in the cold. Jin looks around and sees a LEBO coffee shop down the street. "Tell her to meet you there."

"What if she says no?"

"Don't give her the option."

The coffee shop is bright, cheery, and warm. Soft acoustic music plays over the sound system. Jin nods at an empty table at the back. "Go stake your claim. I'll take a seat in the corner by the door."

"You're not going to be with me?"

"Better if she thinks you're alone. She might be more open to speaking honestly. Go sit and I'll bring you a coffee."

Sun doesn't want any coffee. Her stomach is roiling. But it *is* a coffee shop. "Tea?"

"Sure."

Sun sits at the table. She takes out her phone and dials Fan's number. It rings. No answer. Probably because Fan doesn't recognize the caller. Or she's busy. Sun gets voice mail. She hangs up and tries again.

Fan answers: "*Wei?*"

Sun's mind goes blank.

"*Wei?* Who is this? *Wei?*"

Fan abruptly hangs up.

Jin, in the drink line, gives Sun a questioning look. She shrugs, embarrassed. He motions his encouragement. Sun takes a breath and rings Fan again.

Fan answers testily: "*Wei?* Who is this? Why do you keep calling me?"

"It's the person you left a note for," Sun says.

Sun hears a sharp intake of breath on the receiver. "I don't know what you're talking about," Fan says. Then she hangs up—again.

Ma de!

Jin arrives with three cups in a carrier. He sets two down. "I hope she likes tea."

"She hung up. Twice!"

"Persevere, Constable Sun. Persevere!"

Jin finds a seat in front where he can stay out of sight. Sun dials Fan again. No answer. Sun texts: *If you don't pick up the phone, I'll come knock on your door.* She calls a fourth time.

Fan answers, subdued. "What do you want?"

"I'm at the coffee shop down the street. Come. Let's talk." Sun hangs up, before Fan can say no.

Fifteen minutes pass. Sun decides Fan isn't coming. Then Fan enters, her head swiveling. She spots Sun. She walks over cautiously, like she's picking her way through a minefield. She sits.

Sun pushes a cup of tea, now cold, across the table. "You left me a note for a reason. Tell me what you know."

"I don't want to get in trouble."

"This conversation is off the record."

Fan looks down at the cup. She pulls it toward her but doesn't drink.

Sun reaches out and touches Fan's hand: "You were a first respondent at the scene of Cai's death. Let's start there."

Ma enters the lobby of the widow Pang's building, flashes her ID at the concierge, and asks him to summon the elevator. She doesn't tell him her destination and he doesn't ask—no doubt he can guess where she's headed.

Upstairs, she knocks on the Pangs' door. After a long while, the door opens to reveal a bloodshot eye. "It's me again, Mrs. Pang. Dr. Ma, CIB."

"What do you want?"

"To speak to you. Alone. It's just me this time."

"It's late."

"I know. I'm sorry. But may I take five minutes of your time?"

The widow groans, closes the door, unlocks the safety chain, and opens the door again. She waves Ma inside, then shuts and relocks the door. "Wine?"

"Why not?"

A half-empty bottle of red is already sitting on the coffee table. The widow goes into the kitchen and retrieves a fresh glass. She brings it back, pours for Ma, and refills her own glass.

Ma sips. "Very nice."

"Where are your friends? The big ugly one and the normal-sized cute one?"

Ma smiles. "The cute one is on other business. The big ugly one is *not* my friend. You know his name, don't you?"

"Aren't you working together on the case?"

"I'm not sure if he's working with me . . . or against me. Perhaps you have some thoughts about that?"

"I'm not sure what you mean."

Ma sets her glass down. "I'm guessing Detective Han came here after the death of your husband, maybe in the company of another large man who goes by the nickname Pangu—and suggested that if you know anything about why your husband was killed and by whom, to keep this information to yourself."

"Why do you guess that?"

"Mrs. Pang," Ma says, "I am not interested in causing you any legal or emotional distress. Nor do I want to indict your husband for any crimes postmortem. But I *do* want to find out who killed him and bring the perpetrator to justice. And if there happens to be some connection to the local PSB . . . I'd be interested in knowing that."

"I don't know anything beyond what I told you."

"Believe me when I say I am sympathetic to your situation. Widowed. Fearful for your future. Perhaps pressured by powerful men. But also believe I won't hesitate to bring you in for questioning. To put you in a detention center if you don't cooperate."

"You wouldn't."

"In a heartbeat."

"What an awful thing to threaten."

"Someone locked your husband in a giant vat of cooking oil and boiled him alive. I saw the results firsthand. It wasn't pretty. Help me find his killers."

The widow sobs into her wineglass.

Ai! Tears were not Ma's intention. "I'm sorry."

The widow Pang sets her glass down and covers her face with her hands. Her shoulders shake.

Ma is more comfortable with conflict than comfort, but she shifts over to the couch and places a hand lightly on the widow's back. She waits out the bout of tears, then goes into the kitchen, finds a roll of paper towels, brings them back. The widow takes one and blows her nose.

Ma picks up the widow Pang's wineglass, offers it to her. The widow drinks, sniffles, takes a breath. "I was accustomed to my husband frequently going out at night for meetings, social events, whatever. If he needed me to come along for official wifely duties, I would—otherwise he went alone, and I didn't ask too many questions. After so many years of marriage, I'd already heard all the answers. Drinks with so-and-so. A committee meeting. Dinner with such-and-such." She gulps wine. "But last month he suddenly stopped going out. Like, abruptly stopped. And he walked around with a cloud over his head. Moody. Cranky. I could tell he was worried. Stressed. I asked him many times what was wrong. And finally, he told me."

The widow picks up the bottle and refills her glass.

"Which was?" Ma asks patiently.

"He was scared."

"Scared?"

"That someone was after him."

"Who?"

"He didn't know."

"Why did he think that?"

"A couple of his close friends had been attacked recently. It almost appeared that someone was targeting his social circle."

"Why would someone be doing that?"

"I don't know. He didn't speculate. Many reasons, I suppose."

"Such as?"

"I don't know!"

"Were your husband and these other people involved in something together? A business venture of some kind?"

"I don't know. He kept his outside affairs private."

"Do you think he was involved in something illegal?"

"I told you, I don't know!" the widow screeches. Then: "I'm sorry."

Ma touches the widow's arm. "I apologize for asking such personal questions. But it's necessary to pinpoint a motive for his murder. Did he mention the names of the friends who were attacked?"

"Just one. A man named Zhao. We sometimes socialized with him and his wife."

"What exactly happened to Mr. Zhao?"

"Someone cut off his hand!"

"Good heavens! When?"

"Last month."

"And the culprit was never caught?"

The widow shakes her head. "Then a few weeks went by, and my husband

decided maybe it was . . ." She shrugs. "Personal to Zhao. He'd offended someone or . . . or, I don't know."

"What else can you tell me about Mr. Zhao?"

"He is head of the district Building Investment Corporation."

Another Nangang official. "What about Han? He warned you not to talk
to us, didn't he?"

"He said my husband may have been involved in some type of criminal
activity and that's why he was killed. He said Nangang protects its own, but
if I talked to the press or you and bad things came into the light, I could lose
everything." The widow grips Ma's hand. "My husband had his indiscretions.
Perhaps he . . . pushed the envelope. But he was a good man. He didn't deserve
to die like that."

"I agree, Mrs. Pang—no one deserves to die like that."

THIRTY-FOUR

By the time Lu reaches the Korea Town Market, it has closed for the night. He squints through the glass door and spies a narrow shop with shelves on either wall. The shelves are haphazardly filled with an assortment of food supplies, kitchen and home goods, and handicrafts.

Lu pulls up the email sent to him by Sergeant Bing. It lists Kim's address and phone number—turns out she lives in the same building as the market, four floors up. Lu calls her phone. No answer. He calls again. She answers with an annoyed, "*Wei?*"

"Is this Kim Myeong?"

"Who's this?"

"Public Security Bureau. I'm downstairs. Buzz me up."

"Public Security? What do you want?"

"The door. Now."

Kim buzzes and Lu walks up four flights. He finds a middle-aged Korean woman dressed in pajamas, her face shiny with the smeared remnants of a thick moisturizing cream, waiting in the doorway of her apartment. Lu feels like he's entered a time warp and is viewing his grandmother thirty years ago.

Kim has the presence of mind to ask for Lu's ID. He shows it to her. She lifts her glasses and squints.

"Raven Valley? Where's that?"

"I'll explain once you invite me in."

"It's not convenient to talk just now. Can you come back tomorrow?"

"You know better than that." Lu pushes his way inside. Kim *tsks*, but steps aside. The first thing Lu sees is a huge crucifix on the wall. "Have you not heard,

Mrs. Kim? Religious iconography promotes a delusional obsession with the su-
pernatural and keeps citizens in a state of backwardness and poverty. Better to
rely on our president and party for guidance and comfort."

Sister Kim shuts the door. "I'll replace that old thing with portraits of
Chairman Mao and President Xi just as soon as they arrive in the mail."

Lu fights the urge to smile. "You live alone?"

"Yes. I'm a widow."

Lu conducts a quick search. Living room, kitchen, bedroom, bathroom.
The place is spotless. He sees a few photographs of what he assumes are family
members in formal Korean clothes. What looks to be a wedding photograph—a
much younger Kim and a pleasant-looking man.

"I see you're not in uniform," Kim says, following at his heels. "Are you
here on official business?"

"I'd just like to ask a few questions, and then I'll get out of your hair."

"How shall I address you?"

"Inspector Lu is fine."

"Tea, Inspector Lu?"

"That would be lovely."

Kim offers Lu a seat at the kitchen table. She adds tea bags into a pot, then
water from an electric kettle. She opens a cupboard and removes two teacups.
Lu asks her a few background questions. Birthplace, occupation, deceased
husband's occupation. "You and your husband didn't have any children?"

"No." Kim sits and pours the tea. "We weren't able to. I wasn't able to."

Her forthrightness causes Lu slight embarrassment. He's used to prying
into people's lives, but only so far as the answers directly relate to a crime. He
sips from his cup. "Barley?"

"Imported from South Korea. I sell it downstairs if you'd like some." She
clears her throat. "Not to be rude, but I've had a long day and was looking forward to a quiet night. Surely you didn't come to ask me about my childlessness?"

"Do you own a Dongfeng Minister van?"

This out-of-the-blue question takes Kim by surprise. But she recovers
quickly. "Yes. I use it for my business."

"How about on the evening of Sunday, October fifteenth? Did you use it
then?"

"Who can remember a specific night that far back?"

"Perhaps you have a calendar on your phone?"

"I prefer the old way of doing things." Kim goes over to a paper calendar she has tacked on the wall. She turns a page and marks the date with her finger. "That was a Sunday. The shop was closed, and I didn't write down any appointments, so I'm guessing I had no need of the van."

"Then why was it on the Tongjiang Expressway around midnight?"

"Was it? There must be some mistake." Kim resumes her seat, picks up her teacup, and sips. Lu notes that her hands are steady.

"No mistake, Mrs. Kim. What's more, I suspect the vehicle was used in the commission of a serious crime. A homicide."

"That's . . . why, that's preposterous."

"Have you ever heard the name Sung Jongmin?"

"No." She gives Lu a look of admonishment. "Not every Korean in China knows every other Korean, Inspector."

"Obviously. But Sung's from Harbin. And I'm thinking he took his last ride in the back of your van before someone dumped him on the side the road and lit him on fire."

"Why would someone do such a violent and horrible thing?"

"Because Sung was a sexual trafficker of female North Korean defectors."

Kim is silent for a moment. Then, her lips firmly set, she says: "If that's the case, he deserved what he got."

"Can I quote you on that?"

Kim smiles thinly. "For the record, Inspector, I don't know and have never heard of Mr. Sung, and I have no knowledge of my van being used in a crime."

"Who else has a set of keys?"

"No one but me. I occasionally lend it to friends or hire a young man to use it for picking up and delivering goods, but I wouldn't have done that on a Sunday."

"In other words, someone hot-wired your van, took it for a spin to Raven Valley with a body in the back, then was kind enough to return it to where they found it?"

"I think it's more likely you are mistaken about the van."

"I have a photo from a traffic cam. It looks like someone tried to disguise the license plate, which is itself a crime. Luckily, they failed."

"I see." Kim takes another dainty sip of her tea. "And yet, here you are. Sitting at my kitchen table. Having a civil conversation rather than putting me in handcuffs and hauling me away. Why? It is because . . . you are out of your jurisdiction? Or is the van only part of the reason why you're here?"

Lu experiences an odd moment of déjà vu as he realizes Kim not only looks like his grandmother, she smells like her, too—a combination of peppermint liniment and mothballs. But, whereas Lu's grandmother was a bit doddering, Kim is as sharp as a tack.

"Let's cut to the chase, then," he says. "First, you should know, jurisdiction is not an issue. I'm working with the Criminal Investigation Bureau. If I wanted to arrest someone in Hong Kong for throwing a gum wrapper on the street, that would be within my power. But the truth is, I am less concerned about the murder of Sung and more interested in his sex-trafficking ring. I want to know about its roots and branches, so to speak."

"I don't know anything about Mr. Sung or his roots and branches."

"If that's going to be your attitude, I'll make a call to request a warrant for your arrest. You'll be in custody within the hour." Lu takes his phone out and sets it on the table. "Perhaps you'd like to reconsider your statement."

Kim doesn't answer for a moment, then says, "Biscuit?"

"Why not?"

Kim collects a tin and sets it on the table. "Have you heard of a man named Tang Fuqiang?"

Lu is careful to maintain a neutral expression. "Who's he?"

"The biggest gangster and sex trafficker in Nangang District. He owns brothels, cybersex dens, massage parlors, outcall services. Chinese girls, Korean girls, Vietnamese girls. He gets them from brokers and forces them into prostitution to pay off their debts, which they never can. Then he sells them off into an even worse situation when they are no longer able to bring in a daily minimum."

"You're well informed."

"As you could tell from the crucifix in my living room, I'm a Christian.

I volunteer with various charities, so have had many occasions to hear about Mr. Tang and the poor girls he uses and abuses."

"Do you have any proof?"

"The proof is all around you. Walk into a barbershop or a brothel. Interrogate the manager, question the girls."

"If it's so easy, why isn't he in jail?"

"Because he pays off the local Public Security Bureau."

"Do you have proof of *that*?"

"Nothing that would hold up in court."

"So you've decided to take matters into your own hands, is that it? Start offing Tang's cybersex pimps?"

"No, of course not." Kim takes a delicate nibble of her biscuit.

"But you know who killed Sung. Maybe someone who is associated with one of these 'charities' you mentioned."

"Inspector, if you really want to do some good in this world, you should be investigating Tang, not the death of, as you put it, a cybersex pimp."

"Why do you think I'm here, Mrs. Kim?"

"Perhaps you could clearly state your intentions?"

Lu finds himself warming to Kim. She's clever and forthright. The question is—what exactly does she know? "Sung is not my primary concern. I want to see Tang behind bars . . . as well as whoever he might be bribing in the PSB. What can you tell me?"

Kim takes another bite of her biscuit, chews meditatively. "Are we making some sort of deal?"

"What do you propose?"

"Let's say I heard a rumor that this—what was his name? Sung?"

Lu smiles and nods, playing along.

"A rumor that this Sung was killed by someone who took a very, very dim view of his enslavement and trafficking of helpless young women."

"A dim view indeed," Lu agrees.

"And the person who did this is of no danger to the general public."

"Go on."

"And this person also made a recording in which he questions Mr. Sung about his filthy business—and Sung implicates the Nangang Public Security Bureau."

"Where might I find a copy of this recording, Mrs. Kim?"

"I could possibly turn up a snippet or two, but I don't think it will be much use to you, legally speaking."

"Even if it's not an official interview by a proper authority, it might prove valuable in building a corruption case."

"I doubt it, Inspector. You see, the questioning took place under torture."

THIRTY-FIVE

They sit at the kitchen table, a pot of tea and tin of biscuits at their elbows like two old friends on a lazy Sunday afternoon, while Kim plays Lu a recording on her phone. It is in Korean, of course, but despite not understanding the language, it shakes Lu deeply.

It starts with a male voice telling Sung to identify himself. Then silence, followed by a meaty smack. Sung gives his name. He begs for his life. This earns him another slap.

Fast-forward. The interrogator asks Sung to reveal who he bribes to operate his cybersex den. Sung denies paying anyone. The interrogator shouts angrily. "He's threatening to cut off a finger," Kim translates. A moment passes, followed by a nauseating sound like a knife chopping through a thick carrot. Sung screams. "He's made good on his threat," Kim says. She might as well be telling Lu the weather in Saigon.

Lu counts two more fingers before Sung, sobbing, tells the interrogator Tang Fuqiang sends a man around every week to collect thirty percent of Sung's profits, in exchange for which he keeps the cops off Sung's back. Sung doesn't deal with the PSB directly, but he's heard Tang's *guanxi* goes all the way to the local chief, a man named Hong.

Kim stops the recording. "I don't think I need to go on. The point is, like I said, Tang is behind the cybersex den, and Hong gets paid to look the other way."

Lu is both disgusted and disappointed by what he's heard. Rumors and hearsay obtained by torture. The interrogator is vicious and cruel. Whether or not he is a danger to the public or just to Korean pimps is beside the point—he's a cold-blooded killer.

But Kim obviously has connections to some sort of underground anti-trafficking operation. She might yet prove useful. "I'd advise you to tell whoever the person is on this tape to cease and desist," Lu says. "If I hear of any more fingerless bodies, regardless of what terrible people they might be, I'll find this person and see him brought to justice."

"I understand," Kim says. "Please know I had nothing to do with what you just heard."

"Aside from lending out your van, perhaps?"

Kim slips her phone into her pocket. "I told you, Inspector. You must be mistaken."

Lu puts his card on the table. "Congratulations. You are now my confidential informant. If you hear of anything regarding Tang or his associates or the Harbin Public Security Bureau, I'll expect a call. Don't make me come back here with a detention order, Mrs. Kim." He takes a last swallow from his cup. "Thanks for the tea—it was delicious."

Lu takes a taxi back to an agreed-upon meeting spot and Monk picks him up in the van. The others are already inside, and, judging from their faces, have something to share. Their news must wait until they are safely back at the hotel, however.

Monk drops them off a few blocks away and they enter the lobby by means of the same ruse. Once Monk has escorted Lu and Jin upstairs, he leaves, taking his bag of women's clothes with him.

Lu volunteers to get take-out food. He runs down to a nearby restaurant—now shadowed by a plainclothes cop—and the team reconvenes in Jin's room thirty minutes later. Jin is uneasy at the sight of so many Styrofoam containers of dumplings, soup, noodles, and steamed vegetables. Not to mention the bottles of Harbin lager Lu has procured. "Don't spill on my floor!" he warns.

Lu laughs with his mouth full. "It's a good thing I passed on the 'Three Stinks of Ningpo' special."

Once everyone has filled a plate, Sun starts: "Fan was terrified to speak to me. But she knows what she saw, and it wasn't the scene of a suicide."

"How can she be so sure?" Ma asks.

"When she and her partner found Cai's body, it was lying in the middle of the floor. There was a cord around his neck, but it wasn't attached to anything. And she confirmed there was nothing suitable overhead to use as an anchor."

"Meanwhile, the report clearly shows photos of Cai hanging from an overhead pipe," Lu says. "So, if what Fan says is true, the scene was staged, and badly so. What was the chain of events after she and her partner responded to the scene?"

"They called in a suspicious death. Then confirmed the body was Cai's—he had ID on him. Almost immediately they got orders to secure the scene and not allow anyone else in. Chief Hong arrived soon after, and then Xu."

"That in of itself is strange," Lu says. "For a suicide."

"Yes. Xu told Fan and her partner that, given Cai's identity, it was a sensitive case and to not speak to anyone about it."

"You don't think Xu or Hong killed Cai, do you?" Jin asks.

Lu shakes his head. "If it was them, they'd have staged the scene from the get-go, not let a couple of constables show up to poke holes in it. They obviously falsified the incident report, though. Which means we are looking at the murders of two high-ranking Nangang officials—and a conspiracy to cover it up."

"Make that three Nangang officials," Ma says.

A dumpling nearly falls out of Lu's mouth. "What?"

"To be more accurate, two murders and one amputation." She tells them about Zhao.

"*Tian!*" Jin says incredulously.

"Brother Jin, could you look up Zhao's incident report?" Lu asks. "I'm certainly curious to know how they swept *that* one under the rug."

Jin logs into the provincial crime database and finds the incident listed as an attempted carjacking. Zhao and his driver have both provided statements to that effect.

"*Ta ma de,*" Lu growls. "Imagine having your hand chopped off and then having to lie about the circumstances." He stops suddenly. "Wait a minute. Zhao's hand was amputated. Cao was strangled. Pang boiled. Get it?"

"Get what?" Jin asks.

"The Five Punishments."

The others are at least vaguely familiar with the Five Punishments—a generic term used from antiquity up until the twentieth century to describe various penalties levied on criminals. Over the centuries, the Five Punishments varied as legal codes were revised, but they included, at one time or another: tattooing on the cheek; beating with a light stick; beating with a heavy stick; cutting off the nose; amputating a hand or foot; castration; exile; penal servitude; and various capital punishments, including strangulation, being boiled alive, decapitation, and Death by a Thousand Cuts.

This final method was particularly brutal—the offender was tied to a post, stripped, and the executioner contrived to cut off bits of his or her flesh, one ounce at time, drawing out the inevitable death from shock or loss of blood for as long as humanly possible. The last documented case of such an execution took place in 1905.

Ma frowns. "I don't know, Lu Fei. That's kind of a wild conjecture."

"Sure, but it fits the evidence we have. The widow said there were how many other attacks?"

"Undetermined," Ma says. "She only knew of Zhao for certain."

"Never mind," Lu says. "The pattern is as clear as the nose on your face. District mayor, procurator, head of the building agency. The perp is targeting high-level Nangang officials. We should run a search on any district functionaries of a supervisor rank and above to see if they've suffered any mysterious accidents. The more names we can link together, the better chance we have of establishing a connection between them—and therefore a motive for the crimes."

"And about interviewing Zhao?" Sun asks. "Since we know he's lying about the carjacking."

"If we do that, Xu and Hong will know we're on to them," Lu says. "Their men are already crawling all over us like ticks on a dog. Better we keep a lid on our findings as long as possible." He stares around the faces in the room. "If Xu knows what we know, he might be forced to do something . . . rash."

"Like what?" Sun asks.

"Never mind, Constable," Ma says. "The inspector is being dramatic. Xu would never dare lift a finger against a CIB team."

"He would if he felt threatened," Lu says. "And if he figured he could get away with it. Which is why I think the sooner we go big, the better. It's time to get Deputy Director Song involved."

"No." Ma crosses her arms. "Everything we have so far is unsubstantiated, speculative, unproven. If I took this to Song, he'd laugh in my face, then bite my head off. I need something solid."

"Song should at least be informed of what we suspect," Lu says.

"Sure, as soon as we have a shred of evidence to back it up," Ma says.

"Perhaps you're being overly cautious because this is the first case you're lead investigator on?"

An uncomfortable silence descends over the room. Jin pauses with a clump of noodles on the tip of his chopsticks.

"I've made my decision." Ma's gaze is sharp enough to cut glass. "Understood?"

"You're the boss."

"That's correct. And if you go over my head and call Song yourself, I'll boot you from the team."

Lu and Ma glare at one another for a moment. Then Lu picks up one of the beer bottles and holds it out. "Refill . . . boss?"

Ma's smile is guarded. "Getting me drunk won't change my mind, but yes." Ma holds out her glass and Lu pours. "Perhaps now you would be so good as to share with us your adventures this evening? No doubt, they were completely relevant to our investigation?"

Lu chooses his words carefully. "I met with a source to discuss the sex trade in Nangang."

"What's that got to do with Pang and Cai?"

"Not sure. But it has a lot to do with the Nangang PSB. The source told me the trade is controlled by a guy named Tang Fuqiang." In answer to Ma's questioning look, he nods. "Yes, *that* Tang Fuqiang." He turns to Jin and Sun: "Tang was a player on the scene back when I was here. At the time, he was under the protection of the Nangang PSB chief—a guy named Xu. Yes, *that* Xu. And now, according to my source, Tang has a deal going with Chief Hong. I'm certain the three of them—Tang, Hong, and Xu—are up to their grotty little scrotums in the same fetid pool. It wouldn't surprise me to discover Pang and Cai were involved as well. Maybe Pang took bribes in exchange for cutting through red tape when Tang wanted to open a new brothel. Maybe Cai squashed any legal proceedings against Tang that popped up."

"Who is your source?" Ma asks.

"For the time being, they must remain confidential."

"How irritating. And what proof does this source have?"

"Nothing we can put into a report."

"In other words—nothing."

Lu makes a sound of exasperation. "Everything we've learned so far is pointing in the same direction—a major conspiracy involving top officials in the Nangang administration and the local Public Security Bureau. Who knows how high this goes? The mayor of Harbin? The party secretary? The governor?"

Ma raises an eyebrow at Jin and Sun. "By this time next week, Inspector Lu will have us kicking down doors in Zhongnanhai and dragging state leaders out into the streets in their underwear."

Sun picks unhappily at her food—she thought this was going to be a simple murder case. Working shoulder to shoulder with a team of seasoned CIB investigators. How exciting! What an opportunity!

Instead, it's much darker and more frightening than even a brutal murder. Sun feels exposed and imperiled. She suddenly longs to be back in Raven Valley fielding phone calls from old ladies who can't find their eyeglasses.

"Let's assume for the moment you are correct about the Five Punishments," Jin says. "They are, historically speaking, a means to punish criminals. Which, according to your conspiracy theory, Mayor Pang, Procurator Cai, this Mr. Zhao, and whoever else, are—criminals, I mean."

Lu agrees. "That's right."

"So the killer is a vigilante."

Lu nods. "A modern-day Judge Di."

"I'm not convinced," Ma says. "The motive here seems more intimate than a faceless entity punishing wrongdoers. I think we can agree there's an element of fury present in boiling a man alive, no?"

"Perhaps," Lu allows. "It may be our perpetrator has been personally harmed by the actions of the victims. A daughter caught up in the sex trade, for example. And whether he is using the Five Punishments to strike fear into his targets or to justify his actions as some sort of old-school pursuit of justice is immaterial. If we can find a specific crime that links Pang, Cai, and Zhao to Tang, Xu, and Hong, we should be able to narrow the field of suspects."

Jin wipes his mouth with a napkin and folds it neatly on his plate. "It seems like it would be a narrow field indeed. We're looking for someone who shares a personal connection with all these officials . . . and has the resources, logistical know-how, and ill will to carry out such a diabolical scheme."

Lu suddenly thumps his forehead with his palm. "When you put it like that, Brother Jin, the answer is obvious. I know just such a person."

THIRTY-SIX

There is a midnight knock on Kim's door. Despite the hour, and the fact that there was no buzz from downstairs, Kim opens it. She finds Hak standing outside, wearing a coat, a hat, a face mask. Kim quickly ushers him into her apartment. "No one saw you?"

"I was careful. What's the emergency? No, let me guess. Dalian."

Kim glares. "I told you no, but you did it anyway."

"I saved seven lives."

"How many did you take?" Kim puts up a hand. "Don't answer. I don't want to know. Your recklessness has put all of us in danger. The Chinese authorities will react aggressively. They'll round up every Korean pastor they can get their hands on."

"And none of them know a thing. It'll blow over." Hak takes off his mask and hat and plops onto Kim's couch. "It's cold out. How about some tea?"

"You do what you want and damn the consequences!"

"Listen to me, Sister Kim. Every time I go on a mission, I fully expect to get arrested or killed. And I accept those possible consequences. What I cannot accept is sitting around and doing nothing while these women and girls are abused."

"Even if your actions lead to the exposure of people like me?"

"If arrested, I'll never talk. You know that."

Kim hisses in annoyance and lowers herself into a chair. "I didn't call you here to discuss Dalian. There's another problem—of your making. A policeman visited my home tonight. He has proof you used my van to transport Sung."

"What proof?"

"A photo from a traffic camera near where you apparently dumped him off."

"I disguised the license plate. His evidence is circumstantial. He will not be able to prove it was your van."

"Do you understand you are in the People's Republic of China?" Kim protests. "The police can prove anything they want!"

"So, why didn't he arrest you?"

"He's after something bigger. Sung's network. Tang. The local PSB."

"Then we're on the same side."

"No cop is on our side, Brother Hak. Especially with the trail of dead bodies you leave behind. He'll milk me for whatever information he can get, then try to squeeze me for your identity. I might be taken away to a detention center any moment."

Hak considers this. "Is he working alone?"

"Stop," Kim says. "The answer is no. You are not allowed to kill him."

"Fine. Then have you considered the possibility he has some sort of personal vendetta? Perhaps there's room for cooperation."

"He is not your concern. The best thing you can do now is just disappear."

"Sister Kim—"

"I'm serious," Kim says. "You're too rash. Too impulsive. Too violent. We can't risk working with you anymore. We're cutting you off."

Hak is shocked by Kim's words. Without her network and the intelligence and financial support it provides, he's vulnerable, exposed, alone. "You can't do that."

"I'm sorry, Brother Hak."

Hak's expression turns to stone. "You are making a mistake."

Kim feels a chill run up her spine. She is fully aware Hak could murder her in her own living room. Effortlessly. And not lose any sleep over it. But she is resolute. "I warned you not to go to Dalian. Now you've risked the exposure of the entire underground network. And there's this policeman sniffing around. Our situation is perilous." She sighs. "Brother Hak, I don't say this lightly—but the best thing you could do now for the girls you want so badly to help is just . . . go away."

Hak watches her, his eyes narrow slits, reptilian in their cold scrutiny.

Kim stands and goes to the door. "Goodbye, Brother Hak." She opens it and waits.

Hak doesn't move from the couch. Kim wonders if he's debating the pros and cons of snapping her neck. Minus the funds and information she provides, she's of no use to him. In fact, she's a liability.

After a moment fraught with uncertainty, Hak stands. He walks to the door. He looks at Kim. Then he walks out without saying another word.

Kim gently closes the door. She locks it and turns the dead bolt.

Although she knows, if Hak wanted in, no lock could possibly stop him.

THIRTY-SEVEN

The same night Kim and Hak dissolve their partnership, the Nangang Benevolent Association—what's left of it—meets at a downtown restaurant in which Chairman Yu owns a half share. It is the first time they've all convened since Cai's murder and some of the members were quite reluctant to come out of hiding. But Xu insisted.

Tang arrives in the company of his chief of security, Diesel. They are ushered by the obsequious restaurant manager into a private back room. Already present are Xu, Hong, Chairman Yu, Deputy Mayor Wan, Judge Ren, and Zhao. Both Liu and Chen have made excuses for not attending. Liu is, in fact, away on a business trip, while Chen's burgeoning agoraphobia has recently become debilitating—he's been holed up in his house for weeks and is one step away from locking himself permanently in his bedroom and relieving himself in plastic water bottles.

Drinks are served and cigarettes lit. Xu launches right in:

"They know about Cai."

"Who knows?" Chairman Yu asks.

"The CIB."

This elicits curses and gasps around the table.

"How?" Tang asks.

"I'm not sure how, but we've been periodically monitoring Cai's case file to see who's accessed it," Xu says. "We got a hit earlier this evening—the CIB tech, Jin." Xu turns to Zhao. "They also referenced your incident report."

Zhao pales. He self-consciously keeps the stump of his left arm concealed beneath the table. "What? Me? Why?"

"Obviously they are connecting the dots between the attack on you and the murders of Cai and Pang." Xu's ponderous lips droop unhappily. "Given the circumstances, we have to assume they suspect the report of Cai's death by suicide is falsified."

"*Wo kao!*" Deputy Mayor Wan mutters.

"Now what?" snaps Chairman Yu.

Xu sips from his glass of whiskey. "If we could be sure they haven't written their findings into a report or discussed them with higher-ups, I'd suggest we kill them. All of them. Tonight. A hotel fire, perhaps."

"You can't be serious," Wan says.

"Before taking such extreme measures, let's think this through logically," Judge Ren suggests. "Brother Hong, you never filed any reports concerning Brothers Chen and Liu, correct?"

Hong nods. "Correct."

"Brother Xu, you are confident the pathologist who performed the autopsy on Cai won't change his story?"

"Yes," Xu says. "But I'll warn him CIB might have some questions."

"And Brother Zhao, you and your driver will hold firm to the carjacking story?"

"Of course," Zhao says.

"Then regardless of what CIB suspects," Judge Ren concludes, "they *know* nothing for sure. And they can *prove* nothing."

Xu frowns at Hong. "What if one of those constables told them about Cai?"

"I'll look into that," Hong says. "If so, I'll handle them."

"You're not going to kill them, are you?" Judge Ren says.

"No, of course not."

"There is one other security issue to consider," Chairman Yu says. "Gao. Even if he is not the Magistrate—which we can't be certain of—what he knows of us could prove damaging. Should the CIB knock on his door and threaten to send him back to prison for what little remains of his life, he might spill all. Perhaps it would be prudent to . . . make sure he's not in a position to speak to them."

"No," Xu says.

"Brother Xu," Yu says. "Don't let your personal affection for Gao cloud your normally ruthless inclinations."

"We owe him," Xu says. "All of us, to some extent or another."

Deputy Mayor Wan holds up a hand. "What Brother Yu says is true. Gao knows enough to cause us all major problems. And he *could* be the Magistrate. Perhaps eliminating him would kill two birds with one arrow."

"He deserves better than that," Xu says.

"Well, unlike our great country," Tang says, "the Nangang Benevolent Association is a democracy. We all get an equal say. And I agree with Brothers Yu and Wan. Gao's time has come."

Xu bristles. "Perhaps you'd like to see to Gao, then, Brother Tang, since you're already seeing to his wife."

"Gentlemen," Judge Ren says. "Please."

Xu angrily stubs out his cigarette. What Tang says is true—if a simple majority votes to kill Gao, he won't be able to prevent it. "I would ask you, humbly, to wait. Let's make a contingency plan—I'm sure Brother Tang can impose on Uncle Number Three or Ice Pick Brother to have a shooter standing by. In the meantime, Brother Hong will deal with the two constables, and I'll send a man around to remind the widow Pang to keep her mouth shut. As Brother Ren says, that should sew up any potential leakages quite nicely."

"And then what?" Chairman Yu asks.

"Then we wait. CIB resources are considerable, but not unlimited. And surely there are other cases requiring their urgent attention. If they don't get traction on Pang's homicide—which is ostensibly the investigation they are here to conduct—they'll have to move on. In a week, maybe two."

"What about Lu?" Hong says. "He's looking to flatten you and is using the power of the CIB as his own personal steamroller."

"For a certainty," Xu says. "But if it comes to my word against his, I can make a case that he resents me for terminating him all those years ago. He may well end up making wild accusations without any evidence to back it up. While that would doubtless be unpleasant for *me,* it might prove fatal for *him,* career-wise. And as for that bitch Ma . . ." His lips curve into a crocodilian smile. "Let's spark a rumor that they're sleeping together. That should trash her credibility."

Chairman Yu laughs. "There's the ruthlessness we know and love, Brother Xu."

Xu lights a fresh cigarette. "Aren't you glad I'm on *your* side?"

THIRTY-EIGHT

Lu emerges from the lobby entrance the next morning, solo and coatless, and walks up to an SUV idling out front. "We're not going to headquarters this morning," he tells the sergeant sitting behind the wheel. "Come back after lunch."

"Wait, what?"

Lu turns and disappears back through the lobby doors. The sergeant hesitates, then takes out his cell phone and starts making calls.

Inside the lobby, Lu waits beside the elevators. One of the carriages opens, disgorging Ma, Jin, and Sun. Sun hands Lu his coat and then follows him out the back entrance of the hotel. Ma and Jin exit through the front.

Once they step outside, everyone splits into different directions.

Confusion takes root among the PSB surveillance crew. The sergeant sticks his head out of the SUV window and calls to Ma and Jin. When they don't answer, he shifts into gear and backs out of the hotel roundabout. He motions for the unmarked car parked across the street to go after Jin. He drives off in pursuit of Ma.

Out back, a man on a motorcycle pulls up to the curb. Lu hops on behind him and the motorcycle speeds off. Sun runs out into the street, blocking pursuit by the second surveillance vehicle—as well as normal traffic. Horns blare. She gives Lu a sixty-second head start, then moves out of the way, accompanied by the angry shouts and curses of drivers.

Han is riding the elevator up to the widow Pang's apartment to deliver Xu's fresh warning when he gets a call from the sergeant stationed at the hotel. He answers but immediately loses the signal. Whatever—it can wait.

He exits the elevator and walks down to the widow's apartment. He gives the door a violent pounding with a balled-up fist. The kind that lets the occupants know someone with authority is outside. When the widow answers, Han takes her by the elbow and propels her toward the living room. She attempts to reclaim her arm, but fails.

Han pushes her onto the couch. "You've been talking to our friends in the CIB, haven't you?"

The widow is depressed, frightened, and slightly hungover, but she's not stupid. "No! Of course not!"

"They only want to dig up dirt on your dead husband, you understand? And they'll use whatever they find against you, too. Your bank account— confiscated. This apartment—gone! All your assets—poof!"

"I haven't spoken to them since the night you were all here."

"Don't lie to me!"

"I'm not. I even threw out the card that woman gave me. If you want to dig through my trash bin to see if I'm telling the truth, feel free."

Han leans close. The widow can see the individual pores in his nose. Dark pits in a chalky white surface, like the surface of the moon. He reeks of cigarette smoke and morning breath. "If you want to keep drinking your expensive wine and living in your luxury apartment building, you'd do well to keep your mouth shut. And if CIB or anyone else shows up and starts asking questions—call me immediately."

"I will. I swear."

Han stands to his full height and looks down at the widow. "I'm only telling you this for your own good, Mrs. Pang."

"I understand. Thank you, Detective."

Han grunts distrustfully and heads for the door.

After he's gone, the widow goes into the kitchen and guzzles a sizable glass of wine to steady her nerves. Then she pours the rest of the bottle down the sink.

Her period of mourning must tragically be cut short.

It is time to look to the future. Protect her assets. Convert cash into gold or buy property overseas. Whatever it takes to keep what is rightly hers out of the capricious hands of the government.

She calls her personal banking representative to make an appointment for later that morning, then rushes to take a shower and get dressed. It will be a busy day.

The motorcycle driver parks down the block from Gao's apartment building and flips up his helmet shield. He's a young guy with an eyebrow ring—one of the bartenders at the Black Cat. "Tell Monk thanks," Lu says.

The driver salutes and rides off.

Lu enters the building. It wasn't hard to find Gao's information—after all, he's an ex-con. As always, if he's not going up more than five flights, Lu takes the stairs.

He reaches the third floor, walks down the hall, and knocks on Apartment 338. A fit-looking young man dressed in a sweater and scrub pants answers.

"I'm looking for Mr. Gao," Lu says. He flashes his ID.

"What is it with you guys?"

"What do you mean?"

"Why are you harassing Mr. Gao?"

"I wasn't aware that we were."

"Two visits in the space of about three weeks seems like harassment to me."

"Were the other people who came here tall and unpleasant, or short, with a face like a fish, and likewise unpleasant?"

Kong gives Lu a strange look. "The second one. Shouldn't you know that?"

"Is Mr. Gao here? If you'll let me in, I'll explain."

"How about explaining before I let you in?"

"What is your name?"

"Kong."

"And you are?"

"Mr. Gao's home health care aide."

"I see. Well, please move aside, Mr. Kong. This is official business."

"Who is it?" a voice calls from within.

"Police," Kong answers over his shoulder.

"Again? *Ta ma de*. Well . . . the sooner you let him in, the sooner you can let him out."

Kong curtly gestures for Lu to enter. Once inside, Lu sees an old man sitting on a rattan couch with the TV on.

Lu has never met Gao but assumes this is who the old man is. "Mr. Gao?"

"If I'm not, I probably shouldn't be in my apartment, sitting on my couch, watching my TV," Gao says. "Who are you?"

Lu flashes his ID again. "My name is Lu Fei. I'm with the Public Security Bureau, currently assigned to the Criminal Investigation Bureau."

"Two bureaus is a lot for one man," Gao says.

Lu looks at Kong, then back at Gao. "Your assistant here said Xu visited recently?"

Gao shrugs unconvincingly. "I don't recall. I'm old."

Lu smiles. "I wonder, Mr. Gao, if I might speak to you in private for a few moments."

"Why not? All my other uninvited guests do. Kong, if you wouldn't mind?"

"Are you sure?" Kong says.

Gao waves a hand. "I won't smoke any cigarettes, if that's what worries you."

"That's not what worries me."

"I won't be long," Lu says. "And I promise not to rough him up too badly." He sees Kong tense. "That was a joke."

Kong agrees to wait in the hall. "Five minutes." He goes out and shuts the door.

Lu sits across from Gao. "Where'd you get that one?"

"A lot of people want to know. Unfortunately, he's one of a kind. What can I do for you, Mr. PSB-CIB?"

"Why was Xu here?"

"Don't you know?"

"Answer the question, please."

Gao picks up the remote and shakily turns off the TV. "Is there a problem at home? Mama and Baba aren't talking?"

For all his apparent infirmities, Gao's tongue remains sharp. "You know how this works," Lu says. "I ask the questions."

"I am not at liberty to discuss a confidential conversation with a member of law enforcement, for legal reasons. Even to another cop."

Lu is unsure of how to play this without knowing the status of Gao's relationship with Xu. "I used to work in Harbin as a detective. Many years ago. Under Xu."

"Oh, really?"

"We didn't exactly get along."

"A shame."

"This was not long before Xu was promoted to Nangang chief. I never had occasion to meet you then—I wasn't one of Xu's favorites. But I was aware of your patronage. And the fact that you subsequently went to jail for corruption. Meanwhile, Xu has done quite well for himself, hasn't he? Last time I saw him he was wearing a Rolex."

"When our friends win, we all win."

Lu laughs. "The one thing they can't take from you in prison is your sense of humor."

Gao coughs dryly. "They can certainly take nearly everything else, can't they?"

"Indeed." Lu knows from Gao's file that he's just turned seventy. His hollow cheeks, sunken eyes, mottled skin, make him seem much older. "There's a killer loose in Harbin. Have your heard about that?"

"You are referring to the premature passing of Mayor Pang."

"So, you are aware."

"It was in the news. Everyone in Harbin is aware."

"And there are . . . others." Lu watches Gao carefully.

Gao's eyes narrow. "Who?" He seems genuinely curious.

"I am not at liberty to say. But Pang is not the only Nangang official who has been targeted. I'm beginning to think someone has it out for a select group of powerful men. Men who share a specific connection."

Gao looks down at his gnarled hands. "You mean, apart from the fact that they are district officials?"

"Yes. The victims are spread across different government offices. Administrative, legal, business investment. I'm thinking, perhaps they all rose through the ranks as protégés of an influential local leader. A man who greased the wheels for them. And now they are reaping the benefits. Meanwhile, their benefactor has . . ." Lu looks around the apartment. "Fallen from grace."

Gao runs a desiccated tongue across chapped lips but doesn't answer.

Lu forges ahead. "I know for a fact that you and Xu were tight, back in the day. It must have been a hard blow when he turned his back on you in your hour of need."

Gao smiles thinly. "That is how the game is played. No hard feelings. No sense in everyone suffering."

"How noble of you."

"I'm an old man, and my time on this earth is limited, so let's cut to the chase, shall we? You're here because you consider me a suspect in this little revenge scenario you've cooked up. Well, I have absolutely nothing to hide." Gao waves around the spartan apartment. "What you see is what you get."

"May I be honest with you, Mr. Gao?"

"An honest cop. That's a first."

"Do you know anything about my personal history with Xu?"

"I've never laid eyes on you before today. I didn't even catch your name. I don't really care to."

"Like you, I have good reason to be very cross with Xu. I wouldn't mind seeing him get some comeuppance. Although being boiled alive might seem a little extreme."

"You want to join forces, is that it?"

"No. But if you know something about these assaults . . . and Pang's murder . . . I might be sympathetic to extenuating circumstances . . ."

"Oh, let's clarify that statement, shall we? In other words, if I killed Pang, and did whatever to whoever else, you'll let me go with a slap on the wrist? Long as I promise to behave from now on?"

"I'm saying . . . I am looking to land a shark, not an old catfish content to go where the current takes him."

Gao knuckles his bloodshot eyes. "I'm tired, Mr. PSB-CIB. I don't know anything about Pang's murder. Go bark up another tree. Please tell Xiao Kong to come back inside."

Lu waits to see if Gao has something more to say. But Gao reaches for the remote, turns the TV back on, slumps back into the couch cushions. Lu sighs, stands, goes to the door, opens it.

Kong is waiting in the hallway, arms crossed. Lu admires the corded muscle of his forearms. "Are you an athlete, Mr. Kong? Powerlifter?"

"I work out. Why?"

"What did you do before working for Mr. Gao?"

"Worked for another old man."

"Before that."

"I was in the military. A corpsman."

"Ah. Let me see your identification card."

"It's in my coat, inside."

"Go get it, please."

Kong does. Lu takes a photo of it with his phone. "Thanks for your time."

"Can you people leave Mr. Gao in peace from now on?" Kong says. "He's already paid for his crimes." He shuts the door before Lu can answer.

THIRTY-NINE

The surveillance team outside the hotel finally manages to round up Ma, Jin, and Sun and escort them to PSB headquarters. Han and Pangu await them in the lobby.

"The chief would like a word," Han says through clenched teeth.

They ride an elevator upstairs and walk down a wood-paneled corridor laid with blood-red carpet. Han knocks at a door. A voice calls for them to enter.

The office is furnished with an ostentatiously large desk, pictures of Xu with various dignitaries on the wall, and two rows of leather armchairs facing one another across a glass-topped coffee table. Xu is already sitting in a slightly more grandiose chair at the head of the coffee table. His face is a mask of cold fury. He motions curtly toward the chairs. "Sit."

"Is that an order?" Ma asks.

"Please, Dr. Ma. I'm not in the mood. Take a seat. Detective Han, shut the door."

The three investigators sit. Han and Pangu stand in the background like palace guards.

"Where is Inspector Lu?" Xu asks.

"He had other business," Ma says.

"What business?"

"Business that is no business of yours," Ma answers. "We are not your subordinates, and it's not necessary that we ask you for permission to go where we please. And I'd like to know, why the hell are you having us watched and followed?"

"For your own protection," Xu says.

"*Heng!*" Ma growls.

"Someone in Harbin has killed a district mayor," Xu says. "Who is to say your own lives would not be in danger if the perpetrator learned the identities of the investigative team trying to track him down?"

"We can take care of ourselves," Ma says.

"Really? Are you currently carrying firearms?"

"No, of course not."

"While you are in Harbin, your safety is my responsibility. Can you imagine the negative impact on public stability, not to mention, excuse me for saying, my reputation, if some misfortune were to befall you? Frankly, Dr. Ma, your actions this morning were juvenile and irresponsible. We are supposed to be working together, not playing childish games."

"You're the one who is playing games, Chief Xu."

"How so?"

"Withholding information, at best. At worst, actively interfering with our investigation."

"Why do you say that?"

"It's just a feeling I have."

"Well, nothing could be further from the truth. I'm guessing Inspector Lu has been whispering dark thoughts into your ear. It's no secret that he has a personal vendetta against me. Perhaps your relationship with him is starting to color your *own* perceptions."

"What do you mean by that?" Ma snaps. "My *relationship*?"

Xu holds up a hand. "Only that you have worked with him in the past. You trust him. And like him enough to bring him aboard your team."

"*Like* has nothing to do with it."

"If you say so. My only wish is to cooperate with you to solve this case. After which, we can part ways in a respectful manner."

"Certainly, Chief. You can begin by calling off your watchdogs."

"As I said, the officers are there for your personal protection."

"They seem more like jailers."

"Nonsense."

"Nevertheless. Call them off."

Xu gazes coldly at Ma. "Where is Lu?"

"I told you—that's his business."

"Dr. Ma . . ." Xu's thick lips curl into a frown. "I feel I really have no choice but to call Deputy Director Song and tell him you are treating us in an adversarial manner."

"Go ahead." Ma stands up. "In the meantime, if you need me, you'll know exactly where to find me. Won't you?" She strides for the door. Jin and Sun abruptly lurch to their feet and follow. Ma does not wait for Han to open the door—she does it herself and stomps off down the hallway, with Jin and Sun at her heels.

Xu motions to Pangu. "Go with them."

Pangu nods and follows.

"Shut the door," Xu tells Han. He gets up and walks over to sit behind his desk. He switches on a powerful air filter that rests on the floor and lights a cigarette. "Nasty, arrogant bitch."

Han comes over to stand in front of the desk. "What should we do, boss?"

"First, tell the surveillance team they've done a shit job. Get some new faces in there. Some women, if you can."

"No women in the Homicide squad, boss."

"I know that, idiot! Pull them from somewhere else. They don't need to know details; all they need to do is keep watch without being obvious."

Han isn't sure how he's going to carry out that order, but now is no time to argue with Xu. "Yes, boss."

"And start spreading rumors that Ma and Lu are spending nights at the hotel humping like dogs in heat. Far and wide, got it? I want to lay the groundwork for claiming Lu is unduly influencing Ma."

"I'll put the word out."

"Meanwhile, I'll call Song and tell him Ma's being difficult. That's all we can do for now. Dismissed."

Han turns and heads for the door. Before he can make his escape, Xu slaps the surface of his desk and shouts:

"And find that bastard Lu!"

FORTY

Lu comes away from his encounter with Gao none the wiser. Does Gao know something about the murders, or does he not? Is the muscular Mr. Kong his hatchet man? Does Xu suspect Gao, or was he just delivering a warning to him?

While Lu feels no closer to unraveling the mystery of Pang's killer, there's one thing he's certain of: Xu is, at this very moment, shitting white-hot rage-fueled balls of fire. And all that heat will be directed at Ma, as she's the team leader. If Xu could get away with it, Lu thinks, he'd stick Ma in a black jail, hook battery cables to her nipples, and crank up the juice. Fortunately, the CIB's authority outweighs that of a city Public Security Bureau.

Regardless, these next few hours might be the only time Lu will be able to operate unsupervised and unimpeded. He might as well make the best of them.

He stops into a café for coffee and a steamed bun. He thinks as he chews. Gao appeared old, poor, miserable, and physically infirm, but still in possession of all his mental faculties. And he has a strong motive for the murders—revenge.

But does he have the means?

On the face of it, no. However, money can be sequestered and hidden in a variety of ways.

Lu takes a sip of coffee, a bite of bun. Chews, swallows. Was Gao pretending to be surprised when Lu mentioned that other Nangang officials apart from Pang had been targeted? If not, he must be legitimately estranged from his former protégés. Certainly, given his living conditions, they don't appear to have provided much financial support following his release from prison. He may well be, as it appears, isolated, friendless, alone apart from the protective Mr. Kong.

Lu knows from reading Gao's official records that he has no siblings, no children. Only an ex-wife. Of her, Lu has only a hazy recollection—younger than Gao, pretty, a lounge singer of some stripe. Suitable arm candy for a man of power and influence.

Lu goes outside and finds the nearest public bus. He boards and rides it half a dozen stops. It doesn't matter where it's going, he just wants to get some distance from Gao's apartment building. He disembarks, switches on his phone— he's previously switched it off to prevent Xu from tracking his movements—and texts Jin.

Need address and info on Gao Yang's ex-wife. Can't remember her name, but there is only one. I'll check my phone in thirty minutes. Also, Gao's aide. Texting you picture of his ID now.

Lu's phone is suddenly flooded with a dozen texts from Han—they grow increasingly irate and profane as they progress chronologically. Lu doesn't bother to read them, but he gets the gist. He laughs to himself, sends a picture of Kong's ID to Jin, then switches off his phone.

He starts walking, searching for another café. He's got some time to kill.

Xu sits behind his desk and smokes cigarette after cigarette. A noxious cloud swirls above his head. He normally limits the amount he smokes in his office— it's against regulations, of course—but if he didn't have a cigarette in his hand, he'd probably be punching a wall.

If it was only Ma to contend with, Xu wouldn't be half as worried. Even if word of Cai's murder leaked out, even if one of those constables talked, there's no way to prove the death scene was staged to look like a suicide. Ma might have suspicions—but producing concrete evidence will be as elusive as catching a fish in a rushing stream with a pair of chopsticks.

And absent evidence, Ma has the diplomatic sense to not point fingers and waggle her tongue.

Lu, however—that leprous dog's prick—is a different story. He knows the territory; he knows the players. He knows about Xu's connection to Tang Fuqiang; and he's aware of the dead cybersex director, even if he can't connect him to Tang directly.

He just knows entirely too damn much.

Xu stops mid-smoke; he's suddenly had an awful, terrible notion.

He turns on his monitor and opens a link to the camera Hong has installed in the hallway outside Gao's apartment. He rewinds the feed and watches. *Cao!*

He stubs out his cigarette and unlocks a drawer in his desk. He takes out a burner phone and makes a call.

FORTY-ONE

When Lu checks his phone thirty minutes later, there is a terse message from Jin listing Ling Wei's basic details: name, DOB, address, employment ("entertainer"). No criminal record, no children. Marriage status: divorced.

Jin has provided similar information concerning Kong. Lu sees that Kong was telling the truth about his military service—five years in the PLA. And he's been working for a home health care agency since his discharge seven years ago. No criminal record.

Experience tells Lu it's unlikely Kong has gone from never having so much as jaywalked to premeditated murder—but stranger things have happened.

Lu turns off his phone, flags a taxi, and gives the driver Ling's address.

The driver takes him to an upscale apartment building. A uniformed attendant sits at a gleaming desk in the glass-fronted lobby. Lu shows his ID. "I was never here."

"Certainly, sir," the attendant says. "Which resident did you want to see?"

"Don't worry about that."

Lu boards the elevator and notes the camera in the ceiling. He gets off on the fourteenth floor, walks down a flight, then locates the door to Ling's apartment and knocks.

She answers, a perplexed look on her face—a strange man at her door and no warning from downstairs. "Hello," she says. "Can I help you?"

Lu shows her his ID. "I'm working with the Criminal Investigation Bureau. I'd like to ask you some questions."

Ling's eyes widen. "About?"

"May I enter?" He smiles pleasantly. Ling retreats. Lu steps over the threshold. "Are you alone?"

"Yes."

"Mind if I take a quick look?" Lu does. He sees a bedroom, bath, living room/kitchen. Modern appliances, floor-to-ceiling windows. Good-quality furniture with lots of homey touches—a knitted afghan, fresh flowers. A couple of framed posters for Ling's cabaret performances on the wall; no photos of her and Gao. Or her and anyone else, for that matter.

They sit at her dining table. Ling offers Lu tea. He accepts.

"Do you know a man by the name of Pang Wenbin?"

"I know who he is. Was. I read about his terrible murder."

"You knew him personally?"

Ling hesitates. "We'd met, some time ago."

"When you were married to Gao Yang."

A shadow crosses Ling's face. "Yes."

"When's the last time you spoke to your ex-husband?"

"Almost six years ago."

"Just after he was arrested."

Ling nods.

"You were quite the pair, weren't you?"

"What do you mean?"

"Come, now. The ambitious politician. The beautiful chanteuse. I'm sure his *guanxi* greased more than one wheel for you. And then, in his hour of need, you dumped him like yesterday's news."

"It wasn't like that."

"What was it like, then?"

Ling stares down at her teacup. "He was a criminal. I didn't want to be associated with that."

Lu feels no personal animosity toward Ling. He doesn't know her at all. But intimidation is a useful tool for prying the truth out of hidden recesses. "That's a laugh. You used him, and when he no longer proved of use, you turned your back to him."

Ling looks up, angry. "What do you know about it? Are you here to ask me about my ex-husband, who I haven't seen or spoken to in six years?"

"I think Pang's murder is connected in some way to Gao. What do you think?"

"I don't understand. My ex-husband went to prison. He was stripped of his position and benefits. His property was confiscated. How could he be involved in a murder all these years later?"

Lu leans back in his chair. "I want you to make a list of Nangang government officials who traveled in Gao's circle back in the day."

"He knew a lot of people."

"I guess you'd better get a thick pad of paper, then."

"I can't remember them all."

"Do your best. I'll wait."

Lu sips his tea while Ling grudgingly jots down names. This exercise might be a waste of time, but it's worth a shot. When she's done, Lu has a quick look. Zhao is listed, but not Procurator Cai. There are a handful of other names he remembers from his time in Harbin. Lu folds the paper up and puts it in his pocket. "This is a nice apartment. How do you pay for it?"

"I work."

"So, if I checked your financial records, I'd see your rent listed on your expenditures?"

Ling grips the pen in her hands until her knuckles turn white.

"I'm waiting," Lu says.

"The apartment is paid for."

"By?"

"An LLC."

"Do you work for this LLC?"

"Not exactly."

"So why don't you stop wasting my time, Ms. Ling, and tell the name of the person who owns this apartment and allows you to live here?"

Ling holds out for a moment, and then says, in a whisper: "Tang Fuqiang."

Whatever Lu was expecting, it wasn't this. "Tang Fuqiang? Nangang's biggest brothel owner and pimp?"

"I don't know anything about that," Ling says.

"Sure you don't. I suppose you're always deaf, dumb, and blind where your boyfriends are concerned. How long did it take for you to hook up with Tang once you dumped Gao? Were the sheets even cold?"

"I'd like you to leave now."

"We'd all like something, Ms. Ling. I'd like a magical gourd that never runs out of Shaoxing wine. Do Gao and Tang know each other personally?"

"I believe they've encountered one another in the past."

"But Tang's name isn't on your list."

"You said to write down Nangang officials."

"So I did. What was the nature of their relationship—when you were married to Gao?"

"I don't know. Social acquaintances, perhaps."

"Business dealings?"

"I knew nothing about my ex-husband's business."

"I suppose you'll claim the same regarding Tang?"

"Tang is a property developer and a restaurateur."

"And a sex trafficker and probably a murderer."

"Please go now. Please."

"One last question. Does Gao know about you and Tang?"

Ling's eyes well with tears. "I haven't spoken to my ex-husband in six years."

"I wonder what he'd say."

Ling unexpectedly reaches across the table and clutches Lu's hand. "Please don't tell him. He's suffered enough. Leave him in peace."

Lu pulls his hand away. Ling is correct, it's time for him to go. Not out of deference to her feelings—but because if Gao really does have dirt on Tang and his Nangang cronies, this tantalizing new tidbit of information might be just the thing to crack him open like an oyster shell. "Don't tell Tang I was here. Or anyone else. The CIB has ways of punishing you that are positively medieval. I'll see myself out."

The attendant downstairs gives him a polite nod when he comes out of the elevator. As soon as Lu is through the lobby doors, he dials a number on his cell phone.

FORTY-TWO

Tang is in the middle of his monthly lunch meeting at the Little Red Palace with his brothel managers—they are feasting on roast chicken, stewed beef, abalone and sea cucumber, tofu and mushrooms, noodles, hot and sour soup—when Xu calls. He excuses himself from the dining room and goes into the hallway. "To what do I owe the pleasure?"

"Lu's been to see Gao."

"What? *Wo kao!* Where's Lu now?"

A pause on the line. "I don't know."

"What do you mean, you don't know?"

"He engineered an escape this morning."

"*Ta ma de!* How could you let this happen?"

"I didn't let anything happen, Tang. He escaped!"

"Your damned incompetence will cost us dearly!"

"Watch your mouth. I'm not one of your lackeys or whores."

Tang squeezes the phone in his hand until he hears it crack. He wills himself to speak calmly. "Do you now agree it's time to make that unpleasant phone call to Ice Pick Brother?"

There's a pause on the line, followed by Xu's heavy sigh: "Make the call. Tell him to have someone on standby, but not to pull the trigger until we say so. Gao didn't tell me anything, and I doubt he told Lu anything, either. We'll sit tight and see what happens. In the meantime, I have a camera in Gao's hallway, and I'll send Han around to keep watch outside. And we're currently running a search on the citywide surveillance system. It's only a matter of time before Lu's in hand."

"A man like that can do a lot of damage before he's caught."

"Call your friend. But tell him to wait for our signal."

Tang makes his excuses to the managers and goes up to his office. He takes a burner phone out of his desk and is about to dial Ice Pick Brother when he gets a call on the house phone from Diesel.

"I just got word that someone fitting Lu's description is at Ling's apartment," Diesel says.

Tang curses and abruptly hangs up. He types a password into his computer and opens a spyware file that allows him to listen in through Ling's cell phone. He catches the second half of Lu and Ling's conversation. *Gan!*

Furious, and alarmed, he phones Ice Pick Brother. No more debate. It's time for an old man to die.

Han and Pangu are on the way to Gao's building when Han receives a call. He carries two phones—one official, and one unofficial. The call comes on the unofficial one. Han knows to follow certain protocols, number one being, no names. "*Wei?*"

"Where are you now?" Xu asks.

"About fifteen minutes out."

"Listen very carefully. The circumstances have evolved. Be on the lookout for our missing friend. I expect he is on the way to your destination. Also, a third party has been dispatched for the purposes of sanitation. Do not interfere with that third party. Understand?"

Han's pulse quickens. "If that's the case, won't it be odd for us to be in the vicinity?"

"No. Our friend was spotted on a surveillance cam at that destination earlier this morning. We are, of course, very concerned about his welfare, so you have been ordered to keep watch on the location in case he returns."

"Got it."

"In the meantime, should you, while keeping an eye out for our friend, hear reports of shots fired, you'll be conveniently situated to respond to the scene and secure it for further investigation."

"And if our *friend* happens to be on the scene while this is happening?"

Xu has already discussed this very matter with Tang. After reluctantly agreeing that they have no choice but to kill Gao, Xu suggested they use this opportunity to murder Lu as well, should he arrive at an opportune time.

Tang vetoed that idea. "Sorting a disgraced old man without friends or social status is one thing. A high-level bureau investigator is quite another. I don't want to be in debt to Ice Pick Brother for the rest of my life."

Xu had to accept this reasoning. "If a golden opportunity presents itself, take it," he tells Han now. "But don't be reckless. If it doesn't fit into the narrative, just take him into custody—you know . . . for his own safety."

"Understood." Han hangs up.

"What going on?" Pangu asks.

"What's going on is someone's coming to snuff Gao, and if we get a chance, we're going to snuff Lu, too."

Pangu's mouth drops open. He's loyal to Xu, but has never killed anyone before, let alone a fellow police officer. "That's . . . that's crazy!"

"Don't worry. All you have to do is keep your eyes open and keep your mouth shut. I'll take care of the rest."

When they reach Gao's apartment building, Han drops Pangu off in back. "Stay out of sight. Call if you see Lu."

Han drives around front and parks down the block.

Unlike most PSB officers, Han routinely carries a concealed firearm. He eschews the standard nine-millimeter revolver with its six rounds in favor of a more substantial QZ-92 automatic with a fifteen-round capacity. He draws his pistol and cocks it. He lights a cigarette and waits.

There are no taxis to be had outside Ling's building, so Lu summons a car service. Traffic is atrocious. Lu sits in the back, gritting his teeth with impatience. When they finally reach Gao's building, Lu shows the driver his ID. "Circle the block. I'm looking for any suspicious people hanging around, or vehicles with guys sitting in them for no apparent reason."

"Cool," the driver says. He's a young guy with a fashionable haircut and he seems jazzed to find himself part of a police operation. "But don't you guys usually have your own cars for this sort of thing?"

"Long story," Lu says.

The driver noses his car around the block. He spots Han's SUV before Lu does. "That guy we just passed. His engine's off, he's just sitting there smoking."

Lu scrunches down. He sees the SUV, recognizes it as the same make and model Han drives, but can't see the person inside clearly. "I'll take your word for it. Pull over at the far corner."

The kid parks and turns around in his seat. "What now?"

"I need something I can use as a disguise. What do you have?"

The kid laughs. "You serious?"

"Dead serious. You're about my size. Let's trade coats."

"No way. This is a Moncler Genius. It cost nine thousand yuan!"

"How the hell does a driver afford a coat that costs nine thousand?"

"Hey, Brother, don't be rude."

"You're right, I'm sorry," Lu says. "How about a sweatshirt or something?"

The kid roots around and comes up with a camouflage hoodie. The lettering on front reads PROPERTY OF RIKERS. The hoodie is woefully inadequate for the outside weather, but it's better than nothing. Lu ends up paying not only for the ride but adding an extra three hundred yuan for the hoodie. He shrugs into it and pulls the hood up.

Lu gets out and heads for the apartment entrance. As he's walking, a young man in a motorcycle rides up, parks at the curb. He's wearing a coat, gloves, motorcycle helmet, and carrying an insulated food delivery pack on his back. He reaches the lobby before Lu and disappears inside.

Han doesn't know who will be coming for Gao, but when he sees the motorcycle rider, he figures him to be a likely candidate. He watches as the rider enters the building, then another man in a hoodie approaches and stops to hold the door for an old woman. Despite the hood, Han quickly recognizes Lu. He texts Pangu: *He's here.*

Han gets out of the SUV and hustles for the lobby, the pistol concealed under his coat.

Lu takes the stairs. He can hear footfalls receding above him, then the slam of a door. When he reaches the third-floor landing, he opens the door leading to the hallway, sees the guy in the motorcycle helmet walking down it, eases it mostly shut, peeks through the crack.

The guy in the helmet stops, knocks on a door. The door opens. Lu realizes, too late, the door is Gao's. He hears a muffled *pop!* The guy in the helmet disappears inside.

Lu throws open the door and runs, stops.

He's unarmed. The guy in the motorcycle helmet is not.

Lu looks for something he can use to even the odds. He spies a fire safety box on the wall, yanks it open, frees the fire extinguisher. He rips out the safety pin as he rushes down to Gao's apartment, registering the sound of another suppressed gunshot.

He reaches the door, bumps it open with his shoulder, gets a flash of Kong lying splayed on his back, tendrils of bright blood spreading across the floorboards, Gao on the couch, clutching his stomach. The shooter has a gun in his hand and the barrel is pointed at Gao's face.

Lu squeezes the trigger on the fire extinguisher hose. A great gout of white foam erupts. The shooter throws up an arm, turns, aims.

Lu slips on Kong's blood, plops on his ass. The fall saves him. A bullet whips through the space he was occupying a split second ago, thumps into the wall.

Lu fires off another torrent of foam. It hits the shooter dead-on. He flails his arms, trips over a chair.

The hose sputters. The fire extinguisher is spent. Lu gets up, skates across the slick floor, smashes the butt of the canister into the shooter's helmet. It makes a dull clang. He drops the canister, goes for the gun. He and the shooter wrestle for control. Foam covers their hands and clothes, making it impossible to get a solid grip. The shooter wrenches free of Lu's grasp, runs for the door, slipping and sliding. He trips and falls halfway through the door.

Lu takes a step toward him. The shooter rolls to his back and levels the gun. Lu dives. A bullet shatters the window behind him.

By the time Lu has regained his feet and reached the doorway, the shooter is gone.

FORTY-THREE

Lu confirms Kong is dead. A round in the chest, another in the head. And Gao has sustained a stomach wound.

Lu switches on his phone and calls emergency. He gives the operator the address and says to hurry, then hangs up without answering any other questions.

Gao lies on the couch, blood leaking through his fingers, chest heaving. Lu grabs a dish towel from the kitchen, lifts Gao's hand, and presses the towel to the wound. "Hang in there, Mr. Gao. An ambulance is coming."

Gao groans.

"Who did this?" Lu asks. "Is it because you know something about the murders?" Gao's eyes flutter. Lu lightly pats his cheek. "Mr. Gao, talk to me."

A voice barks from the door: "Get away from him!" Lu looks up.

It's Han—and he's got a gun in his hand.

Lu's first thought is, *That was fast.* The second is that Han was the shooter in the motorcycle helmet. He quicky discards that idea. Han outweighs the shooter by thirty kilos, easy. "I'm trying to help him."

"After you tried to kill him? Likely story. Move away."

"Did you see a kid in a motorcycle helmet? He must have run right past you."

"I don't know what you're talking about."

Lu sees Han's finger tight on the trigger. The sick grin on his face. "Wait," Lu says. "Don't be stupid."

"You're the stupid one. Shooting a defenseless old man. And why? You couldn't find any proof to back up your beef with Chief Xu, so you try to frame him for murder?"

"What? That's . . . absurd!"

"Move away from Gao. Now!"

Lu raises a hand, sticky with Gao's blood, and steps away.

The prospect of dying is bad enough. The thought of *Han* killing him is intolerable. "You'll never get away with it. I'm not even armed."

"Then what's this?" Han reaches into his coat pocket and extracts a pistol with a suppressor attached to the barrel. "You dropped it in the stairwell before running back here and pretending to help Gao. Really, Lu? How stupid do you think we are?"

"That's not mine, and you know it."

"Right. That's what they all say."

Gao's breath rattles. A siren wails. Animated voices burble up from the courtyard.

"What now, Han?" Lu asks. "You're going to shoot me in cold blood?"

What, indeed? Han isn't sure himself. He could easily put a couple rounds in Lu, place the other gun in Lu's hand, fire a shot off into the ceiling. Make it look like a fair fight.

He'd probably get a medal. Courage under fire, that sort of thing.

And it would be deeply satisfying to watch Lu die. To be the instrument of his death.

But, no—it's *too* easy. He wants Lu to suffer. To be stripped of his dignity, his reputation, his self-respect.

To lose everything.

Then he can die.

Han smiles. "You're under arrest for the attempted murder of Gao Yang."

Pangu arrives, wheezing and sweating, thirty seconds later. Lu has little choice but to let Han frisk him and confiscate his phone. Han pulls out a set of handcuffs, but Lu says, "Not on your life." Han doesn't push it. He makes Lu sit in one of the chairs while Pangu stands guard.

Two EMS medics arrive. They perform a quick triage, get Gao on a stretcher, and take him downstairs.

"All right, Lu," Han says. "Let's go."

"I'll make you a deal," Lu says. "Let me call Ma, and then take me to the hospital where they're taking Gao. After we see if he lives or dies, I'll comply with all your instructions."

"You think we're going to put a pillow over Gao's face while he's in surgery?"

"I wouldn't put it past you."

"You know how this works. You go to central processing—in cuffs."

"I'm working for the CIB. If you show me a little professional courtesy, they might do the same later when they arrest you for your various crimes."

Han laughs. "You're a real cutup, aren't you, Lu? All right. I'll play along. But no bullshit. You make a run for it, and I'll gun you down."

"I'm not going to make a run for it."

Han and Pangu take Lu downstairs and put him in their SUV. They drive to the hospital with lights and sirens. Pangu hands Lu his phone. Lu calls Ma, tells her Gao's been shot, he's on the way to the hospital, and Han is trying to frame him.

Pangu quickly snatches the phone back. "That's enough."

At the hospital they are directed to a waiting room in the surgical ward. A family sits there, fidgeting with worry, waiting for news of a loved one. Han asks around and finds an empty room across from the nurses' station, commandeers it. He searches inside to make sure there's nothing Lu can use as a weapon, then waves Lu in.

"I could use some water and a hot drink," Lu says. "Coffee or tea will do, I'm not picky."

"What am I, your damned servant?" Han growls. "Inside!"

Lu enters and slumps into a chair. Han slams the door, leaving him alone to stew in silence. When Lu raises his hands to massage his temples he notices they are stained with Gao's dried blood.

Fifteen minutes pass. Lu hears voices outside. He opens the door to find two constables standing guard.

"You're supposed to remain in the room, sir," one says.

"I need something to drink. And a wet cloth to wipe my hands off with. Please."

The constables exchange a look. The first one speaks again: "We'll see what we can do."

Another fifteen minutes pass. There's a knock on the door. Lu opens it and the constable hands Lu a bottle of water and cup of tea.

"Thanks," Lu says. "How about a towel or something to clean off my hands?"

"Sorry. They'll want to swab you down."

"I see. Any word on Gao's condition?"

"Nothing yet, sir."

Lu drinks the water and tea. He paces, wondering where Ma is, expecting to hear her ripping a few new assholes outside—but it doesn't happen. Eventually he pokes his head out of the room again, to find Han standing in the corridor.

"Where's Dr. Ma?" Lu asks. "Why isn't she here?"

"Your team is sequestered at the hotel for their own safety," Han says.

"Trying to isolate me, is that it? That's going to end up poorly for you."

"It's working out fine so far," Han says.

"Ma's going to skin you alive."

"Her prized investigator's been pinched for attempted murder. If she intervenes it'll look like there's more to you two than a strictly professional relationship." Han waggles his tongue.

"Good luck making that stick, asshole."

"Seems like you're the one who could use some luck, Lu."

"Gao knows I didn't try to kill him."

"Then I guess you'd better pray the old bastard lives."

The evening wears on. A PSB supervisor whom Lu doesn't know arrives to take his statement. Han sits in. Lu explains that he went to visit Gao to ask him questions regarding a murder investigation—saw the shooting go down—saved Gao's life.

"Han was there," Lu says. "Conveniently waiting outside. Odd. Have you asked him what he was doing there? And the shooter must have run right past him. That's how Han got his hands on the gun. Speaking of which, you won't find my prints on it."

Han gives the supervisor a grin that says, *Will you get a load of this guy*?

"We will run a GSR test," the supervisor says. "Have you fired a gun recently?"

Lu thinks of a ghost town on the southern border—heat, humidity, and the stench of death. "Not since July."

A CSI tech is summoned. He brings a gunshot residue kit, swabs Lu's hands and clothes, packs up, and leaves.

After another interminable wait, a surgeon finally appears. His scrubs are sweat-stained—his face is lined from wearing a mask and cap. He seems surprised to find himself facing a scrum of men, two of them in constable uniforms.

"Is anyone here family?" the surgeon asks.

"No," Han says, flashing his ID. "What's the story? Is he alive or dead?"

"The patient is out of surgery and stable . . . but critical. We've placed him in a medically induced coma. If he makes it through the next twenty-four hours, his chances of recovery are good."

Lu feels like a jerk for asking, but he does so anyway: "When will it be possible to get a statement from him?"

"He'll remain sedated for at least twenty-four hours. Perhaps longer. And when he awakes, he will be experiencing confusion and brain fog. I'd say, to be safe, seventy-two hours minimum."

"May I have a moment in private with the doctor, here?" Lu asks Han.

"As if," Han says. He turns to the surgeon. "Please take good care of Mr. Gao. His health is of the utmost importance to us."

"Do you know if he has any family here?" the surgeon asks again.

"Yes," a voice says. Everyone turns. Ling Wei stands at the mouth of the corridor. Lu is surprised to see her. Judging from Han's reaction, so is he.

"And you are?" the surgeon asks.

"His ex-wife. I got a call from the hospital—I'm still listed as his emergency contact."

"I see. You heard what I told the officers?"

Ling nods. Then she covers her face with her hands and begins to sob.

The surgeon shifts tiredly on his feet. "His chances of recovery are good."

Ling brings herself under control, nods, and wipes tears from her cheeks. "When can I see him?"

"He's in the ICU now. Perhaps tomorrow."

"I want to see him now. Please."

The surgeon considers. "All right, for just a few minutes. You'll have to put on protective gear and be accompanied by a nurse."

"That's fine."

"Why don't you have a seat and I'll send someone to get you when we're ready?"

Ling withdraws into the waiting room. The surgeon gives instructions to one of the nurses and then says his farewells.

Han removes a pair of handcuffs from his belt and dangles them from a forefinger. "All right, Lu. Time to go."

"I want to call a lawyer."

"You know the drill," Han says.

Lu does. Under Chinese law, a suspect can be detained for several days before the police are obligated to file an arrest request with the procuratorate. Once the procurator has approved it, a suspect may be held for as long as 13.5 months while a thorough investigation is carried out. Suspects do not have the right to have a lawyer until after the initial interrogation, and in some cases not even until the case goes to trial.

"No cuffs," Lu says. "I won't make trouble. And I want to make one more phone call."

"After you're processed."

"Fine."

Han and Pangu take Lu to central processing. There he is photographed, fingerprinted, and placed in a cell. He asks again to make a phone call. Han says he'll arrange it.

No surprise—he doesn't.

大雪
HEAVY SNOW

FORTY-FOUR

Later that evening, a guard brings Lu dinner—a bowl of rice with stringy vegetables and mystery meat, a thin soup, a weak cup of tea. Tasteless, but Lu eats. He knows he's not getting anything else until morning. He knows he might be here for a while.

They've taken his watch, belt, shoelaces. He has no way to mark the passage of time. He imagines Ma raising hell on his behalf, but even she is bound by law and procedure. The Harbin PSB is under no obligation to let Lu see or speak to anyone until after the interrogation process has begun.

After dinner, Lu sits on his cot, dozing off for want of anything better to do. He hears the jingle of keys and hollow footsteps. He stands and goes over to the cell door, which consists of crisscrossed steel bars. A guard approaches, followed by Xu and Han.

"Thanks," Xu tells the guard. "Give us a minute."

When the guard is gone, Xu turns to Lu. "I always knew you were crazy. But to kill an old man you've never even met simply because he was something of a father figure to me?" Xu clucks his tongue and shakes his head.

"You going to try framing me for Pang's murder, too? How about Cai's fake suicide?"

"What are you babbling about? Cai's death *was* a suicide. Open-and-shut. And as for Pang, I guess you didn't hear. We made a collar."

"What collar?"

"Some scumbag who owes Pang hundreds of thousands in gambling debts. Yes, sadly it's true, Pang had a gambling problem. Nobody's perfect. But we caught his killer, so all's well that ends well. Except for you."

Lu thrusts his arm through the bars. Xu recoils. Han jumps in. There is a brief wrestling match and Lu is forced to yank his arm back before Han manages to break it. He shakes it out and winces in pain.

Xu straightens his tie and smooths his hair back. He curls his lip. "The next time you see daylight will be when they take you outside to put a bullet in your brain."

"You won't get away with it, Xu!"

Xu and Han walk out of view. Lu hears a heavy door open, then slam shut. He punches the wall and leaves a smear of blood on the cement.

That evening, Ling Wei manages to spend a few moments with Gao in the ICU. She is horrified by his appearance: a breathing tube snaking down his throat, ventilator rhythmically whooshing and clicking, IV lines and monitoring wires grafted to his flesh, Gao's body dwarfed and dehumanized by the machinery working to keep him alive.

Ling touches Gao's arm with a gloved finger—it feels as cold and inert as a fillet of beef in a supermarket meat bin. Gao shows no awareness of her presence.

The nurse eventually ushers her out and Ling takes a taxi home. When she reaches her apartment building, the attendant downstairs greets her with an uneasy nod. Ling, distracted, barely notices.

Upstairs, she unlocks her door and steps into her apartment. The lights are on. Strange. When she left it was still daylight—she wouldn't have turned on the lights.

Then she smells cigarette smoke.

She finds Diesel sitting at the kitchen table. "Good evening, Ms. Ling," Diesel says. He taps ashes from his cigarette into a cup he's using as an ashtray.

"What are you doing here?" Ling snaps.

"You're to come with me."

"Why?"

"For your own safety."

"I'm perfectly fine. Please get out of my apartment."

"Don't be silly," Diesel says. "Go pack. Take everything you need. You might not be coming back here for quite some time."

* * *

On the morning following the shooting, Constables Fan and Zheng arrive for an eight-to-four shift. They are immediately summoned into different interrogation rooms where Chief Hong takes turns accusing them of fabricating details about Cai's suicide and leaking them to the CIB.

Zheng swears on his ancestors that he didn't speak a word about Cai to a single soul. "Not even my wife!" he says. "Not even my girlfriend!"

Fan puts on a brave front, but Hong can smell the fear on her. "Unless you want to go to jail for disobeying a direct order . . . ," he threatens, "subverting police authority . . . revealing state secrets . . . you'd better confess."

Fan isn't sure how she could possibly be accused of revealing state secrets, but nevertheless, she pictures herself in a prison uniform, head shaved, performing hard labor in a copper mine in the desolate reaches of Inner Mongolia.

Fan tells Hong that Sun approached her to ask about Cai's death, and she had no choice but to reveal her suspicions that he was murdered. She has the presence of mind to omit the fact that it was she who alerted Sun by leaving an anonymous note in her folder.

"So, how did Constable Sun know to question you?" Hong asks.

"I'm . . . I'm not sure."

"I don't believe you. And were you not told that this was a highly sensitive case and to keep your mouth shut?"

"She's working with the CIB! I had no choice."

Hong concludes the interview by placing Fan on administrative leave and sending her home with a warning: "Another word to Sun or anyone else and you're finished."

Fan doesn't know it yet, but she's already finished. Hong will give it a few weeks, then sign an order for her immediate termination, citing perjury, dereliction of duty, and corruption charges. She'll never work in law enforcement again.

FORTY-FIVE

Lu has experienced what follows many times—only from the other side of the bars.

They let him twist in the wind for three days before starting interrogations. Then comes rapid-fire questioning while he's chained to a "tiger chair." It's all for show, of course—everyone knows what Lu did and didn't do.

Between sessions, he's kept in a private cell. His repeated demands for a phone call are ignored. He assumes Chief Liang knows about his arrest by now, but even he is unable to break through the bubble of concrete and steel surrounding Lu.

On the fourth day, Han and Pangu come down to his cell in the company of two guards. "Good news," Han says. "The procurator has approved your arrest. You're going to be transferred to the city detention facility."

"You're violating my rights by not letting me speak to a lawyer."

"They'll let you call when you get there. Turn around so I can cuff you."

Lu is escorted through the bowels of the PSB to a back lot, where he's loaded into a van with a couple of other arrestees.

Upon arrival at the new facility, they are stripped, searched, hair shorn, allowed to take a shower (Lu's first since his arrest), issued prison uniforms of dark blue with thick white stripes on the shoulders and pants, and brought to a room where they stand at attention as the warden addresses them.

Lu barely pays attention. He knows the routine. They must strive to be model inmates. Rehabilitate themselves through a sincere study of socialist principles. And so on. When his lecture is done, the warden dismisses the other inmates but tells Lu to remain behind.

"I see you were a deputy chief of a township."

"I'm still a deputy chief. And I'm innocent."

"That is for a trial to decide. In the meantime, I don't want any trouble here. Don't tell the other inmates you were a cop. That might make you a target."

"Thanks for the sage advice," Lu says.

"You'll address me as Warden."

"Yes, Warden."

The warden nods tersely. "Dismissed."

"I'm owed a phone call. And a lawyer."

"Later."

"You know I'm close personal friends with a deputy director at the Ministry of Public Security, don't you?"

The warden stands nose to nose with Lu. He is short but has the pugnacious air of a street fighter. "I don't give a donkey's balls who you know, inmate"—the warden looks down at the serial numbers on the breast of Lu's prison blouse—"Eight-nine-three-four-five. I don't play favorites. Within my jurisdiction, justice is blind. Got it?"

"Yes, Warden."

"Dismissed!"

Lu is placed in the four-by-four-meter cell that will serve as his bedroom, bathroom, and living area—along with nine or ten other men—for the foreseeable future. The walls are painted a sickly green. Bunk beds line the walls. A narrow window high up in back casts an anemic rectangle of sunshine across the floor. A hole in the floor serves as a toilet. A camera watches from the corner of the ceiling.

Only one of the beds is free—the one closest to the toilet. A few necessities supplied by the facility are laid out there—two thin towels, a set of sheets, a toothbrush, and an enamel cup.

The other inmates are elsewhere—perhaps in one of the reeducation classrooms enduring a lecture about "The Fourteen Principles of Xi Jinping Thought" or singing patriotic songs. Lu sits on the thin cotton mattress, smells the odor of old food, unwashed bodies, and shit. He blows on his frozen fingers; the cell is not heated.

He suddenly feels crushed beneath the weight of despair. He might never get out of this place; might never see Yanyan again. The thread of his life prematurely and unnaturally severed.

Soon he hears the tramp of feet, guards calling out orders, cell doors opening and slamming shut. A guard admits his fellow cellmates, locks the door behind them. A thickset guy comes over and jabs a thumb at his own nose. "I'm Meng Quan." *Mad Dog.* "Boss of this cell. Got it?"

"Sure."

"Say it!"

"You're Meng Quan. Boss of this cell."

"Don't forget. What I say goes. Understand?"

"Understood."

"You cause trouble, and *I* get in trouble. And if *I* get in trouble, I'm going to hurt you."

"I'm not interested in causing trouble."

"What's your name?"

"Lu."

"What're you in for?"

"Nothing. I'm being framed."

Meng Quan smiles, revealing a few missing teeth. "Me, too. Right, boys? We're all being framed."

The others respond with good-natured shouts of, "Me, too!" "I was framed!"

Meng Quan slaps Lu on the shoulder, rocking him a bit. "Keep your nose clean, do what you're told, and we'll get along fine, all right, Qingbai Lu?" This is the nickname by which Lu will be known for the rest of his tenure in Meng Quan's cell: *Lu the Innocent.*

After a barely edible dinner, Lu is finally allowed to make his phone call. He badly wants to call Yanyan back in Raven Valley but calls Ma instead. There is no pretense of privacy—a guard stands watching a few feet away. Lu tells Ma what he knows. She says she's doing everything she can to get him free on bail.

"I need a lawyer," Lu says.

"On it."

"And I need you to call Yanyan for me."

"I'll will. I'll explain everything."

"What can Song do to help?"

"We've talked about it. He's making phone calls, but we're going to have to let this play out. We may have to go through the motions of a trial."

"But that could take months! A year!"

"We can force it through faster than that."

"The case is such bullshit, Xiulan. Can't we just get it dismissed?"

"The procurator has already approved the arrest and indictment."

"What about Gao? Hasn't he cleared me?" There is an unnerving silence on the phone. "Well?"

"He's made a statement that it was you who shot him," Ma says.

"That's ridiculous!"

The guard butts in: "Time's up."

"What are you talking about? I just got here!"

"Time's up!" The guard fingers the baton holstered at his waist.

"I have to go," Lu says into the phone. "Please call Yanyan."

"I will. Keep your chin up."

Lu laughs bitterly and hangs up.

FORTY-SIX

Life in the detention center follows an unvarying routine. An alarm sounds at six thirty. Meng Quan claps his hands and shouts for everyone to get up, giving those who are more difficult to rouse an encouraging kick.

Everyone makes their beds, then stands at attention, shivering in the cold, sometimes for ten minutes or more, while the guards complete a morning head count. Afterward, inmates are let out of their cells to brush their teeth and use the facilities in the cell block's single restroom, which is outfitted with a trough sink, a similar urinal, four holes in the ground for other business, and rough showers. As there are more than a hundred inmates, this process takes a while, and is accompanied by much shoving, complaining, and urging of the inmates in front of the line to hurry up.

Morning toilet complete, the inmates shuffle in sloppy unison outside for a flag-raising ceremony and a rendition of the national anthem played over loudspeakers. This is followed by thirty minutes of physical exercise—a few half-hearted calisthenics and a lot of military-style marching.

Next comes breakfast in the cells—a watery rice gruel with bits of pork fat and bitter vegetables, fried bread, sometimes a turnip. The rest of the day is filled with menial chores and study sessions. The sessions remind Lu of his ideological and political education classes in high school and university. Long, droning affairs. Lu hasn't slept more than an hour at a time since his arrest and fights to stay awake during these lectures, but he sees what happens to those who do not—the instructor points to the offender, and a guard, who is likewise on the verge of dozing, springs to life, strides forward, and doles out a rap with his stick.

As bad as the study sessions are, they pale in comparison to the continued interrogations. These might take place at any time. First thing in the morning, just before bedtime, in the middle of lunch, while you're scrubbing the urinal. A team of guards arrives, calls your name, and hauls you off to a windowless room, where you are locked in a tiger chair and asked question after question for an hour, maybe two, sometimes three. In Lu's case, it's shouted accusations regarding Gao's shooting. It doesn't take Lu long to understand that the guards are essentially reading from a script. They aren't personally acquainted with the case—for all they care, Lu might have been arrested for pissing in a corner of Mao's mausoleum—but their job is to coerce a confession from Lu.

Lu knows better than to confess. And the guards know he knows better, so the interrogations become a pantomime in which they try to break his will, but secretly have low expectations of succeeding. Nevertheless, in his first week of his incarceration, he endures no less than eight interrogations.

One cold afternoon, two guards come to collect Lu. He expects to be taken to yet another windowless cell and interrogated, but instead they escort him into a visiting room, where Ma and a balding, bespectacled man in a rumpled suit wait on the other side of a plexiglass barrier.

There is a phone receiver on either side of the window. Ma picks hers up and motions for Lu to do the same. She smiles through the scratched glass, her voice tinny in Lu's ear. "How are you, Brother Lu?"

"Glad to see you. Otherwise, I have one or two complaints. All right, a *lot* of complaints. Have you spoken to Yanyan?"

"Yes. She understands the situation. She said to tell you . . . to take care of yourself. And, that she loves you."

Lu looks away for a moment. When he has composed himself, he turns back. "And Chief Liang?"

"He said he knows you are an idiot, but there's no way you did what you're accused of."

"Sounds like him."

"Let me introduce you to Mr. Shi—he will act as your lawyer."

Shi takes the phone and has Lu recount the events leading up to Gao's shooting and the shooting itself. Also, what he knows about Gao, Ling Wei, Tang Fuqiang, Chief Xu. As Lu lays it all out, Shi looks increasingly distressed.

He writes furiously on a notepad and stops frequently to mop sweat from his receding hairline.

"What do you think?" Lu says, when he's done.

"I think it's a difficult case."

"How so? I obviously didn't shoot Gao. I mean, there's really no way Xu can prove I did."

"I'm not so sure."

"What do you mean?" Lu is growing agitated.

"He's presented some compelling evidence. A PSB detective witnessed you entering Gao's building just before the shooting."

"Yes—Han. And the shooter must have run right past him on the way out. Maybe even handed off the gun to him."

"That will be quite impossible to prove," Shi says.

"So he just happened to be there at that time?"

"According to Han's statement, you disappeared that morning. Or, to be more exact, you ran away from police escorts who were provided for your convenience and safety."

"*Fei hua!*"

"You didn't run away?" Shi says.

"Yes, all right, I ran away. But those cops were there to spy on us, not keep us safe."

"Their intent," Shi says, "cannot be proven in court. In any case, that morning you visited Gao's apartment. They know this because a camera was installed some weeks ago in Gao's hallway."

"Then they should have video of Kong shutting the door in my face when I left after speaking to Gao—and of the actual shooting later that day!"

"They have footage of your first visit. But the video feed cuts out before the shooting occurred. There is speculation that you somehow disabled it."

"*Ta ma de!* That doesn't even make any sense! Why would I have gone to see Gao, left, and then returned several hours later to murder him?"

Shi shrugs. "I'm not sure. But as their narrative goes, Han and his partner were dispatched to Gao's apartment on the off chance that you would return because they were concerned for your safety. And thus were already on the scene when the shootings took place."

"How convenient. And my motive?"

"You are still bitter about being transferred to Raven Valley and blame Xu. In your quest for revenge, you've tried to pervert this case into one about police corruption. You know of Gao from your time in Harbin, and in a desperate attempt to harm Xu you went there to try to force him to incriminate Xu in some manner. When Gao refused, you shot his health care aide, who was trying to defend him, and then Gao himself."

"A constable third class could clearly tell from the crime scene and position of Kong's body that the shooter fired as soon as the door was opened."

Shi sighs unhappily. "I'm telling you what their report says."

Lu runs a hand across his close-cropped scalp. "All right. But there's no direct proof I shot Gao. No footage or eyewitness account."

"They have the weapon used in the shooting. With your fingerprints."

"I never touched that gun!"

"I don't know what to tell you, Inspector. Perhaps they lifted the prints from something they had—a teacup, for example—and transferred them to the weapon."

"*Tian!*" Lu moans. Then: "I took a GSR test at the hospital."

"And it came back positive for gunshot residue."

"I haven't fired a weapon in months!"

Shi spreads his hands. "But you see what we're dealing with? Motive. Proof you visited the victim earlier in the day. A weapon with your fingerprints. A positive GSR test. Detectives who place you at the scene immediately after the shooting. Gao says you did it. You even had his blood on your clothes. As I said, it's a tough case."

"Very reassuring, Lawyer Shi. When's my execution? Next Tuesday?"

Ma takes the phone from Shi. "I'm afraid there's more bad news."

"How could there possibly be *more*?"

"Given the fact that someone has been arrested and confessed to Pang's murder, our investigation is officially closed. And I am not allowed to directly involve myself in your case due to a conflict of interest. In fact, I'm currently under disciplinary review for bringing you aboard, given . . . the outcome."

"*Cao,*" Lu mutters.

"Of course, Deputy Director Song and I believe you are innocent. We'll do what we can behind the scenes. But . . ." It's not necessary for her to finish her sentence—Lu gets the point.

"What about the guy who says he killed Pang?" Lu asks. "No doubt he's just some patsy Xu and company have drummed up. Maybe he's got a gambling debt he can't repay or they're threatening to kill his family. If we can get to him and force him to tell the truth . . ." Lu sees the expression on Ma's face. "What?"

"The suspect committed suicide in his cell several nights ago."

"You mean someone murdered him!"

"Probably. But we have no way of proving it."

"That odious prick Xu has me pinned to a wall like a butterfly."

"I wish I had better news."

"That makes two of us."

FORTY-SEVEN

Days bleed into weeks. Lu's despair deepens. Some nights, it's all he can do to keep from dashing his brains out against a wall.

Meng Quan runs the cell like a petty king, distributing chores, mediating conflict, extracting tribute. Lu does as he's told without complaint. His fellow inmates keep digging for the reason why Lu is incarcerated, and he finally tells them he was arrested for murder but is innocent. Most of them are there for far less serious crimes—theft, gang activity, attempted rape, extortion. Lu's murder rap earns him a touch of deference, as if it's assumed he did it and is lying about it after the fact.

When asked what he did "on the outside" for work, Lu says he was in sales for a beer distributor. It's an odd enough gig that he's unlikely to encounter anyone in the same industry, and he knows enough about beer to lend himself an air of credibility.

Three afternoons a week, weather permitting, inmates are let into a yard for some exercise. Lu usually takes a brisk walk, stretches, moves around, but avoids practicing any martial arts—he doesn't want to make himself a target for any tough guys looking to scrap. Most of the other inmates are attached to some group or another, generally whatever gang they belonged to on the outside. Lu skirts around the edges of these affiliations, not wishing to be part of any particular crew, but also aware that loners are easy pickings for abuse.

Before long, Lu notices he's getting some unwanted attention from a couple guys from another cell on the block. Both are sizable customers, one bald and missing half an ear, the other with a huge Buddha tattooed across his ample belly. They circle him during yard time like sharks. One pass, then another; then a third. They don't say anything, they don't make a move to touch him, but their dark looks communicate a palpable sense of menace. Lu doesn't call them out—he's not looking for a confrontation—but later he asks Meng Quan if he knows who they are.

"The bald one's called Ha and the one with the Buddha on his stomach is called Heng."

Lu recognizes these names as having been borrowed from the two guardian statues usually found outside Buddhist temples—fierce-looking warriors who, despite the pacifism of the Buddhist faith, are vested with the authority to use violence to combat evil. Ha is depicted with his mouth open, and Heng, mouth closed.

"I guess Ha does all the talking," Lu says.

Meng Quan laughs. "You got that right."

"They've been giving me the eye."

"Oh? Best watch out. They are a pair of real bastards."

"What do they have against me?"

"Not sure. Maybe they think you're pretty. I'll ask around."

Two days later, Lu wakes in the night, sensing movement in the dark. Before he can react, rough hands grip his wrists and ankles, drag him to the floor, press him down, cover his mouth. Lu struggles, but there are too many to fight. He feels a sharp point jabbing into his throat.

"Be still!" Meng Quan hisses. "Or I'll slit your throat."

Lu stops struggling.

"I heard a rumor," Meng Quang whispers. "That you're a cop."

Ta ma de.

"Is that true?"

Lu considers. Will saying yes make Meng Quan more or less inclined to murder him? He finally gives a short nod.

Someone says: "A fucking cop!" Another says: "Kill him!"

"Shut up!" Meng Quan growls.

"I can explain," Lu whispers.

"Good," Meng Quan says. "Quietly."

Lu knows the next words out of his mouth will determine whether he lives or dies. "I told you the truth. I was framed for murder. By the chief of Harbin Homicide."

Meng Quang laughs. "Framed by another cop? That's rich. Well, I'm not partial to cops, even ones who claim they were framed."

"Don't kill me. I can help you."

"Help me?" Meng Quan laughs again. "Says the man lying on the floor with a shiv held to his neck."

"I have friends in high places. The Ministry of Public Security."

"Bullshit. If that were true, would you even be here?"

"I told you," Lu says. "I was framed. It will take some time for my friends to work things out. But they will. And when I'm free . . ."

"What?" Meng Quan scoffs. "You'll get us all pardoned?"

"No. I can get you lawyers. Look into your cases."

"Don't bother. We're all guilty. Of something. Besides, if I kill you now, I'll earn a hundred cigarettes. That's pretty good!"

"What are you talking about?"

"That's the bounty on your head, Qingbai Lu. A hundred cigarettes. That's how I knew you were a cop."

"I'll send you a case. That's ten thousand cigarettes."

"A hundred cigarettes guaranteed, versus ten thousand promised. Hmm . . ."

"You don't like cops, right? Well, I'm going to take a lot of them down. Nangang PSB, Harbin Homicide. Some of them might even end up in here for a spell. It would be open season."

Meng Quan *pffts*.

"Xu—head of Homicide," Lu says, hoping the name will register. "No? Chief Hong, Nangang PSB? How about some guy who goes by Pangu? Detective Han?"

"Han!" someone mutters in the dark. "Big guy? Used to be in the Vice Division?"

Lu doesn't know if Han used to be in Vice. And Han is a common enough name. But he's getting a positive reaction, so: "That's right. He's part of it, too."

Lu feels the tip of the shiv lift away. "I know Han," Meng Quan says. "He knocked out two of my teeth."

"Sounds like something he'd do. Last year, he even attacked me. I used his own sap on him. Hit him behind the ear. Knocked him clear into the Ming Dynasty."

Meng Quan laughs. "Is that right?" He sits back on his haunches. "All right, boys, let him up."

Someone protests. Meng Quan tells them to shut up. Bodies climb off Lu. He sits up and massages his rib cage. "Thank you."

"You owe me," Meng Quan says. "Ten thousand cigarettes. And not that cheap Chinese shit. I want Marlboros."

"Deal."

"Everyone go to bed."

The inmates shuffle back to their bunks.

Lu touches his throat to see if there's any blood. His finger comes away dry. "Who put the bounty on my head? Did you get a name?"

"Why should I tell you?"

"Because I'm going to kill whoever it was."

"Good luck with that. You know this guy?" Meng Quan makes a fist and then moves it in a downward stabbing motion.

"I don't understand."

"Ice Pick Brother. Heard of him?"

"Can't say I have."

"He's a gangster. Part of the Big Circle Boys. Untouchable."

"Nobody's untouchable."

"Sure, Qingbai Lu." Meng Quan claps Lu on the shoulder. "In the meantime, best watch your ass. I'm holding out for my ten thousand cigarettes, but a lot of the other guys in here aren't as greedy. A hundred will do them just fine. Get some sleep. Tomorrow you're on toilet detail."

Lu climbs into his bunk. Meng Quan does the same. Lu sees the last inmate standing has a small broom that he's holding up to the ceiling to block the camera lens. Once Meng Quan and Lu are lying down, he lowers the broom and gets into his own bunk.

Before long, the cell is filled with the sounds of snoring men. Lu does not sleep the rest of the night.

FORTY-EIGHT

Lu's life is not the only thing hanging on a razor's edge—so, too, is Dr. Ma's career.

Lu's arrest prompts a disciplinary review at the Ministry of Public Security. Ma is temporarily suspended from duty, pending a hearing—and forced not only to prepare a case in her defense for bringing Lu onboard the investigation, but also against rumors of an affair between them.

Deputy Director Song, her direct superior, is also not immune from the scandal. His boss, the director general of the Criminal Investigation Bureau, calls him onto the carpet and demands answers. Song, uncowed, vociferously defends both Ma and Lu.

The director general is neither satisfied nor convinced: "This is a great loss of face! And a public relations disaster. Even if what you say is true—and your claim of a conspiracy is not only outlandish, but difficult to prove—the optics for us are catastrophic. Dr. Ma will certainly receive a demerit, perhaps a demotion. That's assuming she's found innocent of charges of malfeasance and negligence. I suggest you cut off all contact with her until this plays out."

"What about Inspector Lu, sir?" Song asks. "If he's innocent—"

"That is out of your hands. What I said about Ma goes double for him."

"Isn't there anything you can do?"

"I'm doing it. Keeping my head down as the shrapnel flies past!"

Song knows the only way to save Ma's career—and Lu's life—is to prove Lu's innocence. But, given the case against Lu, and the lack of concrete evidence indicating corruption in Nangang, that is an exceedingly tall order.

Despite the potential political fallout it may entail, Song makes an unofficial trip to Harbin and pays Xu a visit. They sit in Xu's office, where Xu, seated in his ostentatious chair, looks down on Song like a petty king.

Song notes the presence of an ashtray on the coffee table. "It is permitted to smoke in here?"

"Not really. But I find smoking clears the mind, so I do on occasion." Xu gets up and switches on the air purifier. It whooshes soothingly.

Song removes a pack from his pocket. "Chunghwa?"

"No, thanks." Xu resumes his throne and takes out a pack of Marlboro Reds.

Both men light up.

"I am here to discuss Lu Fei's case," Song says.

"I figured. I know you have some affection for him and that he even saved your life on one occasion. But I am sure you are also aware of his deep-seated animosity for me. Sadly, it's clear he's just gone off the deep end in search of revenge, even resorting to attempted murder."

"If it's you he's after, wouldn't it be easier to just shoot *you,* rather than this man Gao Yang?"

"It's not my death he's after, Deputy Director. It's my humiliation. Disgrace. Downfall."

Song brushes ash off his pants leg. "To be clear, you deny that there is a killer at large in Nangang District who's targeting various officials?"

"If you're referring to the man who murdered Mayor Pang, we caught him and he confessed."

"And then hung himself in his cell."

Xu shrugs. "It happens."

Song is not in the mood for games. He leans forward and points with his cigarette. "There's no way Lu shot that old man. You're railroading him, pure and simple."

Xu's expression hardens. "Prove it, Deputy Director. Otherwise . . . I'm busy. If there is no other business to discuss?"

Song stands. Xu follows suit. Song is the taller of the two, a fact that Xu seems to have forgotten. As Song takes a step toward him, some of Xu's bravado dissipates.

"Tell you what, Xu," Song says. "Ask your friend Gao to change his tune.

When Lu's released, I'll make sure he fucks off back to Raven Valley and never bothers you again. Then you and your boys can deal with whatever's really going on behind the scenes here by yourselves. I'm sure it will end badly for you either way, regardless of Lu's involvement."

"That sounds like an attempt to subvert justice, Deputy Director. Shameful a man in your position would make such a suggestion. Perhaps I should record our conversation next time."

"Have it your way, Xu." Song takes a last drag of his cigarette. "But make no mistake, you just made yourself an enemy. And I'm going to crush you like . . ." He drops his cigarette to the carpet and grinds it under his shoe. "Like *that*. I'll show myself out."

FORTY-NINE

Two nights later, after dinner, a pair of guards come for Lu. "Get your stuff and come with us," one says.

"Where to?" Lu asks, immediately wary.

"Don't ask questions, Eight-nine-three-four-five. Just do as you're told!"

Lu exchanges a look with Meng Quan. Meng shrugs.

The guard draws his club. "Don't make me ask again."

Lu has no belongings apart from a toothbrush, a cup, and a change of clothes. He collects these items and says goodbye to his cellmates. They start to clap—Lu realizes they think he's been released.

Is it true? He follows the guards down the corridor, not daring to believe it. Inmates in the other cells pick up on the clapping, adding their own, until one of the guards tells them to quiet down.

So—maybe not.

The guards take Lu to see the warden. The warden is waiting at his desk, drinking tea. A TV plays in the corner of the room. An evening musical variety show. Lu stands at attention.

"Word is going around you've been made as a cop," the warden says. "That means your life is in danger. I'm transferring you to solitary for your own safety."

"I'd feel safer with my cellmates."

The warden laughs. "You've made friends, eh? Good for you. But your cellmates, like ninety-nine-point-nine percent of the detainees here, are a bunch of liars, thieves, and cutthroats. And apparently there's a bounty on your head. I don't want you killed in my facility, so—solitary confinement."

The guards lead Lu through several locked doors, into a different wing of the facility, and finally into a block lined on either side with half a dozen small cells furnished with a single bed, a sink, and a hole in the floor.

As Lu is marched down to the far end, he can't help but notice only two of the other cells are currently occupied—one by the man called Ha, and the other by Heng.

"Wait," Lu says.

"Get inside," one of the guards says, opening the door to the last cell.

"Those men—"

"Don't worry about them. They're locked up."

"But—"

"Are you going to give us trouble?" the guard says. "Because if you do, we'll put you in the 'culture room' and let you stew for a few days."

Lu hasn't been to the culture room, but he's heard horror stories about it—inmates strapped into a tiger chair so tightly their hands and feet swell dangerously, left in the dark to piss themselves, no food, no water. Sometimes the guards "season the air" by giving it a good dose of pepper spray. Sometimes they shock you with a Taser in the arms, the nipples, the testicles.

Inmates have been known to go mad from this treatment.

Lu reluctantly shuffles into the cell. The guard shuts the door and locks it by means of an old-fashioned metal key, then he and his partner depart, the sound of their shoes slapping on cold, hard cement.

Lu places his cup and toothbrush in the sink. He makes the bed with rough sheets. In due course, there is a click and the light goes off.

For security reasons, it's never full dark inside the detention facility. As Lu stands at the barred door of his cell, he can see the dark mouth of the cell opposite, the faint outline of the empty cot, the dull gleam of the steel sink. He hears the distant clanging of heavy doors; a trickle of water; a dry cough, from either Ha or Heng. After a moment he returns to the cot, sits, takes his shoes off, lies down.

Nothing to do now but sleep.

Time passes. Hard to say how long without the benefit of a clock or watch. Lu hears a screech. The sound of metal hinges. He sits up.

Now whispers, echoing off the floor and walls. Footsteps. Approaching.

Lu puts his shoes back on. He stands and faces the cell door.

Ha and Heng materialize out of the gloom. Ha carries a sheet that has been twisted into a makeshift rope. Heng carries a key. He fits the key into the lock on Lu's door and twists.

"Don't do it, boys," Lu says.

Heng opens the door and comes through. Lu thrusts his fingers toward Heng's eyes. Heng reacts by throwing up his hands. Lu kicks him between the legs. Simple, direct, devastating. Only it doesn't work. Heng grunts but doesn't go down. A shooting pain travels up Lu's leg.

Lu has heard of some old kung masters who train to take blows to the groin or carry heavy weights from their genitals. To Lu, such a skill is an example of one in which "the juice is not worth the squeeze."

When Heng stops to adjust something in his pants, Lu understands he doesn't have iron balls—he's just got some sort of protective cup in there. Cheating bastard.

Lu retreats, but there's nowhere to go. He attacks Heng with an old standard. Jab, cross, left hook. The cross and hook get through, but Heng just grunts and lashes out with his own flailing strikes. Lu covers up—the impact of the blows sends him careening around the cell. Heng snatches at Lu's shirt, ripping the sturdy cotton fabric. Lu pummels his midsection. Heng lifts Lu off his feet and slams him hard against the wall, drops him, wraps his thick hands around Lu's neck, and squeezes. Lu pries at Heng's fingers and wrists. Air whistles in his throat. Black spots crowd his vision. Lu finds one of Heng's eye sockets with a thumb, digs in. Heng shouts, turns his head away. Lu slaps Heng's arms aside, claps his palms to Heng's ears, elbows him in the jaw.

Heng stiffens and tips over onto the cot.

Before Lu can reset, Ha's hammer-like fist comes in hot. Lu covers up. Ha's knuckles thud into Lu's shoulder and his head ricochets off the wall. His knees buckle. Ha loops the makeshift rope around Lu's neck, succeeds in getting it halfway down Lu's face, cinches it tight. The rough fabric bites painfully into Lu's mouth and jaw. Lu stomps Ha's foot, to no effect. Ha twists the rope tighter, drags Lu out of the cell, worries him back and forth like a dog with a chew toy.

Lu rams the heel of his hand into Ha's groin. He feels only a hard object there, same as with Heng. He reaches down and grabs the inside of Ha's thigh with his fingertips, pinches *hard*. Ha squeals and his grip on the sheet momentarily slackens. Lu wraps an arm around Ha's waist, steps in ass-first, throws Ha over his hip. It's sloppy, but that works to Lu's advantage—Ha hits the floor headfirst. Lies there, stunned.

Lu steps back, untwists the sheet from around his neck, works his jaw open and shut to see if it still works.

He hears movement and turns just as Heng bursts from the cell. Lu whips the end of the sheet into his face. Heng's head snaps back. Lu steps out at an angle, kicks the side of Heng's knee, follows up with a left cross and an uppercut that aims for the moon.

For a second time, Heng stiffens and goes down—a giant oak, felled by a well-placed ax.

Now Ha groans and rolls to his hands and knees. Lu spins around behind him, loops the sheet over Ha's neck, grips it like a pair of reins. Ha bucks. Lu slides his feet inside Ha's hips, rides his back. Ha lurches up. Lu drops his feet to the floor, kicks out the back of Ha's knee, yanks on the sheet. Ha falls on his butt. Lu drags him backward into the cell.

Once inside, Lu puts a knee between Ha's shoulder blades and pulls hard on the sheet. Ha's thick fingers scrabble frantically at the fabric. He gurgles. Lu keeps the tension on until Ha's arms go limp. A few more seconds for good measure, and he releases the sheet.

Lu hears Heng moan. *Ta ma de!* As soon as one goes down, the other gets up. Lu steps over Ha's prone body, exits the cell, reaches down, grabs Heng's ear, and twists. Heng cries out and clutches at Lu's wrist. Lu forces him up and into the cell, like a bull with a ring in its nose. He gives Ha a sharp kick in the ass for good measure, then hops outside the cell and slams the door. The key is still in the lock. Lu twists it, pulls it out, slips it into his pocket.

Ha sits up and rubs his chafed neck. Heng spits blood. Lu takes a moment to catch his breath. "Who paid you to kill me?"

"Your mother," Ha growls hoarsely.

Pretty much the answer Lu was expecting. He unzips his pants and aims a stream of piss through the bars of the door.

Ha and Heng shout angrily. Lu arcs the stream high and waves it back and forth to reach as much of cell as he can. Ha and Heng climb onto the cot like rats seeking higher ground. Lu finishes and zips up. "Sleep well, boys."

He walks down to an empty cell near the door and stretches out on the bare cot there. Ha and Heng shout abuse until they can shout no more, and then fall silent.

FIFTY

A pair of guards enter at six thirty the next morning to find Lu in an open cell, Ha and Heng in a closed one. Lu tells them his side of the story. Heng and Ha lie their asses off. The guards lock Lu up and leave; Lu can't be sure they aren't in on the whole thing. They return fifteen minutes later with reinforcements and take Lu, Ha, and Heng to separate rooms for interrogation. Lu recounts the night's events several times, doing his best to hold together the tattered edges of his waning patience.

The warden arrives in time for Lu's fourth retelling. Afterward, he sits back in his chair and lets out a long, aggrieved sigh.

"I thought the idea was to move me for my own protection," Lu complains. "If I didn't know better, I'd say you were angling for a hundred cigarettes."

"Don't take that tone with me," the warden barks.

"Isn't there a camera in the solitary block?"

"Yes. But . . ."

"Let me guess. It was on the blink."

"I run a straight ship," the warden says. "I'll get to the bottom of this. If there was foul play, heads will roll."

"Unless it is possible for a human to shit out a perfectly functional metal key," Lu says, "I'd say the chances of foul play are rather high."

Later that day, Lu is returned to the same cell block. The guards attempt to put Lu back in his original cell, but he protests. "That one smells like piss."

Lu remains in solitary for the next two weeks. He waits anxiously for the next attempt on his life. But, while a handful of inmates pass through, none of them try to murder Lu in the night.

There is no further word from the warden. No mention of the attack, a subsequent investigation, disciplinary actions. And, of course, no apology.

As for Heng and Ha, perhaps they've been sent to another cell block, or even another facility. Lu does not see them again.

The wheels of justice grind slowly in the People's Republic. But in some circumstances, such as particularly heinous or notorious crimes, the process can be quite speedy. Arrest, trial, sentencing, in quick order. Lu's case falls into this category.

One morning, Lu is brought to the visiting room for a meeting with Lawyer Shi. Shi informs him the trial will begin in two days' time. "It will be presided over by the president of the Nangang People's Court," Shi says. "His name is Ren. He's what American Westerns used to call a 'hanging judge.'"

"Don't sugarcoat things, Shi, give it to me straight."

Shi spreads his hands. "I'll do my best for you, but the odds are stacked against us. You're not a Christian, by any chance?"

"I'm a servant of the state, and therefore an atheist."

"Then I'll say a prayer on your behalf."

The trial is a straightforward affair. It takes place in a small room with a few rows of seats in the back for observers. Lu stands at a podium, facing a long bench where the presiding judge, Ren, and two "people's representatives" sit. Together, these three will hear the evidence and issue a verdict.

The people's representatives are a man and woman in their fifties. Unlike Judge Ren, who is wearing a black judge's robe, they wear regular business attire. Lu doesn't recognize either of them, but assumes they are someone connected to Xu's *guanxi* network and understand their role is to find him guilty as charged.

The procurator presents evidence, including statements by Han placing Lu at the scene of the crime, Lu's fingerprints on the gun, his positive GSR test, and, most damning of all, Gao's statement that Lu was the one who murdered Kong and shot him.

Lawyer Shi has the right to cross-examine witnesses—but Judge Ren determines Gao and Han's statements are sufficient, which is within his authority, and so neither bothers to show up at the trial.

Deputy Director Song, Constable Sun, Chief Liang, and Luo Yanyan all watch from the benches. Dr. Ma does not make an appearance—as per Song's advice—but has submitted a statement verifying some of the anomalies and suspicions she and Lu uncovered during the investigation of Pang's homicide

Naturally, Judge Ren rules that her statement is unsubstantiated hearsay and bars it from being entered into the court records.

In the end, the verdict is a foregone conclusion: guilty.

Given the crime, the sentence should come as no surprise, but even so, hearing it spoken by Judge Ren sucks the very oxygen from Lu's lungs.

Death.

Lu hears someone—maybe Yanyan—cry out. Lawyer Shi manages to get a quick word in before Lu is hustled out a side door by the court policemen: "We can appeal."

"Don't bother," Lu says, and then he is gone.

FIFTY-ONE

Post-trial, Lu is transported to his new long-term place of incarceration, Harbin Prison. He's placed in a cell block much like the one in at the detention facility, with the exception that his fellow inmates are all on some form of death row, pending appeals or commutation to life in prison.

The atmosphere here is a bit laxer; the guards recognize most of the inmates have nothing left to lose, so threats of consequences for rule-breaking have little effect. The inmates spend most of their days sitting around, smoking cigarettes, chatting, or just thinking silent thoughts. As Lu has already been convicted and sentenced, there is no longer the need for periodic interrogations.

It is now dead winter—the prison grounds, or at least the narrow swath of them that can be seen of them through the windows, are covered with snow. Lunar New Year is just around the corner. A time of renewal and fresh beginnings.

Even for the men in Harbin Prison, who have little hope for the future, there is an incipient sense of excitement. If nothing else, there will be a performance of singing, dancing, and skits by some of the prisoners, and a fresh orange or some other treat to enliven their dull, unappetizing meals.

A week or so after Lu's transfer, Song throws his weight around and secures a visit. He brings Yanyan with him and stands off in the distance for a moment, giving them as much privacy as is available to a condemned prisoner. Lu is overjoyed to see Yanyan—but she can't stop sobbing. Watching her in distress, unable to reach through the plexiglass to touch her, is among the hardest things he's ever had to do.

"It'll be all right," Lu says. "Song and Ma will think of some way to help me."

Yanyan mops her eyes and nods. "Yes. And when you get out . . . maybe we can plan a wedding?"

Now it is Lu's turn to mop his eyes. Song comes over and takes the receiver. He tells Lu an appeal has been filed, a new trial date set. "Don't lose hope, Lu Fei. We are doing our best for you."

Two days later, Lawyer Shi arrives for a pretrial meeting. He doesn't have much in the way of fresh legal strategies. Lu can't really blame him. The case against him is as tight as a lead-lined sarcophagus.

Shi does have one interesting piece of news. "I received a phone call at my office. No caller ID, and the man did not give his name. He said he had an important letter for you and asked that I hand-deliver it. I agreed. The letter appeared in my mailbox a few days later."

Shi passes the letter to a guard, who inspects it and then brings it to Lu.

Lu breaks the seal and removes a single piece of paper. It reads:

Lu Fei

As the saying goes, "a candle lights the way for others, but is itself consumed." This might well sum up your situation—in attempting to right wrongs and seek justice, you are now on the verge of being snuffed out.

Admittedly, I bear a heavy responsibility for your plight. In my youth, I was a greedy, arrogant, and immoral man. And I attracted men of similar low character to me like a magnet.

Now, I am old and all I desire is to live out my few remaining days with a modicum of dignity and comfort. Knowing those few who I still care for are safe.

Which brings me to our current predicament.

Know this—I only accused you because I was left with no other choice. The person I value most in the world is being held against her will. She is the reason I provided testimony against you.

I am told she will be released when your appeal is denied, and your fate finally sealed.

But I would be foolish to leave her well-being in the hands of men who have proven themselves so disloyal and untrustworthy.

So, here is my proposal. I will recant my testimony. I will tell them the real shooter was a boy in a motorcycle helmet, and that you, in fact, saved me. There will be questions, of course. I will explain them away as best I am able—an old man, in shock, befuddled, and coerced by the police who were seeking a quick end to the case.

I cannot tell the whole truth—not yet.

But once the person being held against her will is free, I will reveal everything I know. The names of all the parties concerned. Past misdeeds. The current plot against you, as I understand it.

My recanting should be sufficient to secure your release. As soon as that happens, you must engineer a daring rescue without delay. Swear that you will do this, and I will call for your release forthwith.

I feel regretful that my past actions have contributed to your distress. And that I must now come before you, hat in hand, begging for help, using your very life as leverage. But desperate times call for desperate measures.

Should you agree to my proposal, call the number below. There are men who stand ready to help you in this quest. Good luck.

There is no signature at the bottom of the letter, but Lu doesn't need one. "Write this down," he tells Lawyer Shi. He recites the phone number. "The moment you leave here, go buy a prepaid phone. Call that number. I doubt anyone will answer, but just leave a message. Say 'Lu agrees.' Got that?"

"What's this about?"

"Just do it. Please. Then throw the phone away."

Lu spends another few days twisting in the wind. No word from Lawyer Shi. No way to know if Gao has done what he said he was going to do. But one morning, following breakfast, he is informed by a guard that he has fifteen minutes to gather his belongings.

Lu's first thought is that the order for his execution has been finalized, damn his appeal. He wonders what method will be used—shooting or lethal injection. Nowadays, lethal injection is favored. Less mess. There are even portable "execution vans," which provide a cheaper and cleaner alternative to transferring condemned prisoners to a special facility.

Lu pictures himself being led through the corridors of the prison, out a back door, and into a police bus that bears no special markings. Inside will be a slide-out bed with straps. Cameras to record the proceedings. A technician will insert a needle. A prison official will press a button. Quick. Easy.

Afterward, a prison physician might remove Lu's heart, lungs, kidneys. It's a billion-dollar business. U.S. dollars, not yuan.

"Where am I going?" Lu asks the guard.

"I don't know, just pack your stuff."

"I'm packed." Lu doesn't, in fact, have any belongings to speak of.

"Then sit on your bed and wait."

It is another thirty minutes before a guard comes to collect him. He's taken to an administrative area, where he's processed, the belongings confiscated from him upon arrest returned (phone, keys, wallet), and he's allowed to change into his old clothes, including the PROPERTY OF RIKERS hoodie—still stiff with Gao's blood.

He signs some papers and is let out into the parking lot.

It's freezing out, but the sun is shining. Lu squints against the glare. He smells car exhaust. His feet crunch on dirty snow. He's out. Alive. He starts walking, fast, just in case they realize they've made a mistake and come back for him.

No one has been notified of his release, so no one is there to greet him.

Lu turns on his phone—delighted to find it still has power—and calls a car service. He sends texts: to Yanyan, Song, Ma, Lawyer Shi. A stream of responses quickly flood in. He doesn't read them. It's too overwhelming. He turns off his phone.

The car arrives and Lu goes to the train station. He purchases a ticket for Raven Valley, and while he waits for its departure, he buys a bowl of noodles from a food stand, eats the first real meal he's had for weeks. He washes it down with a beer, even though it's not yet noon. He wants another, but resists. He hasn't had alcohol since his arrest and doesn't want to find himself unexpectedly drunk so far from home.

The train arrives, Lu boards. He reads the texts on his phone as he rides. He tells Yanyan he'll be back in Raven Valley that afternoon. Lawyer Shi confirms he has been notified that Gao recanted his accusation and essentially cleared Lu of the shooting. There is some confusion regarding the rest of the evidence presented against him, but given Gao's statement, a judge—not Ren—ruled Lu must be released.

Lu arrives in Raven Valley, takes a car service to his apartment, goes upstairs, showers, and calls Yanyan. She buzzes from downstairs twenty minutes later. He lets her up and when he opens the door, she wraps her arms around him and squeezes. Then, wiping away tears, she leads him to the bed.

She tugs off his shirt and runs her hand across his stomach. "Didn't they feed you in there?"

"Steak and cognac every night."

"Idiot." She kisses him and pulls him down on top of her.

Afterward, they lay sore and spent. "What happens now?" Yanyan asks.

"Paperwork. Filing of motions of dismissal. I don't know. Lawyer stuff."

"But you're free?"

Lu thinks of the bargain he's made with Gao. "More or less."

"And now that the case is dismissed, you'll get your job back?"

"I don't see why I wouldn't."

Yanyan nestles herself into Lu's shoulder. "Maybe you should retire. Help me run the bar. You're always getting into trouble. I don't think I can take it anymore."

"I'd drink all your stock."

"Probably."

"Remember what you told me when you came to visit me in prison?"

"Yes. I said to dry your hair after you take a shower so you don't catch cold."

Lu playfully flicks her ear with his finger. "The other thing."

"Sorry, I have short-term memory loss."

"You said we'd plan a wedding."

"I did? I must have been delirious."

"Yanyan . . ."

She laughs. "All right." She props herself on an elbow and kisses him. "A promise is a promise."

FIFTY-TWO

After Yanyan leaves to go open the Red Lotus. Lu lies in bed, loath to part from its warmth and Yanyan's lingering scent. Finally, duty calls.

He dresses and goes downstairs and walks to a nearby convenience store, where he buys a prepaid burner phone. Back in his apartment, he cracks open a bottle of beer, pours himself a glass, drinks deeply, then calls the number he's memorized. As expected, no one answers. He leaves a voice mail: "It's me. I'm out and ready to get to work."

The call comes thirty minutes later. A man whose voice he does not recognize. Heilongjiang accent. "Where can we meet? Can you come to Harbin?"

"I'd rather not."

"We'll meet you partway, then."

"We?"

"There are two of us."

"Is the other one Gao?"

"No."

They agree on a service area off the expressway a few kilometers beyond the outskirts of Harbin. Lu doesn't want to deal with Chief Liang just yet, so instead of taking one of the PSB patrol vehicles, he rents a car and drives there, arriving in the early evening. He parks outside a large food court—the appointed meeting place—and watches the entrance for about twenty minutes. He has no idea what he's looking for, so he gives up and goes inside. He buys a cup of tea and sits at a corner table, away from other patrons.

He sees a few families, and three or four men sitting by themselves, having a quick meal or hot drink. Five minutes pass. Two of the men stand, as if by some unspoken signal, and walk over to Lu's table. One is tall and the other is short. Lu is certain he has never laid eyes on either of them before tonight.

"Good evening, Inspector," the tall one says. "May we sit?"

Lu gestures for them to do so.

"You can call me Zhang," the tall one says. "And you can call my partner Li."

"All right, Zhang and Li."

Zhang turns to make sure none of the other patrons can overhear. "Tang Fuqiang is holding Ling Wei against her will at his compound in Nangang District. Tang said he'd release Ling when your death sentence was upheld on appeal, but Gao doesn't trust him."

"Then why did he make a statement that I shot him in the first place?"

"He was in the hospital. Defenseless. Bullied by Xu's thugs. Tang had Ling in his clutches. What was he to do?"

"Now he's come to his senses, is that it?"

"Once he was out of the hospital and had space to consider, he concluded that Tang and Xu would wait a suitable amount of time after you were dead, then murder him as well and make it look like an accident, or a heart attack."

"I'm guessing he doesn't know that Ling and Tang are a couple?"

Zhang laughs. "They are not a couple."

"Really?" Lu scoffs. "He owns her apartment, and she lives there rent-free. I'm sure he gets *something* in return."

Li speaks for the first time: "Know your enemy, and even if you fight a hundred battles you won't lose."

This is a slight misquote of Sun Zi, but Lu gets the picture. "So, Ling was a spy for Gao, is that it?"

"Tang lusts after Ling," Zhang says. "She used his lust to control him. But they were not romantic partners. As much as Tang wishes they were. And Gao did not know—she kept this arrangement from him so he wouldn't fret."

"I don't understand. Didn't she divorce Gao the moment he was arrested? So what's her game?"

"Gao instructed her to divorce him," Zhang says. "For her own protection. Otherwise, she'd be caught up in his prosecution. But she still cares for Gao. And has always, in her own way, sought to watch over him."

"Has Ling secretly been in contact with Gao all this time?"

Zhang shakes his head. "Before the shooting, she hadn't spoken to Mr. Gao or laid eyes on him since he was detained all those years ago. As was necessary to make her repudiation of him look genuine."

"And now?"

"Now circumstances have changed. And Tang must be dealt with for both Ling and Gao's sake."

"Why hasn't Tang killed her already, since Gao rescinded his statement against me?"

"I told you," Zhang says. "Tang is in love with Ling Wei. He won't kill her. But . . . there's no telling what other things he might do to her."

That thought turns Lu's stomach. "Who are you two to Gao and Ling?"

"I was Gao's bodyguard before he went to prison," Zhang says. "Old Li here was his driver."

Lu looks at the two men. He estimates them both to be in their early fifties. They don't look like the hardened killers he knows them to be. "And the assaults and murders? Gao's revenge for what? Going to jail while others did not? And you two did the dirty work because why? Personal loyalty?"

"Are you inquiring as a policeman? Is it your intention to arrest us on suspicion of those crimes?" Zhang leans in. "Or are you here to help us free Ling and get your own revenge on Tang Fuqiang? And Xu. You want Xu brought to justice, don't you?"

"I'm not a fan of your brand of justice. The Five Punishments went out of style a long time ago."

"I'm not sure what you're referring to, Inspector."

"I'm referring to boiling Mayor Pang like a potato."

Zhang makes a face. Regret or disgust or annoyance, Lu can't be sure. "Do you intend to keep your end of the bargain or not?" Zhang says. "Time is of the essence. Tang will use Ling as leverage to pull Gao out of hiding, and then he will kill him. Gao can only hold out for so long."

"Let's assume Ling is rescued and Gao goes public with what he knows," Lu says. "Names, dates, criminal offenses. He knows this might send him back to prison?"

"It might, it might not," Zhang says. "He's already done five years. He can make a deal with the provincial procuratorate."

"And you think his testimony will be sufficient to net fish as big as Tang and Xu?"

"Not just his testimony," Zhang says. "There are also tapes."

"Tapes?"

"You see, the Little Red Palace—"

"The what?"

"That's what Tang calls his compound. The Little Red Palace."

"Cute."

"Yes. It's not only Tang's home, but also a brothel and casino. And Tang has the rooms where his girls service clients under surveillance. At some time or another, most everyone in Tang's circle has been caught on video doing something . . . indiscreet."

"Including Tang?"

"Of course not. But you can bet Xu's on those tapes, as is the man who handed you a death sentence, Judge Ren. That should clear your reputation, don't you think?"

"It won't hurt."

"Tang saves the juiciest footage on hard drives. He even labels them for easy reference. 'Chancellor Du, Harbin Technical Institute.' 'Chairman Yao of Harbin Steel.' 'Chief Xu, Harbin Homicide.'" Zhang smiles. "Tang is nothing if not meticulous."

"And you know all this how?"

"The compound was built when Mr. Gao and Tang were still friendly. Gao helped provide construction permits. He knows everything about the place. It was he who suggested the hidden cameras. For a rainy day."

"Is Gao on any of the tapes? Is that what this operation is really about?"

"No," Zhang says firmly. "Mr. Gao was faithful to Ling Wei."

Lu grunts skeptically.

"Doubt if you want to," Zhang says. "Once inside, you can see for yourself."

"All right—so we get inside and steal the tapes. Then what?"

"Not all the tapes, just the relevant ones. We'll make copies, send them to the provincial authorities. And your contacts at the CIB. If we spread the manure wide enough, it will produce a fertile crop."

"Unless the authorities decide it's not in their best interests to let those tapes ever see the light of day," Lu says.

"You're quite the pessimist, aren't you, Inspector Lu?"

"I'm a realist."

"The authorities may well engage in a cover-up, but they'll still move to arrest and prosecute whoever's on those tapes. Quietly, perhaps, but they'll do it. The very real possibility of word getting out will force their hands. And . . . we'll help them along by leaking snippets of the tapes to the press."

"The press will suppress the story. Censors would never let them get away with doing a story on the corruption of an entire district government."

"Maybe so," Zhang allows. "Or maybe we can find a journalist willing to risk it for fame and fortune."

Lu grunts. "Is it just supposed to be the three of us? Please say no."

"Just us three."

"Against how many?" Lu asks.

"Tang has a security detail of about ten men. Guards posted at the front and back gates, at the the entrances to the residence, and one in a control booth where surveillance cameras are monitored, a couple watching things inside."

"Armed?"

"Handguns, mostly, though they may have access to a few automatic rifles."

"Three against ten," Lu says. "Bad odds."

"We'll have the element of surprise."

"How do you propose to get inside?"

"Does this mean you are joining us?"

"I haven't agreed to anything. I'm just evaluating the chances of success. And I'm not interested in killing ten or more men. I'm a police officer, not a commando."

"Black cat, white cat," Zhang says, referring to Deng Xiaoping's famous dictum. "It doesn't matter if a cat is black or white, so long as it catches mice." In other words, *the end justifies the means*.

"Catching mice is one thing," Lu says. "Slaughtering them is another."

"We aim to keep the slaughter to a minimum," Zhang says. "The two objectives are Ling and the tapes. In and out, as quickly as possible."

"I still don't like the odds."

Zhang shrugs. "We can't very well post a want ad online asking for hired guns."

Lu thinks for a moment. "I know someone who might be interested."

"An outsider? We're only including you because you have law enforcement experience and a vested interest. We can't afford exposure."

"This person has skills. And, from what I know of him, plenty of motivation. And good reason to avoid the authorities."

Zhang looks at Li. Li gives him a shrug. "We'll trust your judgment," Zhang says. "But if you're going to speak to him, it has to be soon. We do this tomorrow night."

"So soon?"

"Every passing second Ling is imprisoned at the Little Red Palace is an agony for Mr. Gao. And tomorrow a snowstorm is expected. Anyone with common sense will remain inside, warm and cozy. The Little Red Palace won't have many customers, and the storm will help mask our movements."

"Let me make a call."

FIFTY-THREE

The three men part ways in the parking lot. Lu sits in his car and calls Kim. She answers on the third ring. He tells her he wants to meet the man who tortured and killed Sung. "Don't waste my time pretending you don't know how to contact him," Lu says. "This is urgent."

Silence on the phone.

"Listen," Lu continues. "I need him for a very specific kind of job. The kind that, once it's done, will ensure I'm in no position to turn him, or you, in to the authorities. Get my drift?"

"I hear you," Kim says. "But I cut off all contact with him following a . . . disagreement. I can reach out, but I'm not sure he'll respond. I have no idea if he's even in Harbin."

"Try. I want to meet him tonight, if possible. Oh . . . one other thing."

"Yes?"

"Does he speak Chinese?"

"Passably."

Lu hangs up and considers what to do next. It doesn't make sense to drive back to Raven Valley if there's a chance of meeting Kim's contact. He heads for downtown Harbin.

He just can't seem to quit this place, no matter how hard he tries.

Kim calls back by the time Lu is near the railway station. "He wants to know where to meet."

"Is he in Harbin now? How about the mezzanine of the railway station? I'll find a table at the café."

"Give him an hour."

*   *   *

It's more like two. Lu has been nursing a cup of coffee for some time, watching travelers come and go, picturing what this man might look like. He sees a few possibilities—rough-and-tumble-looking characters—but none of them approach his table. Then Hak materializes from the crowd, dressed in dark, muted clothing, a ball cap, a cotton face mask. He sits and fixes his eyes on Lu.

Lu can't see much of his features or his build, but his impression is of a man of average height and broad shoulders. "I'm Lu."

"Hak."

"Would you like something to drink?"

"No. Why am I here?" Hak's Mandarin is accented, but understandable.

"Let's take a walk."

"I lead."

"Sure," Lu says. "As long as it's not down any dark alleyways."

Lu follows Hak downstairs, through the cavernous station, and out the north entrance. Hak finds a remote spot in the enormous plaza outside, removes his mask, and lights a cigarette. Lu sees that he's got a square jaw, strong features, if a bit drawn out. A week's worth of beard growth.

Lu shivers and rubs his hands together. Hak smiles. "Cold?"

"You're not?"

"I'm used to it." Hak's cigarette glows red in the dark. "I'm listening."

Lu explains. About Ling Wei, Tang, the Little Red Palace.

"You want to make a deal?" Hak says. "I help you, you forget about the dead Korean?"

"I think you are familiar with Tang," Lu says. "And given the fact that you yanked out Sung's teeth and cut off his fingers, I'm guessing you aren't fond of sex traffickers, especially those who pimp out North Korean women. Sound about right?"

In lieu of an answer, Hak smiles again. Smoke dribbles from his mouth.

"I'm giving you a chance to help me take out the biggest trafficker in Nangang District," Lu says. "Perhaps in all of Harbin."

"And Sung?"

"You get a pass on that one. But next time you torture and kill someone, even if they deserve it, I'll hunt you down."

"You'd never find me."

"I'm pretty good at my job. But I suppose you could always go back to North Korea. Though you might get a cold reception there."

"I told you—I'm used to the cold."

"What do you say, Mr. Hak?"

Hak finishes his cigarette, squeezes the cherry between his fingers, deposits the butt in an old candy tin he keeps in his pocket. "Can I kill Tang?"

"This is not a hit job. We will kill only if necessary."

"What happens after you get this woman out? Tang is free to go about his business?"

"He has tapes. Of clients with prostitutes. We'll get them to the authorities. Tang will be arrested. Probably executed."

"Or he'll just run off to Thailand. Or the Middle East."

"Even if he manages to escape, his days will be numbered."

Hak grunts. "How many men do we have?"

"Four. Including you."

"Who are the other two?"

"They work for someone who wants the woman safe."

"You trust them?"

"I trust that they are who they say they are."

"When do we do this?"

Lu hesitates. "Are you in?"

"Yes."

"Tomorrow night."

Hak makes a face. "Not enough time. We need a plan."

"They say they have one."

"And weapons? Do they have those?"

"I don't know."

"Call them. We meet. Now."

Lu phones Zhang on his burner phone. Zhang gives him an address.

Hak has a motorcycle. He accompanies Lu to his car, then disappears. Lu waits, his engine running for warmth. Ten minutes later, Hak rides up and waves Lu onward.

They head south. Lu follows his GPS to a residential neighborhood, a small house. He parks at the curb. Hak parks down the block. Lu gets out of his car, but Hak jogs up and tells him to wait. "I will have a look first."

Seems like a prudent plan to Lu. He climbs back into his car while Hak fades into the darkness around the side of the house. Five minutes pass. Lu starts to worry. He considers starting the car and driving away. It might be the sanest course of action.

The front door to the house opens. Zhang stands framed in the doorway, backlit. He waves. Lu gets out of his car. Zhang turns and disappears into the house.

Lu approaches the door. He sees only a rectangle of empty hallway. He enters, shuts the door. It's warm inside.

"This way," Zhang says over his shoulder as he walks toward the back of the house.

Lu follows, passing stairs on the right, a living room on the left. He is conscious of the fact that he might be walking into a trap. No weapon, not even a baton.

When he reaches the end of the hallway, he hugs the wall, peeks into the kitchen. He sees Hak and Li, sitting at the table, smoking cigarettes. Hak has a black pistol by his elbow. Li is holding a bag of frozen vegetables to his cheek.

Lu looks at Zhang. He notices that Zhang is sporting a fat lip. "We met your friend," Zhang says. "You're right—he has skills." He smiles. There's blood on his teeth. "Beer?"

"Sure." Lu takes a seat at the table. "Everyone all right?"

"No harm done," Li says. He pulls the bag away from his cheek to reveal the beginnings of a nice shiner.

FIFTY-FOUR

Zhang serves beers all around and then spreads a floor plan of Tang's compound on the table.

"Where'd you get this?" Lu asks.

"I told you, Mr. Gao helped with the construction permits," Zhang says.

The compound is rectangular in shape and enclosed by a two-meter wall. It sits in the middle of an ordinary residential block like a cancerous tumor, surrounded on three sides by other properties, mostly standard suburban houses with modest yards.

"These other houses," Lu asks, "they don't belong to Tang?"

"He owns one or two," Zhang says. "Some of his staff live in them. The rest are just regular citizens."

Hak stubs out his cigarette. "How many entrances?"

"The main gate is to the south. It opens onto this courtyard with a fountain in the center, a carport to the west, garden to the east. Then comes the main residence. I'll come back to that. Behind the residence are more gardens, and outbuildings. This one, to the west, is for male staff. Self-contained, with apartments, restrooms, a kitchen, recreation room. Opposite it, on the east side, are dorms for female staff and hostesses. Same thing—completely self-contained. At the back of the property is more green space and a north gate. The north gate is accessible only by a narrow lane between these other properties, barely large enough for a single vehicle. Both gates, north and south, are high-quality steel construction. Camera surveillance and an armed guard on duty twenty-four hours a day."

"So how do we get in?" Hak asks.

"Hold your horses," Zhang says. "Let me finish the tour first." He points. "The main residence. Three stories. The front doors open onto a huge foyer. On the first floor you have a lounge, gaming room with card tables, *mah-jongg*, roulette, and so on, a conference room, a full-service kitchen, and a dining room.

"A staircase in the foyer leads up to the second floor. To the west are half a dozen rooms where the girls service clients. Apparently themed. High school classroom, office, dungeon, what have you. The east wing is accessible only through a door secured by a key card scanner—it houses offices for the staff, including Tang, and the control room. The control room, also secured by a door with a key card scanner, is where all the camera feeds are monitored and the master tapes are stored."

"Then that's our main objective," Lu says.

"Yes. That and Ling Wei."

"Where's she being held?" Lu asks.

"We suspect the third floor—where Tang has his private quarters. Master bed and bath here, a living room, two guest rooms. A balcony that looks over the back garden. A staircase runs directly up from the first floor at the rear of the residence—like the east wing, it is accessible only by key card. We suspect just a few people possess a key card that will unlock *all* the doors. Tang and his head of security, most likely. Perhaps his housekeeping manager."

"Then how do we gain access to the control room?" Lu asks. "You have explosives?"

"No. We'll have to get our hands on one of those key cards."

"From?" Lu says.

"Tang or his head of security."

"That's the plan?" Hak says. "What if Tang is already upstairs? What if the head of security is upstairs with him? Or in the control room?"

Li drops his bag of vegetables on the table. "So it's not a perfect plan. Nothing is. We adjust as we go. Chances are, Diesel will show his face at the first sign of a break-in—"

"Diesel?" Lu says.

"Head of security's nickname. Ex-fighter. Hits like a truck, or so they say."

"Then we don't fight him," Hak says. "We shoot him."

"No indiscriminate shooting," Lu warns. He nods at the floor plan. "How do we get inside the compound? Climb over the wall?"

"Exactly," Zhang says. "Through a neighbor's yard."

"Which one?"

"This one." Zhang points to a narrow plot of land that terminates at the wall not far from the female dormitory.

"Who lives there?"

"A married couple. Ordinary citizens. In their fifties. No children. No parents. That's why we chose it. They won't be harmed."

"What other security measures does Tang have?" Hak asks.

"Additional cameras at the entrances to the buildings, and stationed around the grounds. We don't know all the locations, but it's not a problem. We have a portable jammer. And tomorrow's forecast is for heavy snowfall. Ten or more centimeters. In that kind of weather, the camera feeds might not show much, even without the jammer."

"Might," Lu says. "A lot of mights and maybes."

Zhang shrugs. "Another beer?"

"That's a given," Lu says.

Zhang grabs fresh bottles from the fridge. He, Li, and Hak light fresh cigarettes.

"All right," Lu continues. "Over the wall. And then?"

"We catch one of the staff or a security guard, grab his key card, get into the main residence," Zhang says. "Find Diesel or Tang. You and Mr. Hak handle the control room. Lao Li and I will get Ling Wei." *Lao* means "old," and Li is certainly no fresh-faced youth, but in this context Zhang means it as an affectionate form of address. "Then back out the way we came in."

"Will the staff fight?" Hak asks.

"Cooks and bartenders and so on? No. But the security guards will."

Hak inhales through his teeth. "Tough operation. Many unknowns." He taps his cigarette ash into a dish everyone is using as an ashtray. "What experience do you have?"

"I was a senior sergeant in the PLA," Zhang says. "Lao Li was a cop."

Lu pricks up his ears. "In Harbin?"

Li nods. "Before your time."

"Did you know Xu?"

Li smiles thinly. "He was coming in as I was going out. But he was a bit of a shit even then."

"Either of you kill before?" Hak asks.

Zhang and Li look at one another, but do not answer.

"Oh, they've killed," Lu says. "You'd probably approve of their creativity on that score."

Hak shrugs, apparently satisfied. "You have weapons?"

"A couple of those." Zhang nods to the gun on the table. Lu recognizes it as a Type 92 automatic, 5.8-millimeter rounds, twenty to a clip.

"No good," Hak says. "We need more firepower."

"It's what we have," Zhang says.

"You give me cash and I get better guns."

"Now?"

"Yes, now."

"How much?" Li asks.

"Fifty thousand yuan."

Zhang chokes on his beer. "*Wah!* So much?"

"I can get four submachine guns, with suppressors. Ammunition."

"We have maybe . . . thirty thousand."

"Give it to me. I'll do my best."

Li and Zhang exchange a look. Zhang shrugs. Li gets up and walks down the hall.

"Give me your car keys," Hak says to Lu.

"No way."

"You want me to carry guns on my motorcycle?"

"I'll drive you."

"Better you don't. Trust me."

Lu fishes the car key out of his pocket and hands it over. "Don't speed. And don't wreck it."

Li soon returns with an envelope. Hak puts it in his pocket. "Might take two or three hours." He stubs out his cigarette and leaves without further comment.

Zhang goes to the refrigerator and collects more beers. "I hope your friend didn't just run off with our cash."

"Something tells me he didn't." Lu yawns. "What now?"

"Have you eaten?" Li asks.

"No."

"I'll make something." Li gets up and fills a pot with water.

"Lao Li is an excellent cook," Zhang says.

"Lifelong bachelor," Li says.

"After we eat, I'll make up a place for you on the couch," Zhang says. "You'll want to get a good night's rest. Tomorrow is going to be a long day."

Lu sighs. If he'd known he was having a sleepover, he'd have brought a change of underwear.

FIFTY-FIVE

Li makes noodles with pork, cabbage, spring onions, mushrooms, carrots. As promised, the meal is quite tasty. The three men eat in silence, and then Zhang puts a blanket on the couch for Lu, and another on the floor for Hak.

Lu doesn't expect to sleep, but he does. He startles awake in the early hours of the morning, disoriented, thinking he's back in Harbin Prison. Then he processes his surroundings—the living room, couch.

Hak snoring softly on the floor.

Lu falls asleep again and wakes at dawn to the sound of clanking and rattling in the kitchen. Hak's spot is empty. Lu goes to the window and looks out—a light snow is already falling.

He walks down the hallway to the kitchen. Li is busy at the stove. Hak and Zhang are drinking tea at the table and smoking their first cigarettes of day. "Pull up a chair," Zhang says.

Breakfast is served: rice porridge with leftover pork and vegetables, toast, fruit, tea. Afterward, Hak shows them what he's bought.

"QCW-05." He holds up a squat black submachine gun. "Less than three kilos. With suppressor attached, accurate up to fifty meters. Fifty rounds per clip. Even with the suppressor it makes a sound, but it won't burst your eardrums. Unfortunately, I was only able to buy two. And I'm using one of them. You three can decide who gets the other."

Li looks at Zhang. "You trained with such a weapon, right?"

"An older model. But I've used a submachine gun before, yes."

"Any objection?" Li asks Lu.

"No," Lu says. "What did you get for the rest of us? Sticks and stones?"

Hak reaches into the duffel bag at his feet and removes two of the North Korean Browning pistols he favors. "For me and you." He looks at Zhang and Li. "You two have handguns already, yes?"

Zhang nods. "Yes."

Hak sets the Brownings on the table, takes out a pump-action shotgun with a pistol grip and a fat magazine. "Twelve-gauge. No suppressor, very loud. Got two for the price one." He smiles, pleased with himself.

For his finale, like a magician pulling a rabbit from his hat, Hak produces four bulletproof vests. "Good against handguns. Rifles, not so much."

"Money well spent," Zhang says.

Later, Lu steps outside to make a call. The snow is already up to his ankles. He dials Yanyan.

"Hey," she says sleepily. "I thought you might come by the Red Lotus last night."

"Sorry, you wore me out. I fell asleep."

She laughs. "Will I see you tonight?"

"Tomorrow?"

"Why tomorrow?"

"I have a couple of administrative things to clear up."

Yanyan's tone changes. "What *things*?"

"Nothing important. Meet my lawyer in Harbin, collect some stuff I left at the hotel where I was staying. Like that."

"I got all your things from the hotel. Me and Constable Sun."

"You forgot my favorite sweater."

"We did?"

"Anyway, tomorrow night I'm all yours."

"I really hope you're not doing something stupid, Lu Fei."

"Who, me?"

"I'm serious. If you do something stupid and end up in prison again I'm not coming to visit you. I'm not sending you a care package. And I'm not marrying you."

"You really know how to hit a guy where it hurts. I'll see you tomorrow. And . . ."

"Yes?"

"I love you."

Yanyan sighs into the phone. "I love you, too."

The snowfall worsens as the day wears on. Hak dozes on the couch. Zhang and Li pack their belongings and clean house—wiping down surfaces, mopping the floor. Regardless of what happens tonight, it's clear they won't be returning.

Lu watches with amusement. "Any CSI team worth its salt will find your DNA within fifteen minutes."

"We know," Zhang says. "But this place has served its purpose—time to move on. And we don't expect anyone to connect the two quiet bachelors renting this place with a break-in at a notorious gangster's compound."

"After tonight, where will you go?"

"Elsewhere."

"You, Li, Ling, and Gao, one big happy family, is that it?"

Zhang shrugs.

"Did you used to do this kind of work for Gao in the old days?" Lu asks.

"Mr. Gao was a businessman and politician. Not a thug. Rough stuff was rarely required."

"You took to it like a duck to water."

"Are you trying to rile me, Inspector?"

"No. Just trying to understand. What you did to Cao and Pang. The level of sophistication—and brutality. It wasn't the work of amateurs."

Zhang gives Lu a deadpan stare.

"Let's say you rescue Ling and reunite her with Gao," Lu says. "And then? You go back to bodyguarding? And Lao Li to driving?"

"No. Lao Li and I will take a well-deserved retirement. Move to the country and plant snow peas. Enjoy the passing of the seasons." He recites a poem by a Song Dynasty poet named Zhu Dunru:

I've been around the world.
Seen what lies beyond.

Nowadays I don't get lost among the flowers.
Or drink overmuch.
And when the show is over,
I'll strip off my costume
and toss it down to the fools.

"Why, Mr. Zhang," Lu says. "You're a killer *and* a poet."
"You should see my calligraphy," Zhang says with an enigmatic smile.

At dusk, the men have a small meal of roast pork buns, washed down with tea. No more alcohol until the mission is complete. Zhang distributes balaclavas and latex gloves. He and Li dress in police uniforms that look indistinguishable from the real thing and even include fake ID numbers over the left breast pocket. Everyone straps on a bulletproof vest.

Zhang, Li, and Hak enjoy a final communal smoke. Their unspoken camaraderie is such that Lu wishes briefly he were a smoker, too.

And then it's time to go.

Lu and Hak will travel together in Lu's rental car. Zhang and Li will take their own vehicle.

Outside, Lu finds the snow is already up to mid-calf. He worries the rental car isn't up to driving in these conditions. He and Hak must first dig out the wheels before they can pull away from the curb.

Lu follows Zhang's taillights through suburban streets, his windshield wipers whisking to and fro. The neighborhood is a ghost town—everyone is wisely encapsulated in brightly lit and heated homes. The only other vehicles they pass are snowplows.

The journey to Gold Mountain Village takes forever—and yet is over much too soon.

They park on a side street. A neat row of houses on other side, mostly two stories, porches in front, tiny front yards. Zhang gets out and walks to Lu's car.

"Wait here," Zhang says. "We won't be long."

Zhang and Li pass through a gate leading to one of the houses, knock on the front door. When the door opens, Zhang and Li force their way inside.

Five or six minutes later, they come running out to their car, Zhang giving Lu a thumbs-up.

Lu gets out and opens the trunk of his rental. He hands Hak his submachine gun, takes a shotgun. He and Hak trot up to the house. Zhang and Li follow, carrying their own weapons, and an extendable ladder.

In the entryway, Lu sees an umbrella stand, shoes in little cubbies. "Where are the owners?"

"Safe," Zhang answers.

"Show me."

"No time."

Lu grips Zhang's coat. "Show me."

Zhang hands the ladder to Li and takes Lu upstairs, into a bedroom. A man and woman lie on the bed, facedown. Wrists and ankles zip-tied. Some kind of makeshift gag in their mouths.

"You sure they can breathe?" Lu asks.

"I'm sure."

Lu and Zhang go downstairs and out the back door. They follow Li and Hak's trail through the snow across the backyard—leafless trees, their limbs festooned with icicles, a garden shed, and then, looming in the darkness—a wall. Li has already unfolded the ladder and set it in place. He's holding his shotgun in one hand, a black device with a row of antennae in the other.

"Where's Hak?" Zhang hisses.

"He went over," Li says.

Zhang curses. "What's his hurry?"

Li jerks his head. "Go."

Zhang starts up the ladder. His foot slips and he nearly falls. He steadies himself, reaches the top, drops out of sight.

"You next," Lu tells Li. "You have the jammer."

Li puts the device in his pocket and starts up. Lu holds the ladder still. Li slides over the top and disappears.

Lu puts a foot on the bottom rung.

He thinks of Yanyan, dressed in red, amid the raucous atmosphere of a packed banquet room. Gold dragons and phoenixes and double happiness characters on the wall.

Then he pictures himself lying in Tang's garden, a red stain blossoming in the white snow beneath him.

"*Ta ma de,*" he mutters. He starts climbing.

小紅宮
THE LITTLE RED PALACE

FIFTY-SIX

Lu peeks over the top of the wall. He sees trees and snowdrifts and the bulk of a building ahead—Li below, knee-deep in white powder, hissing at him to lift the ladder over. Lu straddles the wall, hauls the ladder up, hands it down to Li. Then he jumps, holding the shotgun one-handed. A soft landing. He and Li move forward.

The building is red brick with white accents and a red tile roof, two stories. Hak and Zhang are standing at a side door, a woman caught between them. The woman is wearing a winter coat and holding a cigarette. The lenses of her cat-eye glasses are beaded with melting snow. Her lips tremble with cold . . . and fear.

"Caught this one having a smoke," Zhang tells Li and Lu.

Hak reads a laminated ID card the woman wears on a lanyard around her neck. "Su. What is your job here, Su?"

"I . . . manage the girls."

"And this key," Hak says. "Opens what doors?"

"Doors?"

Hak gives the lanyard a sharp tug. "Doors! Third floor? Control room?"

"No. All the other ones." Su's teeth chatter like keys on an old-fashioned typewriter. "Please don't kill me!"

Hak drops the lanyard. "If you want to live, you will cooperate."

The group snakes through courtyards dotted with manicured trees and bushes, decorative rocks, birdbaths, naked statuary.

They reach the main residence and crouch in a grove of bamboo. Lu reads characters, limned in snow, inscribed on a rock that rises from a nearby pool of frozen water: FEN FA ZI QIANG.

He snorts.

Hak nudges Li and points at a camera that looms over the back entrance. Li holds up his little black device and nods.

Hak grabs Su by the collar and hustles her over to the door. He tugs off her key card, hangs the lanyard around his own neck. He holds the key card to a scanner set in the wall.

Here we go, Lu thinks.

Hak opens the door, pushes Su inside.

Lu immediately hears a pop. Not loud, but enough to give him a start. He rushes past Zhang and Li and through the open door, where he sees a young man in a dark suit and white shirt lying on the floor, a bright splatter of blood across the wall.

Su regards the body with abject horror; Hak holds a hand over her mouth to cut off a scream. Lu glares at Hak.

"He had a gun." Hak nods with his chin. Lu sees an automatic on the floor.

Zhang and Li squeeze in behind Lu. Li closes the door, cutting off a blast of frigid air.

Lu takes note of the surroundings. A small foyer, three doors—the one they've just come through, one to the right, one straight ahead. Zhang points his submachine gun at the door on the right.

"That leads up to Tang's quarters. Try the key card."

Hak warns Su not to make a sound before taking his hand away. He holds the key card up the scanner and tries the door. It doesn't budge.

"Where's Tang?" Zhang asks Su.

Su's eyes are still locked on the dead man, her mouth a thin white line. Hak grabs the collar of her coat, jerks her around to face him. "Tang!"

Su shakes her head. "I don't know. Maybe the lounge."

"You have customers tonight?" Zhang asks.

Su hesitates. Hak gives her lapel a rough shake.

"A few," Su says. "Three or four."

"In this weather?" Zhang says, incredulous.

"It's Chief Xu's birthday."

"Xu's here?" Lu says.

Zhang looks at Lu. "It's your lucky night." He turns to Su. "Where's Ling Wei?"

"Upstairs. Guest bedroom."

Zhang nods at the third door. "The lounge is that way. Let's go."

Hak pushes Su over to the door. He holds the key card to the scanner. The lock clicks as it disengages. Hak opens the door, shoves Su over the threshold.

Zhang goes next, then Li. Lu follows, into a carpeted hallway. He sees a swinging door on the left with a glass window at head-height. The kitchen. And another swinging door opposite, also with a glass window. Lu peeks inside as he passes and spies a round table with seating for twelve, a wood-carved chandelier, wall panels decorated with lucky symbols and Chinese zodiac animals.

They pass through a door at the end of the hallway and into a grand foyer. Double-height ceiling. A staircase with an ornately filigreed banister running up to a second-floor mezzanine on the left. The floor is marble, laid out in a black-and-white diamond pattern. A life-sized sculpture of a peach tree squats dead center, the delicate pink hue and dark green leaves of the peaches expertly rendered in carved stone.

Across the foyer are heavy wooden double doors, painted lucky red, leading out to the front courtyard. On the right, another red door, closed. The gaming room. A third door on the left, cracked open.

The lounge.

FIFTY-SEVEN

Hak leads the way, Su his human shield.

The lounge is womblike. Wine-red carpet. Velvet wallpaper. Red mood lighting. A bar at the back. A karaoke stage in front. Plush seating all around—couches, armchairs, low tables. A haze of cigarette and cigar smoke.

A small group is clustered in front of the stage. A handful of men, twice as many hostesses. Lu recognizes some of the faces. Chief Hong sits with a young woman in a cocktail dress on his lap. He's got one hand wrapped around a glass, the other cupping the woman's breast. Kitty-corner from him is Judge Ren, a fat cigar between his stubby fingers.

The singer onstage absolutely butchering "Country Roads" is Xu.

At first no one notices the intrusion. But then a young man in a dark suit and white shirt—Lu now recognizes it as the muted uniform of the LRP's security detail—emerges from a dark corner, hand extended to impede their progress.

Hak angles the barrel of his submachine gun, fires two quick rounds into the young man's chest.

Xu cuts off mid-warble. A man sitting in a chair with his back to the door whips his head around.

Tang Fuqiang.

Lu hasn't seen Tang in ten years. But he'll never forget that face—its conventionally handsome features concealing the true nature of the man. Like an executioner wearing the mask of a matinee idol while gleefully lopping off heads.

Zhang fires a sudden burst at Xu. Xu leaps offstage. Hak gives Zhang a hard shove. "No!" Hak shouts. "You'll hit the women!"

A big man sitting at the bar has already come off his stool and is running toward the stage. Lu sees a flash and hears the roar of an unsilenced gun. Li goes down. Lu fires his shotgun from the hip. Bottles of imported booze explode.

Another security guard pops up from the back of the room. Zhang fires a burst. The guard flies backward.

The men near the stage take cover. The big guy with the gun—Diesel, Lu assumes—leaps over a couch, pushes Tang under a table. He squeezes off a shot, intended for Hak, but hits Su. She makes a sound like "Oh!"—then collapses. Hak ducks for cover.

Lu scrambles behind a chair. Zhang runs for the far side of the room, seeking to outflank Diesel. Diesel shoots and Zhang dives to the carpet.

A brief lull. Everyone hunkers down.

The air smells of ammo propellant. Lu's ears are ringing. Even so, he hears the slap of leather-soled shoes coming from the foyer. He turns in time to see two men in dark suits and white shirts rush in. They look young, their off-the-rack suits too big for their frames, like teenage boys at their first formal event.

But they have pistols in their hands.

Lu rapid-fires, pumping out spent shells. By the time his magazine is empty, the edges of the doorframe are splintered and pocked, and both men are splayed on the floor.

Lu ejects his magazine, slaps in another. His last.

He checks everyone's position. Zhang is pinned down across the room. Li huddles behind a couch. He sees Lu looking at him, taps the bulletproof vest below his coat, gives Lu a thumbs-up.

Hak is to Lu's right. As Lu watches, Hak slowly stands up, submachine gun leveled.

Lu thinks, *Get down, idiot!*

Then he sees that Diesel is also standing up, his gun held to the temple of one of the hostesses.

"Drop your weapons or I'll kill her," Diesel says.

"Then you will all die," Hak says.

"Isn't that the plan anyway?" Diesel asks.

"No!" Lu calls out. "You can all walk out of here. We just want Ling."

Someone—Lu thinks it's Tang—curses Lu's ancestors going back eighteen generations. Someone else—Lu thinks it's Xu—says, "Is that Lu Fei? *Gan!*"

Diesel speaks over his shoulder without taking his eyes off Hak. "Everyone grab a girl—these bastards won't risk shooting and hitting one of them by accident. We'll head for the door. Stay close. Stick together."

The group arranges itself into a jumble of heads and torsos and legs, each of the men sheltering behind a hostess, gripping her hair, her cocktail dress, her neck—whatever point of purchase proves expedient. They move forward in a ragged clump.

Hak tracks their progress with the barrel of his gun.

When they reach the foyer, Diesel turns and stands guard, facing Hak, his thick forearm wrapped around the neck of a young woman in a sequined party dress while the other men and their captive hostesses file out two-by-two.

So much for the element of surprise, Lu thinks. By now the entire compound must be on high alert. The entire security detail mobilized and armed.

Hak shuffles to the left.

Diesel understands Hak is maneuvering for a better angle. He hesitates, then swings the muzzle of his gun away from the hostess's temple, points it at Hak.

Hak fires. An expert shot. His round just nicks the edge of the hostess's earlobe and blows a hole in Diesel's cheek. Diesel shouts, spins, and falls. The hostess shrieks, drops down on all fours, crawls off in search of cover.

Diesel claps one hand to his cheek, pats the rug for his gun with the other. Hak runs forward, firing as he goes. He hits Diesel twice in the chest. Diesel grunts and goes slack. Hak takes one last step to stand directly over Diesel's body, puts a final round in Diesel's forehead.

A shot rings out from the foyer. Hak doubles over. Lu gets up and rushes to the doorway, sticks the barrel of his shotgun through it, fires blindly. He risks a quick glance, spies movement behind the peach tree—a guard crouched there. When the guard pops up for another shot, Lu fires again. A stone peach explodes. Lu fires twice more. The guard hits the floor, his gun clattering across the marble.

Lu feels a waft of cold air, looks left, sees that the double doors leading outside are wide-open, framing a dark rectangle of night. The last of the fleeing hostesses is just now tottering over the threshold on high-heeled shoes more suited to a fancy ballroom than a severe winter storm. Naturally, she immediately slips and falls, but quickly gets up, and escapes into a whirling gust of snow.

Hak tugs Diesel's key card from around his neck, offers it to Lu. "Take this. Go."

"You're hit? How bad?"

"Take it!"

Lu hears the crack of a gun and a slug thuds into the doorframe a few centimeters from his head. He looks up and sees a guard standing where the hostess was a few seconds ago. Another shot, this one close enough to crease the fabric of Lu's balaclava. He returns fire, emptying the magazine of his shotgun. The guard drops out of sight. Lu tosses his shotgun aside, draws his gun, runs for the double doors. He slams them shut, finds a sliding bolt, locks it in place.

Ta ma de, close shave!

He turns in time to see two men on the mezzanine struggling to open the door leading to the east wing. And then Zhang bursts out of the lounge, sees the men, opens fire with his submachine gun. The men jerk and flail and stray bullets stitch the wall and ceiling as empty shell casings skitter across the marble floor. Zhang runs up the stairs, switching out his magazine as he does so, Li at his heels.

Lu runs after them, then detours to check on Hak. Hak is on his feet, holding his left shoulder. "How bad?"

Hak shakes his head. "Doesn't matter. We finish the mission." He hands Lu the key card, then heads for the stairs. He ascends slowly, leaving a trail of bright red droplets behind.

When they reach the mezzanine, Lu sees that one of the men Zhang has shot is Judge Ren; the other is Chief Hong.

Ren is already dead, eyes glazed, lips curled into an aggrieved grimace. Hong is unconscious but still alive, his breathing rapid and shallow.

Zhang aims his submachine gun at Hong's chest. Lu pushes the barrel down, then snatches his hand away—it's hot to the touch. "No."

Zhang shrugs. "He'll be dead soon anyway."

Lu drags Ren's body aside, holds Diesel's key card to the scanner, opens the door to the east wing. Inside is a long hallway, doors on either side. He, Zhang, and Li start down it, opening doors, finding only empty offices. Hak brings up the rear.

The two doors at the far end are constructed of steel and secured by key card scanners. Zhang nods at the one on the left. "Tang's office."

"Maybe he's hiding inside," Hak says.

"He's not a priority," Zhang says. "I want to get upstairs, find Ling Wei." He motions toward the other door. "Control room. Let's get inside and you two can grab the tapes while Lao Li and I head upstairs."

"Whoever's inside will be waiting for us," Lu says. "Probably armed."

"Just unlock it and I'll stick my gun in and empty the magazine," Zhang says.

"You might hit a hard drive."

"We don't have the luxury of time and precision, Inspector. They could be spiriting Ling away as we speak."

Hak offers Lu his submachine gun. "Here. You might need this." Lu puts his pistol away and reluctantly takes it. He holds the key card to the scanner, hears a click. He grasps the knob, turns, and flings the door open.

FIFTY-EIGHT

A fusillade of bullets zips across the hallway and peppers the door to Tang's office. Lu wisely stays out of the line of fire.

There's a brief respite when the shooter realizes he's wasting ammo on empty space. Zhang takes advantage of this opportunity to extend his submachine gun around the doorframe and unload the remainder of his magazine. He quickly withdraws, pops out the spent magazine, slaps another one home, tugs the charging lever.

Heavy silence.

Zhang motions for Lu to look inside the control room. Lu shakes his head. Zhang takes a cautious look, nods. "He's down. Come on."

Lu follows Zhang into the room. A young man in a white shirt and dark pants is slumped against the wall, chin on his chest. Blood on his shirt, blood on the wall.

Zhang prods the man to make sure he's dead. He is. Zhang holds out his hand. "The key card." Lu hands it over. "Get the tapes and get out," Zhang says. "We'll get in touch later."

Zhang and Li run down the hallway and disappear through the door leading to the mezzanine.

Lu takes stock—there's a row of monitors with split-screen camera views. Communications equipment. A computer workstation. A metal cabinet against one wall. Secured by a combination lock.

Hak shuffles in, examines the cabinet. "Keep watch outside."

Lu goes to the doorway. "Noise!" Hak warns. He shoots the lock with his pistol, then pries open the cabinet to reveal shelves holding row after row of hard drives.

The hard drives are neatly labeled. And Lu has a shopping list. Xu, Hong, Wan, Yu, for starters. He stuffs hard drives into a messenger bag he's wearing under his coat, keeping an eye out for the names of other high-ranking officials—the mayor of Harbin; the party secretary; Chief Wu, Xu's boss. Any provincial leaders. He doesn't see them, and doesn't have much time, so he just takes what he can and says, "Let's go."

In the hallway, Hak motions at Tang's office door with his Browning. "I want to see if Tang's in there."

"No time."

Hak doesn't care. He fires several rounds into the lockset, nudges the door open with his foot.

The office is empty apart from a polished desk, a leather couch, and matching armchairs.

"Satisfied?" Lu says. "Come on!"

Lu rushes down the hall, slowly opens the door leading to the mezzanine, glances down at Ren and Hong's limp bodies. He pokes his head out farther and looks down at the foyer. He sees the doors leading outside are still closed. Good. And the guard beside the peach tree is splayed, unmoving, in a pool of blood. Unfortunate, but also good.

He starts down the stairs. He's almost to the bottom when he realizes Hak is not behind him. He turns.

Hak is crossing the mezzanine.

"Hak!" Lu shouts.

Hak stops. "Bring the car around front. I'll meet you there."

"Hak!"

Hak opens the door leading to the west wing and steps through it. Lu hears a woman scream, a man shout.

Then a gunshot.

Despite his obvious skills, recruiting Hak was a mistake. He's insane and out for blood.

Lu runs to the front doors, unlocks them, cracks one open. Snow swirls into his eyes. The front gate is open. Two cars idle in the courtyard, steam billowing from tailpipes.

Lu exits onto the porch. He hears a gunshot. He runs forward, takes cover behind the fountain at the center of the courtyard. Another shot, and a bullet cuts across the lip of the fountain, spraying plaster.

Lu stays low as he shuffles two meters over, then has a look—he sees a guard crouched in a booth beside the gate. The guard sees him and fires. Lu answers with a short burst from his submachine gun, lowers his head, shuffles over another meter, stands, empties his magazine at the booth.

It's like shooting fish in a bucket.

Lu tosses the submachine gun aside, draws his pistol. The two idling cars speed off through the gate. Lu starts to follow, intending to run around the residential block to his rental car, when he hears the roar of an engine. He turns as an SUV pulls out of the garage. Lu fires at the windshield. The SUV swerves left into the fountain, crunches to a halt. Lu squats in the snow, waits. Ten seconds pass; the driver climbs out out of the SUV, hands high, fear on his face.

"Run," Lu says.

The driver runs.

Lu walks to the SUV, looks inside. Empty. He climbs in, sits behind the wheel. The messenger bag digs painfully into his side. He shrugs out of his coat, lifts the strap of the bag over his shoulder, tosses it onto the backseat.

He shifts into reverse, executes a three-point turn, points the nose of the SUV at the open gate. Time to go. *Goodbye, Hak.*

Lu tightens his hands on the steering wheel—then shifts into park. He will give Hak thirty seconds.

It's warm inside the car. The seats are high-quality leather, or some reasonable facsimile. There's a little perfume diffuser on the dash—it smells of lavender.

Lu counts to sixty. No Hak. *Ta ma de.* Lu starts over. Counts to sixty again. *That's it.*

He shifts into drive, takes one final look in the rearview mirror, sees Hak come through the double doors into the courtyard.

Lu rolls down his window and waves frantically. Hak trudges tiredly through the snow. He opens the passenger door, slides onto the seat, closes the door. He's panting from exertion or pain or a combination of both.

"Idiot," Lu says. He drives through the gate, turns left. He circles around the block. Zhang and Li's car is already gone. Lu hopes that means they were successful in rescuing Ling. "I'll get the other car started, then come get you."

Hak doesn't respond. His eyes are closed. Lu can't tell if he's passed out or dead.

Lu gets out, forges a path through the snow to the rental car, unlocks it, slides behind the wheel, starts the engine. He pulls abreast of the SUV and gets out to retrieve Hak.

But as he reaches for the door of the SUV, it rolls forward. Through the fogged glass, Lu can just make out Hak behind the wheel.

"Hak!" Lu shouts. "Hak!"

The SUV picks up speed.

Lu rushes back to his rental car. He shifts into gear, presses on the gas. The car lurches violently, fishtails wildly. Lu works the wheel, pumps the brakes, regains control. He takes a breath, resets, cautiously accelerates.

But by the time he reaches the end of the street, the SUV is gone.

And with it, the hard drives.

FIFTY-NINE

Lu drives to Sister Kim's. It's the only place he can think of where Hak might go.

It is a long journey, in the driving snow, visibility poor, the rental car not designed for these conditions. When he finally reaches his destination, he parks, strips off his bulletproof vest, takes the Browning. He buzzes Kim's apartment from downstairs and demands to be let up.

When he reaches the fourth floor, he finds Kim waiting for him in the open doorway, dressed for bed, her face shiny with cold cream. But unlike his previous visit, her manner is not deferential. "What are you doing here at this hour?"

Lu pushes past her, searches the apartment. "Have you heard from Hak?"

"I contacted him yesterday, like you told me to."

"I mean tonight."

"No."

"Let me see your phone."

"I don't talk to Hak on my phone, Inspector."

"How, then?"

"A messaging app."

"Show me."

Kim sucks air through her teeth, but boots up her laptop just the same, opens a VPN browser, shows Lu. "I've erased all my correspondence. I'm not a fool."

"Message him now. Tell him you need to speak to him. Urgently."

"What happened, Inspector?"

"Just do it!"

She does. "What now?"

"We wait."

"Until what?"

"Until he replies. You can go to bed if you want."

"With you sitting on my couch?"

"I won't make a peep."

"I'm an elderly widow. It's highly indecent."

Lu laughs tersely. "I'll make sure the neighbors don't see me. Got anything to drink?"

"Tea? Lemon water?'

"Something stronger."

"I don't drink alcohol."

"Just my luck."

Kim goes to bed. Lu sits on the couch and waits. Hak doesn't message. He doesn't knock on the door. Lu, exhausted, eventually nods off. Kim rises before dawn, clucks her tongue, makes Lu tea and breakfast. He sneaks out of the building just after first light. He drives back to Raven Valley, stops near where Hak dumped Sung's body, and tosses the Korean Browning into a ditch.

He returns the car to the rental agency and takes a taxi to his apartment. He showers and drinks a beer, even though it's not yet noon. He scans the news for reports of the chaos at the Little Red Palace. There is nothing. It won't remain so for long. No way to hide that level of violence. Even in Nangang.

Later, Lu checks his burner phone. No calls from Zhang. He texts. *Status*? Zhang texts back an hour later. *We are safe. Where are hard drives?*

Lu: *Our mutual friend has them. Whereabouts unknown.*

Zhang: *Need drives!*

Lu: *I am aware!*

That evening, Lu makes an appearance at the Red Lotus. He's not in the mood for socializing, but to do otherwise would be suspicious.

The Red Lotus is busy, but Yanyan has reserved him a table. She gives him a kiss when he comes in. Lu feels the eyes of the other patrons upon them. Is it because the pretty widow is kissing the deputy chief, or because the deputy chief has just recently been freed from prison after being accused of committing a murder?

Lu is halfway through his second beer when Chief Liang shows up. Liang stamps snow off his boots, waves at Yanyan, takes a seat across from Lu. "Figured I'd find you here."

"Careful, somebody might mistake you for a detective of some kind."

"You've been avoiding me."

"Just processing things, Chief. It's been a weird couple of months."

"You can say that again." Yanyan brings Liang his customary beverage—a tumbler of whiskey. "Thank you, Ms. Luo. Don't be shy about bringing me a refill without being asked."

Yanyan laughs. "Of course, Chief."

When she's gone, Liang leans in. "Reports of big doings in Nangang District."

"Oh?"

"Massive shooting at a residence belonging to Tang Fuqiang. You know Tang, don't you?"

"Sure. Every cop who's worked in Nangang in the past fifteen years knows Tang."

"Seems the head of the Nangang PSB, Chief Hong, was on the premises at the time and got hit. He's alive, barely." This news surprises Lu. Last time he saw Hong, he looked like a goner for sure. Liang drains half his whiskey glass. "Any idea who could have done it?"

"No."

"If I did a GSR test on you right now, what might I find?"

"Salt from this dish of peanuts? What's the working theory? Regarding the shooting?"

"Well, everyone knows Tang's a gangster. I suppose the assumption is it was a gang war thing."

"What was Hong doing in the crossfire?"

"You tell me."

"I did already. You and everyone else. And I ended up framed and on death row for my trouble."

Liang tosses the last of the whiskey down his throat, frowns into his empty glass. "These things seem to be getting smaller and smaller." He sets the glass down on the table. "You might find yourself a suspect as the investigation develops. If you don't have an alibi, you should consider getting one. It would be a shame to see you go off to prison again so soon."

"I agree. Who else was shot?"

"A lot of people."

"Tang?"

"In the wind."

Lu thinks of Hak's words the night they met at the Harbin Railway Station: *He'll just run off to Thailand. Or to the Middle East.*

"Do you know if Xu was at the scene?" Lu asks.

"I'm sure he was—he's chief of Homicide, and there were lots of dead people."

"I mean, during the event."

Liang's expression turns cagey. "Why do you ask?"

"Hong and Xu are tight, that's all."

"Right. Sure."

Yanyan arrives with Liang's second whiskey. Liang drinks it quickly and wipes his mouth. "Be smart, Lu Fei."

"I am, Chief."

"Then why do you do dumb shit all the time?"

"The heaviest burden falls to those who can carry it."

Liang scoffs. "As a penalty for saying that, you'll pay for my whiskeys."

"That's fair. And thanks for the heads-up."

Liang says his farewells. Lu drinks another beer, then tells Yanyan he's going home to get some rest. She kisses him goodbye. Two kisses in public in one night.

Given the current situation, it feels like a bad omen.

Lu goes back to his apartment and takes a long, hot shower, scrubbing his skin until it is red and raw. Afterward he dresses in comfortable clothes and lies in bed staring at the ceiling, expecting a pounding at the door, a team of investigators barging in bearing evidence collection kits, hauling him off to another detention center.

But nobody comes that night . . . the next morning . . . or in the days that follow.

Lu eventually decides he is a can of worms Xu no longer desires to pry open.

Lu spends the next few days handling administrative matters relating to his reinstatement as deputy chief of Raven Valley. The county PSB chief, a tough old bird named Bao, will eventually make the final decision on that score, but first Lu must gather paperwork, testimonials as to his character, and the judge's release order.

It is toward the end of the week when Lu finally receives an email from an address he does not recognize. He opens it to find a link and a password. These lead to a series of video files which are labeled *Xu, Hong, Wan,* and so on.

Lu opens the file for Xu. It shows an overhead view of what looks like a miniature classroom. A blackboard. School desks.

A young woman sits at one of the desks, in a high school uniform. A man stands behind her, toying with her ponytail. He grips it, yanks, pulls her head up, leans down to place his mouth on hers. He releases her, walks around to the front of the desk. Reaches down toward his belt.

The man is Xu.

Lu doesn't need to see the rest. He closes the file.

He calls Dr. Ma. She is happy to hear from him. At first. They talk of his prison release, and her upcoming disciplinary hearing, which looks to be just a formality now that the charges against Lu have been dropped.

Then he tells her about the videos.

"Where did you get them?" Ma asks sharply.

"An anonymous sender."

"We can't use something like that without knowing its provenance."

"I get that. But you can use facial recognition to identify the women. You could get addresses, run background checks. If you pulled one or two in for questioning, they might have interesting stories to tell. Some of them may be doing this work willingly, but others may not."

"What pretext would we have to questioning them without referring back to the videos?"

"I don't know. You're clever, you'll think of something."

"I don't know. Sounds radioactive."

"You have the faces of major Nangang officials on tape, having sex with prostitutes. Get one girl to go on the record and the whole house of cards will fall."

Ma thinks. After a moment she says: "You have any media contacts?"

"A few."

"Send them the files and have them call the Harbin mayor's office, PSB, and CIB for comments. That should kick it off."

"Will do. And, Xiulan? Thank you. For everything."

"Don't forget to invite me to your wedding."

"I won't. Let me know if you need help finding a date to bring with."

"Are you kidding? They're lined up down the block."

Lu laughs. "True enough."

Lu calls Annie Ye, a scrappy young journalist he's had a mildly adversarial relationship with in years past.

"What a turn of events, Inspector," she says. "Usually I call *you,* and you don't bother to answer. Are you hoping I'll do a redemption piece regarding your recent arrest and conviction for murder?"

"*Overturned* conviction. And no. I've got a scoop. Big one. Massive. One that will make your career. Interested?"

"Does a cow have teats?"

"I haven't been on a farm for a while, but last time I checked, yes."

"So, tell me."

"I'll send you a couple of video files. Watch them in private and then give me a ring."

Lu hangs up and sends Ye an email. Five minutes later she calls back, sounding like she's just sprinted a mile. "This is . . . incredible!"

"I have more. Once you view them, you'll start making phone calls to the Harbin mayor's office, PSB, CIB. CCDI."

"Yes. Yes, of course!"

"Congrats, Ms. Ye. You're about to become a very famous journalist."

SIXTY

The provincial media censors attempt to keep a lid on Annie Ye's story, but salacious details and video screenshots leak through online chat groups. It eventually grows too large to suppress.

Subsequent events pop off like a string of firecrackers.

Most of the remaining NBA members go into hiding. Deputy Wan issues a video denial of everything. Internet wags pair it with screen shots of him tied up in the LRP's second-floor dungeon, one of Tang's hostesses in full dominatrix gear applying metal clamps to his nipples.

Gao provides testimony to the procuratorate regarding the members of the Nangang Benevolent Association, their myriad business interests, connections to Tang, and illegal activities at the Little Red Palace.

Eventually investigators circle around to question Lu—not about the shooting at the LRP, but to inquire about his knowledge of corruption in Nangang.

City and provincial authorities are eager to get the case over with and out of the public view as quickly as possible, so the hammer of justice falls swiftly. Arrests are made. A few of the NBA's lesser members who do not appear on Tang's tapes—Chen, Zhao, and Liu—just lose their jobs and membership in the Communist Party. Han and Pangu are stripped of their badges and sentenced to five years each. Xu, Hong, Yu, and Wan all get suspended death sentences—basically, life in prison.

Tang's whereabouts remain undetermined.

Lu wonders where Hak has disappeared to—perhaps holed up in some illegal sublet, biding his time until the next opportunity to torture and kill a few sex traffickers. But Lu doesn't go searching for him. Where Hak's concerned, he figures it's better to let sleeping dogs lie.

Lu is eventually fully reinstated to the Raven Valley PSB and even awarded a citation for meritorious service. On his first day back at work, even the normally sullen and rebellious constables Yuehan Chu and Big Wang seem pleased to have him back.

"It was a real shit show around here while you were out," Chu confides.

"The chief was in an awful state," Wang confirms. "Foaming at the mouth and barking at us like a rabid dog."

"I'm strangely happy to see the two of you also," Lu says.

"Let's not get carried away," Chu says.

"Yeah," Wang agrees. "We're just looking forward to some peace and quiet around here for a change."

That afternoon, while in the squad room discussing an incident report with Constable Sun, he spies a small photo of a man on her desk. He attempts to look at it without being obvious. It's definitely not her fiancé, Yao Jun. Finally, he asks: "Is that a cousin or something?"

Sun looks embarrassed. "No. It's . . . my boyfriend."

"Constable Sun, you cheeky devil. A fiancé and a boyfriend! Where do you find the time?"

"I broke up with Yao."

"Such a shame."

"Don't sound so disappointed."

"He wasn't right for you," Lu says. "If you don't mind me saying."

"Oh, I agree."

"And this one? Where'd you meet him?"

Sun smiles. "His name is Tian. He's a detective in Harbin."

"He's *what*?"

"I met him at the mayor's office during the investigation. Don't worry—he's one of the good ones."

"I wasn't aware there *were* any of those in the Harbin PSB."

"Well, I know of at least one other policeman who got his start in Harbin and turned out to be a pretty good guy."

"Ah. Well . . ."

"And speaking of that," Sun continues, "should you ever find that you want to add another detective to the team here—I'm sure Detective Tian would be open to a transfer."

"I will absolutely keep that in mind, Constable Sun!"

SIXTY-ONE

Contrary to Hak's prediction, Tang is not in Thailand, or the Middle East—he's in New Jersey.

To be specific, he's residing in a small town called Fort Lee just across the George Washington Bridge from Upper Manhattan.

By now Tang has heard word regarding the fate of his brothers in the Nangang Benevolent Association. And he suspects the Chinese government will soon issue an Interpol "red notice" to the U.S. authorities requesting his extradition back to China to face some unpleasant music.

But he knows such matters typically move at a glacial pace. His plan, which he is now in the process of executing expeditiously, is to sell off his U.S. investments and fly to South America, where he will make a new home for himself without possibility of extradition. To be sure, he is not looking forward to the tropical heat; he doesn't speak a word of Spanish; and he expects to find a critical shortage of young, attractive, Asian females to keep him company. But life in distant exile is certainly preferable to a cold Chinese prison cell followed by a hot injection of potassium chloride.

One of Tang's local business ventures is part-ownership in a Manhattan club that caters mostly to Japanese businessmen on an expense account. He leaves the day-to-day management to his partner, a yakuza gangster, but occasionally likes to drop in to check on things, make sure the staff isn't slacking off, the girls are pretty and welcoming, the drinks aren't too watered down. He generally sits at the bar and drinks a high-end whiskey, and, if so inclined, has quick and impersonal sex with one of the girls in the manager's office, then goes to an *izakaya* nearby for some comfort food.

Tonight he visits the club, spends fifteen minutes with one of the hostesses, enjoys a meal of potato croquettes, yakitori, and a bowl of soba, and drives back to Fort Lee in a relaxed mood. Along the way, he listens to the Mandarin broadcast on WKDM 1380 just to hear his native tongue. Eventually he grows tired of the tedious talk radio program and switches to a pop station.

When he reaches the northern tip of Manhattan, he turns onto Harlem River Drive, crosses the GW Bridge, exits at Fort Lee, and finally enters the parking garage under the luxury high-rise where he owns a penthouse apartment. He yawns as he rides the elevator up. He's ready for a hot shower, a nightcap, and bed.

Tang's apartment is not large—one bedroom, a combined kitchen and dining area, a living room. The real selling point is the view—floor-to-ceiling windows looking toward Manhattan. When Tang enters, he throws the dead bolt on the door, drops his keys and phone on the kitchen counter, kicks off his shoes, fills a tumbler with ice and two fingers of whiskey. He pads down the short hallway to his bedroom, then stops.

Something's not right.

The lights are off in the living room, but he can see dark shapes outlined against the gray light coming in through the windows. A standing lamp, an armchair, a floor vase.

Is that the silhouette of a person? Tang walks over, flicks on the overhead light. He finds a man sitting in one of the chairs, one leg casually crossed over the other.

"Who are you?" Tang says, in English. "How did you get in here?"

Hak speaks in Chinese. "My name is Hak. Sit down." Hak points to the couch.

Tang hears an accent. He guesses Korean but isn't sure. "Get the hell out before I call the cops."

"You're not going to do that. Sit." Tang notices the gun in Hak's hand. A fat cylindrical suppressor on the end.

Tang sits and places his glass of whiskey on the coffee table. "Whatever it is you want, we can work it out."

Hak shows Tang a photograph. "Remember her?"

The photograph shows a girl, maybe fifteen or sixteen, in a school uniform, bob haircut. Tang thinks, *Who is the girl to this man? Daughter? No, he is too young for that. High school girlfriend? Sister?* "No. Who is she?"

"I watched your tapes," Hak says. "She was in two of them. The last one was dated more than two years ago. Where is she now? Dead?"

Tang honestly does not remember the girl, but if she made an appearance in his secret tapes, and then disappeared from his stable of hostesses, she is either dead or he sold her off to someone else. Either way, a grim fate. "I don't know. I've never seen her before. I swear."

"Your answer is not satisfactory."

In Tang's transactional view of the universe, every insult, every transgression, every sin is redeemable by cash money. The only question is, how much? "I don't know this girl, but maybe I can help you search for her? I have money. Lots of money."

"Not money. I want my sister back." Tang starts to rise, but Hak springs out of his chair and smashes the butt of his gun into Tang's forehead. He climbs on top of Tang, pinches his jaw open, and jams a pair of socks he's taken from Tang's bedroom into his mouth. He smashes the gun against Tang's temple again, stunning him, flips him over, zip-ties his wrists. He takes a roll of duct tape from his coat pocket and winds it around Tang's head to keep the gag in place.

The whole procedure takes less than thirty seconds.

Hak manhandles Tang into the bedroom and onto the bed. He sets his gun on the nightstand.

Tang mewls through the gag. Hak returns to the living room. Tang hears the TV, switching channels. A music video. Something heavy, industrial. Drums like jackhammers. Guitars like buzz saws.

Hak returns with a backpack, removes a pair of elastic bands. He sits on Tang's chest, loops one end around Tang's neck, twists it into a makeshift noose, ties it off around the headboard. He turns and sits on Tang's legs, loops the second band around Tang's ankles, then climbs off the bed, tugs it tight, and ties it off on a footpost.

Next, Hak takes a pair of scissors from the backpack, shows them to Tang. Tang attempts to beg, but the gag reduces his words to gibberish. He struggles against the restraints, but he might as well be encased in cement.

Hak uses the scissors to cut off Tang's pants. His silk shirt. His Calvin Klein underwear.

He leaves Tang his socks.

Hak reaches into his backpack, removes a set of plastic coveralls, shakes them out, slips into them. Booties go over his shoes. Latex gloves on his hands. Tang watches all this from the corners of his eyes, rigid with fear.

Then Hak shows Tang a knife.

Tang has an appreciation for the finer things in life. Expensive liquor, beautiful women, crystal glassware, high-end cutlery.

He recognizes the distinctive pattern on the blade—Damascus steel. Very strong. Very sharp.

Hak climbs onto the bed, straddles Tang, and gets to work.

清明

CLARITY

As the weeks pass, Lu settles back into a routine in Raven Valley. Come spring, his imprisonment and the violence at the Little Red Palace slowly take on the quality of a strange and unpleasant dream.

But Lu occasionally thinks of Gao Yang and Ling Wei. Where are they now? Are they together? What of Zhang and Li?

Curiosity finally inspires him to track Gao down. It's not hard—Gao still must register his whereabouts like any other citizen. His new address is in a suburb south of Harbin. One Saturday morning, Lu takes a patrol vehicle and drives there. He arrives to find a modest but well-kept house on a small plot of land.

He opens the gate and walks up to the door. He knocks. When it opens, Lu finds himself facing Ling Wei. She is not pleased to see him.

"I'm sorry to intrude," Lu says. "I've just come to see how you and Mr. Gao are getting along."

"Fine," Ling says. "Thanks for coming. Goodbye." She starts to shut the door, but a voice calls out from behind her. Gao appears at her shoulder.

"Well," Gao says. "Mr. PSB-CIB."

"I'm not representing any government agencies today. I'm just here to pay a social call."

"Are you? I guess we'll have to invite you in."

Ling shoots Gao a dark look. Gao touches her arm and nods reassuringly.

He smiles at Lu. "Let's go in back. It's a pleasant day."

Lu follows Gao through the house and into the yard, where he's got a small porch with a couple of chairs overlooking a garden. "Sit. Beer?"

"Sure."

Gao disappears inside, reappears with two beers. He hands one to Lu, then an opener. Lu pops the cap on his bottle. "Would you mind?" Gao says, holding out his own bottle. His hand trembles slightly.

Lu hands Gao his opened bottle, takes the other, pops the cap. "*Gan bei.*"

"*Gan bei.*" Gao drinks, wipes a dribble of beer off his chin.

"Nice place," Lu says.

"Peaceful."

"I guess the procurator didn't see fit to throw you back in jail."

"The state found my testimony useful. Besides which, I had already served time for corruption and there were no new charges against me."

"Right."

"Speaking of jail, have you been to see your old friend Xu? Reveled in a bit of a gloat?"

"I've considered it. I'd like to look him in the face—while his is behind bars. But that seems petty. Maybe in a year or so, when he's had time to reflect upon his bad behavior." Lu sips from his bottle. "Think he'll ever get out?"

Gao shrugs. Then sighs. "You know what really pains me about the events of this past winter?"

"Aside from the obvious?"

"Kong. Remember him? Good man. Only wanted to protect me. He didn't deserve that."

"I guess Ling is your nurse now? Or is she your wife again?"

"Less than a wife. More than a nurse. We are partners, of a sort. We trust each other. Share a deep affection. Would do anything for one another. And I have told her she is free to go when she wants, where she wants. Start over, if she chooses. But for the moment, she chooses to stay here, with me. For which I am grateful."

"How are Mr. Zhang and Mr. Li? Or whatever their real names are."

"Happily retired."

Lu shifts in his chair to look Gao in the face. "Do you feel any remorse?"

"For what happened at the Little Red Palace?" Gao shakes head. "Weiwei was freed. You got the hard drives. None of you was killed. And as for that insidious gang of miscreants in Nangang—they were a cancerous lesion on the soul of Harbin. A lesion I had a hand in creating, yes. But through you and Zhang and Li, and the mysterious Korean you brought to the party, that cancer has been excised."

"I'd like to believe your kindly old reformed gangster act. But I just don't understand what kind of man gets revenge on another by boiling him alive."

"I don't know, either, Inspector."

"Why pretend at this point?"

"Pretend what?"

"That you didn't tell Zhang and Li to deep-fry Pang. And strangle Cai. And cut off Zhao's hand."

"Because I did not do those things. Did they say I did?"

"Of course, not. I'm a police officer. They wouldn't confess to me."

Gao turns stiffly to meet Lu's stare. "I don't know who killed Pang. Or Cai, or who cut off Zhao's hand. It wasn't me. I wasn't even in touch with Zhang and Li until after I was shot."

"Somehow I find that hard to believe."

Gao's eyes narrow. "When it was clear that I was going to be arrested, convicted, imprisoned, I gave Zhang and Li a sum of money and sent them away. I told them not to inform me where they were going, and not to contact me, for their own protection. Same with Weiwei. And whether you believe it or not, that was the last contact I had with any of them until after I was released from the hospital—which is when Zhang and Li came to see me. By that time Tang had already abducted Weiwei and I'd signed that damned statement incriminating you." He leans back in his chair and returns his gaze to the garden. "I knew in my heart Tang would never let Weiwei go. And he'd try to kill me again. Not that dying holds any fear for me. But I couldn't allow him to do that to her. So I turned to two old friends and a policeman with very few options, for help." He waves at his vegetable patch. "And here we are."

Lu digests this. If not Gao, then . . . *who*?

They finish their beers. Gao asks if Lu wants another. Lu says no, he has to drive.

It's pleasant on the porch, basking in the warmth of the sun. A distant smell of woodsmoke.

Lu rests his eyes for a moment, and when he opens them he sees Gao is asleep. Lu quietly gets up and goes into the house.

Ling is sitting in the kitchen, smoking a cigarette.

"He's asleep," Lu says.

"He sleeps a lot these days." Ling stubs out her cigarette and stands. "I'll see you out."

"Not just yet."

Ling sighs and her shoulders slump.

"I want to know why," Lu says.

Ling hesitates. "You wouldn't understand."

"Try me."

It takes Ling a moment to marshal her words: "My husband—my ex-husband—was no saint. But the man I loved, and who loved me, was a kind and gentle person."

"Who paved the way for pimps and criminals."

"He ensured I was not part of that world."

"I guess it's easy to look the other way when you're getting what you want."

"I guess I am no saint, either."

"Understatement of the century."

"Yang was no more guilty than any other government official. The system itself is corrupt. Men like him just find a way to swim with the tide."

"That's a cop-out."

"Not everyone has the luxury of being honest and forthright, Inspector."

"*Fei hua!*"

"Believe what you want."

"I will, thanks. So, Gao went to prison and his protégés prospered. And you felt that was . . . unfair? Unjust?"

"Despite his many transgressions, Yang was not like those others. He was a businessman. A politician. Corrupt, yes, but also benevolent and charitable. I could give you a list of all the wonderful things he accomplished on behalf of the people of Nangang District, but I don't think you'd care."

"You're probably right."

"As for Xu and Wan and Pang and the others—when my ex-husband was their big brother, their ambitions and greed were kept in check. But as soon as Tang assumed that role, they turned into slavering beasts, without the slightest hint of humanity."

"Meanwhile, Gao was the epitome of a Confucian gentleman."

"He sought power and influence, but not just for his own benefit."

"Sounds like you're splitting hairs. Criminals are criminals."

"You may think so, but I had a front-row seat to witness what happened after Yang was sent away."

"As Tang's mistress."

"I was never his mistress. I kept him close, like Zheng Pingru." Lu understands the reference—Zheng was a pretty socialite who hobnobbed with Japanese military officials to gather evidence for the resistance after Japan invaded China in 1937. She was executed at the age of twenty-two. "And Tang made it easy," Ling continues. "No sooner was Yang locked up than he came sniffing around, like a dog with the scent of fresh meat in his nostrils."

"And that made you cross, so you decided to have him and everyone in his little boy's club murdered."

Ling sets her lighter down on the kitchen counter with a sharp click. "Yang was corrupt. The others—most of them—were evil. There is a difference."

"I'm not sure I see the distinction."

"That is because you are a Great Sage, able to wade through the muck and filth of the world without staining your garments."

"Hardly. I just have principles and I stick to them."

"I did the people of Nangang a service. No innocents were harmed. Whether you agree with my methods or not is beside the point."

Lu asks Ling the same question he asked Gao. "Do you feel no remorse?"

"Does a surgeon feel guilty when he cuts out a malignant tumor?"

"But the barbarity . . ."

"When the balance of social order is disrupted, it can only be restored by punishing the offenders. And the punishment should fit the crime."

"Who would have expected a nightclub entertainer to be such a hard-core legalist?"

"You may look down on me if you wish, Inspector. But, like you, I have my principles."

"Except for where Gao Yang is concerned."

"He paid his debt. He went to prison for five years. He lost is health, his property, his social standing. Nearly everything."

"But not you."

Ling's lips form a faint smile. "No. Not me." She shakes another cigarette out of her pack, puts it in her mouth, then sets it down on the counter. "What now?"

Lu doesn't answer. He's not sure.

"Just to be clear," Ling says, "I've retired from my position as the Magistrate."

"Magistrate?"

"Never mind. The point is, what you see here is what you get. Gao Yang and I only want to live our days quietly, enjoying our garden and our little patch of sunlight."

"How idyllic."

"Have you considered, Inspector, that perhaps it is time for *you* to look to the future—and let go of the past?"

"If only it were so easy."

"Why isn't it?"

"You and Zhang and Li murdered two people."

"Two criminals. And through our efforts, justice was served. An entire gang of corrupt officials arrested. Nangang District, and Harbin, will ultimately be better for it."

Lu thinks of Xu sitting in a prison cell, dressed in an ill-fitting uniform of blue and white, head shorn, the indignity of squatting over a hole in full sight of his fellow inmates while relieving himself, eating watery gruel, enduring lectures on socialist principles and the role of the individual in society.

He can't deny what Ling says is true. Harbin *will* be better for Xu's imprisonment.

"We are no danger to anyone," Ling says. "I ask, humbly, Inspector—allow Yang to live out his remaining days in peace, with me at his side."

After a long moment of silence, Lu finally says, "I have to be getting back."

Ling walks Lu to the door. She opens it, turns, and fixes Lu with an intense stare. "What happened in Harbin is history. When you leave here and I shut the door, that's the end of it for me. How about for you? Can you drive off and not look back? Keep your eyes on the road in front of you? Because that's where your life and future await. Not in your rearview mirror."

Instead of answering her question, Lu says: "I was wrong about you, Ms. Ling."

"You thought I was a whore."

"*Whore* is too strong. *Gold digger,* perhaps."

"And now?"

"And now I see that your love for Gao is as deep as the Qinghai Lake. And, in its own way, just as cold."

"Love takes many forms, Inspector."

"So it does. Goodbye, Ms. Ling."

"Goodbye, Inspector."

Lu walks outside. Ling shuts the door behind him. He goes to his car, starts the engine, backs out of the driveway.

He drives past suburban homes, open fields, pig farms. He knows he should probably turn the car around. Put Ling in handcuffs. Launch a new investigation. One that would surely end with her execution for murder.

But he doesn't. Despite his misgivings about Ling's actions, her words ring true: Harbin is history. Time to let it go. And focus on what lies ahead.

Lu boards the expressway toward Raven Valley. Although it's against regulations unless there's a valid emergency, he turns on his flashing lights and speeds to the point of recklessness.

He can't help himself. He suddenly wants nothing more than to be home.

ACKNOWLEDGMENTS

A shout out to the stellar team at Minotaur, and especially my editor, Keith Kahla, for his continued guidance and support. Gratitude to the many journalists, scholars, and commentators whose works inform the Inspector Lu Fei series. A big hug to my family and friends for their encouragement and (sometimes tough) love. And it can never be said enough—thank you to the readers who have joined me on this generally delightful, often frustrating, but always worthwhile adventure.